THE AMERICAN TERRORIST
Book One: Vengeance Rising

Forthcoming from R. Carl Irwin
The American Terrorist Book Two: Freedom's Twilight
The American Terrorist Book Three: The Nemesis of
Truth
Destined Liberty
Jurisdiction
The Gray Gloom: Part I
The Gray Gloom: Part II

THE AMERICAN TERRORIST
Book One: Vengeance Rising

R. Carl Irwin

THE
AMERICAN RENAISSANCE
Publishing Company

Denver ▪ Colorado ▪ USA

All rights reserved.
Published by The American Renaissance Publishing Company, LLC
757 E. 20th Street, Suite 370, Denver, Colorado, 80205, USA

Visit Us Online

TheAmericanTerrorist.com
TARPC.com

Library of Congress Cataloging-in-Publication Data is on file with the Library of Congress.

ISBN 978-0-9916064-1-2

First Edition

This book contains an excerpt from the forthcoming title:
Freedom's Twilight – Book Two of The American Terrorist by R. Carl Irwin. This excerpt has been set for this edition only and may not reflect the final content of the forthcoming edition.

For My Wife

Chapter One

Saturday, September 14

A radioactive dispersion bomb, also known as a dirty bomb, isn't a weapon of mass destruction; it's a weapon of mass disruption. Hasan Muhammad Ismail didn't care about the name, but he cared about his mission. It was Allah's mission for him, and his destiny of seventy-two virgins awaiting him in gardens of rippling streams inspired his work and provided significance to his life. Sweat dripped off his brow, and he wiped it away as he loaded another box of TNT into the RV.

The day of reckoning had arrived. Ismail was the keystone in his terrorist cell. Most people thought of a terrorist cell as a group of Muslims located in one place at one time, plotting to bring down another landmark. Few understood the reality: a cell in time, constructed by people working together over time and dispersed over distance, sometimes without ever communicating. His cell, a component of Universal Jihad had planned and prepared for this attack for several years. Their exalted leader, Mansur Ghazali, devised this scheme to strike a signature blow at the Great Satan, and it had worked to perfection so far.

The original cell member bought a warehouse in the border town of McAllen, Texas, with a simple mission: build a small, specially insulated room under the floor of the warehouse to store radioactive material. A second cell member bought a modest home in an ethnically diverse neighborhood in Miami, also with orders

1

build an insulated room for the storage of explosives.

The McAllen cell and its successors easily accumulated the radioactive material. Several Al Mukhabarat Al A'amah officers provided all the necessary material from a stock of rubidium, cesium 137, and strontium 90. The House of Saud had collected as much of the material as possible to construct a grid of destructive power covering their vast oil fields as well as their refineries and ports. The reason for the grid: to trigger remotely all their oil assets if invaded. The royal family thought it better to contaminate the area rather than allow an invading army, particularly an American army, to steal their oil. If they couldn't have it, no one else could, and the royals, confident their supply of radioactive material would pollute the fields for decades, left plenty around.

Hispanic or Latino-featured people smuggled most of these materials across the Mexican border at will in various quantities over the years. The brief exchange between the warehouse owner and the smuggler, apparently an ordinary business transaction, was the only contact these terrorist brothers and sisters would ever have.

The warehouse owner eventually sold his operation to a dark-skinned man, who sold to another Hispanic-looking couple after eighteen months. These conveyances looked so innocent no one ever suspected all these people had ardently devoted themselves to Universal Jihad.

The Miami cell operated in the same manner. The home sold several times over the years, nothing unusual for the neighborhood. No unusual activity, no unusual noises, just normal people successively living in a diverse Miami neighborhood. But inside the insulated room, they had incrementally accumulated a massive store of TNT and Semtex.

Mansur Ghazali had appointed Hasan to complete the mission and bring glory to Allah and Universal Jihad. Another bead of sweat dropped to the concrete floor as Ismail placed his final box of explosives in the RV. He wiped his brow again and then considered the task at hand. Connecting several boxes of explosives would be simple; he just needed to finish it in thirty minutes so he wouldn't fall behind schedule. As he reached for the first wire to attach to the detonator, he thought of all the other members of his cell. They had vanished long ago, and he hadn't met a single one. Once they had obtained their required accumulations and then sold the property, they moved to random places in the US and ultimately slipped quietly out of the country back to their homelands. Ismail could feel their prayers for his success; he was the chosen one.

After wiring the detonator, he glanced at the other side of the RV. The radioactive material sat innocently hidden in the leather couches. It had arrived in Miami from McAllen in small doses, transported by several unseen Universal Jihadists. His exposure to radiation didn't matter; his life in this world would soon end. Other cell members took precautions, a superior once told him, but even if they did contract radiation poisoning, they would simply sell the property and silently fade away. This Jihadist didn't fade away; he would go out with a bang.

Hasan latched the folding couches over the explosive stash and scanned the RV to insure that the bed, the shower, and the kitchen were in order. The mixture of TNT and radioactive material concealed by the RV's amenities awed the terrorist; it would create optimal destruction, and he hugged himself in zealot glee.

After a shower, Ismail knew the time had come. He calmly stepped inside the RV and took the wheel. The engine purred. Ismail had made some alterations to increase the RV's power; his childhood background helped him immensely. His father had raised him with hopes of him becoming a mechanic, and he had learned the vocation well, yet Ismail had different dreams. That life was forgotten when he joined the Saudi Arabian intelligence agency, Al Mukhabarat Al A'amah, and there he thought he would feel satisfied with his choice. But it wasn't enough. When Ghazali recruited him for Universal Jihad, he knew he had found his new earthly home. It was a lonely existence with conviction his only companion, promising an eternal destiny with his loving Allah in heaven with those gardens of rippling streams.

Ghazali, the consummate terrorist, had recruited many of his captains and lieutenants from the intelligence services and secret police of several Middle Eastern, African, and Central Asian countries. From Universal Jihad's birth, Ghazali vowed never to threaten any Islamic government. By declaring war on the West, particularly the Great Satan, Ghazali earned these regimes trust, performing as a terrorist proxy when convenient for them, and thereby forestalling any counter-terrorism measures. He soon found sympathetic ears in many governmental agencies, giving him much-needed space and time to build his network.

Through these sympathies, Ghazali cultivated an unspoken alliance, a bond, with these governments, and he found fertile recruiting ground among those who could overlook the religious differences among the numerous Islamic sects. Ghazali's creed, a dedication to destroy the Great Satan, offered a salve to heal sectarian wounds. Inside the upper echelon of his organization, the Jihadist bound himself in blood to wage war against the infidel and never persecute fellow Muslims. Universal Jihad didn't discriminate among Muslims; if you hated the Great Satan, you were a devoted member. It was universal.

Many soldiers did not fully understand this, but the captains and lieutenants, wise to the ways of the West, knew the Great Satan constantly worked at dividing the Ummah, the worldwide Muslim community. Universal Jihad boldly resisted those efforts with frenetic passions and a willingness to sacrifice life to end the dominion of evil. These leaders—Shia, Sunni, or Sufi—whether they remained in their respective agencies or quietly retired with the blessings of their governments, as Ismail did, proved quite capable of implementing Ghazali's directives. They recruited soldiers in their own religious sect without ever disclosing the close association their Jihad had with other sects, and their war marched on. No questions, no excuses, and no failures became the motto.

Ismail merged onto the relatively clear I-95, driving south. He checked his watch, confident he had plenty of time to spare. Arriving at 11:00 a.m. wasn't unusual for a 3:30 p.m. kickoff on a hot Saturday for these American football games. The big intrastate rivalry was expected to draw a capacity crowd of nearly sixty thousand screaming infidels, who always crammed the parking lots early and swilled vast quantities of the blasphemous alcohol, drinking themselves into immoral oblivion.

The traffic slowed slightly as he turned onto the Dolphin Expressway, but it didn't worry him. After a little less than a half mile, the Jihadist maneuvered into the right lane and took the off-ramp to NW 12th Avenue, where the congestion started, but he expected it. As he crept steadily ahead, Ismail squinted to read the street signs and knew the stadium entrance was close.

The city's expanded and renovated major league baseball park transformed into the nostalgic Orange Bowl for a few Saturdays every fall to accommodate its favorite university's football team when playing its intrastate rivals. Today it would become Ismail's deadly playing field. The gate loomed ahead where a parking attendant wearing a yellow jacket and tan shorts stood checking passes. Ismail reached to the dashboard and found his ticket and parking pass. He smiled to himself. The car ahead rolled past the attendant, and he was next. Glancing in the mirror, he noticed no perspiration and nodded at his apparent Hispanic complexion.

"Morning," the attendant greeted.

"Morning," Ismail replied politely. "Hot one today," he added as he handed the infidel his parking pass.

"Feels like it," the attendant responded as he tore a small coupon from the bottom and handed Ismail the remaining portion. "Just put it on your dash, all's good."

"Thanks," replied Ismail, and he slowly drove to the parking area reserved for RVs. He pulled into a space near the stadium, turned the engine off, and, after switching on the TV, settled back on a couch. His instructions ordered him to execute the plan after halftime. Apparently Ghazali believed that moment maximized the stadium victims and the game's television audience.

An hour before kickoff, Ismail ambled into the stadium, bought a Coke, and climbed to his seat high in the first tier. The game started, and he cheered for the local squad when appropriate, blending nicely into the crowd. As the second quarter wound down, the home team was about to score, sending the crowd into a frenzy. Down twenty-one to seventeen, a touchdown would put them ahead at the half. The close game fit perfectly into his plan; it meant most spectators would rush back for the second half. Hasan had to resist the urge to return to his RV, since his departure at that point certainly would draw some curious glances.

On the next play, the team scored and the crowd erupted; Hasan played along by high-fiving his drunk and grinning neighbor. With only a few ticks left on the game clock, many fans started for the food stands and restrooms. On cue Ismail left the stadium with many others who preferred to guzzle booze rather than liquor gap for the entire game. The Jihadist inwardly cursed the infidels. What a disgusting existence, he thought as he innocuously joined the parade to the parking lot.

Just at the outer edge of the concrete sidewalk, where the thick concrete poles stood guard, Ismail dropped to one knee and started tying his shoe. He furtively reached into his pocket for the malleable C-4 clay explosive, and switched to his other shoe and tied it as well. Glancing around to make sure no one noticed, he furtively clumped the C-4 to the base of the concrete pole farthest right. It looked like a wad of gum. He stood and then leaned down once more to wipe dust from his shoe, and as he did so, he pressed a tiny detonator into the clay.

Wiping his hands, he stood and walked toward his RV, checking with peripheral vision whether anyone had spotted him. The oblivious infidels swarmed toward their trucks, vans, and RVs. Once at his RV, he stepped inside and abandoned his game-day demeanor. Now the sweat dripped under his arms and beaded at his brow again. He shrugged and stretched his back with nervous indifference, since no one would see him again.

Ismail waited silently on his couch for twenty-five minutes. When he finally glanced out the window, the drunken infidels had vacated the parking lot and returned to cheer on their insignificant teams in the stupid game. He smiled, settled into the driver's seat, and turned on the engine. Revving it gently, he shifted gears, slowly pulled out, and turned toward the stadium. The parking lot lanes guided him to the concrete post where he had planted his C-4, and as he approached he quickly glanced at his two trigger devices. The one on the left for the concrete post, the other for the TNT and the Semtex in his RV. He shrugged again and took a deep breath to steady himself. Allah waited for him and so did the virgins. He shivered and inhaled sharply several more times, nearly hyperventilating, and the perspiration dripped freely down his face.

He gunned the accelerator; the engine responded with a roar, and the vehicle launched toward the concrete post. He next pressed the left button on his trigger, and a small cloud of smoke burst in front of him. Easily ramming past the damaged pole to Ismail's delight, the RV hurtled onto the concrete sidewalk with its powerful engines humming. A few startled stragglers gaped at the vehicle in shock, and the terrorist screamed maniacally.

The RV thundered into the side of the stadium, sending a shudder through the massive structure and spraying debris everywhere. Hasan knew he had penetrated deeply enough to create maximum damage. Forcefully punching the right button, the suicide bomber yelled to Allah that he was blissfully on his way to his garden of rippling streams, and the RV exploded in a horrific ball of fire.

Chapter Two

Sunday, September 22

The hazmat suit fitted her snugly, intensifying the hot day. Agent Melissa Dellendale stepped over some wreckage left by the devastating radioactive dispersion bomb. All the talk, all the speculation about an attack at home had ended. No one now doubted it could occur, and the confirmed death toll had already reached 27,595. The immediate shock had killed thousands of fans, kids, football players, parents, and grandparents, and the radiation killed several more within hours. She shook her head, thinking it could have been worse. The bomb had contaminated up to a mile radius around the temporary Orange Bowl, but the mild winds that day had isolated the radiation. Experts now believed they could have the area decontaminated much earlier than originally predicted, and people could return sooner than thought to restart their lives.

She hated the suit, but why risk it, she thought. The FBI had issued every agent a newly developed anti-radiation pill, useful before exposure to radiation, but the drug company hadn't proved its effectiveness conclusively. And it wouldn't help the hundreds or thousands or tens of thousands of people over the next several decades whose cancer diagnosis would confirm the fear that they had lived with for so many years. She didn't want to be one of those victims; her heart sank into her stomach thinking of all the misery.

"Hey there. Dellendale turned to find a tall man whose face was hidden behind a glaring hazmat screen. Cocking her head to peer inside the plastic shield, she recognized Daman Pryce's twinkling blue eyes, always smiling, even now. Just the way they are, she thought to herself. No one could smile at this horror.

"What you are you doing here?" she asked curtly.

"CIA's going to be all over this, Mel."

She had to strain a little to hear him, but she understood what he said. "I know. You need to be. I want any information you have. Screw FISA, Daman." The Foreign Intelligence Service Act, though clarified and better understood after the Patriot Act and subsequent legislation, sometimes still operated as "the wall" between criminal prosecution and foreign intelligence, especially with the old-timers. But Miami had just bulldozed that barrier.

Daman Pryce nodded again. "We think we know where he is."

"Iran?"

"How'd you know?"

"Doesn't take a genius to figure that one out."

"No, guess not."

"So can you get him?"

Daman nodded. "We think so. Special Ops thinks it's difficult, but definitely possible. Several plans are in the works. Right now, it's my department leading the effort, and we have to find his exact location."

"Iran's a large country, Daman."

He nodded a third time, less decisively.

"So you really don't know where he is."

"We think he's in a remote area north of Tehran. Got a glimpse of him, looking old and haggard, but with the beard and robes, we couldn't make a positive ID. Yet. Once we do, we can move in."

The FBI, NSA, DIA, and CIA had identified the author of this act just hours after its commission. A few days later, they had unearthed the entire plot back to its nascence, years earlier. The players, the explosives used, the transactions were all now known, two weeks too late.

Melissa had seen enough of the devastation. Her inspection was more perfunctory, since the true crime scene experts had already pored over myriad microscopic pieces of evidence for the past week. She needed their reports more than anything; her visit today rested with a personal need to witness the tragic damage inflicted on her country by yet another terrorist act. "So when you do find him, are they going to let you kill him?"

Daman's chuckle ended in a grimace that indicated frustration, not amusement. "That's the million-dollar question, Mel. You know that." He paused. "We voted in all these doves, and now we have to live with it."

"Things have changed, Daman. Just look around."

"Yeah, but not inside the Beltway. The first words out of the Speaker's mouth? 'Don't overreact.' With the war hawks screaming bloody murder, she won't back off and look like she called it wrong, so she's hardened her soft appeasement language. Odd how she can be so intransigently weak, isn't it? And it's permeating Washington. The Senate majority leader bowed his head like a good little boy and trotted right behind her."

Melissa sighed heavily, twisting the ring on her right pinky finger as she so often did when thinking. The president also had campaigned on an antiwar platform. Although not a part of the Speaker's flock, he probably couldn't walk down the war path with the hawks either.

Maybe some had it right at election time and some wrong, Mel thought. Who cared now? Politics had to fold to the demands of the day, the real demands of a real world outside DC and inside the Miamis. "The country's not going to live like this, Daman."

"Yeah, but it recovered from this quickly, Mel. The markets bounced back in a week. Especially when everyone down here responded so professionally. The first responders, the National Guard, the military, all of them reacted so efficiently. The country is proud of the response. That takes some of the edge off the attack."

Melissa rolled her eyes. "That's inside the Beltway talk, Daman. And this attack didn't target the economy. Ghazali went for effects. To kill kids and their families, American football, and our whole way of life. More terrifyingly symbolic than anything." She paused for a moment as she scanned the scene. "Yes, the country is proud of how it responded, and it has recovered quickly. This area may be up and running with ninety-nine percent or more of the radiation removed much sooner than anyone ever expected. But people still burn inside. Under all that pride and all that courage and all that stoic efficiency is a simmering rage. They're just not going to tolerate it. I see it, Daman. I see it in the eyes of these Miamians. They're quietly going about their business, but their tolerance is finished. And people in other cities? They're not demonstrating, they're not marching, and they're not screaming bloody murder like the war hawks in DC. It's more eerie than that. They're quiet, and they've resolved not to let this happen in their cities. Yet the politicians misunderstand that. It's not acceptance of Miami; it's a stark understanding that they're under attack, and they know who is responsible, and they're going to start demanding accountability. And if none comes, you mark my words, something is going to happen. Something frightening, Daman."

Chapter Three

Tuesday, September 24

The face gradually appeared in the mirror as long strands of beard piled up in the sink. After the trim, he peeled away the cosmetic wrinkles around his eyes. He scooped up the heap of robes and threw them into a corner with satisfaction. No one would recognize him. Even if he had kept the tangled hair and frayed beard, people wouldn't detect him in this city.

His unremarkable features had always worked to his advantage: medium height, medium build, brown eyes, and black hair meticulously manicured to present a mundane appearance. It fooled everyone; it always had. Although a select few knew who lived in the slightly upscale apartment, the rest of the city wouldn't connect the man with cropped hair and trimmed beard with the same long-haired, wild-bearded terrorist plastered on TV screens everywhere in the West. The most infamous face in the world was transformed. As insurance, he pinched a colored contact lens from its case and placed it in his right eye. After placing its companion in the left, he blinked several times; the eyes were still brown, just a different shade.

Mansur Ghazali smiled inwardly as he chanted in Arabic. He then repeated his promise to Allah again: to rid the world of the infidel and make the language of Allah the only language on Allah's earth. He loved Arabic—its melodic resonance, its inherent beauty. All other languages paled in comparison to its richness and depth.

And it was the language of the Qur'an and Mohammad. Arabic's eternal timelessness demanded surrender to the tenets pronounced in the words and acts of the last and greatest of all the prophets, Mohammad. Those words held not only justification but the commands to eliminate those who worked against Allah's will. Ghazali lived the warrior's life to fulfill the Qur'an and the Prophet's promises.

His daily prayers to Mecca always raised the hair on his neck. The ritual inspired him and filled him with confidence and life, knowing he did Allah's work here on earth. The Miami bomb was the first of many acts designed to destroy the Great Satan. He had worked diligently to construct a network that would overwhelm the Westerners and especially the Americans. He hated them; he hated all of them. Not just the politicians, not just the nasty warrior crusaders, but all the petty little people, all those infidels. They did not honor Allah; instead they worshiped liberty, private property, the pursuit of happiness, capitalism, constitutions, individual rights, free enterprise, free press, free speech, free morals, free everything. He despised all of it and all who embraced it. Disgust permeated his body and fouled his heart, a heart originally born and cleansed in Arabic, the Qur'an, and the Hadith, yet in life contaminated by the infidel. Restoring his purity by vanquishing the source of that disgust breathed life into his soul and gave him meaning.

The TV screen blared with more news out of Miami. The hated Americans had responded better than he expected, better than he wanted, but still the triumph was his. The exultation he felt from the suffering he had inflicted on the hedonistic city—the city of so many obscene lights, so many decadent clubs, so many frivolous young people—partially purged his soul. He had radiated them with poison, and they died an empty death cheering at a meaningless game. The young and the old, the black, the white, the Christian, and the Jew all died. The horror it must have evoked, the terror it must have spawned when the explosion rang in their ears while millions watched, appalled, on American TV. It delighted and empowered him.

This act inside the Great Satan was scaled to the fantastic, and the evil fools expected another show of shock and awe. The Miami bomb plot had been complicated and time consuming, taking many years to implement. In the process, he had infiltrated the American borders with several other operatives and cells, still waiting for instructions. He had many grand schemes and would soon begin planning the next massive assault, killing perhaps forty or even fifty thousand nasty infidels. But for his next attack, he had other ideas. It wouldn't take years, not even months before he lashed out again. No, he didn't have to kill twenty-seven thousand people for his next act; but he must strike terror in their barren hearts, and he had to convey his hatred in a more personal, intimate manner.

He returned to the mirror to splash his face with cold water and stare at Allah's latest messenger. He began chanting again in his beloved Arabic while dabbing his cheeks with a towel. After dressing in modern but plain attire, he inserted the padding in the oversized waistline that provided a tad more identity insurance. Smiling, Ghazali donned a pair of sunglasses and trotted down the stairs to join a bustling crowd on a sunny sidewalk.

Chapter Four

Saturday, October 11

The view across Lower Michigan Avenue from the cable news office impressed Thomas Spencer. He ran a finger across the window. The building had the latest energy-efficient nanotechnologies built right into the glass. The view across the gap into another sleek row of energy-efficient office spaces, towering above the street below, paid homage to man's ability to define where and how he chose to work. Thom faintly smiled.

"Are you ready, Mr. Spencer?" the show's producer asked from behind him.

Nodding, he turned from the impressive vista and eyed the empty chair on the stage. Invited by the host of *Weekend Talk*, Spencer would pull no punches in this debate. Peter Dickson had loaded the deck against him with the other guest, Hamid Khalid, a local Islamic scholar, and they eagerly waited for Thom to enter their little den.

Spencer had made an offhand comment several days ago, which many interpreted as anti-Islamic. Rather than apologize or claim some reporter had misquoted him or taken the words out of context, he defiantly confirmed them. As CEO and majority shareholder of a successful nanotechnology firm, his words caught the attention of the Chicago media and caused a local political ruckus. Since Spencer didn't much care about his public image, he didn't retract his statement, and Dickson asked him on his show to defend what he had said. Without qualms, he accepted the invitation, and surprisingly Spencer received more public support than either Dickson or he expected.

He smiled and laughed aloud when a few of his friends warned him a few days before the show about the scholar's appearance. Thom had read widely on the subject of Islam, but he wasn't an authority, and certainly Dickson and Khalid would try to expose his ignorance and preach their own agenda to the audience. Namely, that Spencer, a greedy corporate CEO, was narrow-minded and inflammatory, not to mention ignorant of complex religious issues. Anyone with a kernel of understanding and tolerance must reject such foolish, politically incorrect views, according to them. But Spencer believed the two men sitting on the stage didn't understand how to play the game. He would direct the dialogue, as he had learned to do throughout his career. Control depended on demeanor and a refusal to allow the opponent to recover from an onslaught. Provoke, jab, and pull no punches, he reminded himself as he sauntered to the chair.

Both men nodded to him and looked at each other with thinly veiled smirks contorting their lips. Spencer folded his hands together.

"Three, two, and one, and you're on the air." The director first zoomed in on the scholar, and then cut to Spencer's lightly salted but more peppered hair, tight square jaw, and steel-blue eyes. As Dickson started speaking, the camera panned to frame all three men.

"We've returned now with Hamid Khalid, a respected Islamic scholar, and the controversial Thomas Spencer, owner of a nanotechnology firm here in Chicago," Dickson smiled into the camera.

He turned toward Spencer. "Mr. Spencer, you're here to defend your now-infamous statement. You said that the Muslim terrorists aren't radical at all, that their acts are clearly justified by the words of the Qur'an, and that any Muslim could easily interpret those words as license to kill unbelievers. These statements seem to indict the entire religion instead of those few individuals that pervert the religion. Do you really believe what you said?"

Spencer grinned. "First, to answer your question directly, yes. Second, I'm not controversial; my statement is controversial. Third, I don't need to defend the statement when the statement is true. Fourth, it's not an infamous statement; it's infamous to you only, Peter. Finally, we both know you're biased against me. You invited an Islamic scholar to refute me, knowing full well that this isn't my area of expertise, but I'm still right, despite anything either of you say."

The host glared at Spencer for co-opting the opening statement with such ease. "Well, Mr. Spencer, maybe you shouldn't have said what you did?" he groused, trying to reassert himself.

Thom knew he already controlled the host; Dickson's defensive posture revealed his anger. Give no quarter, he said to himself. "Well, as I said, yes, I am right, and I'm here to tell you and your scholar why. And, by the way, I have the right to say it, wouldn't you agree, Peter?"

Dickson froze, unable to counter the pugnacious sallies. He abruptly turned toward Hamid Khalid, surrendering the debate to the scholar. "And what is your response to Mr. Spencer's statements?"

In a slight accent and with a smarmy smile, Khalid replied smoothly, "First, I would like to ask Mr. Spencer a few simple questions: Have you read the Qur'an?"

Surprised the scholar would open the door to him by starting with a question, Thom smiled inwardly. "Yes, I have, Mr. Khalid," he answered.

"And did you read it in its original Arabic?"

"No, sir, I didn't. I read an English translation."

Khalid shook his head. "Well, you see Mr. Spencer, there's a problem right here. You couldn't possibly understand it. Did you know that you're not supposed to read the Qur'an in anything but Arabic? Only Arabic captures the pure style of the Qur'an, and many believe to imitate style is sacrilegious."

Spencer paused and smiled. The scholar didn't want to address what the Qur'an said; instead, he was trying to divert discussion to the actual reading of his holy book in English. Spencer would oblige him for now. Drilling with his steel-blue eyes, he said, "Well, then I suppose I and millions of Americans don't understand the Bible, since we can't read it in Hebrew or Greek. But, you see Mr. Khalid, in this country we're not only allowed to read the Bible—or the Qur'an—in English, we have that right. And, Mr. Khalid, what bothers me is that I don't think you respect that right."

Khalid pursed his lips. "It's simply not respectful to read the Qur'an in anything but Arabic, Mr. Spencer."

The scholar stopped to phrase his next thought. Seizing the pause, Spencer launched. "No, Mr. Khalid, *you* are not respectful. In a Muslim country, maybe you cut off a tongue for chanting the Qur'an in English, or poke out an eye for reading it in a language besides Arabic. But here, where you are right now, you need to respect our right to read the Qur'an or any other book in any language we choose. It's disrespectful for *you* not to respect our values."

Khalid gritted his teeth, though he kept his tone even. "Mr. Spencer, we don't cut out tongues and poke out eyes for such acts. I think you know that. You're being inflammatory."

"No, I don't know if your native country does that or not," he retorted, shrugging. "I hope it doesn't because, you see, in this country I also have the right to judge that kind of act, and I can only say if your country persecuted people like that, it's barbaric."

Khalid glanced at the host and, with a sardonic look, shook his head. "If your guest and your countrymen persist in reading adulterated versions of the Qur'an, Mr. Dickson, then such misinterpretation, misunderstandings, and problems will always persist."

Spencer leaned forward in his chair. "Mr. Khalid, you don't have to speak through our host, you can speak directly to me. First, I don't think *we* have the problem. I think it is *you* who have the problems. I am quite confident that I understand what the Bible says even though I haven't read it in the original. Likewise, I am certain I grasp the themes of the Qur'an even though I haven't read it in Arabic. You see, Hebrew and Arabic are both Semitic languages, and neither these languages nor Greek are undecipherable esoteric codes incapable of translation. I and many others can understand what the words mean. And it's quite clear that the Qur'an in several places—and in several translations—commands that Muslims fight or kill infidels. Let me explain it to you. It starts early on, in Sura 2, The Cow, verses 191 and 192. Admittedly, those verses require the infidel to commit the initial aggression, but as one reads further into the Qur'an, the language becomes more demanding. Sura 4:76 requires the Muslim to fight against those who don't believe in Allah. In Sura 9:5, non-Muslims have to repent and pay the zakat or are attacked. In fact, those verses later in Sura 9, verses 71 through 90 or so, impose an absolute duty to fight. What about Sura 47:4, where there is a command to smite the necks of unbelievers in a clash? Muslims have declared war against the West and others in so many capacities that there's a perpetual, unconditional requirement to decapitate all these unbelievers. Sura 48:29 says those who are with the Prophet are severe with infidels. And it continues, not just with commands to kill, but so much of your holy book is dedicated to demeaning the unbeliever. Are you going to deny this, Mr. Khalid?" Spencer had memorized those verses—his only preparation for the show—so he could provide specific references.

Khalid, who wouldn't deign a scholarly response to an illiterate infidel—illiterate since the man couldn't speak Arabic—scoffed loudly. Immediately realizing the audience wouldn't appreciate his arrogance, he ineptly recovered his unctuous grin and asked, "You've mentioned your own Bible, Mr. Spencer? And you've read it?"

"I'm no scholar, but, yes, I've read it, and I get its gist."

"Did you know that your own Jesus Christ commanded to have those who wouldn't have him as king brought forth and killed? Did you know that? Your own Jesus Christ."

Spencer, shifting his eyes back and forth, searched his mind for a passage where Christ had given such a command. Finding none, he shrugged. "Well, I think he's your Jesus Christ as well, if only as a prophet, but I have to admit, I can't think of where that was written, Mr. Khalid. Please tell me?"

"Luke 19:27."

"You mean the parable of Minas?" Spencer asked skeptically.

"Yes."

Spencer shook his head. "Christ is quoting the king in the parable, not making the command himself."

"Ah, so am I taking that out of context. Am I misinterpreting it?"

"Of course you are, and you don't need any hermeneutical Hebrew magic to decipher that. We all understand it, including you. Now here's the question: where am I taking the quotes about killing or fighting the infidel out of context; where am I misinterpreting that?"

"Well, Mr. Spencer, you are."

"All right, then explain this to me. Christ is nearly to Christianity what Mohammad is to Islam, correct? Both titular heads in the least of their religions?" Khalid didn't respond, and Spencer continued without the admission. "Don't you think there is a significant difference between the one who died on the cross rather than kill anyone and the other who rose up out of the desert with sword in hand and killed to establish his religion? You see, I don't think Christ killed anyone. Yes, he said he didn't bring peace, but a sword, but that was a metaphor. He never had an actual sword, never used one, and I certainly can't find where he ever commanded anyone to behead an unbeliever. In fact, Christ commanded his followers not to fight when he was arrested. Even Peter had to sheath his sword. Now, I think we can find several historical instances where Mohammad orchestrated several killings and surely he instigated several battles and maybe he even partook personally in few killings himself. No doubt he was a warrior, right?"

Khalid hesitated. He raised an eyebrow and asked, "What about Revelations, Mr. Spencer?"

Spencer scoffed. "Hasn't happened, Mr. Khalid. And in Revelation—not Revelations—I don't think it's Christ the man who is acting, but Christ as God. And I'll admit God in the Bible—and in the Qur'an—kills people. But again, I don't recall any circumstance of Christ's requiring his followers to kill unbelievers."

The tension mounted, and Peter Dickson maneuvered nervously in his seat. Before he could interject a calming segue, Khalid blazed back. "How arrogant of you, Mr. Spencer! This is your problem. You believe your religion superior, incapable of error, free from any violence, any aggression, and you use it to justify your aggression, your intimidation of the countries in this world. Yet, Mr. Spencer, your history definitely suggests otherwise. The Crusades and your Inquisitions don't reflect well on your religion. You and your media easily gloss over those subjects, but they are indelible fixtures in our minds. You have no innocence."

"Ohhh, those Crusades again. I don't understand your arguments there. I always thought the Jews then the Christians lived in the Holy Land long before the Muslims. By at least six centuries or so, wouldn't you say? And, by the way, who do you think converted or killed all those Jews and Christians, Mr. Khalid? But let me tell you something else, we know that the West isn't innocent.

The West itself has roundly criticized the Crusades and the Inquisitions, and you know why? Because we allowed something known as rationality to enter our culture, and through it we improved, we progressed. We recognize that some acts and values in the Old and perhaps even the New Testament aren't right. With the Qur'an, you can't do that."

"And that makes you better than us?" the scholar asked, maintaining the smirk.

"Yes. You don't see Christian children taught in our schools to kill Muslims, Buddhists or Jews. You don't see Jewish children taught in their schools to decapitate Christians or kill Hindus. We don't have schools like your madrassas where the young are taught to kill. It's not prevalent, common, condoned, accepted, or tolerated in our society. Period."

Khalid leaned back in his chair, inhaling deeply and gesturing professorially as he started to respond.

Spencer leaned a little further forward in his chair and cut him off before he had a chance. "And you know what else Mr. Khalid? If one of our religious leaders tried to impose any sort of temporal sanction on someone supposedly violating doctrine, moderates and fundamentalists alike would rise up in protest. Yes, that sort of thing did happen in the past, but not now. We wouldn't tolerate it. And you know what else we wouldn't tolerate for a moment?" Spence didn't wait for an answer. "A Christian sect that used women and children as shields to protect themselves for any reason whatsoever; we wouldn't need any Muslim nation or Hindu army to eliminate that group; we'd do it ourselves, and we'd do it immediately. And, maybe, just maybe, those women and children somehow have consented and do it freely for your terrorists, but what kind of statement does that make?

"It's completely different for you. That behavior, the fighting of infidels, the killing of infidels, is entirely acceptable because it's not only an easy interpretation of your Qur'an, but a natural one. Any Muslim can read it for himself—or herself, if she's allowed to read—and justify those sorts of barbarous acts. That's why you don't see Muslims around the world protesting against violent terrorist attacks committed by Muslims; that's why you yourself, Mr. Khalid, mumble and mutter justifications instead of harsh recriminations against the likes of Ghazali. Down deep, you and so many in your faith really don't think they're immoral or wrong."

Khalid drummed his fingers, appalled at the other guest's temerity. "I am dumbfounded, Mr. Spencer. Your values, your religion, your philosophy aren't better than ours, but you think they are. And that is your and your country's mistake."

"Mr. Khalid, I'm not a cultural relativist, and you aren't either. You think yours is a far better way of life, but I am here to tell you that you are wrong. Absolute right and wrong exist, and Western culture is superior to yours in nearly every way, and it took us centuries to get here. And to get here, we had to forge a Renaissance from our Greek and Roman heritage, experience a Reformation, embrace Enlightenment, spark two Revolutions, the Scientific and Industrial, before we had a decent foundation for progress, but progress we have. And we have more work to do, but our answers, the world's answers, do not lie with your culture or with your religion. Period. A little-known fact about the West: our religions coddled reason even though the very essence of reason threatened its foundation. Yet, out of this protection, the Church helped create the University, and among the Church, the universities, and all the various kings, princes, and burghers, the individual emerged. The individual emerged because of the odd separation of powers among all those forces, and not one of them could monopolize the culture or our history.

"Yours is a monolithic existence, and in that existence, I don't find any space where the individual can breathe. With that kind of oppression, no progress will occur. Only what existed at the point of your historical beginning—July 16, 622, in the Western calendar, known as the beginning of the Islamic Era or Anno Hegirae— matters. And in 622, your religion not only condoned but passionately embraced killing the infidel, slavery, and a host of other morally reprehensible acts. You can't escape your history, Mr. Khalid. But you want to know what the real problem is? You don't want to escape that history; you want everyone, the entire world, to reject their own history and culture and adopt yours and live it eternally, but we stand in your way."

Khalid cleared his throat. "It sounds as if you require us to change our religion, in its entirety, to accommodate you."

"Yes, I do. I demand you reform Islam so it doesn't justify killing me simply because I don't accept it. But that's the problem with your religion, Mr. Khalid. Because the Qur'an is the timeless word of Allah, you can't reform it, so the world is stuck with an ultimatum: either submit or perish. That is a fair and natural reading of your God's words. But I'm here to tell you I choose neither. I'm not Christ for certain, Mr. Khalid. And, I'm not Peter. Turning the other cheek and sheathing swords are for God and saints."

"That sounds like a threat, Mr. Spencer," Khalid said in a contemptuous voice.

"It's just a fact."

Spencer's blunt words hung among them in stunned silence, as both Khalid and Dickson sat astonished, and the cameras continued to roll.

Chapter Five

Tuesday, October 14

Ghazali clipped a few more hairs from his beard, trimming it neatly. Arabic satellite news blared in the other room. The newscaster relayed a report from the United States where a national controversy had erupted over a debate on a local TV talk show. A reporter cut to the footage, and Ghazali stepped into the living room to hear the entire exchange between an American CEO and an Islamic scholar. The next clip translated a later interview on a national daily cable news show, where a less combative Thom Spencer justified his antagonistic demeanor with the Islamic scholar, but the controversy still simmered.

Although Ghazali was fluent in many Middle-Eastern languages, he didn't understand English. He wouldn't learn the filthy language; others in his organization had that job, but, even in translation, he clearly understood the American's position. Smiling, he couldn't help but agree with him, especially the quarrelsome version. This Spencer had interpreted the Qur'an correctly; Ghazali had not only the right but the duty to exterminate the infidel. War existed between Muslims and all those who refused to accept the blessed word of Allah. Those who denied the words and deeds of the Prophet attacked his religion, his very way of life, and they had to die. Yes, this Thomas Spencer understood.

Returning to the bathroom, Ghazali suddenly stopped short,

struck by another idea. The newscaster was giving his commentary, but Ghazali didn't hear any of it. Lost in thought, he wandered to a window and scanned the busy street below without seeing it.

The Muslim scholar Khalid was also correct. Spencer had committed an abomination against Allah by reading the sacred text in the vile English. The arrogant American's image hung in his mind, and he recalled the man's last words. He had said 'It's just a fact' with such gall! An elegant plan formed in Ghazali's mind, and the next assault against the Great Satan suddenly started to emerge. His imagination conjured up the worldwide headlines, and he nodded to himself. This impudent American, violating the fundamental principles of Islam, had provided him with his next extraordinary statement.

After wiping his face, Ghazali quickly dressed and left his apartment for the nearest phone. Activation of the terrorist cell required little effort, and, if his soldiers executed the plan properly, he would send a terrifying message to the unbelievers. As he quickly walked along the bazaar, the sunlight warmed his shoulders, yet he felt a cool tingle of a chill shiver down his spine.

Chapter Six

Monday, November 10

Tears rose in her eyes, but Toni Spencer determinedly continued chopping. She blinked several times, which helped relieve the discomfort, though the strong odor still tainted the air. She loved cooked onions, Thom loved them too, and, surprisingly, the kids complained if she didn't include them even if preparation of her famous spaghetti sauce was an all-out attack on her senses. Scraping another batch into the large sauce pan, she lifted her head out of the intense smell at the sound of a car coming to a stop outside.

"Jennifer," she called, "get your sister up and come down and set the table. Now I'm not going to tell you again." She waved her towel to pull in more fresh autumn air from the open window. A little warm for this late in the fall, but glad for it, she thought to herself.

Rose came into the kitchen lugging a full basket of laundry and cheerfully offered to help. "I can do it, Mrs. T. Let her play."

"Rose, you can't do everything around here, and she needs to learn responsibility. Get a little discipline in her privileged life. I haven't changed my mind on this. Next summer is going to be different from this last one. You mark my words," she said confidently.

Rose responded with her patented grimace. "I have marked them. Doesn't mean I've changed my mind, either. Don't be too hard on her. Kids gotta be kids."

As a full member of the family, Rose exercised her right to object whenever she disagreed. She had been there from the beginning as Jennifer's nanny and then little Michelle's, and Toni respected the older woman's wisdom. But regarding Jennifer's responsibilities, Toni was resolute not to relent, and the disagreement was a mild point of contention between the two women. Thom's support vacillated between them, usually siding with Rose when a chore interfered with his all-important father-older daughter movie nights.

She interrupted her internal conversation by cocking her head, thinking again about the car. Out here in the boondocks, cars were a rarity unless it belonged to them, which she knew wasn't the case.

"Did you hear someone pull up, Rose?" she asked, walking to the window to investigate the noise.

Rose shook her head, intent upon folding all the sheets before dinnertime.

Without warning, a crash shook the house. Toni dropped her knife and whirled toward the nanny, who had thrown the sheet into the air. Shock registered on both their faces, and together they dashed out of the kitchen. In the large foyer, the splintered front door barely hung on one hinge, and debris littered the floor. A man clad in black, including a black handkerchief covering his face, brandished a handgun.

Wild eyes conveyed utter depravity. The man aimed the firearm at Toni's face and shouted, "Lay down now!"

Rose shrieked, raising trembling hands to her face as she dropped to the floor. Toni's heart sank into her stomach. In a flash, she grasped the man's intention and its outcome, yet she refused to cave to emotion. Instead, she glared into those maniacal eyes and seethed in a cool, distinct voice, "You coward."

He lunged at her, flinging her down on the cold marble. She glanced up to see another man filming the entire scene. Screams erupted from upstairs, and she tried to push herself to her feet, but a blow to her neck from the butt of a gun sent her reeling. Through the bright stars dancing in her eyes, she saw her children marched down the winding staircase by two more men, also dressed in black.

Another intruder—Toni had lost count of how many there were—stepped from behind the cameraman and grabbed Rose. He roughly dragged her next to Toni, while the two terrorists from upstairs shoved the girls down and pushed them across the slick marble floor. Little Michelle didn't cry, but the four-year-old's bewildered expression silently shouted fear to her mommy as Toni stared at her helplessly. Jennifer's screams stopped abruptly when her captor slapped her mouth; her whimpers echoed in her mom's ears. Fighting through the stars, she caught her older daughter's attention and tried to give her an assuring look. Jennifer suddenly stopped all emotion, and her eyes widened in instant understanding; she knew they were all going to die. Strangely, Toni's inner voice futilely replayed Rose's recent advice and her retort about Jennifer's life. None of it mattered now. Bile formed in the pit of her stomach; surreal sensation fought down the revulsion.

The terrorists bound their ankles and their hands behind their backs with practiced ease. Rose still didn't understand what was happening, but she had stopped her screeching. Courage replaced fear, and she shouted angrily. "Who are you? What is the meaning of this?" A blow to the back of her head immediately shut her up.

The black-clad men formed Toni, Rose, Michelle, and Jennifer into a line on their knees, and the cameraman stepped back to get all four in the shot. A terrorist stepped to the side of each victim. Perspiration dripped from Toni's executioner to her arm; the foul stench assaulted her senses. As he grabbed her hair and wrenched her head back, she caught the flash of steel and from the corner of her eye saw three more blades. Deadly silence saturated the air. Then Toni convulsed as vomit surged from her stomach, shattering the eerie stillness. Tears burst from her eyes. Blessed blackness came quickly; she never witnessed the horror.

Chapter Seven

Monday, November 10

Pools of blood had congealed on the floor; violence and death infected the entire home, and Deputy Sheriff Dan Weaver found it impossible to avoid them. He didn't recoil when he accidentally caught the edge of a blood specimen with his boot heel, since the crime-scene unit had already spent several hours examining that area. Surveying the foyer again, Weaver tried to calm his churning stomach.

Called to the scene during the attack, he had arrived at a bloody and appalling sight. The entire gruesome killing spree had unfolded live right in front of the startled surveillance company personnel. They dispatched security personnel as soon as the terrorists stepped from their car, simultaneously notifying local law enforcement. Weaver, a close friend of the Spencer family, had instantly recognized the address when the call came in. The Spencer estate was outside the northwestern suburbs of Chicago in an area generally considered rural, although still close to all the amenities of city life. When he jerked his vehicle around and hit his siren, he calculated it would take eight minutes at high speed.

As he pulled into the driveway and leapt from the cruiser, he heard other sirens wailing. Seeing the front door hanging open, he drew his gun as he ran up the steps. The scene shocked him; he didn't take time for emotion. With no need to feel for decapitated victims' pulses, the search for the murderers inside the home became his immediate priority. He followed a trail of bloody footsteps toward the stairwell. As he started up, another officer hurried through the door, his gun also drawn. Nodding, he communicated to Weaver he had him covered.

Before Weaver got two steps up, a violent explosion flung him backwards onto the marble. His partner was thrown against the splintered door. With alarmed expressions, they scrambled to their feet and launched themselves up the stairs. The wide hall was already filled with smoke and still more billowed out of a room Weaver knew was Spencer's office. Windows were blown out of their frames; body parts had splattered in every direction. A security guard breathlessly arrived behind them and all three scanned the destroyed office in bewilderment, wishing it was a shared nightmare, but the acrid smell and their burning eyes told them otherwise.

Four hours later, that odor still hung in the air, and his eyes remained bloodshot.

"Dan."

The sound of his named jolted him from his trance. "Yeah, Bill."

"I think we know why they went to the office."

Dan looked at the investigator with revived interest.

"Well, you know how on the surveillance company's video we noticed one of them with a camera?"

Dan nodded.

"Well, he took his film and uploaded it to some site. Spencer has a T3 out here, so it didn't take long at all. Not sure yet which site, but the whole thing is on the web. After they made sure they had done that, bang, they triggered their bombs and blew themselves up. Obviously they knew about the surveillance and knew they wouldn't get out alive."

Weaver sighed. It had actually taken him just a little longer than nine minutes to get to the house, and he now rebuked himself. The surveillance company's digital clock indicated just eight minutes had elapsed between their arrival and the decapitations. If only he had arrived sooner he could have prevented the upload. Hell, a few minutes earlier, he might have prevented the murders, but then he realized the terrorists would have simply set off their bombs right away, still killing everyone.

"Hey, Dan," another deputy called, "you better come out here. We know you're close with the Spencers."

Weaver stepped outside to see Thomas Spencer escorted through a crowd of first responders. The man looked up toward the corner of his home, and Dan glanced back to see wisps of smoke still wafting into the air. Looking at his friend, he could only notice Spencer's ashen appearance.

Grinding his teeth, he started to speak; Thom Spencer interrupted. "They're all dead, aren't they, Dan."

Weaver exhaled heavily and dropped his head. "Yes, Thom, they are."

Aside from the pale face and clenching fists, Spencer showed no emotion. He nodded once curtly and then asked, "Are you going to let me in?"

Dan pressed his lips tightly together. A warm fall breeze ruffled the leaves on the large oak trees. Hoping to avoid this conversation, he glanced at the grove, wondering if somehow the wind could wipe the day from existence. He swallowed, and the surreal situation caused his eyes to gloss over. He started the perfunctory response. "You really don't want to go in there."

"Are you going to let me in or not, Dan?"

Dan's glossed eyes stared at Spencer's deadpan expression. Useless for him to try to persuade Spencer otherwise; instead, Weaver nodded, turned on his heel, and led Thom Spencer into the foyer.

Spencer's eyes raked the scene. To Dan's horror, Thom immediately walked to the spherical objects covered by white sheets. Peering under the first sheet, Spencer paused for several moments. As if to imprint the image on his mind, he blinked several times, though he did not flinch or turn away. One after the other, Spencer mechanically repeated the procedure with each sheet. When finished, he took one step toward the bodies and then turned sharply away and walked toward Dan without looking back.

"What happened upstairs?" he asked, his voice flat.

"The killers blew themselves up."

"Are you going to let me see?"

"They're still investigating, Thom."

"Are you going to let me see?"

Dan's shoulders wilted, and again he nodded and led Spencer

upstairs to view that carnage.

"Hey, we're not finished up here," an investigator complained as they walked down the hall. Dan waved him off without a word.

"Try to be careful up here, Thom."

Thom nodded. He stopped at the door and looked into the destroyed office, but didn't linger long. Again without speaking, Spencer turned and made his way down the stairs and then right out of the house, pushing through all the deputies, officers, and investigators who still crowded the driveway. Dan followed until Spencer stopped among all the vehicles and turned to his friend. "How long ago did this happen?"

"Close to four hours. We've been trying to get a hold of you, Thom."

"I know. I turned my phone on and saw all the messages. I was at the office working. I turned everything off before taking a nap, and I didn't turn any of it back on when I went to workout and run. No one knew where I was."

"Thom, you couldn't have done anything. I was here in just minutes. They were already…well, you know. If you were here, you would have been killed too."

"We all know who did this, Dan, and I wasn't the target. They planned for me not to be here. They wanted me to see it, to live it, not to die from it."

Dan agreed. The sheriff tried to peer behind those blank steel-blue eyes. No emotion surfaced. Shaking his head slightly, he asked, "Thom, are you…well, are you all right? I know you're not all right, but you seem so, so detached."

Thom looked at his friend. Before he could answer, another government-issued sedan rolled into the driveway. Two people stepped out of the car. A striking woman, harmonizing athleticism and feminine elegance, with shoulder length blond hair, crystal blue eyes, and a smooth, tanned complexion, approached Weaver. "Deputy, I'm Special Agent Melissa Dellendale, FBI."

Dan had anticipated their arrival. The FBI field office had notified him DC agents would investigate the crime scene personally as soon as a Bureau jet could fly them there. "Yes, Agent Dellendale. We've gathered all the evidence, so you can review it. If you speak with Investigator Loo inside, she'll give you the information you want."

"Thank you, Deputy. Our investigators will arrive shortly as well," she replied. But instead of marching toward the home as her companion did, Dellendale hesitated. Turning the ring on her little finger, she sighed as she stared at Thom Spencer. "I'm not certain what to say to you, Mr. Spencer." A neo-pager beeped, and she pulled out a thin flexible device that automatically unfolded. She glanced at the number. Annoyed yet resigned, she asked for a minute to make the requested call. Mel reached for her phone and her contact card from another pocket. Harried, she dropped both in the mud. Thom picked them up and wiped off the dirt. Appreciative of his politeness, she smiled, but it faded as she momentarily stared into cold eyes. It sent a chill down her spine. After a quick phone conversation, she returned. "My heart and my prayers go out to you, Mr. Spencer. I'm so sorry. I know that seems rather hollow and useless right now," she said compassionately.

Thom cocked his head and shook it. "It just seems that way, Agent Dellendale, because we all know that words and tears aren't adequate responses to evil. But for right now, they're all we have, so I appreciate and thank you for them."

Thom was sincere with Dellendale, yet his demeanor was so antiseptic. Dan could feel Agent Dellendale's discomfort. She handed Thom her card. "Sorry for the stain, but I don't have any more. If you need anything, Mr. Spencer." She walked quickly toward the house, and Spencer pocketed the card without looking at it. Dan stared at his friend. The Thom Spencer he had known for so many years had disappeared, and a different man stared back at him.

Chapter Eight

Tuesday, November 11

Dan Weaver and other investigators had asked him to stay nearby in case of questions. While sitting in his vehicle alone for several hours, in between desperate spurts of despair and sadness, an incredible idea formed. No one even glanced at him, and Thom decided to leave without speaking with Dan. His friend would understand. Not many vehicles traveled Randall Road at 2:30 in the morning. Spence sped to his office, outside Batavia, Illinois, where a nanotechnology corridor had spontaneously evolved over the last few years near the Fermi accelerator lab. People had thought it would benefit them or was nostalgic to build where so much physics had been discovered and learned. Spencer had built his company's campus there because he liked it, and it wasn't too far from home. He never considered moving south; the commute didn't last more than about forty-five minutes, and it always gave him time to think. This time of night, he would make it in thirty minutes, allowing him to reflect sporadically on his developing plan, and conveniently cutting short the time to play the gruesome scene over and over in his mind.

Images of those contorted, sunken faces eventually consumed his focus during the drive. He recognized them; then again he didn't. When he left that morning, he took the time to say goodbye and kiss everyone, as he always did. His oldest daughter, Jennifer, kissed his cheek while little Michelle nuzzled his neck, asking in toddler talk why he had to go to the office. Answering with the usual, "I always do," they frowned, even Jennifer, but then smiled when he told them he'd try to be home early. Toni kissed him as he patted Rose on the shoulder on his way out the door.

He always described his family life as perfectly imperfect. His love for Toni had quickly transcended the romantic and grounded itself where making love didn't make the love. Passion remained, but trust and friendship placed their love beyond the ordinary and in the realm where it easily rebuffed those momentary lapses of anger and biting exchanges husbands and wives inevitably visit upon each other. They had found their own special kingdom of love.

He loved his work also; he loved his family more, immensely more, yet he still would miss Jennifer's soccer game where she scored the winning goal. All he could do was buy her a congratulatory pizza and ice cream while inwardly berating himself for his absence as Michelle played kissy-cheek with him. "You now give me a kissy on my cheek, Daddy!" Rose laughed forgivingly when Daddy played kissy-cheek, no matter that Daddy had missed the game. They all still smiled and loved him despite his foibles, despite him sometimes forgetting the priorities. Perfectly imperfect.

Those smiling and loving faces he now juxtaposed to the mutilated heads hidden underneath white sheets. Those smiling and loving faces were gone, destroyed so suddenly and absolutely, and the void threatened to engulf him. He tried concentrating on the living moments with his family, the faces he forever wanted to remember, compartmentalizing the grotesque, disfigured heads into the recesses of the mind. It was important, he told himself, to remember the life and not just the death of his family. He never even felt the tears streaming downs his cheeks.

Campus lights outlined the buildings as he approached the gate. Security guards waved him past without question and then did a double take when it struck them who actually had just arrived.

Entering the main building, Spencer approached the guard station on his way to the elevator. The guard looked up and his eyes widened. The familiar figure, always so athletic and assured, suddenly seemed haggard and spent. Old even. "Mr. Spencer." He paused. "I'm so sorry, Mr. Spencer."

Thom stopped and studied the sincerity in the guard's face.

Without realizing his eyes had puffed up and reddened, he rubbed them once more. "Terrance, thank you." He breathed heavily a few times to steady his voice. "I won't be long. I have to get a few things from the office, and I really didn't want to come here during the day. Especially a weekday."

"I understand, Mr. Spencer. I don't know what else to say."

"You've said all that can be said, Terrance. Thank you."

The elevator whisked him to the fifth floor. Again rubbing his eyes, Spencer put aside his anguish and focused on the tasks at hand. He sat at his desk, logged onto his personal computer, and accessed a few personal files, more as a decoy than from an actual need for the information. He swiveled in his chair to face the business desktop. Next, he plugged an untested photonic device developed by Tyler Washington into a USB port and started typing in his codes, accessing monitored databases and files.

His best nano-scientist and closest friend, Washington had worked on photonic computing for many months. Processing based on the photon rather than the electron opened a fantastic door into quantum computing. Still in its infancy, the technology still was finding its way and most people in the industry believed it wouldn't be viable for at least a few years. Yet, Tyler had designed, built, and programmed a device to work within normal electronic computers, more as a game than anything. Plug the device into a port and obtain information without detection. Because of several bugs, neither thought it was ready for commercial application, but it did theoretically allow the user to operate an electronic device invisibly with proper access codes or passwords. Once on the web, inside a program, or in database, the user could mine, deposit, or even alter information without being traced. A dangerous tool, with far-reaching implications, it would have more applications when photonic computing further developed. Until then, Tyler and Spence had kept the program essentially dormant.

With the download completed to his thumb drive, Spencer took a deep breath. Now for the tricky part: confirming the device had removed his computer trail. He exited the database, logged off his computer, and disconnected the photonic device. If it didn't work, no way could he reconnect it. His log in, all the time logged, as well as the downloaded data would appear on security reports. Spencer pressed a button on the device, and after a nervous moment a LED flashed twice, confirming the device had scrubbed all traces. He then rolled his chair to his personal computer to finish the download of those personal files. It finished. Instead of immediately leaving, he walked to the liquor shelf and poured himself a half shot of whiskey. After sloshing the alcohol around his mouth for a few moments and then swallowing, Spence set down the glass and picked up his photonic and thumb drives, and walked to the elevator.

Back down in the lobby, Spencer leaned on the guard's desk and sighed heavily, but spoke clearly enough that the guard wouldn't stop him from driving. "I'm not certain when I'll return, Terrance. I have many things to do, you know."

The guard smelled the liquor, but could tell Spencer wasn't intoxicated. A drink or two after what had happened to him didn't seem like such a bad idea. "You take care of yourself, Mr. Spencer," Terrance said sympathetically.

As Spencer pulled out of the campus parking lot, he spoke Tyler's name, and his phone dialed automatically.

"Hey, I've been trying to find you all day, Spence. No one would allow me near your home, so I drove back to work for a while to console all those people. I finally told them to go home. We all felt helpless. I went home, miserable. Kept calling you, but no one answered. Same with Dan Weaver. No one called me."

"Been a long a day, Tyler."

Tyler's silence revealed how he was struggling with his emotions. After a few moments, he choked out, "I loved them as my own, Thom. You know that. Hell, you guys are the only family I got."

Thom ignored his friend's pain. "Are you still at home, Tyler?"

"Yeah. Been sitting here waiting for your call."

"Sorry I didn't call before now, but I want to talk."

"I can come meet you. Might be easier."

"No. I'll be there in a half hour or so."

Spence arrived at Tyler's expensive, high-end town home well before sunrise. When he walked through the door, Tyler sighed heavily and leaned down and grabbed his friend in a strong embrace. Spencer wanted to keep this meeting sterile, devoid of emotion. The tears were gone, or so he thought, but when Tyler refused to let go, they reappeared and flowed steadily down his tired face, and for the moment, Thom allowed himself to cry.

The two men finally parted, a little uncomfortable in their mutually exposed vulnerability. Redness surrounded Tyler's brown eyes, and his voice trembled with intensity. "Those dirty bastards, Thom. Those dirty, filthy bastards."

Thom and Tyler shared many of the same thoughts and opinions about politics. Frustration and anger sparked in Tyler just watching the evening news, and several times innocent conversations would end with Tyler banging his fist and declaring with a snarl his blood pressure had risen too high, and he didn't want to talk anymore. The world just made him too damned mad.

Tyler froze for a moment, staring absently at the floor, and then more tears welled up. He blinked furiously, releasing them to his already wet cheek. "What in the world do I say to you, Thom?" he asked, swallowing his anger.

Thom reined in his emotions. "Tyler, there isn't anything to say. There's only something to do. I'm not here to cry, but to do something about it."

His friend peered into Spence's tired eyes as he rubbed his jaw. "Do you want a drink?" he asked, waving his friend to a seat on the couch.

Thom shook his head. "You remember when we talked about weaponizing the Bio-nano Utility Sequencer?"

Tyler paused at the abrupt change of tone. Bio-nano Utility Sequencer? The BUS, he asked himself. The inapposite question brought him up short. "Are you serious? Talking business now, Thom?"

"It's not business, Tyler. This is personal. Just answer the question, and you'll soon see where I'm going."

A quick breath and shake of the head cleared Tyler's mind, allowing him to placate his friend. "Sure, sure I remember. I think I'm the one who first suggested we use the BUS for a weapon, wasn't I?" Thom nodded. "There's still no real good way to trigger the catalyst, though. The trigger riddle still kinda gnaws at me. We thought the Department of Defense might figure something out if we sent the schematics to it."

Thom didn't respond. Tyler peered at him awkwardly. "Did you ever do that?" he asked apprehensively, more concerned about his friend's state of mind than an answer.

"No, I didn't."

"Well, now that we've finished the prototypes, we probably could," Tyler offered ambivalently.

"No, absolutely not." Spence paused a moment, reflecting on what he was about to say.

Several moments passed, and Tyler waited patiently for his friend to resume. Finally, Thom sighed heavily and said, "You know what I thought about when I got the message from Dan?"

Shrugging while shaking his head, Tyler couldn't fathom his friend's shock.

Thom's eyes slightly squinted. "I blamed myself. I immediately knew what had happened, and I blamed myself for their deaths. If I hadn't opened my big mouth that one night, then Dickson's and those other shows wouldn't have happened, and no one would know me from Adam. I drove to my home in a stupor, dizzy from pain, knowing I would walk into some sort of earthly hell. And I did. Much worse than I imagined. Yet something came over me the moment I arrived. In that single instant, when I walked up my driveway and looked up and saw smoke coming out of where I knew my office once was, I stopped blaming myself. Not some sort of rationalized cure, just…the sight disgusted me so much, the thought that people in our own country couldn't exercise their own rights… I knew this wasn't my fault. I was right, and that sort of cowardly act confirmed everything I thought about them. They are to blame, Tyler. Not me. I don't feel guilty anymore, and even though it only happened a few hours ago, and I could have many years to live with this, I know I won't. Ever. You want to know what I felt?"

Tyler rubbed his jaw, understanding. "You felt rage, my friend. You felt rage."

Thom nodded. "Simple rage. But not emotional, fiery rage. Cold and calculating rage. When I walked around my house, I made sure to imprint in my mind what they did. I didn't cry, and I didn't rant or cause a scene. I just observed. Intently. Then I left, and as I was standing outside with Dan, an FBI agent showed up. She said the usual things, sincere and genuinely upset. I could tell from her expression, her eyes mostly. You know what happened?"

Tyler shrugged again, unsure where this was leading.

"Her pager went off. And she looked at her phone and asked if I could wait a minute or so. I had nowhere to go, so I didn't care. As I waited for her to finish the call, just standing there, I don't know why, but it hit me. Frequency waves. Her neo pager was compact and flexible. It unfolded into an electronic device much thinner than a credit card. You know what it reminded me of?"

Tyler's expression changed; he thought he understood where Thom was going. "Nano-tape."

Spence nodded. "Material thin as Scotch tape, containing a power source and emitting frequency waves, trigged by…"

Tyler finished the analysis. "Light, sound, touch, almost anything. I know. I worked on all of it."

"Right," Spence nodded again. "And it also could be triggered by time. The strip's power source could be set to a timer."

"No doubt," Tyler agreed.

"Don't you see? This solves the trigger riddle. The nano-tape could trigger the BUS by a timer."

Tyler's eyes widened in understanding. "Of course. The nano-tape emits encoded complex frequency waves after a programmed amount of time, and puff, they catalyze our BUS, and it goes to work." Tyler sighed, unsure of the implication, especially in light of the circumstance. "I still assume you don't want to involve the DoD."

Spence shook his head. "No."

Tyler frowned.

Spence pressed on dispassionately. "We already have the nano-tape. The reconfigurations would take a couple of days at most to design."

Tyler thought for a moment and agreed with a curt nod.

"And we have much of the BUS already. Designing it to react to the nano-tape, that's the tricky part. I need you to do it, Tyler. Not DoD, and not the company."

Tyler leaned back in his chair. The man across from him had just lost his entire family to an ungodly terrorist act, and here he was asking for help building a nano-device. The surrealism inundated the moment, and Tyler couldn't help smirking. "Thom, are you listening to yourself?" he asked.

"Very clearly. I know it sounds strange, but do you think you can do it…well, actually I know you can, but will you is the question?"

With his arm resting on the chair's arm, Tyler stroked his jaw while thinking about the health of his friend and, oddly, the possibility of his request. "I don't know," he finally answered. "Can't start from scratch, you know. I would need the entire BUS program. I know I designed much of it, but a team built a lot of that. We keep that tightly secured. Just going in there and taking it for a new project's going to raise some serious suspicion."

Thom reached into his pocket, withdrew the external photonic drive and the thumb drive, and threw them next to his friend. "It's all there."

Tyler wrinkled his brow, focusing more on the photonic device than the thumb drive. "You used it to hide your download? Did it work?" he asked.

"Seemed to, but I guess we'll find out tomorrow or the next day, won't we?"

Tyler raised his eyebrow. Security programs and personnel strictly monitored every download, authorized or not, and Tyler and other executives received a report every morning describing all system activity. "Yeah, guess so. If it's found out, they'll come a-calling." Other formidable concerns about the proposal popped into the scientist's head. "I'm going to need a team of technicians, though. I don't think I can do it alone; that would take months."

"For some of the initial components, maybe, but with the BUS, I think a lot of that work is already completed."

Tyler rubbed his jaw again, considering.

Spence didn't interrupt.

"Probably so," Tyler eventually surmised.

"But you have to process the final pathogen, Tyler."

"Yeah, that probably can be done too. Pretty easy at that, now that I think about it." Tyler glanced at his friend, disturbed by his pure detachment. "You've thought this out pretty far, Thom."

Tyler's expression indicated nascent understanding, but Thom knew Tyler didn't grasp the full extent of Thom's intentions. Spencer leaned forward with his hands on his knees and whispered, "I have to warn you, Tyler, it's nothing you could imagine." He abruptly stood and started pacing around the living room. Tyler, patient with his friend's fragile state, still felt a little unnerved by his demeanor, yet he listened without interrupting. "The rage I felt..., well, my plan not only quells that, but stops this insanity. We can no longer live under this terrorist threat, and I'm going to end it. I'm not going to lie to you, Tyler; if we're caught, we're dead. I come to you, Tyler, not just because you're my best friend, but like me, you don't have any brothers, sisters or parents around. And now I don't have a family, either. We're alone, you and I. We don't have ties to keep us around. We can move discreetly.

"If at any time you want out, or you don't agree with what we're doing, or you simply change your mind, then we stop. Not just you; I quit as well. We go only as far as *you* want. If you aren't in now, then it goes no further than this conversation you had with a confused and distraught friend whose family had just been brutally murdered. You must understand this, Tyler. This will go only as far as you want it to go."

Out of the confusion of emotions and fatigue, the moment suddenly converged, and Tyler realized what Thom Spencer was actually suggesting. His friend hadn't visited him to seek comfort and condolences; instead, he was there recruiting him for a mission. Instantly he recognized how feasible it was, and all the placating, all the discomfort and concern vanished. Tyler leaned forward, paused, and then pushed himself out of the chair. He strolled around the room, still faintly massaging his jaw. His scientist's mind raced, calculating the logistics of the operation. While he paced, obstacles tumbled as he mentally pieced together Spence's most recent scientific puzzle, and the initial blurred feasibility materialized clearly. It *would* be easier than he originally thought. He stole a quick look at Spence's eyes, and he could tell his friend already knew it.

Tyler gritted his teeth and cleared his throat. "I thought you came here for a hug. Obviously not. A moment ago, you said 'I couldn't imagine.' Thom, I'm perhaps the most qualified person in the world to imagine what you intend to do. I know exactly what we're making here, my friend, and I know its potency."

Thom frowned. "Obviously a wrong choice of words."

"Obviously," Tyler affirmed, his eyes wide open. He stared several seconds at his friend. Something had changed. Passion remained, but it had turned intensely cold, and time wouldn't warm it up. He knew, because he felt it too.

He pressed his lips tightly together in quiet anger. "Oh, I'm in— so in—Thom," Tyler snarled. "As you probably have already gathered, the tape and serum are quite doable. But there's gotta be more than that. What's next?"

Thom immediately spotted avenging conviction and commitment in his friend's changed demeanor. He smiled. Not a jovial, friendly smile, but one sterile and calculating. "To make my plan work, we have to recruit one other person."

"One person? That's it?" Tyler asked coolly.

"One person."

"Who's that?"

"Jacob Brannan. Major Jacob Brannan."

Chapter Nine

Monday, April 21

Nanotechnology: A new science where man pushed the limits of reductionism almost to the depths of the quantum world and exalted his sublime power. Technology based on one billionth of a meter, a size as small as the molecule, had inexhaustible potential for humanity. When man can build from the molecular level, resequence the matter that makes up the everyday world, he truly had arrived at a place where creativity merged with productivity, art and science united. Imagination need not check itself at the nano-scientist's door, and the world's richness could infinitely increase. Some researchers proposed nano-machines, mechanical devices inserted into the atomic structure of the world to work mechanical magic. Others believed man could restructure matter without machines; scientists just had to redesign a molecule, to make its properties better suited for an intended use. No doubt a complex process, but feasible, and when a scientist hit on the right combination, the result was glorious.

The nanotechnology industry fascinated Spencer, and, although his background was in finance, he understood much of the science. After making a substantial amount of money on Wall Street, he decided to call his undergraduate friend, Tyler Washington, who worked in the field every day and had kept Thom current.

Tyler graduated with a coveted doctorate in nano-engineering, and he had developed a process manipulating rubberized material.

44

When he walked through the corporate door, executives promised him research dollars for his material as soon as other projects were completed. New projects always seemed to pop up, and Tyler kept shelving his invention, and working for a corporation snatched away all the time he needed to explore it further. He had to eat, he convinced himself, and the corporation fed him well. But the day Thom Spencer called and suggested they join forces, Tyler rolled the dice and resigned, and the two began searching for the ideal company to start the journey to success.

Just outside Chicago, a small firm struggling to find its identity had appeared on Spencer's radar. Like many nanotechnology firms, it sputtered in its infancy; the founder had staked all his money in the technology to produce a bullet-proof material. But the science failed, and the company tried converting all its assets to produce another nanotechnology material. Further research demanded more money, and time started running out. With funds dwindling, the company went up for sale.

Thom immediately believed Tyler could adapt his process to the bullet-proof material. Tyler studied the idea for several hours and announced that Thom had a scientist's instinct. The process would work, and the company's existing asset base would provide much of what he needed. Thom had expected the negotiation would require several sessions of tough bargaining; instead, after one twenty-minute meeting where the owner reviewed Thom's offer and nearly cried, Thom bought the company. The former owner couldn't believe Spencer's generosity, and both men left the table exceedingly pleased with the agreement.

With a multi-year facility lease, computers, equipment, and eager employees excited by the new ownership, Thom as Chief Executive Officer and Tyler as Chief Science Officer began their personal adventure into nanotechnology. Two years later, Nanoexelogy had a contract to deliver light-weight, fire-resistant bullet-proof suits and goggles to the United States Army and Marines. With its soldiers nearly invulnerable to fire, bullets, and many kinds of shrapnel, the US kept expanding its military dominance.

Nanoexelogy equipment became standard issue, and next came material designed and manufactured for hot weather, cold weather, and for nearly every environment a soldier, airman, marine, or sailor could face. Law enforcement and first responders quickly followed. For expanded applications, they converted the technology to sports apparel for the professional as well as the casual athlete. The cash flow exploded and transformed Nanoexelogy into a Wall Street darling.

Tyler, since his days as a doctoral candidate, had dreamed of marrying nanotechnology and medicine. He identified nanobiotechnology as the field with the richest opportunities to cure disease and genetic disorders to regenerating human tissue. With the cash cow as the company's stable generator, exploration into nanobiotechnology was a natural progression. Once Nanoexelogy took this next step, a state-of-the-art campus in Batavia, Illinois, provided ample room for both the core business and the nanobio dream. Other companies flocked to the area, and soon synergy created the nanotech corridor.

As Tyler exuded supreme confidence in his science's ability to conquer the maladies of nature, Thom managed the means to bring these cures to the world. Progress in the medical field came quicker than either had expected, and they soon patented several prototype serums called bio-nano utility sequencers. The BUS became the technological basis for Nanoexelogy's foray into nanobiotechnology.

When Tyler first hypothesized applying the BUS to a bio-weapon, Thom agreed Nanoexelogy's mission should incorporate weapons development. But creating a pathogen at the nano level wasn't intriguingly original, and bio-weapons notoriously dispersed uncontrollably, either infecting too many or too few. If they could control contagion rates with timing and toxic penetration, then they had a unique weapon.

Both quickly realized the serum itself didn't pose the problem: infect everyone in an identified region. Who cared if the substance were benign until catalyzed? The trick was developing a trigger that catalyzed an identifiable segment of the infected area, thus controlling the contagion rate. To solve this "trigger riddle," Thom believed he would have to involve the Department of Defense, which had a nasty habit of hijacking any technology introduced to it. Spence made the strategic business decision to bide his time, giving Tyler and his team a chance as he prepared for DoD's nasty habits. It was a fortunate decision.

Visiting New York reminded him of the time he made several of those first deals on Wall Street, generating the seed money for Nanoexelogy. When he and Tyler opened a worn wooden door into a Midtown bar, he flashed back to the lounge where he and Toni had met more than fifteen years ago. Both had a handsome smell; something about New York made all its bars handsome. Tyler and he walked into a narrow space straddled by a long, thickly-lacquered oak bar—bearing the scars of thousands of drinks banged on its edge. It opened into a dual-level back room, with the downstairs decorated in black and white, and the upstairs in dark gray. High definition television sets occupied the corners, and deep, soft leather couches lined the paneled walls, offering a sanctuary from everyday life.

Thom sank into the couch closest to the stairwell as Tyler settled on a chair and glued his attention to a game on TV. Five minutes later, an average-sized man wearing non-descript clothes came in and stopped briefly at the last bar stool. He kept his head down, but his eyes darted toward Thom, and then he bounded up the stairs without hesitation. His extended hand and ready smile gave the impression they were long-time friends who had gone some time without seeing each other. No one gave them a second glance.

"Thom, how about a beer?"

Thom, puzzled by the greeting, frowned, but the man's brown eyes flashed a warning. Spence merely nodded and smiled as well. The waitress heard talk of beer and lazily climbed the stairs, taking no note of either the trite conversation or the men's faces as she listlessly took the order.

"Well, it's great to see you, Thom."

"Been too long," Thom answered, maintaining the charade.

"It has. Been watching the playoffs? I hope to catch a few games." They continued the small talk until the waitress dropped off the mugs of beer and wandered back to her station at the other end of the bar.

After confirming no one could eavesdrop, Thom said, "I didn't know if you would remember me, Major. We met a quite a few years ago in Israel."

"I do remember or I wouldn't be here," Jacob Brannan replied, nodding. "I usually don't meet people under these circumstances. I recall talking with you briefly about a conversation I had with a Muslim friend of mine. We also talked about your company.

Nanoexelogy has helped our troops tremendously, Mr. Spencer."

Thom acknowledged the compliment with a nod of his own. "And you said that then, and you also gave me a card."

"I remember. I remember every card I give out."

"Well, I kept it," Thom said. "And do you recall what you said to your Muslim friend?"

"I do."

"You didn't offer much praise about his religion or his Middle Eastern governments. Do you still feel that way?"

"Yes, I do. And obviously I've been proven correct. Many times over. Unfortunately, and at your and your family's expense." Brannan's expression darkened as he considered what Thom Spencer had endured. "You know, Mr. Spencer, when a lot of people saw your debate on that Chicago news show, they agreed with you. I did. You were tough, but people felt the same, especially after Miami. Then you made your appearance on that national cable news show the following week and admitted that you had been tough, maybe even too tough. But you explained you purposely had taken a brazen approach, because you were terribly worried, and not only about us. You also felt sorry, and concerned, for so many Muslims, because you felt that their own religion had trapped them. Well, that completely humanized you. You had replaced the monster with a kinder face and a gentler man. I thought it was brilliant."

"It wasn't calculated in that way, Major Brannan. I meant what I said."

"Whatever, it worked. And that's another reason why I wanted to meet you. Again."

Thom Spencer sighed. "I'm taking a big risk here, Major. I have done as much research on you as possible, but there's very little, as I'm sure you know. Made me even more confident. Without the card you gave me, I never could have contacted you. I don't know whether you have a wire or recorder or any other electronic device. I don't think you do, but if you do, you could get me thrown in prison for a very long time for what I'm about to say. Or maybe a psych ward."

Brannan thinly smiled. "Mr. Spencer, I don't remember every card I give people because I have a fabulous memory. I remember them because I give out very few. Now, I think we both knew in Israel what my job was. And in light of what has happened since, particularly with your family, I don't think you invited me here to begin a friendship over beer and sports talk. Given what you know about me, Mr. Spencer, I'm guessing you want something…unconventional from me."

Spencer, gauging the man across from him, appreciated the candor. He leaned forward and said, "I need you to kidnap someone."

"Who?"

Spencer's eyes went cold and distant, as if a switch flicked off in his head and pure detachment consumed all emotion. "A Muslim. I don't care who. Your choice, but Major, you have to know up front this man is going to die, and his death could be painful."

The look on Spencer's face made an impression on the major. He rarely saw such a cold and emotionless demeanor, especially among civilians. "So you're going to sink to their level, Mr. Spencer?"

"No, Major, I'm not. Their level is child's play. I'm taking the conflict up to my level. It's a whole new game. And let me tell you, I'm starting with one, hoping that is enough, but the potential is for many, many more to die."

"How many?"

The cold stare gave no answer. "Are you able to infiltrate any major Middle Eastern cities or regions?"

The major didn't flinch. "What do you mean infiltrate?" he responded noncommittally.

"I need to know whether you can gain access to specifically identified locations in the Middle East for extended periods of time."

Access didn't concern Brannan, but duration did. "Extended? How long, Mr. Spencer?"

"You'll need enough time to disperse an airborne virus at those various locations calculated to achieve a certain dispersal pattern. Then you leave. Later, you'll return to that same site with a catalyst that triggers the virus."

Brannan sat across from a man who owned one of the preeminent nanotechnology companies in the world, and he had a general sense of nanotechnology's potential. Brannan asked calmly, "Exactly how many are you planning to kill, Mr. Spencer?"

"As I said, I hope one. My guess is one won't be enough. After the first, you don't want to know, Major."

"I don't? I just deliver the means by which you kill them?"

"Yes. I will give them a choice. I will give them chances to avoid these deaths. But I must make good on my threats if they don't deliver."

"'They?' Who are 'they?' Who needs to deliver what to you, Mr. Spencer?"

"Don't you remember what you said in that conversation in Israel? You said, 'Together Muslim governments have the means to uproot and destroy all the Islamic terrorist organizations in the world. They simply choose not to do it, and in fact, many networks are supported by these governments.'"

"They do support them, although they actually have killed hundreds if not thousands of suspected terrorists, just very selectively. Only those who threaten their own authority. Amazingly, they can always find and eliminate those terrorists. As for so many other networks, they actually rely on them heavily to divert internal attention away from their own centuries-old internal conflicts, their sectarian and tribal disputes to mention just a couple. But these terrorists must focus on a fantastic enemy—a Great Satan, for example—outside the Ummah, and absorb much of that internal discontent and strife. Without those caricatures, even more volatility is turned inward, forcing already teetering governments closer to implosion."

Spencer nodded. "That's right. And people in the know agree with you."

Brannan started to understand the man who sat across from him. He wasn't insane, and he had a plan. No doubt he had developed technology that he could deploy against those governments. "And you're going to demand what, that they surrender all the terrorists and destroy the organizations?"

"Exactly. All of them, starting with Ghazali and Universal Jihad."

"And what if you succeed, and all those government are toppled? What then, Mr. Spencer?"

"Who cares if the terrorists aren't there to replace them? At that point, six one way and a half a dozen the other, right?"

Spencer's assessment was probably correct, Brannan thought. The major then calculated the threat level required before any Muslim government considered the demand. "All right, Mr. Spencer, but you may need a very high casualty count to coerce governments. How many can you kill, Mr. Spencer? I really do need to know that."

"No, you don't, Major. You're just doing a job, as if you were given an order from your commanding officer. Do it, and understand that if these governments don't meet the demands, the consequence is beyond your control. Your hands will be clean."

Brannan knew differently; his hands were already so dirty, no amount of rationalization would ever clean them, but he didn't care about any of that. He understood Spencer had seized the offensive and would deliver to the Islamic community, the Ummah, a message from the West. Brannan, from the gut, believed the time had come.

"You misunderstand me, Mr. Spencer. I'm not asking because of any sense of guilt or moral implications; I'm asking for purposes of feasibility. I don't want to be involved with any endeavor that can't achieve the impact necessary to accomplish your objective. I don't want you to waste my time."

Spencer paused, evaluating the major's dispassionate response. "The count will be high enough, if necessary."

Though he believed Spencer could deliver on his promise, Brannan wanted to confirm a few facts, and confirm toppled regimes lacking terrorist successors would likely be 'six one way and a half a dozen the other.' "Mr. Spencer, I'm not promising anything, but I'm interested in your proposal. How do I contact you?"

Without hesitation, Spencer handed him a card with a telephone number on it. "Please contact me within a week, Major. There's more to discuss. Leave a message. If you don't call, I'll know your answer."

Chapter Ten

Tuesday, April 22

During the trip to La Guardia Airport, Tyler, anxiously spinning thumbs in clasped hands, interrupted the silence by asking, "Do you think Brannan will go to the authorities?"

Spence shook his head. "No, I don't. He wants in, but he's cautious. My guess, he's checking to see if we can do what we claim."

Tyler smirked, "Well, we'll see if we meet any of our FBI friends at the airport. Then we'll know. What happens to all our plans if we never hear from the guy, Spence?"

"Then I've just wasted money and time, Tyler. Have plenty of both these days, and I don't care how much of either I have to spend. We just start over."

Washington understood his friend's laser focus; the loss of his family took its toll. "Speaking of those plans, how are the decoy sites coming?"

Spence nodded. "We're set. If anyone searches, they're going find the best leads in Chiapas, Mexico. After that, it turns into a dead end. Another trail might lead to Brazil. It cost a small fortune, but if they put enough pieces together, they'll break down a door and find a whole lot of boxes with some old equipment, but that's it. What about the serum?"

"The purchases from outside sources weren't a big deal. Even though the market's limited, I confirmed all of them have several different applications, so there shouldn't be any red flags there.

"Anyway, as you know, the BUS has already done most of the work. Four resequences instead of six really helped, and no one raised a stink about our work in our P-4 lab."

Only the most dangerous serums required a Bio-Safety Level 4 protection, where with other safety measures, all personnel wore hazmat suits and used self-contained oxygen units. Puzzled, Thom frowned. "You never told me why you had to use the P-4. We don't have anything that toxic until it's triggered. It should be inert."

"Well," Tyler explained, "after the sequencing stage it is, but during sequencing, it could be toxic. I had to test it. Maybe you'd do that stuff at a coffee table, but I wasn't gonna chance it."

Spence chuckled, understanding the risk, but the Centers for Disease Control and Prevention regulated P-4 lab activity. "Obviously the CDC didn't cause a problem."

"Not one. All couched in related research. And I did it out of precaution more than any real risk, so not a question asked."

"And you're going to use another BUS to sequence the final agent. And you can do that resequencing yourself, right?" Spence asked, confirming the procedure.

"Yep."

"And you're sure you don't need a P-4 lab for that."

"Hope not, because we don't have one of those where we're going."

Spence gave Tyler a sidelong glance at the flippant tone. "Look, Spence," Tyler said seriously, "I told you, I got it handled. It's all about the sequencing process when I combine the four serums. Completely inert and safe, but when triggered, it resequences itself in a radically different order, resulting in the toxicity, and that stuff is deadly. All the dirty work has already been done."

Tyler gave him a confident look, knowing Spence appreciated reassurance. "But, you know, Spence, I've been thinking."

"About what?"

"Well, I farmed out some of that dirty work, hiding it here and there, but if you hadn't downloaded the BUS when you did, and we didn't have that to start with, there's no way we could've done this."

Spence's ruse had worked. The official Nanoexelogy security log noted his arrival and departure time and the download from his personal computer on that dreadful day in November. The guard also scribbled Spencer had had "a drink or two," which accounted for the time he had spent in his office. No one suspected anything.

After the brutal murders, Nanoexelogy employees expected their CEO to take an extended leave, and everyone understood Tyler's periodic absences, since they presumed Spence needed his best friend's support. During that time, however, neither could have downloaded any company data without raising suspicion or risking detection.

The next time Thom walked through Nanoexelogy's front doors, he informed the company he would resign his position as CEO and would vacate his seat on the board of directors for the remainder of the term so he could travel. By itself that didn't surprise anyone, but Tyler's announcement that he was taking a sabbatical at the same time raised a few eyebrows. However, his explanation—that Thom needed his support to cope with the tragedy—made perfect sense. Besides, until the Spencer murders, no one could recall when Tyler Washington had missed work for more than an occasional long weekend. He had earned some time off.

"Everything's still good with the tape?" Tyler asked after they had traveled a few more miles.

Spence nodded. With some help from Tyler, he had made a few simple modifications to Nanoexelogy's basic design, and paid, under a different corporate identity, an outside firm to manufacture the redesigned tape. It had a different use to divert any scrutiny into the actual purpose. "Patent's pending on the fire design. We just have to rework the trigger from heat to time when meet up again."

Tyler shrugged his shoulder. "With that stuff, not a problem." He paused and asked, "Hey, give me the address on the Brazilian decoy site."

Spence reached into his jacket and pulled out a folded piece of paper. "When you go to Brazil, the tape should be there waiting for you."

"I'll just pick up that and my serum ingredients, gloves on and all, and be out of there in no time. No one'll see or hear me or even know I was there."

Spence nodded again. Brazil wasn't as much a decoy as a drop site, he admitted to himself. If the government somehow discovered their trail, the road would lead there, but it wouldn't reveal anything, because by then everything would be gone.

Tyler, always a little uncomfortable with shared silence, blurted, "To have it triggered by time... good idea, Spence. If our major goes along with us, it should give him plenty of time to make his rounds in all the cities. What a shock for those people after a day or so," he mumbled, his voice trailing off.

A few more silent miles passed, but again Tyler couldn't resist. "By the way, I think I've hit on the right change in my computer program. All electronic searches into our little hideout will be scrambled without a trace." He chuckled to himself. "I'll just have to check it after we get there. Won't take too long."

The mundane chatter tugged a faint grin from Spencer. "All right, after I drop you off, we meet at the rendezvous point in a month. You sure you have all you need—ID's, cash, and your itinerary?" Spence inquired.

"Spence, I know it was your idea that we travel through different countries, using different passports and all, but I agreed with it, and I did everything I needed to do."

"Sorry, just checking, Tyler. Sometimes you scientists don't always have those details organized."

Smiling, Tyler nodded in agreement.

The airport loomed ahead, and when the car stopped at the curb, Tyler looked at his friend and simply nodded before stepping out of the vehicle. He then grabbed his bag from the backseat and headed to his Miami flight without a word. Spence pulled away swiftly and drove to JFK. The half-hour drive passed without incident—no sirens or flashing lights, no dark, unmarked FBI sedan with an inscrutable driver wearing dark sunglasses signaling him to the side of the road. Any vehicle matching his imagined FBI tail made Spence shift nervously; it would eventually veer off or pull ahead, and Thom would relax and just drive.

And no FBI agent met him at the gate; no one gave him a moment's notice as he entered the cabin on his long flight to Athens, Greece. As he took his seat next to a window, Spence glanced out and saw tarmac personnel bustling about their tasks. So many innocent people just doing their jobs, he thought, wondering whether their world would be different if he ever returned to the United States.

Sighing, he plugged in the earphones and leaned his head back, trying to relax. The in-seat screen flipped through various ads and program teasers; then a segment caught his eye: a cable news report on Ghazali's failed plot to bomb a famous New York department store. The FBI and NYPD had done a magnificent job, saving so many families from devastation.

But they couldn't and wouldn't save them all. For the first time in days, perhaps weeks, Spencer had time to reflect, and his thoughts drifted to his family. He had shed his last tear on the day of his family's funeral, a small private affair that now seemed many years ago. He kept the memory of his former life locked securely in his heart, but he tucked that heart away in a remote part of his soul. Now cold calculation and unfeeling action possessed him.

The nation had cried out after the Spencer murders. Washington, DC, didn't hear it, and the government's inaction gridlocked the only nation in the world that could challenge the enemy. Everyone knew the recently foiled plot would lead to another attempt, and another until Ghazali again succeeded. The country wanted bold and assertive action before that happened; instead, nothing...until now. Spencer's plan had proceeded with precision, but he had gambled on this next step with a man named Major Jacob Brannan. Confidently smiling to himself, Spence closed his eyes, certain his gamble would pay off.

Chapter Eleven

Wednesday, June 17

The drumming of President Mark Halladan's fingers echoed off the curved wall of the otherwise deathly silent Oval Office. He glared at everyone in turn, disappointment and anger evident in his expression.

Terrorist attacks had all but ceased after the Spencer massacre, and the failed NYC department store plot showed that the government remained on high alert. Since the failed attack on the department store, no agency heard any chatter or picked up indications of another plot, yet all governmental agencies remained vigilant, and protocol required redundant monitoring during these silent periods.

Without warning, a suicide bomber in a St. Louis mall abruptly declared the cease-fire over by killing twenty-nine people. Three days later in the same city, a man walked into a bank and destroyed it, murdering another twenty-four people and maiming ten more. A week later, three suicide bombers in Denver, Newark, and San Diego exploded themselves within an hour of one another. Denver's nightmare occurred in a crowded family sports restaurant where thirty-eight men, women, and children lost their lives in a blast where the survivors recounted the terrorist's call to Allah just before he detonated his bomb. Newark's bomber chose a docked yacht on a night where a prominent non-profit group was hosting a fund raiser

57

for cancer victims. Instead, sixty-two people became victims themselves. And another twenty-seven San Diegans died waiting in line at a post office when a bomber ran into the building screaming "Allahu Akbar!" before he exploded into bloody fragments.

Halladan stared at a TV screen. Reports of the latest attack had initially shocked him into a quiet, desperate, and strangely numb demeanor. And then the anger swelled. The terrorist had chosen a wedding ceremony in a packed Houston church. A well-dressed, polite man had entered the church, made his way up the aisle, and calmly sat down next to an elderly couple, exchanging pleasantries with several guests. After the bride had made her entrance and marched up the aisle, the minister began the ceremony. As soon as the bride and groom began their vows, the polite man detonated his bomb, instantly killing seventy people; authorities had told reporters to expect more casualties.

Witnesses had described all the bombers as Middle Eastern, and after preliminary investigations, officials confirmed direct connections with Universal Jihad. Ghazali was sending a clear message: Universal Jihad will kill Americans wherever, however, and whenever it can. Churches, family outings, sporting events, economic institutions, governmental buildings—everything was fair game as long as it slaughtered Americans, as long as Ghazali spilled American blood.

And, as intended, the violent upsurge put Americans on extreme edge. Palpitating rage permeated the air. They wanted someone to blame, and violence against Muslim-Americans escalated. In a series of incidents across the country, news stories repeatedly reported violent confrontations at mosques. No deaths yet, but the anger mounted, and people now turned to their leaders for more than answers. They turned to the government to do something: not just to stop the terror, but avenge it.

Mark Dominic Halladan, a graduate of Annapolis, a retired Marine colonel, and a former governor of Virginia, had learned patience during his political career. In fact, he had campaigned on a platform emphasizing patience and prudence. Suspending his own hawkish foreign policy credentials, he feared if he didn't soften the hardline message of the last president's policies, then his docile opponent would become the next president of the United States and promptly surrender to the Islamic front. The world whether it liked it or not couldn't afford that kind of capitulation. Halladan had to defeat the dove running against him, and his rich voice and calming message soothed some of the country, and he was elected by a small margin.

But his softer message and narrow victory had opened the door for the doves, and they barged in and dominated Beltway politics. And Halladan had to play their game while trying to insure the government stood ready to protect its citizens. But he lacked support from a legislative branch mired in peace politics rather than security, and he couldn't use the bully pulpit as much as he wished, since he had distanced himself from the hawks. He had thought things would change after Miami and the Spencer murders, but amazingly, the doves entrenched themselves with the mantra that America should never overreact. Any utterance from the White House suggesting a different strategy brought a chorus of criticism, accusing the administration of beating war drums and rash policies. With the media in tow, the doves continued marching to their own drum, dismissing the nation's rage.

Foreign policy had as many entwining difficulties as managing Congress, especially dealing with the Middle East. Upon entering office, he immediately confronted what he called the two-hat syndrome. Many Muslim officials wore two hats: both governmental representative and private operative. These people never officially communicated with terrorist organizations as government representatives, but frequently did so with impunity as private subjects. Whether through madrassas, mosques, charitable organizations, or even the bazaar, they exchanged information, money, and arms through these surreptitious lines of communication; it was common, known, even expected.

To combat it, the president tried the backdoor approach, inviting leaders of Congress to a secret meeting where he exposed the duplicity. Halladan presented the evidence, and undoubtedly everyone understood the danger, and he knew a majority of the overall Congress agreed the country should change direction and challenge these governments. It wasn't enough. Doves controlled both houses, and a majority of the doves claimed the president lacked irrefutable proof. This leadership demanded party loyalty from dissenting members and stymied any legislation changing current policy. Those ready for change didn't have the votes to replace the entrenched leadership and feared for their committee chairs or seats while war hawks tried to plead the case to a sneering media. In all, about seventy percent of Congress wanted new policies, but thirty percent of Congress, ruling with an iron fist, crushed the super majority.

Halladan shook his head at the strange democracy. The latest messages from Congress were the same: "Don't overreact." His anger and disappointment weren't directed toward the people in the room; they were directed toward the terrorists and the House and Senate leadership. Cynically, Halladan wondered if those leaders relished snickering behind his back. Despite the latest violence, the majority doves continued to ignore intelligence reports identifying both low- and high-level bureaucrats and politicians colluding with Ghazali, circumstantially confirming many officials had more than enough unofficial knowledge to expose Universal Jihad. The evidence still didn't amount to official government action or the incontrovertible proof Congressional leadership required.

Halladan watched a tear-streaked face of a bride staring blankly into the nave, still in her white wedding gown stained by the blood of her dead groom who lay limp in her arms. Even with the sound off, the scene sickened him. How easy it would be to launch a sweeping attack on all of those governments; how he wished he could make the call and begin the operation. Tempted, he glanced at the phone.

Sighing heavily, Halladan scanned the room with his brooding brown eyes. The directors of Homeland Security, Central Intelligence, Federal Bureau of Investigation, and National Intelligence, the national security adviser, the secretary of state, the chief of staff, the president's personal information technologist Andy Mahony, and special counsel to the president Harry Stanton all stared at the TV monitor, horrified by the footage. Melissa Dellendale and Daman Pryce were the only operatives present.

"Please brief us, Agent Dellendale." Halladan finally said with no hint of recrimination.

Mel pressed her lips tightly together. She knew no one blamed her, and in fact, many had commended her efforts to track Ghazali's organization. She had unearthed several terrorists, which undoubtedly had prevented appalling attacks, but no one had predicted this bloody wave, and the more she investigated, the more she understood Ghazali had planted the seeds of these attacks long before she had joined the Bureau, even before Universal Jihad became known to the world. The government could close the borders now, but that wouldn't do anything to stop those terrorists who strolled into the country before borders were a tangible concern. Finding them after so many years presented countless obstacles.

Still, she felt guilty, angry with herself, disappointed in her inability to penetrate the web Ghazali had woven in her country. She knew it was irrational, but the feeling rumbled in the pit of her stomach nevertheless. With effort, she put those feelings aside. "Mr. President, Ghazali is fifty-three years old. He started this organization twenty-nine years ago. It was select, very well-funded, and his organizational skill, even at twenty-four, was formidable. We now have identified some of these suicide bombers as second generation, which means parents may still be here, and suggests that his pool of recruits is quite deep. Of course, we're trying to round up all of these bombers' relatives, and have had some success, but, as usual, they plead innocence. They always claim disbelief that their son or daughter would commit such crimes. In some instances, they're probably telling the truth. In many other cases, we know differently. After analyzing the data, it is probable Ghazali can continue to orchestrate many more of these attacks."

Halladan's brown eyes smoldered at her report, but, with a gesture of his hand, he motioned for her to continue.

Melissa leaned slightly forward, twisting the ring on her finger. "Unfortunately, sir, the more attacks he launches, the closer we get to him. And he knows that. We anticipate he will continue on this path a little while longer and then go dark with all his operations for some time, only to resurface at the most unexpected moment, and then we start again. The dark period could be three months, three years, thirty years. We think he thinks in terms of decades, maybe even centuries, with his Jihad, and he perhaps has built an organization that can structurally exist in that kind of time frame."

Agent Dellendale's brief confirmed what other advisors had reported. Though he trusted them, he wanted the analysis directly from the agent's mouth; not just to build a rapport with her, but to get it without director-level or White House-staff spin. "Well, now that's not very good news, Agent Dellendale, but I expected it," Halladan said calmly as he rubbed his temples with his thumb and index finger. He glanced at Daman Pryce. "Mr. Pryce, what can you add?"

Pryce tilted his head up. "Mr. President," he said in a spooky aloof tone that matched his agency so well, "Universal Jihad and Ghazali, as Agent Dellendale so aptly explained, have been around for a long time but haven't been active long enough on our map for us to develop the assets to penetrate the organization deeply. Now, we have some assets placed, but not in the inner circle where we can harvest critical information. If Agent Dellendale is correct in her assessment of Ghazali's time frame, we will succeed in penetrating it at that level, but it takes time, which of course exposes us to many years where he operates as he does now."

Halladan, frowning in frustration, asked, "Can you tell me something I don't know, Mr. Pryce?"

Without skipping a beat, Pryce answered respectfully, "Probably not, sir, but I have never briefed you." He continued his analysis as if the president hadn't posed the question. "As Agent Dellendale said, Ghazali structured Universal Jihad brilliantly. Not only that, he's extremely charismatic and has cultivated an undying loyalty among his close companions. Universal Jihad isn't a movement or a loosely confederated group of cells with a common aim. It's a highly structured organization with elements of both hierarchal control and decentralization. One cell doesn't know another, but they are coordinated from above. No doubt there are government officials aiding his organization, but there's no direct contact with him. All that occurs through those close companions, his inner circle, which make them harder to pin down."

Halladan's lips tightened. "When will we have evidence of that aid to Ghazali? Now, I'm not talking here, Mr. Pryce, about circumstantial claims that governments sponsor terrorism, supported only by rumor and innuendo. I've been through all that. I want to know when we can definitively prove specific people, in their official governmental capacity, directly sponsor Ghazali. When will we have that dispositive evidence?"

"We're getting closer, sir."

"Take a good look around this country, Mr. Pryce," the president said grimly. "We don't have a lot of time here. The country is demanding action. People have gone beyond hiding indoors. They've taken to the streets with guns and bats, looking for those they believe responsible. They see blood running down church aisles, and they're looking to me to do something to stop it. And I'm looking to you."

Pryce shrugged and glanced at his director who gave a slight nod. "Mr. President, we have thought about abducting one of the officials we suspect helps Ghazali. But we're relatively certain Ghazali and his inner circle keep a careful eye on their operatives, and if someone suspiciously disappears, it may tip them, and we get nowhere quickly. All our other immediate scenarios have equivalent—or even worse—defects. They'll fail."

Pryce fell silent, and the president squinted at him with a baffled expression. "And that's it, Mr. Pryce? That's all our esteemed CIA has for us?"

"Yes. We've lost Ghazali's trail, and destroying his organization in the near term is extremely unlikely," he summarized succinctly.

"Any other suggestions?" the president barked.

"We state the accusation of government sponsorship as fact," Pryce bluntly responded.

Back to the lack of irrefutable evidence, and the president's gut churned. "So we just bomb the hell out of them with no clear evidence of state sponsorship. We make the assertion that Ghazali and Universal Jihad are arms of Islamic nation-states and, therefore, we are justified in bombing those countries."

"Yes."

The president rubbed his jaw, considering the option. "I like it, Mr. Pryce. I like the hell out of it, but as you know, I need congressional support for that, and if I'd had that from the get-go, everything would be different, and we most likely wouldn't be in this situation now. But absolutely nothing has changed with Congress. You just heard the first words out the Speaker's mouth: 'We can't overreact.' It's the same old deal as before, Mr. Pryce."

"And I don't think many of our professed allies would join us, Mr. President," Mac Stenberg, the president's chief of staff, interjected. The secretary of state confirmed Stenberg's observation, nodding with a sour expression.

The president rolled his eyes in disgust. "So, we have circumstantial proof of state officials helping Ghazali, but nothing verifiable. And we're certain none of these governments actually control Ghazali or UJ?"

Daman shook his head. "The terrorist is not under any state control. Governments can no more dictate to Ghazali than he could dictate to them. They use each other, but Ghazali serves Universal Jihad and nothing else. His earthly loyalty is to UJ only."

The president knew the answer before the words were spoken, but he still clenched his fists on the desk. His eyes locked on the phone in front of him. The debate still roiled inside him, sitting there staring at that phone. He had the power to remove those people aiding and abetting Ghazali, and he could easily topple those governments. But what then? The governments' demise wouldn't mean the demise of Universal Jihad. In fact, he would have eliminated the assets—as duplicitous as they were—who knew anything about Universal Jihad or could do anything to Ghazali.

He still could order it. Ghazali had killed thirty thousand Americans in cowardly acts. In seeking revenge, without even knowing whether such a war would bring the terrorist to justice, Halladan had no compunctions about killing tens of thousands, perhaps hundreds of thousands of Muslims. He admitted to himself he agreed with that Chicago CEO's claim about Muslims supporting the jihadists' attacks. They weren't innocent…yet how would history judge the killing of so many people in retaliation for shedding American blood? His personal legacy didn't concern him. For that matter, if history would judge only him and not his country, he would do it immediately. But how would other nations judge the United States in the aftermath? How would the world view his country a decade from now, or a century? The world expected a higher standard from his country. It was as simple as that. The world demanded accountability even though it didn't demand it from itself. If America succumbed to visceral violence, all was lost. The United States had to be the standard bearer of humanity.

So there it was. The endgame. Ghazali chipped away at the American ideal—American Exceptionalism—by pitting Americans against Americans, inciting Halladan to ignore Congress and shrug off the Constitution to placate those demanding action and turn that anger toward Muslim nations, killing hundreds of thousands of people, demonstrating to the world that we are no better than they are, that our principles and values aren't of a higher order, and that we will sacrifice them whenever convenient. It cracked the very foundation of the United States.

And perhaps those cracks are levered into huge chasms as the world rethinks the American ideal, and decides republican constitutional societies are really no better than what history previously offered, and follows a different path to supposed enlightenment. Meanwhile the authors of the endgame, the terrorists, enjoying the rapture of the people as heralds of a new era, neatly slide into the power vacuum left by the intervention of the self-righteous Americans. And the American ideal is buried in those chasms, sealed by these new leaders' eulogizing the death of the Great Satan and marking a new dawn where liberty is no longer the pillar of humanity. Halladan gritted his teeth and shook his head. His imagination had taken hold of him and perhaps exaggerated the possible consequences, but he wouldn't risk it. America wouldn't succumb like that, he promised himself. But peace politics, the let's-just-talk appeasement strategy offered by the doves, did absolutely nothing to protect Americans from maniacs who only spoke with blood-stained knives and detonated bombs. More would die at weddings and in stadiums, and the painful, frustrating dilemma mocked him, frolicking in the miserable realm of the unsolvable.

He pulled his eyes away from the phone. "I unfortunately know where Ghazali's loyalties lay, Mr. Pryce. To murdering, mostly. I also know you wanted to provide me with different answers for all my questions." He scoffed, more to himself. "I also know I almost wished you had fabricated some grand CIA scandalous lie that would justify my picking up that damn phone and ordering DoD to launch an immediate and overwhelming strike. Strangely, I just dismissed that option." He massaged his temples again. "So, we can't find Ghazali; we can't yet penetrate Universal Jihad; we can't prove any Middle Eastern government is responsible; and we don't have any real handle on stateside Universal Jihad assets. So all we can do is to react with our first responders after another attack?"

The bleak assessment silenced the room. Standing, the President walked over and, standing akimbo, stared at the gruesome images on the TV. He turned to his advisers. "People, we need another solution."

Chapter Twelve

Tuesday, June 23

Trinidad and Tobago enjoyed a diversified economy. A US Cold War policy exempted large amounts of ethanol produced in the Caribbean from tariffs, allowing the islands to import sugar from Brazil, where the tariff was firmly in place, and then export the refined product to the US, boosting Trinidad and Tobago's already vibrant energy sector. A Canadian company, purporting to locate in Port of Spain to improve refining techniques from sugar to ethanol, arrived and set up shop without suspicion. Within a month of their arrival, Tyler and Spence had their lab operational in a flex space warehouse, equipped with a kitchen, a few beds, and a shower. Because local authorities didn't concern themselves with legitimate business operations, and the minimal US military and law-enforcement presence, Spence felt secure in the capital city.

Heat still stifled the room, despite the noisy fan, and acclimating to the near equatorial weather would take longer than expected, but the heat wasn't what bothered Spencer at the moment. More details about the church wedding massacre swamped the news cycle, and he felt nothing but frustration.

With the recent spate of Ghazali attacks, Spence's mission had acquired another purpose, one that may have lurked in the background, though he had never embraced it. Originally his plan had only been about avenging his family's death, about repaying American blood with Muslim blood. Now he had changed his mind. These new attacks had paralyzed his government, which clearly was the intent. He gave credit to Ghazali; no one would mistake him for a fool. For the past week, Spence played out various game theory scenarios, and it didn't matter how the US government reacted. Ultimately, Ghazali and Universal Jihad prevailed in each sequence. But he knew the game would immediately change once he placed his piece on the board. Since these attacks, both Tyler and he had worked with heightened focus and efficiency, and now Spence was anxious to make his move.

Tyler entered the office, his brow beading sweat. "Well, I've got it working."

Spencer looked up, visibly relieved at the announcement. "What went wrong?"

"A temperamental computer. Don't care how sophisticated they are, they still glitch. Pesky little problem," Tyler replied, rubbing his hands together.

"But the scrambling software works, right?"

Tyler nodded. "With that solved and our decoys, we should be able to conceal our activities for some time."

Spence exhaled. "How long?"

Tyler sighed. "We're digitally intensive. The trail starts when we make that first broadcast. We're not safe forever."

"I say six months, maybe seven max," Spence offered.

Tyler nodded, taking a seat across from his friend. "Probably. It's going to take some real effort for them to find us. But, when we decide to shut this operation down, assuming they don't catch us here, let me tell ya, my exit strategy will have them guessing where we are for years. No one will find us, and we won't even have to go under any plastic surgeon's knife."

Spence folded his hands and leaned his elbows on the table. "And where are you with the serum?"

"Everything's arrived, and I've already started. Processing here is going to be easier than I thought."

"No issues with any materials?"

"None." Tyler looked at Spence, his brow furrowed.

"What is it, Tyler?" Spence asked, turning his attention to the computer screen.

Tyler bit his upper lip. "I'm much more worried about our friend, Major Brannan. We're taking a big chance with him, and you know it's not just today, but every day. He could give us up at any time. I'm still wondering if he contacted the FBI, and they're just sending him in here to collect intelligence or something."

Thom had guessed his friend's discomfort and had a ready answer. "And you or I could give it all up at any time as well. Besides, I don't think the FBI or CIA or any other agency would be planting an operative in our little organization. They would just charge in here and arrest us on conspiracy charges. The allegation and our custody alone would foil the plot."

Tyler leaned back reflectively. "Yeah, if foiling the plot was the intention. Maybe they'd want to get more information on us…all two of us." He lurched forward suddenly. "Or maybe, Spence, they're keenly aware of what we're doing and have no desire to stop us."

Spence's head jerked up at that comment. He looked long and hard at his friend before answering. "You know, Tyler, I don't mind helping our government, but I'm not certain I'd want it to look the other way. That's exactly what we're accusing the Muslims of doing."

"I know," Tyler said, his forehead wrinkled in bafflement. "Perversely, I kinda hope they can catch us at some point."

Spence gave his friend another contemplative look, stretched, and then stood. "We're going to know much more in just a few hours. Brannan will be here soon."

Tyler's uneasy expression about Brannan crept back, but Spence didn't see any reason to continue the conversation, so he made an offer he knew his friend would refuse. "Care to watch the news with me while we wait?"

Tyler's eyes turned cold and the blood pressure rose. "No. Seen enough." He stood abruptly and returned to the lab.

Major Jacob Brannan's route to Porte of Spain had been as circuitous as Tyler's and Spence's. From JFK to Paris, by train to Rome, a plane to Havana, and a sea passage to the island, the trip finally concluded with a cab ride ending near Spence and Tyler's flex space.

When Spence opened the warehouse door, he did not recognize the major at first. The man standing outside looked vaguely familiar, but was unremarkable and nonchalant as any local meandering through Port of Spain. Spencer hesitated, unsure.

"It's me, Mr. Spencer," Brannan said reassuringly. "I slightly alter my looks all the time. Part of the job," he said, stepping through the doorway.

"Well, Major, I'm glad you made it." Spence paused again, wondering what he should do next with his co-conspirator. Finally he shrugged, "I suppose it's useless to search you. I don't think you'd let me anyway, and if you're working for the government, there's no doubt you have enough right here in this warehouse to shut us down cold."

The major grinned wryly as he opened his loose-fitting button-down shirt to expose an unwired chest. "No wire, Mr. Spencer."

Spence chuckled. "But you wouldn't wire yourself anyway, Major Brannan. These days I think there are better listening devices than that."

"Indeed, but I'm here to continue what was started in New York. I guess we have to trust each other from here on out. I get the idea that I'm complicit in a plot that won't win me a Nobel Peace prize and could put me on the dead side of a lethal injection table."

Spence jerked his head toward a door across the room and headed in that direction; Brannan followed at his heels. Inside, a confusion of equipment cluttered the makeshift laboratory. A large black man in jeans and a T-shirt leaned over an odd-looking microscope. He straightened up immediately and turned to greet the two men, removing a pair of special eye goggles.

"The man from the bar sitting in the corner by himself," Brannan said. "Tyler Washington, I presume."

Tyler didn't flinch at the major's recognition; he only offered his hand. Brannan accepted the greeting and stood silent for several moments, surveying the lab. "And now that we have come this far and after all the vague communications, I need specifics, Mr. Spencer, Mr. Washington."

Spence reached into his pocket and withdrew a few sheets of paper. "Fair enough. These are your instructions, Major. I've identified a total of five cities and regions. Once you have infiltrated each location, you must disperse the agent in the manner outlined. You don't have to be too precise, since it is airborne and will spread by human contact. And, as I told you in New York, you will need to identify a target, apprehend that target, and bring that target here. We will then administer the lethal substance to this person. Choose your victim wisely, Major. I think we want someone who richly deserves what he's going to get."

Brannan furrowed his brow. "Are you suggesting I try to kidnap someone like Ghazali?"

"Absolutely not," Spence responded. "That's too difficult. But I'm confident you know some low-level scum who deserves to meet his virgins under circumstances he doesn't choose. That's all we need. A no-name pile of filth."

"Plenty to choose from, Mr. Spencer."

"After you deliver the scum to us, we will give you the trigger device. It won't look like any sort of trigger you've ever seen. Then you will wait for my call, a page to your phone from the telephone number shown. Once you receive that call, you are to go immediately to the first city and begin placing the trigger device. Locations and distances are outlined in the second set of instructions."

"Do I need to place it in a specific position, exposed to something, or in a particular direction?"

Spencer shook his head. "As your instructions state clearly, no to all. But you're to follow the outlined schedule precisely. You must continue the mission no matter what, Major. Your mission will abort only if you receive a page or a call from the second number listed here. And Major, you also must know that I take full responsibility for these actions. You are not to blame."

The major stared at Spence curiously. "As I told you before, I don't care about that. I'm only concerned about how effective it is."

"And I repeat: it's effective enough, and when you see the actual death toll and calculate future numbers, you will have a decision to make. We will know then whether we can defeat them or not. If you can't go forward, you of all people, Major Brannan, then we might as well give up now. Because, let me tell you something, Major." Spence's eyes narrowed and focused icily on the major. "If the Muslims had what we had, they'd use it. They can't, because in so many ways they've rejected the very ability to create what we can, and now they must face the consequence of the war they started. But if a man like you can't deliver the means to end what has to be ended, then we're doomed."

The major didn't respond to the lecture. "You said the toxin is airborne?" he asked impassively.

"Yes," Tyler answered. "It's contagious for several hours and is dormant inside the infected individual for a year or a little more."

"Waiting to be triggered?" Brannan asked.

Tyler nodded.

"Are these infected people contagious again after exposure to this trigger device?"

Tyler vigorously shook his head. "Absolutely not. Couldn't control the contagion limits if that happened."

"I distinctly received the impression in our brief conversations, Mr. Spencer, that I wasn't going to be infected."

"You're not. We're going to vaccinate you. Actually, all of us will be. It's a liquid solution that has to be ingested and present at the same time the toxin is catalyzed to be effective. Very complicated and expensive to process." Spencer answered.

Brannan nodded. "This delivery device. You said it's not like anything I've seen. What is it?"

Tyler opened a glass cabinet and removed a roll of black tape about three inches in diameter and two inches wide. Throwing it to the major, who instinctively caught it, Tyler smiled deviously. "You pull off a strip and slap it on whatever."

The major studied the tape in his hand for several moments. "That's it?" he asked skeptically. "Looks like duct tape."

"Similar, but thinner," Spence responded succinctly.

Exhaling heavily, Brannan surveyed the laboratory, noticing it was not that impressive. Containing several small machines and scientific apparatuses, the medium-sized room did not appear to possess the technology able to produce a potion that could kill the number of people Spencer and Washington implied, much less a triggering tape. "Despite your backgrounds, Mr. Spencer and Mr. Washington, I am not convinced that just the two of you could manufacture such a lethal substance in this laboratory. The process has to take a lot more manpower and a lot more money than all this cost."

Tyler raised an eyebrow. Glancing at Thom for permission, he explained. "We only do the final processing here. The vast majority of the work actually occurred a few years ago when we were studying nanobiotechnology. During some experiments, we discovered this process, but we ran into problems with a catalyst."

"That was solved by the tape, though only recently," interjected Thom.

Tyler continued. "Two components comprise our approach to nanotechnology, Major Brannan: resequencing matter at the sub-molecular level and subsequent self-replication. We discovered a nano-substance, a kind of replicating protein that we could weaponize. We originally thought dispersion through the water system might work, until we discovered that contaminating central water systems was much more complicated than you might expect."

Brannan nodded. "Yes, if you're trying to kill a large number of people. You have to get the toxin into each water source at the right locations and concentrations. Can be manpower dependent. It doesn't appear your operation has much of that."

"I suggested an airborne agent spread by humans," Spence continued. "Tyler didn't think it could work, but some simulations with a small alteration indicated it would, and we got on another BUS."

Brannan didn't understand what BUS meant, but didn't care to ask that question. "And does it affect other things?"

"Well, when you look at it at the subatomic level, you find..."

"I don't think Major Brannan really cares about that, Tyler," Spence interrupted, waving off the detailed analysis. "Just give him the basics."

"Oh, right," Washington responded. "Well, we have structured it so it attaches to human DNA only and can't be triggered without it. Flora and fauna won't be harmed. And humans won't be either until triggered by the catalyst."

"Back to the tape," the major surmised. "I think you cryptically mentioned frequency waves in our last phone conversation, Mr. Spencer."

"Correct," Tyler answered. "These encoded waves, several waves emitted at different frequencies from the tape, will trigger the pathogen. We've encoded it so it's virtually impossible to duplicate them inadvertently. Don't want any mistaken catalysts to occur."

Brannan chortled at the obvious statement with wide eyes and raised eyebrows.

Tyler continued. "Once it's triggered, the protein-like substance is catalyzed, morphing in a way that is fatal to humans. And it replicates on blood cells. In graphic terms, it eats the person from the inside. It's not a pleasant death, but before they die, they should go into a state of shock and become unconscious."

Brannan displayed no emotion. "After it's triggered, how long until death?"

Tyler rocked his head back and forth. "Probably twenty-four hours, a little more or less."

Brannan's eyes narrowed. "So, a person is eaten from the inside for twenty-four hours?"

Tyler shook his head. "No. It presents first with flu-like symptoms. The person dies from convulsions and bleeding in the last several minutes."

"Can you be more precise than 'several minutes'?" Brannan asked.

Tyler shrugged. "We're not sure."

Brannan reviewed the list of cities and regions, all familiar from his travels, quickly calculating the time required for his retreat. "Well, it appears you're true to your word. As you said, Mr. Spencer, this isn't a suicide mission. I'll have about twenty-four hours to get out."

"Actually longer," Spence said. "The tape is time dependent. Once it adheres, it begins emitting frequency waves only after a programmed amount of time elapses. We'll calibrate it so when the criminalists start modeling the outbreak, they won't detect a pattern."

"So where I place the tape first has a longer delay?"

"Correct," Spence answered. "All the instructions are right there. It's simple."

Brannan nodded. Without a discernible pattern, investigators would find it harder to model. He reflected on the timing and said confidently, "I could even wait it out. Not everyone exposed to the waves will have been exposed to the toxin. I wouldn't raise any suspicion by staying."

"You do as you see fit. Obviously, Major Brannan, we need to give you enough time to leave quietly so you're not connected in any manner, and then according to the schedule, situate yourself at the next destination. If hurrying hinders you, and you think a different approach works, be my guest, but you have to meet the schedule."

"Agreed," Brannan said while strolling around the room.

"You've explained the tape. But the actual substance. Is it in liquid form? I think you mentioned something about a vitamin."

"Gel capsules, actually. Easier for you to transport. Looks like vitamin E," Tyler answered.

"How do I disperse it?"

"Put it in water, shake to dissolve, and squirt. A quart of water or less sprayed at each point identified in the grid we've given you." Spencer pointed at a chart on the paper. "You do it at those approximate distances, and the area will be completely saturated in a day or two. It will actually spread well beyond that, but it's the tape that causes the death. If the wave doesn't reach you, you don't die."

Brannan wandered back to look at the paper and noticed the first city had a single point; as he moved down the list, the number of identified points increased. They had nearly convinced him, but he still had a sticking point. "So, you or someone else did most of the work a while ago, and you, what, concoct this deadly solution in this lab?"

"Yes," Tyler nodded.

"And it's not dangerous to do that?"

"Nope. The stuff is inert until that tape right there triggers it," Tyler repeated.

Brannan gave Tyler a contemptuous look. "Right. You have this serum. You've exposed yourself to it, no hazmat suit, just those jeans and all, and there's this tape, just sitting here and emitting all these frequency waves. Yet, you both look pretty healthy. No convulsions; no bleeding. And you really expect me to believe this works?" He knew they could have already taken the antidote, but he hadn't, and he didn't know whether he'd been exposed.

Tyler grinned. "Do you think we've poisoned you, Major?"

Brannan looked askance at Tyler and shrugged.

"I haven't finished the serum, Major," Tyler said reassuringly. "But even when I do, you still have to press a miniaturized button on each segment of the tape. To turn it on in effect. It's designed kinda like an automatic safety on a gun. Among other reasons, that's also why we have you make separate trips: one with the toxin and another with the tape. It's another safeguard against detection and accidents. Again, we don't want any mistaken catalysts."

Brannan nodded his approval and then furrowed his brow. "What about a power source for the tape?"

Tyler shook his head. "None needed. Nano-batteries are built into the tape itself. The emission doesn't take much power since it doesn't last that long. Maybe an hour or so. We want the signal dead after that so we don't have someone detecting waves after the attack, unlikely as that is. It's all there in your instructions. Simple."

"It seems like it, Mr. Washington." Brannan said as he rubbed his jaw, smiling faintly. "You'd think you would need so much more to pull something like this off, Mr. Spencer, Mr. Washington. But, as I said, I've done my research on the two of you as well. There's more on you out there than on me for sure. With your backgrounds, of anyone out there, the two of you could do it."

Spence pressed his lips tightly together. "You're used to studying terrorist organizations, Major. We're not like them. That's the point. We don't need an organization. We need money, technology, brainpower, and mostly will power. Now, we know that we're not untraceable, but with the security measures we created, and the small number of people involved, we think we can complete the operation. We do, however, depend on our delivery system, which is you. Can you do it?"

Brannan leaned against a counter and skimmed through the instructions. "I can do what you have outlined here. You have designed it well. It's quite feasible. I don't have to sacrifice myself, even at the end. I can be long gone when the final area is infected."

"But we need to know you will infect it. Even that last site, Major Brannan. I must have every single one of those locations as viable threats."

Brannan hesitated momentarily, looking directly into Spencer's steel-blue eyes, and asked without yielding Thom's stare, "What time do you want me to pick up my package, Mr. Washington?"

"I'll have it ready by 3:00 p.m. the day after tomorrow." Tyler responded. "Is that good for you?"

"It's fine," Brannan said.

"What about money, Major? How much do we pay you?" Spence asked.

Brannan cocked his head and smiled briefly. "Mr. Spencer, if you had to pay me to do this job, you'd have the wrong person. But you don't have the wrong person. I'll be here at three o'clock the day after tomorrow."

Chapter Thirteen

Monday, September 2

Spencer had numbered Gaza first on his list of five; Brannan had made it his last stop. He gazed out a window overlooking a crowded alley, one of hundreds in this poor, densely populated area. Nearly a million and half people lived in a region of only one hundred thirty-two square miles. The airborne agent would spread rapidly in such a congested environment.

Slipping in took little effort. Brannan's dark beard and complexion fit as nicely in Gaza as in all the other areas he had visited in the last few months. The seedy motel he found advertised air-conditioned rooms, but his AC unit by the look of it had broken several months ago, and no one had touched it. Still, Brannan was lucky to find lodging with working power. Beads of sweat invaded the beard, and Brannan rubbed his square jaw to wipe away the aggravating perspiration. With the sun beginning its descent, standing next to the window gave him some relief, but he wondered how much crowded confines added to the heat. He glanced at the small table containing the capsules, a spray bottle with a quart of water, and an old fan. After dispersing the airborne agent for the last time, he would complete his plan to trap Spencer's first victim of the serum.

He stepped to the table, grabbed the fan, and set it on the windowsill. Fortunately, the cord reached the outlet easily, and steel blades ground out a hot breeze in the otherwise silent room. With ease, Brannan sliced the first gel cap and dribbled the oily substance into the bottle. After adding a second capsule, he swirled the water, and the agent quickly vanished. He took his time pumping the water through the moving air to avoid drawing any attention to the spray. At that pace, emptying the bottle took the better part of half an hour, and just as in all the other places, no one in the street below noticed.

When he finished with the quart of water, he studied the empty container, wondering whether the vaccination would work. He hadn't taken it yet, and wouldn't until just before he was exposed to the emission waves. If it didn't work, he would die and the plot would likely fail. The death Washington had described should have sent a shudder down his spine, but Brannan considered it moderately terrifying compared to other methods he had encountered. Still, he'd rather not be eaten from the inside.

After hiding his materials, Brannan returned the fan to the table and surveyed the room, confirming that everything was in order. After enticing his intended victim, he wanted to leave as quickly as possible. Sauntering back to the window, Brannan saw the café had opened. It was time. He peeled off his shirt and went to the sink, where a trickle of tepid, slimy water wiped away some of the grime, and he donned a fresh shirt.

The café was located just down and across the alley from his room, and he had spent several evenings there, watching and listening. The low hanging doorway made him stoop, but once through, he had space to stand erect. Brannan waved a large billow of smoke from his eyes. The night before last, he had discovered his target, a thug whose reputation he had known from previous trips to Gaza. Sitting at the small bar, he sipped tea and patiently waited for him. Before long, a brooding, muscular man ducked through the door, and Brannan drained his cup as the other man sat in his usual booth. The waiter brought him his tea without being asked, and as the big man settled comfortably into his seat, Brannan slowly rose and walked toward the booth. The intended victim looked at him without turning his head.

"What do you want?" he asked gruffly.

In a perfect Arabic dialect, Brannan asked, "May I take a seat? I have an offer for you."

The man raised his brow and gestured at Brannan to sit, staring at him with expectant eyes. Brannan cleared his throat. "I know you've always tried to play the terrorist game, Ali, yet you never could really make an impression in Hamas, or any other group for that matter. You've just been an everyday soldier, but you want more, and I can give you the chance to make the impression you've always dreamed about. I also know you don't want to be just a simple suicide bomber; you want more glory than that. You deserve more glory than that. A man with your capabilities should be respected and given the opportunity to earn that glory, and do it without having to sacrifice your life."

Ali Abdul-Muiz leaned forward. Dark-brown eyes widened at Brannan's words. The major had grabbed his attention by catering to the man's arrogance and narcissism. He longed for a destiny laden with greatness, but the right path to this glory eluded him, and he couldn't understand why. Known for his cruelty, he hired himself out as an enforcer, and he was quite good at cheerfully slamming heads into the ground.

But that was the extent of his ability, and no one ever trusted him with an important job. Brannan knew if he could bait the man with glory, Ali would jump at any chance to prove his supposed talents, especially if the task involved killing Americans.

"What do I have to do?" Ali asked, distrust thick in his voice.

"I am going to provide you safe passage to the United States. Now, what you do there isn't on the scale of what Ghazali did in Miami, but it will make an impression."

"Like killing that family in Chicago?" Ali's eyes gleamed at the mention of the US.

Brannan had him. "Something like that. The exact plot will be revealed to you just before you enter the country."

Ali's eyes narrowed. "Who is sponsoring this? Are you Universal Jihad?"

Brannan offered an impassive gaze. "Do you really care, Ali? I'm not giving you my name, and you won't get any contact information. Until later. All I can tell you is this: I can get you to America without any questions. You first have to travel to Trinidad on a Mexican passport. From there, with this same passport, you can get into the US with a visa. That will be provided to you in Trinidad."

Ali was just bright enough to pick up the implication. Of course this stranger was from Universal Jihad. Most of his jobs came from Hamas, and while Hamas supported Universal Jihad, it might not appreciate UJ recruiting contract-labor thugs right in its backyard, so no affiliation would be expressly disclosed. But the idea of Universal Jihad recruiting him thrilled Ali. Hamas didn't own him and had never even acknowledged his loyalty. This man sitting across the table offered him his chance. He'd taken jobs from strangers before, and names didn't matter, because they were never real. Without further thought or hesitation, he said, "All right. I think I get it. Now what's Trinidad?"

"A country in the Caribbean."

"That near America?"

"Close enough. And a Mexican national traveling to the US from Trinidad doesn't raise any suspicion. Easy to do."

"Sounds too easy. How'd you get a Mexican passport?"

"It just takes the right amount of money. All we have to do is slightly change your appearance. Make you look a little more Mexican, which won't be hard to do."

"What's that mean?"

"Shave your beard and cut your hair, and put in a pair of contact lenses, and you'll blend right in. I've booked you passage on a ship to Rome, and from there a plane ticket for Trinidad. Once in Trinidad, you make a call and I'll give you an address where we'll meet. From there, I reveal the plot, give you the money and the contacts, and you head to the US."

Worldwide media coverage had reported endlessly on the Miami plot, so Ali knew Universal Jihad had members positioned in the US. And many Arab sources had also advertised the Mexican connection. "You have this passport?"

"In my motel room."

Ali smiled. Confident that Brannan was no match for him if it were a trap, Ali didn't hesitate. "Why don't you show me? Now. Let's see if you have all this as you say you do."

Without saying a word, Brannan rose and gestured at the door. Keeping the haughty smile, Ali pushed himself out of the booth and nodded for Brannan to lead the way. Brannan snaked through the tables, ducked out the door, and strode back to his motel room.

Once inside, Brannan went straight to the battered dresser and rummaged for the passport. He handed it to Ali, who inspected it carefully. The page for the photograph was empty, but everything else looked official. He shrugged more to himself than to Brannan.

"Of course you can't reveal this plan to anyone, Ali. If locals know of it, they won't allow you to go. You know they've held you back all these years, and nothing would change with them. They'd stop you, Ali."

"Maybe, but I'm checking out this passport."

Brannan didn't think Ali was shrewd enough to take this precaution, but had considered it when he formulated the plan. There was always a risk; if something happened, he would just have to find a different target. "Can you do that without revealing why you have it? Can you trust anyone with the fact that you have a valid Mexican passport? They're valuable."

"Yeah. I know someone."

"Very well. We change your appearance, and you get a passport photo. Take it to this person, have it checked, and we'll meet at the café. Then I'll put the final touches on it. By late afternoon tomorrow, all right?"

Ali tapped the passport against his hand, considering, and nodded. "You have those contact lenses?"

Brannan returned to the dresser, took out a contact case and a piece of paper, and then walked to the closet and pulled out a duffel bag. "In here you'll find several changes of clothes. They're more fitting for a Mexican. Cut your hair as instructed on this sheet."

Ali grabbed the paper and the passport and leaned down to pick up the bag. When he lifted his head and met Brannan's gaze, his expression had dramatically changed. The rough and tough demeanor gave way to a look of thoughtful elation. He pressed his lips together and smiled. "Something tells me that I have found the chance I've been searching for. This is my destiny; this will be my mark in this life."

He nodded slightly to Brannan and left without another word. Brannan stood silently in the middle of the drab room, running over the conversation in his mind. Ali could have caused Brannan problems, but now he knew the thug was hooked. Ali would meet him tomorrow eagerly seizing what he thought was a chance to inflict pain in despicable America.

Chapter Fourteen

Friday, September 6

The stars shone brilliantly in the warm Caribbean night. Major Brannan walked slowly up and down the cracked and flaking sidewalk, waiting for the call. He had not yet notified Spencer of his arrival in Port of Spain, since he hadn't confirmed the target's arrival. Stopping at a refreshment shack, Brannan leaned against the counter and ordered a fruit drink. He checked his watch yet again, wondering whether suspicion had trumped ambition, and Ali had returned to the relative safety of Gaza. Of course, he had to consider the possibility that Ali had been detected. Israeli authorities may have stopped him at the border, but Brannan doubted it. Possibly Mossad had Ali on a watch list, but minor thugs didn't usually rate that much attention. With the authentic passport, the border agents and Israeli police probably wouldn't even notice him. As long as he wasn't roving around Israel, it just didn't matter much.

The phone rang, and despite his anticipation, Brannan didn't flinch. He pressed a button. "Yes."

"Made it," Ali said in Arabic. "Caught some weather over the Atlantic."

"Fine," Brannan answered. "I'll call you in five minutes."

Brannan hung up and walked briskly down the sidewalk, stopping at the corner. He peered around the building and confirmed Ali had followed the instructions correctly. He then called Spencer.

When Spencer answered, Brannan gave him precise orders. "I want you and Tyler to leave your building now and don't return until I call. Leave the side door unlocked. Again, do not return until I call you. Do you understand?"

"I don't like leaving the door unlocked, Major. We have a lot of equipment here."

"Not the kind of equipment thieves really want, at least not for the local black market. Anyway, it won't be unprotected very long. We have to take these small risks, Mr. Spencer. You'd better get used to that."

"We'll leave now," Spencer replied.

Brannan hung up and dialed Ali. Flawlessly switching to Arabic, he gave him the address and exact directions to Spencer and Tyler's lab. "Walk there and speak to no one on the way. If I don't meet you there within ten minutes, return to your current location and wait for me to contact you," Brannan tersely ordered and terminated the call before Ali could reply. An expected wait created vulnerable patience in the first few minutes. Brannan glanced around the corner again to see Ali obligingly nod at the instructions, turn, and start walking.

Brannan watched to make sure he went in the correct direction at the same time scanning the street for anyone who might be following the thug. Brannan didn't think Ali was clever enough to provide protection for himself, especially considering the logistics it would require, or that Israeli or other authorities would expend any resources on him, but he took the precaution nevertheless. No one followed.

Ali stopped at a metal door and rapped on it three times, pushed it open, and entered. Brannan pulled out his tranquilizer gun, insuring it was loaded and ready.

Forty-five seconds behind Ali, Brannan burst through the door only to see Ali aimlessly standing in the middle of the entry with his arms lazily folded across his chest. He spun, and, catching a glimpse of the man who just entered, he did not recognize the major, who had altered his appearance again. His eyes widened, not because of the unfamiliar face, but because the person raised a gun and shot him before he could react.

Brannan hit his target in the chest; Ali started to lurch forward, trying to lunge at his attacker. Ali's legs went limp, and he collapsed to his knees, searching his body for a bullet. Surprise creased his face when he found nothing; no bullet, no blood, and then Ali went slack. He pitched onto his face and twitched once before settling motionless on the floor. Brannan holstered his weapon, knowing the special anesthetic pellet had invisibly penetrated Ali's chest. He calmly walked to the body, kneeled, and checked for a pulse. Satisfied, he reached for his cell phone and called Spencer.

"You may return, Mr. Spencer," he said evenly and hung up.

Brannan squatted, lifted Ali up to his shoulder, crossed to the desk, and dumped him unceremoniously in a chair. He then settled himself in the seat opposite, waiting patiently for Spencer and Tyler to return. They opened the door several minutes later and stopped abruptly with raised eyebrows when they saw the slumped body in the chair.

"Wow," gaped Tyler.

"So you brought him all the way from…where?" Spencer asked, simultaneously wondering how the major hadn't even broken a sweat and marveling at the subtle change in his look yet again.

"I didn't bring him anywhere, Mr. Spencer. He walked through that door on his own. Why carry baggage when the baggage will deliver itself to you? You can find dull but ambitious baggage, and with the right incentive it will go where you want it to."

"Who is he?" asked Tyler.

"A thug. No family. Just a foul man who wasn't smart enough to get himself noticed by the people he wanted to impress. He hates the US more than anything, and the only motivation he needed to walk into this room was a chance to kill Americans. Not ugly or mean or bigoted Americans, but any American."

Tyler walked toward Brannan's dupe and stared down at him. "Looks despicable enough to me, Major. What do you think, Spence?"

Spence, emotionless, shrugged without taking his eyes off Brannan. "I trust your judgment, Major. That's why we asked you to join us, and we trust you would target the kind of man you just described." He paused. "So you promised him that he could kill Americans, and he just came running?"

"Right into your warehouse. I provided the travel documents; that was easy. He was bright enough to have them checked by someone. A little risky, but if it failed, I would've simply tried again, just promising somebody else the same chance. It would eventually work; they're a dime a dozen. Just happened to work on the first try."

Tyler shook his head in disgust, turned on his heel, and headed for his laboratory to set up the web feed they would soon stream.

"So, what's next, Mr. Spencer?"

Spence rubbed his jaw and glanced at Brannan. The major had no need to know the details until now, and hadn't asked. "Tomorrow we'll infect him with the pathogen and expose him to the waves. We'll video the death, and then I'm going to make a call to the United States. To a radio show, and I'm going to make an announcement. The video will be out there on the internet, so they get to see for themselves what we have in store for them."

A look of concern flashed across the major's face and then an impassive mask descended again. "A call to the United States? You're exposing yourself, Mr. Spencer."

"It's an internet call. We can cover our trail, at least for several months anyway. Remember those risks you were talking about? We have ours as well, so here we go. They'll crop up along the way. We'll trip up somewhere, I'm sure, but maybe not until the point is made, a point they understand."

Chapter Fifteen

Saturday, September 7

A Caribbean haze blanketed the night sky, cooling the busy Trinidad street Spence wandered as he contemplated the mission Tyler, Brannan, and he were about to launch. No going back after the next step, he admitted, and much of his ambivalence faded. Grim faced, he returned. They had restrained and sedated Ali, and he remained unconscious. Tyler and Spence began preparing the room for the ordeal, hanging ordinary sheets, purchased in the US at a flea market, on three walls in front of the camera. Tyler set up the video equipment, bought at a small pawn shop, advanced, but not professional, and untraceable.

Ali awoke. Drugged from sedatives provided by Brannan, he still had enough strength to hurl invectives. "I know you Americans. I kill you, you family. I rape you women. I cut you mom head off; you dad watch." Brannan strolled over to the prisoner and stared hard at him. Ali continued spewing threats with a little less volume. Undoubtedly the brute would have inflicted as much pain on Americans if given the chance. Stories of his disgusting acts seeped out of his drugged mouth, and Brannan, waiting dispassionately, always nodded, knowing the man didn't have enough of an imagination to fabricate the events. Sympathy and compassion never had chance.

After finishing the preparations, Tyler marched to a refrigerator and took out a vial and filled three syringes. He injected himself, and Brannan and Spencer accepted vaccinations without flinching. "I've also prepared an injection for our thug, despite the fact he probably was infected in Gaza."

Brannan nodded. "Let me give it to him, please, Mr. Washington."

"Be my guest, Major."

Ali fought against his restraint, spitting and yelling at the major, while Brannan administered the pathogen. Spence calibrated the tape to emit immediately and in a minimal radius; the flu symptoms presented within an hour after infection and exposure to the emission waves, with Ali coughing and sneezing. It took another twenty-two hours for the first violent coughing seizure to happen. Tyler and Spence glanced first at Ali and then at each other. Without any expression, Tyler walked to the camera, pressed the record button, and returned to his work.

Spence rubbed his jaw and decided to get some Caribbean air before the final phase. He stopped short in the street and gazed up into another hazy night sky, inhaling and exhaling deeply so many times he felt light headed, and fell against a wall. After calming his nerves, he checked his watch, turned and returned to the warehouse. Brannan and Tyler discussed the pathogen, and Spencer slipped past them and ambled into the thug's small room. The sedatives had disappeared, though the toxin had severely weakened him. Still, his contemptuous brown-eyed stare held no fear.

Sweating profusely, he sputtered, perspiration flying off his lips, "I lay here, and nothing. You pigs do nothing to me. Give weak drugs and just stare at me. So I cough and have ache in back. So what? No guts, no courage do anything. Cowards! Weak infidels! We prove our superiority, we prove we kill you, you can't do nothing to us. We strike down Great Satan, you be destroyed, and we the Muslims rule what's rightfully ours. I would not look you. I carve nose off you face; ears off head, fingers off hand, then head off shoulder. You know it. Seen it. I do it, smile after I does it. Weak pigs!" he ran out of insults and gasped for breath after the diatribe, his wheezing noticeably increasing. Spence silently waited; Brannan and Tyler joined him a few minutes later.

After nearly an hour, punctuated by sporadic outbursts in broken English interrupted by coughing attacks, Ali's expression changed suddenly. He blinked several times, and they could see his stomach muscles tense under his shirt. It had begun; the beginning of the end. The thug caught his breath and smiled, as if the pain had passed, and nothing hurt him. But then his body twitched and alarm burst from his eyes. Something inside his body had happened, something unnatural, and he knew it. Swallowing several times, trying to gain control of his muscles, Ali glared definitely. "What happen? You done what to me?"

The camera continued to roll, and the three waiting men watched intently. Ali trembled in pain for a few minutes, and then a convulsion shook him. Bile rose to his lips, and, and he spit it out in a scream of pain. Fear and agony now filled his eyes as he stared at his captors in disbelief. The convulsion slackened for a moment. The man tried to catch his breath, but couldn't as his insides churned violently in the process of being destroyed. For a moment, he lay perfectly still; then he arched his back violently as blood spurted from his mouth and nose. The force of the explosion popped the veins in his eyes as they bulged from his skull. Pain enveloped the man; he was no doubt still conscious. In the observers, curiosity had succumbed to detached resignation; they wanted it to end despite the merit of the punishment.

The convulsion stopped, and the man tried to roll to his side. He groped blindly at nothing with his hand. "Kill me. Please kill me," he whispered, and another convulsion struck him. More blood spewed from his mouth and nose; the sheet beneath him puddled with blood from his anus. Lips blackened, and he gurgled on blood flooding his windpipes and lungs. The last breath of his life blew out in a silent scream as blood continued to run from his eyes, ears, and mouth.

Spence glanced at his watch. They now had data on time progression. It had taken sixty-four minutes for the initial flu symptoms to appear, another twenty-two hours and eighteen minutes before the first violent convulsion, sixty-seven minutes of intermittent spasms, and then six minutes from the onset of the last phase to death. The man didn't lose consciousness as anticipated during the horrific climax, but it took less time for him to expire than predicted.

Tyler sighed. "One tough son-of-a-bitch. The vast majority of people will go into shock and won't feel much."

Spencer wondered how effective a nearly painless death was as a message to Ghazali and Muslim governments. He grimaced at his own cold calculations. Brannan shrugged. "No one needs to know that, Mr. Washington. Besides, it's not very comforting telling someone he won't feel much pain when he's about to die. Especially with the image of that thug imprinted in his head."

Spence stared at the others without saying a word for a few moments and then reflexively walked out the door. He couldn't see Tyler's ashen face; he only noticed Major Brannan's antiseptic quizzical stare, and its indelible image stayed with him. In the warehouse bathroom, he swallowed several times and abruptly vomited the entire contents of his stomach. Sweat beaded on his forehead as he steadied himself on the sink, trying not to lose consciousness. The wretchedness of the deliberately inflicted agony and his cold indifference to diminished suffering pierced his armored heart. Tears formed in his eyes and streamed down his cheeks. The thug in there was horrible and deserved to die, but not like that. Spence stared into the mirror and saw only an image of evil. Unable to face his reflection, he turned on the tap and stared instead at the cold water flowing from the faucet. He cupped some in his hands and doused himself.

And he reached back into his mind, searching for the place where he had locked away those images of severed heads, the memories of his family's brutal murder. Finding it, he visualized those images, focusing, remembering. Rage nibbled at the edge of guilt and remorse and then abruptly devoured both, and the color returned to his face. He splashed more water on his face, stood, and looked in the mirror. He shrugged. Perhaps evil stared back at him; so be it. He now understood the major's expression when he exited the room. It had asked whether he could stomach it.

Spencer walked out the bathroom and found Tyler and Brannan had decided to leave the dead thug alone. The major paced back and forth a few steps. He had a good idea what transpired in the bathroom, though Spencer did look much calmer now. Tyler appeared somber and withdrawn. Brannan had to determine whether they had the terrorist's fortitude to complete their task. He stopped and crossed his arms, shifting his eyes between his two accomplices, and grimaced. "Now," he said, "the question is whether you can continue, Mr. Spencer, Mr. Washington. Killing the victim in fact is much different than talking about it, planning it, and even taking that first conspiratorial step toward actually pulling the trigger or in this case injecting him with a deadly toxin. I purposely use the word victim here, because even though Ali was the worst kind of human being, he was still a victim. You can never run or hide from that epitaph. And your plan calls for the victimization of countless others. Even though they're victims, Mr. Spencer, Mr. Washington, sometime victims deserve what they get. If you understand that, if you can live with that, then we can move forward. However, if you go forward, you must also realize not all the victims will be as deserving as that person lying dead in there. If you cannot accept that, stop now. I will dispose of the body. No one will ever know either of you was involved in this, and no one will care. You can return to your lives in America and live with your demons, but know that you did eliminate a piece of pure scum. You did the world a favor, and I'm not saying that just to soothe your conscience. I purposely chose this kind of man so you could turn away at this moment, knowing you murdered someone, but someone who wholeheartedly deserved it. That should alleviate any guilt you have."

Spence stared at nothing for several moments. The image of his family's severed heads flashed in his mind's eye again. Ali was the first step toward his revenge. Regret had faded. Guilt had evaporated. Bathroom episodes might repeat themselves, but he would simply return to the place that held the memories of his murdered family, and it would all disappear again. This was a war someone had to wage, and as with every war, there would be victims. His enemies didn't care about their victims, so he couldn't either. But his victims were more deserving than theirs.

Spence turned toward Tyler, who still sat silently, and then focused his attention back on the major. "Major Brannan, I don't enjoy the pain or the suffering I inflicted on that man in there. I don't revel in the thought that others might suffer like that. It made me sick. But it's the most efficient messenger we have to deliver the kind of message that those people understand. Someone has to have the courage to deliver that message, and I am that person. Understand, Major, I don't move forward out of any sense of pleasure. I do out it out of revenge and out of necessity."

Brannan nodded. "How about you, Mr. Washington?"

Tyler hesitated. He dropped his head and sighed deeply, but slowly nodded his assent. "I guess I was just so consumed by all our plans, I lost sight of what our objective really was. I think about that day I found out about your family, Thom, and think about Miami and all the other attacks. All the pain still bangs around my head. And I keep hearing that banging, and, well, it keeps telling me to do one thing: persevere. Even though what we did horrified me, the banging didn't stop."

"How about you, Major Brannan? Can you do it?" Spence asked rhetorically. He already knew the answer. The man had seen victims, murder, death, all of it plenty of times. He had chosen well.

The major smirked faintly. "I'll manage, Mr. Spencer. But right now we need to rethink our strategy a bit."

"What do mean? We've had our plans laid out for months now. Why change?" Tyler asked.

"Because," Brannan responded, "when you make your announcement and stream that image on the web, things are going to change drastically. You see, up until now you've had the luxury of time. Everything you've done has been on the straight and narrow— nothing illegal, nothing suspicious. Your toxin, Mr. Washington, was really the product of several years of work, not just yours but the work of many others, right?" Tyler nodded. "And the computer technology is the same kind of work product? Right?" Again Tyler nodded. "It was absolute brilliance to bring it all together, no doubt, but easily manageable by you and Mr. Spencer. Just like this setup you have here. It took you months, but you two could do it, because what you were doing was just ordinary business. You had the money and the time. My trips to the Middle East were the same: innocuous, unnoticed actions by a man who blends into the background quite easily. No bombs, no deaths, no commotion. Not difficult, because no one was on our trail; no one had reason to be. Three people could accomplish this one kill, because you had money and access to corporate technology, and I had the experience and expertise. And we even got that one victim to show up on our doorstep without even threatening him. All this to kill one man is quite manageable. But with that video, everything will change. The next phase, time won't be on our side. Believe me when I say that to plan and execute the killing of a single person is very different from the scale you have in mind. The full resources of the FBI, the CIA, the NSA, and other agencies you may not even know exist will be hot on our tail. You cannot underestimate the resourcefulness of those agencies. You cannot underestimate the intelligence of the people who staff those agencies. I know you have taken precautions, but they won't be enough."

Tyler looked at the major incredulously. "And why in the hell didn't you tell us all this before?"

Without a flicker in his expression, Brannan said smoothly, "I had to see if you would take this first step. You had a good plan to kill the first target. But if I had laid this at your feet then, you may not have gone through with it."

Spence shifted uneasily. "So you were hooking or trapping us?"

"Yes, in a sense I was, Mr. Spencer. And once you went through with it, I needed to know if you could continue. If you couldn't, then I would clean up the situation we created, no further action would be needed, and I wouldn't need to reveal what I am about to now. I had to keep that option open. You see, I've been down many roads with many different people, and I've learned to read them, and their level of commitment. I believe the two of you will proceed with your plan. And I will help you make it work. However, to do that, I'll need help."

"From whom?" Spence asked skeptically.

"Mr. Spencer, I represent and am a part of an organization that started some time ago. My guess is that if you hadn't chosen me, it would have been someone else in my organization. Some members are military people who have served in different capacities all over the world. Many have seen combat in Iraq or Afghanistan or in other conflicts. Members also include clandestine operatives, as well as diplomats and government officials. Private individuals deeply concerned about America's current polices are also involved. In fact, the organization was started and is funded solely by private capital. One thing they all have in common is a belief in much of what you have said. They know this isn't a war waged by just a few Islamic fascists who have cobbled together these terrorist networks. They understand these networks have broad support both inside and outside governments, and it is only when those people in and out of governments, those not members of the networks themselves, are convinced that changes must happen that the change will indeed occur."

Spence's skepticism persisted. "And you have told this organization about us, about our plan?"

Brannan hesitated. "I informed them that I had an angle, and told them I wanted to pursue it until I could confirm the commitment. Now that I've done that, I need to provide them with more details. With your permission, of course. But Mr. Spencer, Mr. Washington, this laboratory must be dismantled before you make your call and upload the video to the web. We need to move."

"I think we've got it covered," Tyler responded, but he detected doubt in his own voice.

Major Brannan looked coolly at the scientist. "Fine, but do you want to take such a risk before the job is done? Do you want to take that chance when I can offer you a plan that improves the likelihood of success to a much greater degree? We need help, and I know who can provide it."

Washington pressed his lips together. Until now, he hadn't questioned the plan, but something inside him triggered an instinctive nerve, telling him that Brannan was right, and everything would change dramatically the moment Spence made the call and uploaded the video. Looking at Spence, he nodded slightly, silently agreeing with the major's suggestion.

Having projected the plan further out than Tyler, Spence had a vague sense that it all had been too easy, and Brannan had uncovered the reason. They hadn't done anything inherently culpable until Ali walked through the warehouse door. Their situation definitely would change, but Brannan's revelation raised another issue: how to keep control. Private money funding the organization screamed power at Spence, and power meant control, and it bothered him. Brannan's assessment, however, was correct, and trying to find a different operative to execute the plan inside the Middle East vanished once they killed Ali. Like it or not, he and Brannan had jumped into bed together.

Folding his arms, Spence said, "All right, Major, agreed. But who is calling the shots?"

Brannan shrugged. "This is your operation, Mr. Spencer. The organization will only support you. Let's just say it wants to play from the bench. The people involved can't be connected. Period. You will see a few of the members, but just a few, operatives like me. Beyond that, you won't know they exist."

"But they'll know who I am, right?" he asked.

"Yes," Brannan nodded, "as do I, but remember I'm just as involved and responsible as you are. I ask you to trust that I trust them. They will never surrender me to anyone."

"And what exactly are they going to do for us?" Tyler interjected.

"For starters," responded Brannan, "we're going to get you out of here. Quickly and silently."

"Assuming we will go," Spence interrupted, "where do you plan to take us?"

"Mexico City," Brannan answered without hesitation. "I've already established a base of operations there. Nothing that can't be discreetly removed if we choose not to go there. From what I can see, we really don't need most of this equipment. That work is completed, unless you plan to make more of that serum of yours."

Tyler and Spence locked eyes; they hadn't thought about preparing additional batches. Spence pressed his lips together. "Well, if we need more, I'm certain your little organization can provide us with what we need fairly quickly, and probably much safer than trying that here."

"You're catching on, Mr. Spencer," Brannan said with a tight smile. "But for the next stage in the plan, we need more communication than laboratory equipment. Mr. Washington, you once mentioned that you had a photonic device that conceals electronic signals." Tyler nodded. "It will conceal all communication signals sent from any source?" Tyler nodded again. "Good. That will help our setup in Mexico. Once we get rid of all the rest of this, it'll be much harder to trace us from here. By the way, did you set up any decoy sites?"

They nodded in tandem. "One in Chiapas and one in Brazil," Tyler answered.

Brannan thought a moment and nodded more to himself than the other two men. "Perfect," he said. "So, we're agreed? I'm going to call some men in here. Right now. They'll clean everything out except a single computer. I presume you can make the call and send the video from one computer?"

"Yes," Tyler responded.

"Keep your device connected to that computer, Mr. Washington."

"Of course."

"Good. When we stream the video, this warehouse will be empty except for that computer and the three of us. We complete the task, pull the plug, and leave. Simple as that."

"And what do we do with the body?" Tyler jerked his head toward the room holding the dead man.

"These men will dispose of everything, Mr. Washington. And we'll make the call and be on the web in forty-eight hours, and gone in forty-eight hours and ten minutes," Brannan said crisply.

Spence contemplated the major's advice and agreed with him on every count, but still wanted to confer with Tyler. The two exchanged a look, and Brannon noticed the communication. "I'll leave, say, for about a half hour? Will that give the two of you the time you need to talk things over? We're not in any danger of detection at this time. No one in Gaza—or in Trinidad—knows or would even care about Ali's disappearance."

Spence nodded. "Half hour will be quite enough, Major Brannan." With a curt nod of his own, Brannan left, leaving Tyler and Spence staring at each other.

Sighing, Tyler drawled, "You know, Spence, he's right. It seems kind of foolish to think we could've pulled this off without any help. Maybe we could, but the odds are against it. We should take his offer."

"Of course we should, Tyler. But we have to make certain we still have some control over this deal. Make no mistake; we're surrendering a lot of the direction of this operation once these guys enter the picture. We have to keep our hands on the one thing that makes this entire operation click."

"What's that?"

"The serum. All the information we have about it and the delivery system. We have to encrypt it and store it where only you and I have access to it. Brannan's right. It's more about communications now, not the technology behind the serum…but we still protect that information. Keep it ours."

Tyler looked at Spence thoughtfully. "All right, I think I can do that with minimal risk. All I do is send the information to a data storage site, maybe even to one of Nanoexelogy's servers, password protected of course, encrypt it, and keep the key on my photonic device, which is also password protected. Even if someone hacks the site, the data is meaningless. Covering my tracks is also pretty easy; no one will be able to trace the site's address. And the passwords on my device and on the site, well, we can double password them, one for each of us. I'll also put a fail-safe on the site. If we're coerced into divulging the site address, we can give a fake password that will trigger a virus to scramble the data completely, make it undecipherable even with the key."

"And we're going to need another fail-safe."

Tyler frowned. "A backup site or something?"

"No. Nothing like that."

"Then what?"

Spence ambled over to a cloth sofa, patched and worn, and sat. He leaned back, stretching, trying to relieve tension from the ordeal. "We just have to make certain that we can check Major Brannan's organization in case it overreaches. I don't think Major Brannan wishes to expose himself or anyone else. If push comes to shove, we have to have a mechanism to force Brannan and his people to do what we want them to do. We have to stay in control."

"And how are we going to do that?"

"We have to check in."

"Check in?"

"Is there a way to program those sites to release the data to an e-mail address unless we check in every twenty-four hours?"

Tyler nodded. "That's not a problem." He paused a moment, pondering the additional fail-safe. "So let me get this straight. If we don't check in, then all the information, including the serum formula, the targeted regions, the amounts, Brannan's name, the existence of this mysterious organization, all of it is e-mailed to an address?"

Thom nodded.

"And where are we sending it?" Tyler asked.

Thom reached for his wallet and withdrew a business card. "Send it to Agent Melissa Dellendale, Tyler."

"So, Brannan and his organization do what we tell them, or Agent Dellendale gets a whole lot of information. The plot is finished, and they're exposed," he mused, stroking his jaw. "Nifty, Spence. Pretty nifty. It just might work."

"Well, Tyler, it just gives us an ace in the hole, just in case we need it."

Chapter Sixteen

Monday, September 9

Richard Prednow rubbed his head in weary exasperation as he terminated another call. "Bruce!" he yelled, "why can't we get a caller who really has something to say?"

"I know, Richard! But what can I say, it's a slow day," Bruce responded. "Maybe you'll like this next caller."

Richard sneered at his producer.

Wait until he gets a load of this guy, Bruce said to himself.

Prednow waved him on. "All right, we have a guy on the line who's calling himself..." Prednow paused, squinting at the screen to make sure he had read it correctly. "The American Terrorist," he said, laughing. Still chuckling while he looked dubiously at his producer, Prednow asked, "Wow. Okay. What's on your mind, American Terrorist? Can I call you AT?" Chortling at his own sarcasm, he pressed his mute button long enough to jeer, "It's not that slow, Bruce. No more whack jobs."

The American Terrorist spoke. "Mr. Prednow, I have heard your statements against those of the Muslim faith. You have been telling your listeners that we have a serious problem with what you describe as the Islamic fascists."

"True. What's your point, AT?" Prednow asked, still enjoying the acronym.

"The problem isn't with the Islamic fascists, but with Islam itself. We will never end this war until we admit this fact."

Sighing, Prednow answered. "I've been down this path before, AT, but even if you're correct, we can't simply declare war on Islam and start committing religicide, now can we? Lobbing bombs into major Muslim metropolitan areas isn't on the Defense Department's agenda."

"You're right, it isn't on the Defense Department's agenda, but something much worse is on mine."

Prednow shifted in his seat. "And what's that supposed to mean, AT?"

"The Muslims have their terrorists who have declared war against us, and now America has its own terrorist declaring war against the Muslims."

"And how, AT, do you propose to carry out your terrorist campaign against the Muslims?"

The caller continued unruffled. "I won't destroy stadiums or demolish buildings or kill a few families, Mr. Prednow. Please understand, when an American decides to become a terrorist, the actions are magnified; they are escalated. We have far greater capabilities than Muslims, and I will use these capabilities in devastating proportions. My demand is simple: unless the leaders of the Muslim terrorist organizations are surrendered and their networks dismantled, I, as the American Terrorist, will take my war to the Muslim people. We are all aware that Muslim governments could capture these terrorists and destroy their networks, but, Mr. Prednow, they lack not just the will, but the desire. Well, now they must obtain the will and the desire, or face the consequences. The names of these leaders and their networks have been posted on a web site. And also on this web site, Mr. Prednow, you and the entire world can witness the fatal result if my demands are not met. These Muslim terrorists must be surrendered to American officials and their networks destroyed within two weeks. That's fourteen days, or the first attack will follow, and countless Muslims will suffer the death you see shown on the web site."

With his finger hovering over the button to disconnect, Prednow looked at his producer who was engrossed in his computer screen. Something in Bruce's expression made him pause.

Bruce spoke into his earphone. "The guy gave me the web site. I've been skimming through it while you talked with him. I don't know if it's authentic or not, but it looks horrific. This guy in the video may actually be dying, Richard."

Something in the American Terrorist's voice, its sinister gravity and calm intensity, persuaded Prednow to withdraw his finger from the kill button and engage him seriously. Dropping the facetious 'AT,' Prednow said pensively, "So, am I to believe...."

"Please allow me to finish," the caller interrupted. Prednow deferred. "After the first attack, I will continue my assault with each successive attack worse than the previous until my demand is met. The roles have now been reversed. It is now an American who is the terrorist."

The line went dead. Unprepared for the sudden disconnect, Prednow scowled, annoyed at Bruce for losing the call but even angrier with himself for not extending it. Uncertain how to respond, Prednow filled the on-air gap with dismissive chatter about pranks as Bruce hastily patched the next caller through.

"And this is Christopher from Rochester?" Prednow said distractedly, his eyes now on the image that had appeared on his screen.

"Yes, Richard, it is. Hey, before we talk, what's that web site your last caller mentioned?"

As the video played, Prednow's shoulders sagged, and he bit his lip. "Well, Christopher, I think it's better we don't advertise that site. Crackpots occasionally slip by Bruce's keen screening abilities, and I think that's what just happened."

"Yeah, maybe, but you know, what if the guy is for real? Maybe that's what America needs. Its own version of a terrorist; and someone who's not going to screw around."

"Christopher from Rochester, we're going to hold you over the break. We'll be right back in a few."

Prednow shook his head in disbelief as he fast-forwarded through the clip again.

Bruce's face suddenly grew even more concerned. "Damn it, he's advertised his web site through ours. There's a portal there now, Richard. Everyone can see this by just going to our site."

Prednow massaged his jaw. "No way to stop it?"

"I'll call IT, but no way. We can delete it, but all anyone has to do now is make a search for American Terrorist on Prednow, and they're going find it. It's already all over the web."

"Call-back number?"

Bruce rapidly dialed the number he had. "No good. Invalid number message."

"All right," Richard said, "this is probably some sort of hoax, but this guy has chosen us to be his messenger, so I want to play it a little differently. We're going to be more reporter-like here rather than commentators. Let's not put any spin on this. It's on the web, so we just tell people it probably is a hoax, but we don't know. Say our staff is on it, and that's it. Got it?"

Bruce raised his eyebrows, but nodded. "Yeah, got it. But, Richard, what if it is for real? I mean, what if he did really kill this guy? It looks so real."

Shifting uncomfortably in his chair, Richard rubbed the jaw once more. Sighing, he said, "You know, Bruce, something inside me, as bad as this sounds, as terrible as it sounds, something inside me wants it to be for real. That was my first reaction. God. What's wrong with me?" He paused. "We can't let on to any of that, all right? Play it neutral."

Bruce nodded.

"Christopher from Rochester, we're back from the break."

"Did you check that video out? I mean whoa, Richard!" Christopher immediately exclaimed.

"Over the break, we reviewed it. I want you and the entire audience to understand that we did not in any way place the video on our site. It appears our American Terrorist is pretty tech savvy and put it there himself. We know it now will be all over the web, but again, we in no way are promoting this...this...."

"It seems he's more than just tech savvy, Richard," Christopher interrupted. "Looks pretty authentic. Kinda reminds me of those decapitations videos. You remember those, don't you?"

"We don't know, Christopher, if this is real," he reiterated, ignoring the caller's question. "We don't know anything about it. It all could be a sham. We just don't know. This person has used my show for his announcement, and maybe his amusement."

"Yeah, Richard, but don't you kinda hope it's real? I mean, you know, that's my gut instinct."

Prednow's shoulders slumped again. "Well, I don't know about that, Christopher. If it is for real, then it appears to be a pretty awful death, and I don't wish that on anyone."

"Doesn't look any more horrifying than having the old head cut off with a knife, does it?"

Back to the decapitations. Richard's radio life flashed in front of him. He wanted to agree, but the political incorrectness of such a response now could jeopardize his future. So he gritted his teeth and said calmly, "Christopher, we have to figure out what is going on here. If this is a hoax, I want to know why. What does it accomplish? If it's not, then I think we really have to find out what this guy's intentions and capabilities are. We need more facts before we can comment on this." He glanced at Bruce, shrugged, and threw up his hands in the air, admitting his response verged on drivel.

As if he somehow had peered into the booth and seen the host's nonverbal capitulation, Christopher chuckled. "I mean, I know what this guy wants to do. He wants to kill Muslims, and maybe a whole bunch of them."

The thought of "countless Muslims" horribly dying gut-punched Prednow before the dread of ambivalence crept into his thoughts. He couldn't quite brush aside the satisfying tingle and feeling of power at the thought: 'Now we have one of our own, and he's a nasty bastard.' If the American Terrorist really existed.

Chapter Seventeen

Tuesday, September 10

After terrorism hit the shores of the United States, the Federal Bureau of Investigation had significantly enlarged its foreign intelligence operations. The J. Edgar Hoover Building remained the central command for traditional criminal investigation. Counterintelligence was headquartered several miles away, inside the beltway in Alexandria.

The newly constructed modern office complex housed a sophisticated computer network designed especially for people such as Senior Supervising Special Agent Melissa Dellendale. Her bullet-proof windowed office boasted a decentralized computer that as a stand-alone machine was likely one of the top one thousand computers in the world.

Every special agent had one of these mini-supercomputers for individual use. Software included a digital laboratory for scanning and reading fingerprints, DNA analysis, voice recognition, satellite mapping, communication decryption, advanced facial recognition systems, and other intelligence wizardry. Built on a lateral network, an agent could tap into the computing power of idle computers. The system was augmented by a supercomputer, which undoubtedly ranked as one of the top five in the world. It secured the entire system, firewalled each mini-supercomputer, housed thousands of mega-databases, and managed database searches. For agents, the system was easy, fast, and remarkably efficient.

The scientists, Ph.Ds., techies, and analysts who operated the high-tech basement laboratories now had more time to provide comprehensive information to the agents. When these technicians didn't have to bother with the agents' "little stuff," they accomplished many more complicated tasks. And, without having to wait for results from the lab, agent productivity increased. Perhaps Miami and possibly even the Spencer murders wouldn't have occurred if this building had been fully operational.

The country, from the politicians to the cab driver, took pride in the FBI, and rightfully so. Some of the exposed and foiled plots were advertised, but many others were not, and everyone knew it. With the latest terrorist attacks, however, doubt had crept into the esteemed FBI halls and their new technological array.

Light bounced off the mellow yellow walls, giving Mel's spacious office an expansive feel. The basement tech rats had used nanotechnology to infuse the paint with sensors that would detect any sort of surveillance, muted sound and monitored the temperature, providing a secure and comfortable environment. She usually thrived in her office, but today she was distracted. Twisting her ring back and forth, she glanced in her compact mirror. Wrinkles, barely visible, yet still there, bothered her, and she rubbed the skin, absently wondering if she looked old.

But age didn't matter, she reminded herself. Who cared how old she was when her life revolved around the Bureau? Her blond, blue-eyed Scandinavian features attracted many suitors, and she liked a few of them, especially one. But whenever she considered her social life earnestly, the thought of her job wedged in and crowded out all potential flames. How could her personal life matter when the world existed in a constant state of turmoil? She studied people, normal people walking down the sidewalks, and she saw beneath their fierce determination a resigned understanding of the true situation. They were hostages living in a fragile world, and the terrorists had the edge. Her crew of twenty special agents, working under her supervision, tried to live normal lives, but she saw the hostage in each of them as well.

She had never felt insecure growing up because of the support from her parents, especially her father. Her mother, a native Californian, and her father, born in Denmark, had married in the

States after they met in San Francisco. Her father initially split his time between Denmark and America, with his family sometimes traveling with him to Copenhagen. But just after she entered her teenage years, he refused to return to the Danish capital after publishing several articles on the other Jihad committed by Muslims. These Islamists moved to European countries and settled into separate communities while militantly demanding special rights and the application of Sharia law to their segregated colonies. Her dad had predicted that within the next century Europe would return to its war-torn history with Muslims as a majority pitted against the European minority. The European establishment ostracized him, and European life had become too uncomfortable. Though he didn't speak much about politics with her after that, Mel always suspected his convictions had influenced her career choice. She was his pride and joy, and he was her hero.

With her parents' help, she worked her way through college with just a few small loans and landed a terrific summer internship with the Bureau, which was impressed enough to pay for her graduate degree. When she began as a fresh agent after standard FBI Quantico training, the world didn't seem so dangerous. But when terrorism exploded onto the shores of America, when the age of hostage oppression dawned and endured, the sense of security her parents had always provided faded. Until she freed herself and her country from that oppression, she wouldn't let herself go; she couldn't lose her focus, and the tiny lines she rubbed were irrelevant.

Dellendale leaned back in her chair as her door opened, and in wandered Daman Pryce. "Thought I'd come down here and see the office," he announced. "Your assistant let me in."

Surprised by the visit, she smiled, thinking fleetingly about the special one who could make those wrinkles matter to her. "It only took you how many weeks?"

He shrugged. "So, this is where the minilab and super mini-supercomputer you all brag about is," he said, surveying her office.

"Best in the world," she answered.

"Do you really think so?" he smirked with a wink.

She wished he wouldn't do that with those brilliant blue eyes, and for a second her eyes lingered on his lips. A glance at a particular holographic folder snapped her back to the fragile state of the world, extinguishing the flame, and she exchanged her smile with a scowl to counter the snide comment. The man did work for the CIA, and few truly knew what its computer capabilities were. "Yes, as far as a known and certified system, it's the best in the world," she retorted.

Pryce nodded. "Now, on that I might agree with you. So, where is it?"

The smile reappeared, this time glib. Daman only saw an ordinary office desk, but that desk was the mini-supercomputer, and from her vantage its holographic interface had several screens, graphics, photos, folders, and files neatly arranged for her sole review, shared with a simple tap of a holographic button if she chose. The button remained untouched.

"So, why are you here?"

With the FBI computing system established as out-of-bounds, Daman got to the point of his visit. "Well, news travels fast. The word is that they gave you the American Terrorist file."

"And the word is correct. Ghazali's personal trail in the US is so cold, and Universal Jihad is spread out on so many other desks, I don't think I was doing much good. Anyway, I think they wanted to spell me from that front. I'll still be involved, just not exclusively. But this American Terrorist, I think I know who it is, and he's right here on my desk," she proclaimed as she again stared at the holographic file that forced her back into reality.

Puzzled, Pryce looked at a completely empty desktop. He dropped into a chair across from her. "That fast? It just happened yesterday," he muttered, impressed, while still inspecting her desk.

"You know with this new computer system, we work pretty quickly here."

Chuckling, he smiled, revealing perfect rows of gleaming white teeth in retort. "Point taken, but we have to let you do some of the work."

"And I am. In fact, I was just studying a voice recognition test I ran. It came out a match. The boys and girls downstairs are still trying to set the algorithm for their program to run against the database. Pretty confident they would have eventually found the match, but I didn't want to wait."

Pryce gave up on the desk and stared at Mel. "Good for you! Just keeps proving that human intelligence is absolutely needed in more ways than one," he said. "The technology is great, and necessary, but it's only noise without good HI. And there's no doubt you have a lot of that, baby."

She rolled her eyes, but her heart skipped a beat. Even though he flirted, he had delivered a compliment. "Thanks, Daman. You're not one to offer praise to many people."

"Not many to praise, Mel," he said, those intense eyes boring into her own.

She stared back at him, expressionless. He finally dropped his gaze, shook his head, and sighed. "So, I guess my compliments still aren't getting me anywhere with you?"

"Oh, you'll get somewhere with me; it's just not the same place you were thinking."

Pryce nodded, accepting the rejection smoothly. Again. "I am serious about your brains, Mel," he said, offering a cordial retreat.

"I know, Daman," she said softly. "But I'm not sure I can tell you who the American Terrorist is yet. I haven't even told anyone here," she added, reentering the fragile world.

Pryce pressed his lips tightly together and sighed again. Leaning back in his chair, he shook his head, vexed by the reticence of his FBI counterpart. He shifted into CIA spooky persona, leaned forward, and whispered, "Now why are we playing this game, Mel? I'm not here to steal your thunder. If I'm to help, I need to know who this guy is."

Remembering her own words about FISA and how everything had changed, Mel chided herself for even considering withholding information. Though her suspect was an American citizen, she would accept help from any agency, even the CIA. Waving her hand, she abruptly dismissed her own comment. "Relax, Daman. Relax. You're right, there's no need to keep the information from you." The deepened lines on Daman's forehead disappeared. With another wave of her hand, the lights dimmed and the holographic folder floated in midair. She flicked her finger and it opened, offering Daman a view of the documents in super full high-definition. Daman chuckled. "So this is part of your little computer?"

Mel dismissed the question. "You remember the Spencer family murders?"

"Yep," he responded, indifferent to his ignored question.

"I took a sample from Thom Spencer's debate with the Muslim scholar on that Chicago show and matched it against the tape from

Prednow's show. The phone call was definitely digitally masked, but it came out a ninety-nine percent match." She threw up her holographic voice recognition file and ran it.

"Thom Spencer?" Daman asked.

"I think so. I tried finding his current location, and guess what?"

Daman pursed his lips thoughtfully. "You can't find him anywhere."

"You got it. And it doesn't surprise me at all."

"Why's that?"

"I saw him the day his family was murdered, Daman," Mel said reflectively. "His eyes had gone so damned...cold. Frighteningly detached. I still remember them." Mel hesitated; she then flicked her finger, which collapsed all images and brightened the room, and stood. "Come on. I need to go down to the lab then brief some of the upstairs people. We've got to get on this now. Walk with me, all right?" Daman nodded as he rose from his chair.

As the elevator dropped to the basement, Mel gave Daman a rapid synopsis of Spencer's background. By the time they reached the lab, Pryce had learned enough to realize that Spencer fit the profile of the American Terrorist.

"I actually was leaning more toward a hoax, Mel," he admitted. "Our lab guys believe the video is authentic, but that didn't convince me anyone could commit anything more than what we saw: an appalling murder of one man. Now I don't know, especially if Spencer is teamed up with this Washington fella."

"Well, I was put on this case because it's high profile and, like your lab guys, we also think it's genuine. And now maybe we have to give his threat more credibility, because we have a viable suspect who just might pull it off. I'm not clear on what he's threatened, though. What kind of attack will he attempt?"

Daman furrowed his brow and threw her a sardonic look. "Uh, I don't think he's planning on flying planes into buildings or blowing up stadiums. He's going kill a bunch of Muslims with whatever he used to kill that man on the video, Mel."

"You're brilliant, Pryce," she rejoined with a sour expression. "Controlled delivery system, Daman. How's he going to do that? A lot of people can abracadabra a deadly potion, but controlling the rate of contagion and escalation, now that's the question." She stormed ahead as he sauntered behind, chuckling to himself.

After entering Lab 104, she approached a tech. "Billy, I need a facial recognition search on this man from these dates covering airports, train stations, seaports, bus stations, and banks. Whatever you have."

Billy scanned the dates and the places and shook his head. "I'll get on it, but I can't promise much with such broad search parameters."

She flashed a smile, knowing Billy worked a little harder for her when she visited him. "I know. That's why I'm not doing it. You have a better chance down here than I do."

Mel's smile wilted the tech. "I'll give it my highest priority."

She jerked her head, indicating for Daman to follow, and marched out toward the elevators. "I'm heading for the top floors. Anything you want to tell me before I head up?"

Daman shrugged. "Heard from the State Department. I was told that the Saudi minister smirked at the threat. Another overseas person heard an Iranian official literally laugh out loud when he saw the videotape. Obviously, our Middle Eastern friends aren't taking it seriously."

Dellendale nodded. "I didn't expect them to, but that's a good piece of information to give the top-floor folks. Thanks." She stepped into a different elevator this time, and as the door closed, he smiled and winked at her. Her heart thumped, yet her eyes conveyed the fragility of the world, and his smile was left drifting, unrequited.

Chapter Eighteen

Tuesday, September 24

Major Brannan ducked as he entered one of several nondescript yet oddly nostalgic Baltimore taverns in Fells Point. The low-hanging ceiling made it cramped. He avoided the long wooden bar, fortified with steel stools upholstered in red vinyl, many already occupied at two in the afternoon. Instead he marched toward the back, ascended the stairs, and turned right. Again he ducked, thinking his head might bump into another hovering ceiling. A small bar, fully stocked, stood on the right with tables and booths stacked in a row on the left. The black-and-white tiled floor surprisingly gleamed with a clean veneer. Lighting fixtures highlighted a slightly elevated stage framed by a large second-story window with a few streams of light breaking through its slatted shutters. The band didn't have much room to maneuver vertically, Brannan observed, noting their heads would crash through the lightly textured plaster and might even result in a hospital trip if an iron crossbeam interrupted an excited jump.

Brannan slid into the bench nearest the stage and waited. After a few minutes, a shadow played against the stairwell wall, and his contact entered the upstairs. His wavy gray hair and velvety stride exuded unruffled assurance, and the casually elegant clothes connoted a man who had cast aside daily business suits. He strolled to Brannan's table and slid in across from him. Before Brannan could speak, the wealthy man abruptly stood back up and sauntered to the bar to buy two bottles of beer. Upon returning, Brannan nodded his thanks. Drinks provided good cover.

"Well, the two-week deadline passed yesterday, and no one as of yet has surrendered anyone. No one in the Middle East takes our American Terrorist seriously," his contact offered in a deep resonant voice as he took a sip of the beer.

"Obviously," Brannan replied succinctly. "How could they?"

Agreeing, the man slightly shrugged. "So, are you ready?"

Brannan nodded. "We are. I leave tonight. I'll land in Marseilles and then catch a freight ship to Beirut."

"Will it work?"

"How would I know? I'm going to deliver what I need to, and then we'll all see, sir."

"I know. I know, Jacob. I just think some of us are getting a little nervous. I think some hope it doesn't work, to tell you the truth."

Brannan shrugged a shoulder and said blandly, "I understand. It's reasonable to have some misgivings."

"What about Spencer and Washington?"

"Cool, sir. Extremely cool. I thought I might have to calm at least one of them down. It's just not the case."

"Cold bastards."

Brannan shook his head. "That's just it. They're not. They believe in what they're doing, and they think it's the only way. Committed."

Brannan's contact nodded, understanding the passion. "Well, here's the DC update. I heard they identified both Spencer and Washington the day after the release of the video."

"What agency?" Brannan tersely asked.

"FBI."

Brannan took a long pull at his bottle. "Haven't seen any signs of detection."

"No. From what I hear, they're not close to finding them. That's why they haven't released any information. They want those two to feel secure, but if this thing succeeds, you know as well as I do everything changes."

Brannan nodded. "The best they're going to do is trace them to Trinidad. Beyond that, they've disappeared. They haven't been seen or heard by anyone in Mexico, sir. We'll keep them hidden until this plays out."

Brannan peered deeper into the eyes of the man sitting across from him. The small scar on the right side of the cheek glistened a little with a tiny bead of sweat. The major frowned. "What's bothering you, sir? I didn't figure you as one who had reservations about what we're doing here."

His contact smiled. "I'm not worried for the reasons others are, Jacob. I lost those moral reservations long ago. I know what we face. There are just...other possible problems that really concern me."

"Like what?"

"Well, Jacob, what if Spencer succeeds? What if he kills all these Muslims as he's claiming he can? I know before you agreed to proceed our analysis confirmed Spencer's assessment. If he succeeds, it won't matter if a few regimes fall, so long as the terrorists are gone. But, I wonder if they will ever capitulate to the threat, no matter how many are threatened or killed. Maybe they surrender up these terrorists, maybe they don't. If they don't, what do they do then? That's the question that's nagging me. What do they do then? You think they just sit by and do nothing?"

Brannan sighed inwardly and leaned across the table. "I don't think anyone is much prepared for what is coming. And, ultimately, if push comes to shove, there's more of where this toxin comes from, and we just keep spreading it until the job is complete. We're talking about shifting the entire paradigm here, and there's very little anyone can do about it."

The wealthy man leveled his eyes at the major without commenting. He swirled the beer and took another sip. Nodding, he grimaced. "And we go forward, but don't be too sure about that, Jacob. There's always something someone can do."

Chapter Nineteen

Saturday, October 5

Tel Aviv's night lights flickered and flashed through the hotel window. The modernity of the city always impressed Brannan. Below, streets bustled, adorned with expensive cars whizzing through the fast-paced nightlife. Bars and lounges lined both sides of his hotel's street; they opened a little before midnight and the patrons drank until the light of morning crept across the neon. The Israelis had created a little oasis in the desert next to the Mediterranean, and anyone walking around the cultural and economic center of the State of Israel felt its vitality.

Brannan turned away from the window, rebuffing the vibrant milieu, and paced in the interior of his room. The trip from the United States to Marseilles through Beirut and finally to Tel Aviv had been uneventful. The more difficult stage came with his attempt to enter Gaza. Unlike his previous trip to lure Ali to Trinidad, he declined the passport route and opted for furtive access into the Arab enclave. Covert and illegal border crossings into and out of Gaza occurred constantly, but usually required assistance from someone on one side or the other.

The trip into Gaza was the easier, less dangerous of the two. If he were caught, he simply postponed or abandoned the attack. If he were captured escaping Gaza after placing the deadly pathogen's trigger, and wasn't released before the first victim succumbed to the deadly serum, eventually an investigator would dig a little deeper, and not discovering any identity, might figure he had found a possible perpetrator of the outbreak. If detained, the American Terrorist's remaining targets suddenly would become jeopardized.

Brannan's objective was to manage both trips without help, avoiding any possibility of anyone connecting the looming attack with his presence. He proceeded without any assistance, and it paid off; it had been an easier operation than expected. Disguised, he slipped in at a worker's checkpoint in the morning without detection. Posting flyers on buildings with ordinary-looking tape in certain sections of Gaza City didn't require much covert op expertise, and he finished the job in under an hour. He returned to Tel Aviv by a black-market crossing, which he had discovered on a previous trip. After disposing of his workman's attire, Brannan threw on some Ferragamo shoes, no socks, Brioni slacks, and silk shirt. Propping Gucci glasses on his slicked-back coiffure, he strolled to a hotel front desk with an Italian passport in hand.

Nearly thirty-one hours had already elapsed, and silence from Gaza indicated nothing had occurred. He glanced at his gear, packed and ready to go, next to the door. He thought it best to confirm the attack before departing. Why risk the second leg of his Middle Eastern jaunt if the first failed? The TV echoed continuous and repetitive news, and Brannan reached for some bottled water.

Twenty-five days after the American Terrorist made his ominous announcement, the world had not seen or heard from him. When the two-week deadline passed without incident, most wrote off the threats as idiotic blather from an unstable person, and the news cycle quickly forgot about it.

But Spencer hadn't disclosed when he would launch the attack, Brannan thought to himself as he drank half the bottle in one swig and then settled into the couch. The TV screen suddenly flickered with an alert, and a news anchor indifferently started talking. "We have reports out of Gaza of flu-like symptoms infecting numerous people. The latest report indicates that one person fell into convulsions and has died. From what can be determined, it appears the manner of death was similar to that in the American Terrorist video infamously broadcast last month."

Brannan reflexively glanced at his watch, thinking thirty-one hours just a little premature for actual convulsions to begin, but, again, Spencer and Washington had warned him the timetable was only an estimate.

The newsman's co-anchor interrupted. "We have confirmed that report, and now several more deaths have been reported. Those haven't been confirmed, but we now are receiving scores of calls about severe sickness. So far, the reports have been confined to Gaza."

Brannan pushed himself up. Check out-time. He grabbed his baggage and closed the door gently behind him. At the front desk, everything appeared normal; the news hadn't arrived there yet. After paying the bill, he left the hotel, turned right and walked up the avenue. The music from the bar still blared and the customers sat drinking and laughing at their street-side tables. Pleased that Tel Aviv remained indifferent or oblivious to the news, Brannan moseyed past another lounge and confirmed that the same atmosphere prevailed.

He then turned his attention to the street. Several empty taxis lined the curb, and he grabbed the first one he saw. An American band played on the radio station, and Brannan casually asked for a ride to the airport. The taxi whisked him away.

In the thirty minutes it took to get to the private terminal of the David Ben-Gurion Airport, the station still hadn't interrupted its programming with any announcement. The terminals teemed with their usual activity. Apparently no one was taking any significant notice of the Gaza reports. Even airport security posed no problem, so it didn't appear he would suffer a delay. Once he arrived at his gate, he immediately boarded the plane.

The organization had arranged the transportation to Baghdad. The cockpit remained secluded from the passenger cabin; Brannan wouldn't see or talk with anyone during the flight to Iraq's capital. The pilot and co-pilot remained locked in their cabin; Brannan's identity was not revealed to them, and Brannan didn't know who flew him to his destination.

After settling comfortably into his seat, Brannan pulled out his radio phone and scanned the various stations. Of course the news stations reported on the Gaza situation, but the commercial stations happily continued to play their music. Brannan glanced out the window; planes landed and departed, and he felt the jolt of his plane pulling back from the terminal. The pilots had obviously obtained clearance, and they readied the plane for takeoff. His cockpit crew didn't give him any flight instructions; they just flew the plane. The purring engines were his only accompaniment.

Baghdad, as the crow flies, lay about 550 miles from Tel Aviv, and he would land in less than ninety minutes. During the flight, his radio remained operative, and Brannan continued to scan the dial. The number of deaths rose rapidly according to the reports, yet he still found other stations continuing with their original programming. The news stations initiated conversations about the American Terrorist, wondering if he had made good on his threat.

Oddly, no one suggested Israel was in danger, and the reporting was callous. Brannan wondered why the Israelis didn't feel threatened. As he continued to scan the stations, he finally heard a music station mention deaths in Gaza, but only as part of its normal news brief. He shook his head. The drama and trauma over the past several decades had hardened the Israeli citizenship. They lived daily with risk of violent death, whether from missiles or human bombs, and until they saw a tangible threat, they stoically continued their lives. It wasn't that they didn't care; it was just more important to persevere under any circumstance. The American Terrorist hadn't threatened them, and they didn't see any reason to alter what they were doing until something posed a real challenge. So, Brannan obtained his safe passage out of Israel before it closed the borders.

Brannan scanned Arab stations, finding a broadcast from Damascus and another from Baghdad. They were reporting on Gaza and had already concluded the American Terrorist had struck. Yet, these stations gave no indication that either Syria or Iraq had taken any extraordinary action. Brannan faintly shook his head. The entire region lived under severe pressure, and these people had simply adjusted their mindset to cope with incessant threat. Brannan looked out the window, questioning for the first time if the American Terrorist really could penetrate that mentality.

The plane touched down at a private landing strip just outside Baghdad. Once it came to a stop and the bell rang, indicating it was safe to deplane, Brannan rose from his seat, opened the hatch, and lowered the stairs himself.

A warm, strong wind swept across his face. He looked up into the night sky, and the starlight provided just enough light for him to make his way across the tarmac. Having traveled this route many times, Brannan had no trouble finding his way around. After a brisk fifteen-minute walk, the major arrived at a helicopter pad site.

The Blackhawk's engines were already running. The two-hundred mile northwesterly flight would put him within twenty or so miles of the porous Syrian border, where the flow of people and arms went both ways. Brannan wanted to be as close as possible to Damascus before the Syrian government had discovered the full impact of the American Terrorist's attack.

Brannan couldn't distinguish anything behind the pilots' helmets and flight suits, and he kept his face averted as he approached the bird. He climbed aboard, and no one even glanced in his direction; as added precaution, his organization had arranged several decoy flights. The blades started whirring, and quickly the helicopter jumped aloft and darted toward Syria.

This newest version of the Blackhawk cruised at speeds well in excess of two hundred miles per hour. In less than an hour, Brannan would find his car ready for his trip across the border in the dead of night.

A few minutes into the flight, Brannan pulled out his garb for the drive to Damascus. He changed clothes and disguised his face. It didn't require much alteration; just a few changes modified his appearance enough to look like the typical Syrian driving in from the eastern part of the country.

The same wind met him as he stepped off the Blackhawk onto sand-covered concrete. Without a wave or a look back, Brannan scurried off the small pad again under the starlight of the Middle Eastern night. The small box car with a full tank of gas awaited him just as promised.

It whined and then sputtered to life; Brannan immediately turned on the radio. Fortunately it worked, and he spun the dial, searching for news sources out of Gaza, but only static answered him. Sighing, he put the car into first and started his drive to the border, his tires spraying the desert sand into the night air. Tracks weren't a concern; the night winds concealed his trail in moments.

Headlights soon revealed a narrow road, nearly macadamized, and good enough for the trek to the Syrian border. After twenty minutes of cautious driving, Brannan approached the crossing. Thinking he might have to bribe the usual border thug, the major slowed the car, but no one appeared as he crept forward. A glitter of steel caught Brannan's eye, and he finally saw a fence. Two posts leaned drunkenly, held together by a wire loop. Brannan pressed his lips together. "It can't be this easy," he said aloud.

After putting the car in park, he stepped out and walked to the fence. Sure enough, a simple wire held two gate posts together. No lock, no guard, no problem. The major quickly surveyed the area to see if anyone else were near this lame excuse for border protection. He met only the silence and darkness of the night. Brannan pulled the loop up and over the post and pulled it aside, jumped back into the car and drove past the posts, and then hopped back out to close the gate. Chuckling to himself, he hauled himself back into the car and sped down the bumpy road.

According to his intelligence, he would hit a decent highway in an hour or so. The trip to Damascus from the border would take roughly five or six hours, so he would reach the capital of Syria just about sunrise, and city activity would hide his arrival.

Damascus, sometimes called the pearl of the East, perhaps holds the title of the oldest inhabited city in the world, stretching back at least 3,500 years. The four million-plus inhabitants made it the largest city in Syria. He still had to plan carefully, since he had to target solely the Muslim population. On his last visit to the ancient city, he had sprayed the infected water with much less care; when planning the next phase, Spencer, Tyler, and he had defined the area where he would place the tape. His motel/apartment complex sat on the brink of the affected zone, so it wouldn't appear suspicious when the pathogen didn't affect him.

The sun edged over the horizon as the first building appeared on the outskirts of the city. He was familiar with Damascus's roads and alleys and avoided likely points where someone might halt him, though his papers were in order and he had cash ready if a bribe was demanded in the normal course of business.

Just as he pulled off the main highway, he finally found a radio station, and Gaza was the headline. Brannan drove deeper into the city, listening to the devastation. He arrived at the complex without incident and parked his car in a convenient spot. On checking in, the lobby chatter focused on Gaza. The manager didn't give him a second glance after handing him a ring with a metal key hanging from it. Brannan nodded and trudged to his room in the next targeted city.

Chapter Twenty

Monday, October 8

Special Agent Dellendale's mellow yellow wall had ceded space to a super full high-definition screen divided into four quadrants, each displaying different news channels. The hum of her computerized desk masked the sound, and she could barely see through the many holographic interfaces and documents hanging in the air. Daman Pryce sauntered into her office and settled into an empty chair.

Harried, Melissa looked up and shook her head. "It's up to nearly forty thousand people, Daman. Forty thousand lives! They're dead because of this...of this...this American Terrorist. The president now wants me to brief him. It's all hit the fan, and everyone's looking at me. I told them upstairs after we talked, Daman. They just gave me that nod and a polite 'thank you, but that's absurd' routine."

Daman gave her skeptical look. "Yeah, we thought he might pull something off, but this, Mel? I didn't think *this* could happen, and you didn't either."

She glared at him. "You're not helping!"

He shrugged.

Admitting Pryce had a point, she tempered her tone. "We have a very real problem here, Daman. Do you hear the international outcry? People are up in arms! This isn't looking good for us. We're really going to have to commit some serious resources to find this Spencer. I'll tell you, this guy is probably pretty prepared, and I bet we're going to find it difficult...." She suddenly stopped and scrutinized her visitor. "You seem awfully calm. What's up?" she asked, abruptly pressing a button and closing down the holographic images.

Daman slowly crossed his legs and shrugged again. "You know, Mel, the funny thing about my company? We do a lot of listening. But we don't listen to the same things as the FBI. We don't have to. You're hearing a lot of public uproar from other countries and our country as well; domestic disturbances is what I like to call it sometimes. We listen to other people, other places, other things."

Mel peered at Daman. "And what do you hear?" she asked.

He paused. "In a word, fear. Fear from all around the world. Not as much condemnation from where we thought we might hear it— China, Russia. If you can believe it, the talk behind the closed government doors of some of those real big international players is one of fearful indifference. As if they're saying 'Hey, you play with fire and piss off America, you're going to get burned. And, by the way, we don't want to play this game with this American Terrorist fella.' Now, of course, the public face is quite different, but you're not going to hear about a lot of backdoor pressure put on our government."

She found this bit of information interesting. Shifting in her seat, she leaned forward and speculated, "So maybe the polite 'thank you,' from the upstairs folks wasn't a dismissal of the absurd, but one of 'we don't care if it's possible and now go away.'"

He didn't answer.

She eyed her CIA colleague speculatively. For all she knew, Mr. Spook's boss could have sent Mr. Spook to the FBI with a special mission to plant a seed in the lead FBI agent's receptive ear. She still didn't know Pryce's job description or his true title. Few did, she suspected. He would depart DC several times a year for a few days, but much of his time he spent inside the beltway.

She guessed his clearance far exceeded hers, and his name didn't drop too far from the higher echelons at CIA, yet he still found time to stroll into her office. Why? Business or pleasure, she wondered. Both, she bet. "Well, regardless, Daman, we still gotta catch this guy," she finally offered.

"Or at least look good trying."

A cryptic comment and she stared at him hard with her bright blue eyes. "What are you implying? We don't really go after him? Just make it look good?"

Daman squinted, and his eyes glazed just a bit. With his spooky persona appearing, Mel leaned forward, preparing to deal with Daman's business side. Daman lowered his voice. "And act just like some of those Middle Eastern regimes?" He scoffed. "No. Never. Of course not. But you know, Mel, I've talked with some of the people in those Middle-eastern intelligence services, and the information we get from them is worthless. Sometimes you get a contact who really is trying to help, but amazingly doesn't have the resources to get us the information, or simply doesn't have access and never will. And there are others who you know have the information or could easily get it, and they smugly remark how difficult it is for them to find anything at all. It's all a front. They know where these terrorists are; they just don't have the desire to root them out. The roles will now be reversed, I guess. And when they ask me, I can shrug and give them my response. 'Hey, our suspect is an American. I don't have jurisdiction in this matter because I'm not an employee of that domestic bureau.' It'll sound incredibly hollow to those asking, but they're going to feel the bottom of my feet because they'll be walking in my shoes."

Mel cocked her head, placed her elbows on her desktop, and started twisting the ring. "And that will feel good because turn-around is fair play, or because you don't want to find our American Terrorist, since you know what's in store for them?"

Daman smiled enigmatically.

She sighed and leaned back in her chair. "I've had the news turned on. Washington politicians are, of course, up in arms. The Speaker of the House, our friend Wilma Thurlington, was so shrill I had to turn her off. But on the other channels, they interviewed people from across the country. Some were upset. Many others had…well, they kind of had your attitude, Daman. 'Serves them right' or 'I don't care' was what a lot of them said."

Daman shrugged again.

Mel shook her head. "Do you really think that's right, Daman? Should we allow this guy to freelance like this? Whether it's forty people or forty thousand, what he did was hideously wrong, and we have to find him."

Daman's spooky persona faded just slightly, and he assumed a more contemplative expression. "And that's why you have to go after him, Mel. It is wrong, what he did. Just be prepared for various attitudes. I think everyone will support the FBI pursuing this Spencer, but many will remember all the attacks, and others will remember Spencer's family."

Mel rose from her chair and started pacing around the room. Up to the Gaza attack, she had compiled a thick dossier and had a possible lead in Chiapas, Mexico. When she awakened to forty thousand deaths, she expected the Bureau and every agency in the government would provide whatever resources she needed to pursue the trail. Daman was disabusing her of this notion. Since he did walk the shadier and more privileged halls of Langley, he had information, and he was trying to communicate something without telling her outright.

The road to Chiapas and to Spencer might be much more difficult than she had believed: not only because of her adversary's ingenuity, but because she was working against those in her own government who wanted her, and everyone else, sidelined. She glanced at one of the super full high-def quadrants where a reporter interviewed a woman from Atlanta. They spoke of Gaza, and the woman's body language clearly communicated indifference to the victims' plight. She didn't display any vindictiveness, yet she didn't show any sympathy or compassion either.

Walking back to her desk, Mel grabbed a thumb drive. "I have to see the president now. I'm to meet him and others at the White House in a half hour."

"I'm here to drive, Mel."

She chuckled. "Figured you'd be going."

They drove to 1600 Pennsylvania Avenue in silence. After the checkpoints and screenings, the president's personal secretary ushered them into the Oval Office. Familiar high-powered executive elites quietly talked among themselves as they entered. The president hadn't entered yet, so Mel turned to Daman who hadn't looked at anyone, and muttered, "Glad you're here. I need someone important to talk to."

Daman smiled and was about to respond when a side door opened. The president marched into the room with his information technologist, Andy Mahony, trailing. After an incident such as Gaza, everyone understood Halladan's solemn expression. He motioned for them to find a seat as he took the chair at the head of the coffee table. "It goes without saying," the president said, "that what I say now must not leave this room. Period. I cannot have this information in the halls of Congress, and I definitely cannot have it in the press. It will eventually get there, no doubt, but on my timetable. Is this clear?"

Everyone nodded. "I have just heard from our Ambassador to Saudi Arabia. The Saudis, the Iranians, and other Middle Eastern oil-producing countries, are contemplating stopping all oil and gas production if any other American Terrorist attack occurs. Right now it's a rumor and discussion in their elite power circles, not policy, but he brought this to me personally, because in his estimation it had credibility."

Everyone allowed the message to percolate before responding. They had expected discussion on Gaza, and this abrupt dispatch met with shuffling feet and shifting eyes. Finally, William T. Hanson, secretary of the treasury, cleared his throat. "Well, Mr. President, if these countries play this 'oil and gas card' option, it will devastate the world economy. We at Treasury have modeled this scenario, and so have the CIA, the Fed, and NSA. We have all the fossil fuel right here in the US our country needs and more, but because of the EPA, environmentalists, and inane regulations, they aren't developed for commercial production, and we cannot get them online quickly enough. Despite what the Russians claim, they cannot provide enough oil and gas from their remote locations to serve the world markets—and they wouldn't even if they could—and there simply aren't any other relevant producers. The immediate shock to the markets will cripple them beyond the short or even middle term, and the world as we know it today may not reach the long term." Hanson paused, clearing his throat again, and then continued. "Of course, these nations hastily make these threats, but I'm not certain any of them have really calculated or modeled the effects on their own economies. We have, and it's devastating to them as well. However, they have a shorter distance to fall, so to speak, since many of their people live in poverty already."

"Am I to understand correctly, sir," the NSA director, Dave Weathers, asked quietly, "That these people are putting the responsibility of this American Terrorist on the US government?"

The president nodded. "Ironic, isn't it, Dave? If it's their terrorist, we can't blame them, but if it's ours, they demand we assume all responsibility. In fact, Dave, it's so ironic, it becomes the epitome of hypocrisy. I'm not going to stand for it."

Halladan paused a moment himself, and then said, "DoD modeled a different scenario. In the event such a threat was made, DoD modeled what it would take to for us to seize the largest oil fields in the Middle East. Now we're not talking occupation and then liberation, we're talking appropriating these fields with deadly intent. We clear them of any and all inhabitants and keep them clear with prejudice. Shoot to kill if anyone enters our black zone."

The shifts in the seats and shifting eyes occurred again.

"You know what the models say?" the president asked, gauging his advisors' expressions.

They stared at him, most able to infer the answer from their leader's hardened demeanor. "When we don't have to screw around and accommodate political niceties and walk on eggshells and the like, we can accomplish the goal relatively quickly, and without much American bloodshed. It doesn't matter if the fields are booby trapped. It requires some new bombing technology and some inventive logistics, and we would still have to secure the routes, but additional technologies will help. This is entirely feasible. People, if countries make the decision to cut our oil supplies, it's an act of war, and it's a war I'm willing to wage. We're not going to let them destroy the world economy and cause literally billions to suffer. That will not happen. Not on the hypocritical ultimatum they're giving us. So I want each one of you to know we are currently preparing this response plan, and I will expect your input rapidly. We're going to war, people, if we have to."

Mel leaned toward Daman and whispered, "What happened? I thought other countries weren't going to put this on our shoulders?"

Daman responded with a half shrug. "Hadn't heard from any Middle Eastern governments."

"Obviously not. So what do you think those other countries will say now if they hear about this?"

Daman's expression soured. "Their tone might change."

Chapter Twenty-One

Monday, October 8

Spence wiped streaks of sweat from his face. The toilet stank of his puke. News still blared in the other room about the success of his first attack, and nausea was his only response. The Spartan Mexican warehouse echoed loudly with sirens whining from the television, and the loneliness of the moment allowed his guts to express the revulsion he felt when he learned he had caused the death of forty thousand people. Images of severed heads crept back into his mind, and slowly from the guttural spewing came a new resolve. As he stared at the flushed face in the mirror, something in his stomach hardened, and he looked into the toilet bowl and quickly flushed it. No more vomit would come from remorse. When he had killed Ali, he knew his stomach would test his resolve again, and it did, but the images he harbored rescued him, as he knew they would. He recovered much faster this time, and he realized he grew more callous. Remorse, guilt, and regret started slipping further from his emotional inventory.

He stepped out of the bathroom and walked to the couch. Lowering himself as he picked up the remote, Spence started searching for an American news channel. Finally he recognized Americanized English and heard a woman expressing perfunctory sympathy for the Palestinians, and then the woman asked the reporter whether it was a group of Palestinians she saw dancing in the street after the attack in Miami. Clearly her sour expression expressed something less than genuine compassion.

Tyler walked in with Timothy Preston. Both were attired in local garb, and as Thom inspected his clothes and recalled the reflection he had just seen in the mirror, it struck him how easily they had blended into the neighborhood, even Tyler.

"We stopped to watch the news," Tyler said. "Probably would've looked funny if we walked right on by, since everyone was gawking at TV screens."

Preston looked anxious, which alarmed Spencer. He liked Preston. Very much. Preston was Brannan's man, and he possessed a smooth efficiency well masked by his consistently pleasant and at times even jovial mood. Still, beneath the easy-going nature, Thom perceived a man who was committed to this mission, and his eyes conveyed utter confidence in his ability to achieve a desired end.

Deciding he needed to know what had prompted the discernible mood swing, he nodded toward Preston. "Everything all right with you, Timothy?"

Caught off guard by the question, Preston tried to reclaim his confident demeanor. Silently he rebuked himself for revealing any internal turmoil, but merely responded, "I don't want to cause any alarm, but I made a call while we were out, and I've learned some disturbing news. Wasn't sure how to react to it."

Both Tyler and Thom stared at him expectantly. Timothy shrugged. "Someone has to tell you."

"Tell us what?" Thom demanded.

"It appears some Middle Eastern countries have leveled a threat against the United States. A pretty serious threat."

"What threat?" Tyler asked, his brow furrowed.

"To cut off all oil to the US and perhaps the entire world."

"We don't get all our oil from Middle Eastern countries," Tyler remarked.

"Enough, and the rest of the world does," Timothy retorted. "Sources say it would panic the markets and plunge the world into a depression. Psychological as much as anything, but the consequences are just as real."

Thom gazed at Preston intently. Timothy cocked his head and asked, "What ya thinkin', Thom?"

"That those Middle Eastern countries don't know how much

serum we have and how much we can deliver." He paused for a moment. "I think we need another message sent to the world, Timothy. We need to be specific. Our demand remains the same. But we also warn that if any retaliatory action is taken against the US, we will launch another attack. We keep that as a standing threat."

"So if they don't surrender the terrorists, we strike. And if they respond by withholding oil or in any way damage us, we strike again," Preston summed up.

"And you know what, we need to be prepared to do it," Thom added.

Preston pondered Spence's response. This new threat came in a sterile tone, cold and dispassionate. "Could you carry that out?" he asked.

Thom glanced at Tyler who cocked his head, considering. "We would have to set up a new lab. We'd have to obtain more materials. Brannan did tell us he could get what we needed. Could be done."

Timothy nodded. "We can get you what you need. Question is whether we can stay one step ahead of those numerous agencies that are most likely trying to find us."

"Then we have to keep that one step in front of them," Spence declared.

"Well, the odds are that at least some of the oil-producing nations will shut off the spigots after the second attack," Timothy predicted.

"Fine," Thom said. "And they can expect escalating attacks until the oil flows and the terrorists are surrendered. Give them a specified period of time to produce, and if they don't, we attack."

Tyler shrugged. "We may not have to do that, Thom."

"Why?"

"Just my guess, but at some point the US is going to act. If those countries shut off the oil, ten to one they can count on US forces in their backyards in no time."

Thom pressed his lips together. "Then they can count on a very bad day. Even if the US launches an attack, we still proceed with our plan if they don't meet our demands. We must maintain credibility."

Preston pondered Spencer's new plan. "We would have to recall Major Brannan, unless we sent a second operative there."

"I can get him a message, as I am certain you can as well, Timothy," Thom replied. "Anyway, Brannan would return eventually under those circumstances."

Timothy didn't respond. Instead he said, "I'm going to clear this with others. I think we get the OK. We don't have to do a live broadcast. We record it, and deliver it for distribution. You're right, Thom, we have to respond no matter what the US does. If they don't meet our demands, then we hit them."

Thom grimaced. "Timothy," he said slowly, "I'm just going to say this once. I like you, and I know you don't work for us, and that you answer to others. But let me make this clear. We don't work for you, and we don't seek your or your superiors' approval for our actions. Whether we make additional demands, whether we broadcast now, later, live, or taped, whether we even proceed—those are our decisions, and our decisions alone. Not yours. We have the toxin. We have the trigger. You don't. No doubt your organization can kill us. That, however, would quickly terminate this entire operation, now wouldn't it? So you have a choice. You can walk away from us, and even surrender us to the authorities. Or you can accept that I call the shots. Not you, not Brannan, not anyone else. We do this my way, or it doesn't happen. Period. Do you understand this, Timothy?"

Preston flinched. He had been thinking out loud, and had overstepped his bounds, and knew he deserved the reprimand. He had been clearly and repeatedly instructed that he wasn't in control, yet he had let slip what he in his heart believed. Without his organization, the American Terrorist couldn't operate or execute any plan. But Spencer possessed the toxin, and no one in his organization knew how to make it or would risk trying to take it. They had no intention of trying to duplicate or steal the serum. It belonged to Spencer and Washington, and they wouldn't violate that right.

But the organization did want them to wield it, and wield it with a vengeance.

Inhaling sharply, he said, "Thom, you're right, and I didn't mean to sound as if I was taking over the operation. I was just thinking out loud. We do it your way. Just let me know what you want to do, and we'll make it happen."

Thom nodded, accepting the apology. "I agree with your recorded-message approach. Before we send it, I want you to confirm you can get what we need to produce more serum. Then I want to know how fast we can set up shop here. Tyler, make a list of what you need. Get enough material to produce several doses. Timothy, we're going to have to do this quickly."

Preston nodded.

"And Timothy, just to let you know, if anything happens to the toxin, to these new doses, if anything happens to us, the entire operation crashes and everything will be exposed. I call the shots not just because this is my operation. I call the shots because if I don't, a whole lot of information gets sent to places where it doesn't do you or your bosses any good."

Preston digested the information and said slowly, "I understand, Thom." The room felt chilly, and Timothy departed without his usual jovial demeanor.

"Do you think the threat was smart, Thom?"

"Tyler, if it's credible, sometimes you have to let people know in no uncertain terms you have options."

Chapter Twenty-Two

Tuesday, October 16

Special Agent Dellendale leaned on her desk, head in hands as she stared at a blank mellow yellow wall, listening for the fourth time to the taped message from the American Terrorist. She had confirmed that the voice matched the one from the first live message on Prednow's talk radio show.

It was a concise statement: expect another attack with increased casualties if the terrorists were not surrendered and the networks destroyed in fourteen days. But the American Terrorist added a second threat. He promised reprisals, swift and severe, if a Middle Eastern or Islamic nation implemented any policy harming the United States. He would immediately launch additional assaults in response to any stoppage of oil or other act he deemed damaging to American interests.

Spencer had the message physically delivered to Prednow, eliminating any digital trail. The trace evidence on it didn't reveal an origin, but she hadn't expected any clue from that. The mention of oil stoppage, however, instantly caught her attention, and she kept replaying it on her super mini-computer.

Her open door darkened, and before the person even entered, she said without looking, "I suppose you're here to talk about our friend Spencer."

Daman Pryce traipsed into the room, closing the door before he settled into the chair across from her. "Just wanted to let you know we're doing everything we can to find him. Just as I'm certain our good old FBI is doing."

"He's covered his tracks well, Daman. Our leads in Chiapas were a bust. Maybe a trail in South America. Not even worth going down there yet. He could be sitting right in our backyard. That tells me he's getting help." She stared hard at him.

Noticing the accusation in her glare, Daman threw up his hands, palms outward. "Don't look at the Agency, Mel. He's not getting support from us."

"How would you know?"

Daman ground his teeth and rubbed his jaw as he strained his neck side to side. "All right. There are black ops I don't know specifically about, and don't want to know. At all. But, Mel, just because I don't know specifically about a black op doesn't mean I can't catch a whiff of that stink when one is underway. It doesn't matter if it's an inside job or outsourced. I can snoop around and discover who's here and who's not. That gives me a real good idea whether we've got something brewing. With our friend Spencer, too many people *aren't* missing, if you catch my drift."

Dellendale understood and sighed, softening her snappish expression. "Well, he promised an escalation in his first threat, so we undoubtedly can expect an even larger attack the next time. How many deaths do you think we can anticipate?"

Daman shrugged. "One attack doesn't make a pattern. Hard to tell."

Melissa shook her head. "I don't see how we can find him before the next strike, Daman. Despite his threats, another attack may force the Middle Eastern countries to shut off their oil spigots. Do you think they'll really do it?"

He sighed. "Our sources say they aren't idle threats. It's a very real possibility."

Daman's assessment confirmed her FBI intelligence reports. "What does the rest of the world have to say about that?"

Daman exhaled. "It's top-secret information, so other countries can only speculate about something like that right now."

Mel dropped her head and started twisting the ring. "When all the Middle Eastern governments blame us for the oil stoppage because we can't stop Spencer, the rest of world eventually will point fingers at us, you know. What are all these strategic competitors going to say when we respond with an attack on all the oil fields to stop the stoppage? They have to expect that."

Daman tilted his head, thinking. "If they don't openly support it, which some might, they're not going to say anything after Spencer promised reprisals."

Mel looked at him without blinking. "Do you think Spencer was implicitly warning other nations like Russia and China?"

Daman pensively shook his head. "No. Do you?" Mel shook her head. Daman pressed his fingertips together and started bouncing them lightly off each other. "But that threat puts all of them in a predicament, because they realize it could easily be leveled at any of them. I think that's probably been clearly pointed out, Mel. Better for them to sit on the sidelines for this one, is my bet."

Mel considered those countries' options and silently agreed. Russia and China, as well as other nations, would allow the American Terrorist and the United States to settle this conflict with the Middle East without their direct input. Indirectly and discreetly, Russian and Chinese labs would burn late-night candles to backwards-engineer Spencer's pathogen in attempts to discover either a vaccine or antidote. She wasn't sure they would find an answer—she wasn't sure her government could find an answer—but until one of them found one, they very likely wouldn't risk the American Terrorist's wrath.

She paused the ring spinning, squinted at Pryce, and then asked the question that had really been nagging at her. "So, Daman, what prompted Spencer to mention stoppage of oil?"

Daman shrugged.

"You know, it almost seems as though he knew these Middle Eastern countries threatened us. Now, how could that be possible, since that threat was so top secret?"

The question caught the CIA operative off guard; he shifted uneasily in the chair, his eyes darting from corner to corner. Finally glancing at Mel, he ventured, "Oil is their best weapon, so he's also speculating what they might do. Just like other countries might be doing."

Mel creased her forehead doubtfully. "Maybe. But Prednow received this video recording early today. It comes eight days after the president received the threat from the Saudi Ambassador, which supposedly hasn't gone beyond Halladan's close advisors. Coincidence?"

Daman didn't respond.

"And no other agency could sponsor this? Or be involved somehow?" she pressed.

Pryce stared at the floor, stroking his lip. Eventually he replied, "Mel, the CIA would know something was up, whether we're directly involved or not. Nothing is up...and I'm not a big believer in coincidences."

"Neither am I," she said dejectedly.

A White House leak had suddenly sprung onto her desk, and her job became much more complicated. She had no proof, and she didn't have any resources available to investigate it. Just disclosing the possibility created problems, and she glanced at Daman hoping for an answer, but didn't find any suggestions from his drawn face.

Chapter Twenty-Three

Wednesday, October 17

Mansur Ghazali stared at his hands and then pressed them firmly together. Frustrated, he rose from his chair and paced the room. He should have heard from Mohammad hours ago, but Mohammad had solicitously asked him to practice patience. Ghazali did not wait for many people, though he would begrudgingly give his government liaison some leeway. A rap on the door interrupted his impatient irritation, relieving the monotony of the television noise.

Mohammad stepped through the doorway, perspiration already forming on his brow. A brutal thug as a government official, he behaved slavishly in the presence of the volatile terrorist. Smiling diffidently, he nervously bowed.

Ghazali greeted tersely, "You obviously got the message through. They heeded my advice."

Wringing his hands, Mohammad frowned. "Indeed they did, Mansur, and look how that madman, the American Terrorist, responded! He said he would retaliate against all of us for any action taken. Cutting off oil will only get more killed."

"Of course. Don't you see how this proves the US government is involved? How else could he know, Mohammad? No one has publicly announced this as our position. They're behind this Spencer."

"Maybe," Mohammad answered doubtfully.

Ghazali's nostrils flared and his eyes widened.

"I agree with you," Mohammad offered before Ghazali's wrath exploded. "But the Americans of course will deny it. And we do have a problem. We don't have confirmation from anyone that they are involved. If the US government is backing this operation, then it's very well concealed."

Mansur looked indifferently at Mohammad and asked curtly, "Are they going to do it?"

"Cut off the oil?"

"Yes, Mohammad, cut off the oil to the American pigs. And everyone else," Ghazali answered angrily.

"I don't know. I think they're thinking about it seriously, but in the very least they know it will hurt all of us. Even if Spencer doesn't retaliate, the economic consequences are dire. So many of our brethren Middle Eastern Muslim nations depend on the oil. Many that aren't producing it receive American aid, and they're afraid the US will lump them in with us and revoke it. And those of us producing oil can't afford to support them if we're not selling it. We can't lose sight of that. Our brethren aren't."

Ghazali paused and changed tactics, his voice now calm and rational. "Mohammad, it is time for action. Firm and aggressive action. Our brethren governments start with that, and I will also respond. I will take my Jihad to even greater heights. I will inflict pain upon the Americans, pain they've never felt before. We will prevail. America cannot endure what I plan to do to it."

Mohammad sighed. He slowly walked to a chair and wiped his forehead with his hand, feeling the accumulated sweat on his fingertips, before sitting. He stared at the intense man standing across the room—soothing tones flowed from those parted lips, yet raging fire blazed from his eyes. He sighed. "Mansur, we're out of our league. This crazy American has escalated it beyond our means. We don't have an answer for it. At least not one to match his," Mohammad said emphatically.

The words themselves didn't strike Ghazali as much as Mohammad's inflection. Ghazali glared at him. "The man doesn't understand terrorism. This American Terrorist..."

"Has taken the upper hand in a way that we can't answer, Mansur!" Mohammad interrupted. "He killed more people and has inflicted more fear in his first strike than all of ours put together. According to his latest threat, he's going to kill even more Muslims in his next attack!"

Ghazali gritted his teeth. "We can prevail, Mohammad. We *can*. I need to address the brethren governments directly. A hand must be extended to one of the nuclear nations. Give me launching capabilities, Mohammad. A nuclear strike will put us in control."

Mohammad stared at Mansur Ghazali in disbelief. The terrorist had never mentioned a nuclear missile strike before, and Mohammad feared this new tack meant desperation. Diffusing the tension by lowering his voice and assuming a humble demeanor, Mohammad shrugged. "That's debatable, Mansur. We don't know his capabilities. We just don't know what he can do. Who knows, he might trump a nuclear strike. And, Mansur, if America or one of its allies is struck by a nuclear warhead, the US will respond, and I doubt very many people will survive in the Middle East. I don't think we get far with a nuclear response. Too many people die."

"Then so be it, Mohammad. I must address the brethren governments."

Mohammad shook his head. "Mansur, most agree with you and wish to see America destroyed. We all hate it, and them. Despise them just like you, but some lack the conviction, the fanaticism you have, and they won't destroy everything. They're simply not willing to risk it."

Ghazali stared back, unblinking. "You don't understand, do you, Mohammad? Yes, I am willing to risk it. You know why?"

Mohammad shrugged and gestured vaguely, knowing Ghazali would answer himself.

"Because Allah wills it. We are on the side of morality. It may take a hundred or two hundred or more years, but we will prevail, and we must be willing to risk everything; destroy all of it, if we must. When we do, Allah will save us, and we can start a new era, a purer era, more akin to the first year of the Hegira. Those in the brethren governments must be persuaded. It is the time, Mohammad."

Mohammad started to sweat profusely. He had the unenviable job of warning a man who killed in a blink of an eye that the brethren governments, which had benefited from his organization, just might betray him. He swallowed hard. "Mansur, there's a small but growing faction in the brethren governments advocating for severing ties with you. They don't believe now is the time."

An internal alarm suddenly sounded in Ghazali's mind. He hesitated; then he strolled around the room, contemplating the veiled threat the messenger had just delivered. So, the American Terrorist had driven a wedge between his supporters and him. "I certainly hope those in our brethren governments don't think I will accept their betrayal lightly," Ghazali warned. "I will not allow them to sacrifice me to the Americans or anyone else. My resources, Mohammad, aren't limited to actions against the Great Satan. Surely they know this."

Mohammad knew this all too well. Ghazali had always preached deference to the brethren governments, working in concert with them, which allowed his network to expand beyond national and sectarian boundaries. Now, however, they were threatening Ghazali and jeopardizing the mission of Universal Jihad, and Ghazali could easily withdraw the deferential policy. The thought of an internal struggle with Universal Jihad terrified Muslim governments, but it was a considered alternative to the American Terrorist. Only a muffled voice advocated this policy so far, but Mohammad believed it could grow louder very quickly, and he had to forewarn his friend. He shook his head and turned placating palms up. "Of course they know this. It's a small faction right now, Mansur, yet it could increase. Especially if this American Terrorist can inflict substantial casualties. I'm sure they'll protect you, but you're going to have to work with them."

The weakness infuriated Ghazali, and his eyes bored venom into Mohammad, who tried to maintain the terrorist's eyes but couldn't. Ghazali knew Mohammad wasn't responsible, and he forgave him once his eyes dropped to the floor. "Mohammad, you are a good friend. Thank you for the warning."

Mohammad's shoulders wilted with relief.

Ghazali fumed at the cowards; the American Terrorist couldn't go unanswered. He would decrease his contact with the brethren governments and move to a place where he could easily slip past a border, yet not so remote he didn't have access to those he might need. Those many, many loyal operatives inside the brethren governments would alert and help him if any serious opposition to him emerged.

After the relocation, he would accelerate his timetable. Immediate pain in America would force a US government response, and maybe the Americans in a savage act of revenge would destroy those very same cowards who wouldn't act now. If not after this wave of attacks, then after the next. Meanwhile, he would watch as Americans tore at Americans, exposing the country's immorality and hypocrisy, a society destined for historical ignominy. More blood would flow in the American streets, and he smiled to himself at the red rivers of pain he envisioned.

Chapter Twenty-Four

Thursday, November 22

Three successive, bloody attacks left five hundred seventy-five people dead, with each bloodletting so dreadful, even Hollywood couldn't replicate them. The gore and then utter grief consuming each victimized location spawned enormous rage in the heart of most Americans. The seams of sanity stitching together all the streets and roads and alleys appeared ready to burst, fulfilling the dreams of terrorists. Yet, those very seams, when the tension was expanding, growing, and exerting tremendous pressure, grew stronger and cinched up. The strain remained, but those seams didn't burst. And then the unexpected happened: a deflator, and its source was the FBI foiling a fourth attack.

The three attacks occurred within forty-eight hours. Agent Dellendale, still concentrating on the American Terrorist, had kept her hand in the Ghazali and Universal Jihad investigation, and she immediately smelled something wrong when reports flooded her desk.

Putting down the Spencer file, she immediately requested a Lear Jet for visits to the terrorist targets: Ft. Lauderdale; Columbus, Ohio; and Salt Lake City. She swiftly concluded from the evidence that Ghazali had taken the American Terrorist's attacks personally and was playing a game of one-upmanship. But in changing his timetable, small yet perceptible mistakes occurred. With most

Universal Jihadist attacks, mistakes were few and far between, and though the FBI would eventually model the scheme, patterns changed, and trails cooled, eventually fading away. These attacks showed a different mentality: hurried and repetitive. The Universal Jihadists hadn't concealed the evidence as cleverly as before, and it took much less time than usual for investigators to determine the who, the how, and the when.

Mel believed she caught allusions to a madrasa in the attackers' nearly undecipherable notes, uncharacteristically left at hideouts. With this and other information, Mel began to see puzzle pieces falling into place.

On her direction, an FBI SWAT team invaded a mosque in Los Angeles running a madrasa to recruit and teach Muslims a fundamentalist interpretation of Islam. It was on the FBI's list of watched organizations, but its activities hadn't justified any action until Mel's deduction. The tactical unit caught the madrasa with its figurative pants down, and the raid netted enough intelligence for agents to disrupt another cell, which led to yet another unsuspecting mosque.

This mosque was preparing to detonate bombs in Los Angeles International Airport's Terminal 7, and special agents corralled several suspects with ample evidence to prove the case. When the FBI announced the plot to the country, Americans embraced the news as a small but important victory on the stateside War on Terror. No one had any illusion that victory was complete, but it revealed a chink in Universal Jihad's armor. Citizens rejoiced and tensions subsided. Streets normalized without as much fear they would become venues for pitched battles. People returned to the flow of commerce and social gatherings, to the movie theater seats and supermarket aisles, assuming the risk rather than avoiding it in fear.

Although anger still hovered in the atmosphere, demands on the government to retaliate relented, as though the American public intuitively realized the government's hands were tied. People could hang their hopes on someone else to vent their collective anger, and the American Terrorist had assumed a nearly mythic role in the American public as an avenger who wouldn't allow these deaths to go unanswered.

From media interviews to letters to editors, a pervasive theme materialized: "Maybe it's wrong, and we know the American

Terrorist must answer for his actions, but it will undoubtedly be interesting to see his response." The smug tone implied a hope the American Terrorist would indeed inflict a heavy cost on the Muslim world. Others weren't implicit and openly asked the American Terrorist to respond not in kind but tenfold. "Ten eyes for an eye and then give him a medal," was one terse comment by a man in Phoenix interviewed outside a jewelry store after buying a belated anniversary gift, forgotten in the wake of the Jihadist attacks.

A very boisterous minority clamored for the American Terrorist's head, blaming him personally for Universal Jihad's latest attacks while strangely ignoring any calls to decapitate Ghazali. When Speaker of the House Thurlington seized another opportunity to question the administration's will to capture the American Terrorist, she ineptly, though instinctively proclaimed, "It is far more important to get Thom Spencer, the American Terrorist, than any other terrorist." Many ridiculed her remark, but amazingly the press and her admirers gave her a sympathetic pass for the remark.

In a cable news interview, another talking head conveniently dismissed the speaker's comment, nonchalantly blaming her fatigue. Agent Dellendale, listening to the interview, averted her attention from a mid-air document to one of the super full high-definition quadrants on the wall and rolled her eyes. Exhausted, she sighed and tried to refocus on the holographic image. She blinked several times, knowing only sleep would cure the blur she saw. As she reached for yet another cup of coffee, the holographic phone line flashed, and she recognized the incoming number. She couldn't avoid this call. But when she answered, the voice at the other end surprised her. Rather than a presidential aide, President Halladan himself said, "Agent Dellendale, you're in the office late."

"I think, Mr. President, that we should have made these condominium-home offices. I spend more time here than any other place."

The president chuckled. "How about a visit over here, Agent Dellendale? You have a car waiting for you."

"I'll be there shortly, Mr. President."

As Mel entered the Oval Office twenty-five minutes later, Halladan was talking to Andy Mahony, who smiled kindly as she entered and then took his leave quickly. Alone in the Oval Office for the first time with the president, Mel suddenly felt the aura of history engulf her. Blinking a few times, she stepped toward the middle of the room. Halladan offered her a seat on a couch as he rose and slowly walked to a cabinet. "Want something to drink, Agent Dellendale?"

She shook her head. He nodded and poured himself a small whiskey, no ice. He sipped at it as he sat across from her. Leaning back, Halladan tilted his head toward the ceiling and scratched his cheek. "How's the Spencer investigation coming?"

The question caught her off guard, and she frowned. She cleared her throat. "Well, sir, I haven't been putting much effort into that one since the latest attacks. I've been concentrating on Ghazali."

"I know. This country owes you a debt of gratitude, Agent Dellendale. So do I. You do deserve most of the credit." He smiled, though his tone conveyed a strange detachment.

She shook her head "No, Mr. President. We work as a team at the Bureau. I couldn't have done anything without my crew and many others."

Halladan sipped his whiskey and smiled more warmly. "You're a good team player, Agent Dellendale."

She nodded her thanks.

Halladan placed his glass on the table and, leaning forward, said delicately, "Agent Dellendale...Melissa...I need you to shift your attention back to Spencer."

Agent Dellendale's face registered what she couldn't say to the president of the United States.

Halladan sighed. "Ridiculous, you're saying to yourself? You're hot on the trail of Universal Jihad, and taking your eye off this ball isn't prudent. I know. But you are the lead agent on the American Terrorist, and obviously a very good one at that. Your name is nearly household and certainly well-known in Congressional halls. How would it look if we took you off the case and put someone else on it? I can't at all have it appear we condone what Spencer has done. If you close your file on him, then that would be the exact message we would be sending."

Mel twisted her ring. She understood, and he was right. Americans and the world had a legitimate expectation the US government would continue pursuing the American Terrorist. She leaned forward and folded her fingers together, placing her elbows on her knees. "Absolutely, sir. Never considered closing the file."

She stared at the president, sensing ambivalence. "I'm just curious, sir," she asked hesitantly, "but do you wish for me to…to…remove myself from the Ghazali case?"

The president's smile broadened. "Absolutely not, Agent Dellendale. Absolutely not."

Mel grasped the implication: keep up a solid pretense of tracking Spencer, yet put her resources on Ghazali. "Understood completely, Mr. President."

Halladan stared at her, as if lost in a moment of appreciation, and then nodded. "Thanks for coming, Agent Dellendale."

Puzzled, Mel asked, "Did I come here for this…this clarification, Mr. President? A phone call would have saved you some time."

Halladan, with a frank expression, said, "Phone calls may work in the future, Agent Dellendale. Melissa. I just needed to see you in person on this particular occasion."

Mel donned her own frank expression. "You can count on me, Mr. President."

"Yes, I know that now."

Chapter Twenty-Five

Monday, December 10

The din of the Arab night rang in the major's ears as he wandered the alleys and streets of the Muslim district. Effortlessly blending with the Damascenes in his Arab garb, Brannan looked innocent enough as he walked from a wall to a post to another wall to a street lamp, innocuously sticking tape in carefully selected places. A cool evening breeze accompanied the major on his walk of death, and Brannan buttoned his thick undershirt around his neck. As he approached his final spot, a woman with two children stopped to read an advertisement on the lamp post. Barely discernible behind the veil, she smiled kindly at the major and he returned the gesture with a mumbled "hello" in Arabic. When she finished reading and called the children to come along, her eyes flashed the concealed smile again, and Brannan nodded. He waited until she joined her husband some distance away and pulled the tape from his pocket. Hesitating, he grimaced as he looked back at her and nearly returned the roll to his pocket. But images of crumbling homes and destroyed stadiums, littered with the bodies of American children, provoked a flash of anger. His resolve, nearly broken by a veiled smile from a kind woman, returned, and he slapped the tape on the post and walked briskly back to his apartment.

The next morning, Brannan awakened with the knowledge that nearby tens of thousands were infected, and death would arrive in the next twenty-four hours or so. The Gaza death toll had undeniably penetrated the Middle Eastern mentality. Numbers did matter, and, by Brannan's calculation, Damascus would endure more than mere penetration.

Strolling along the nearby street, the major stopped at a small café to purchase a coffee. Early-morning patrons chatted among themselves in the smoke-filled room, and a small table of four elderly Arab men huddled near a television set where the news broadcast a report from the United States. Brannan found an open space at the bar near the table and settled down to listen. The conversation revolved around their visceral hatred of Americans. Brannan wished they were the exception; instinctively he knew better, and any remnants of hesitation remaining after a smile from a friendly face quickly vanished. He swigged the last of his coffee, paid, and walked out the café, a grim smile on his face.

The following morning, a shrieking siren interrupted Brannan's weak coffee and instant oatmeal. He glanced at his watch, raising his eyebrows, and crossed quickly to the window. An odd silence blanketed the neighborhood. He grabbed his jacket, and once outside, he trotted up an alley, hoping to confirm the outbreak. The strange silence still pervaded the street until a man, frothing an odor of fear, turned a corner and nearly knocked him down.

The frenzied man screamed, "It's started. I don't know how many now, but people are falling down spewing blood everywhere! They're dying. The American Terrorist has hit here! We're going to die! We're all going to die!"

Brannan feigned shock. Another wailing siren and then another sounded in the distance as the frightened man grabbed his head and fled, running down the streets still screaming.

Brannan didn't need to wander any further, so he turned on his heel and ran just as the other man had. A show of fear was his best cover, so he raced back to his apartment, as if it would provide protection against an outbreak. As he sprinted, he couldn't help think how prophetic the frantic Damascene's statement was.

Once inside, the major flipped on the TV. Reports had already flooded the local news stations. The Syrian government was already issuing statements; the anchorman advised everyone to stay indoors by order of the Syrian president. Useless, of course, Brannan thought as he prepared for his self-imposed five- to seven-day sequestration.

The next morning, dawning clear and blue, Brannan awakened to silence. No knocks on doors, no yelling, no talking, no traffic noise. Nothing. The street outside his apartment remained empty, though sirens still faintly echoed around the city. When he turned on the television, the hectic scene shot by a cameraman and reporter dressed in hazmat suits clearly indicated a city in the throes of fear and death. With the eerie calm outside, Brannan could barely believe the edge of chaos was only a mile away. The camera showed bodies were piled high and recorded the screams that had turned to thousands of muffled sobs. People scurrying around in the hazmat suits, attempting to help those who were already dead, added to the futility.

The reporter grabbed another person, apparently some official in protected gear, and asked through his suit in a strained and harried voice, "Do you have a body count?"

The official shrugged. "Tens of thousands at least. It's as if a nuclear bomb exploded, killing all these people, but without all the destruction. Just the destruction of life. This American Terrorist, this isn't a man. This is evil incarnate. How can anyone do this? Tens of thousands of people dead. Maybe more. This man deserves to suffer. To die. This has to stop." He turned and darted off leaving the reporter to wrap up with the anchor.

Brannan reflected on the anger the man felt for Spencer and remembered Miami and all the families who suffered the attacks of Muslim terrorists. Abruptly his sympathy dulled. Again. What did the man expect? America hadn't responded, so an American did.

The next ninety-six hours passed slowly for Brannan. The infected neighborhood was still immersed in chaos despite the Syrian government's actions. The number of people dying had leveled off, though bodies kept accumulating. Initially the president had cordoned off an area surrounding the epicenter and had ordered no one in or out except emergency response personnel, but finally, after consulting numerous doctors, he decided to evacuate it. At first people outside the zone feared the consequences of allowing potentially infected people to mingle with the general population, but scientists believed those few who were left alive weren't carriers. Living in the midst of piles of decaying bodies posed a much greater risk. Dead bodies spawned diseases, and the government's goal was to prevent collateral death.

Several agencies predicted a body count in excess of three hundred thousand, but declined to speculate when they would release official numbers. After evacuating the affected areas, emergency responders yielded to cleanup crews for counting, identification, and finally cremation, despite the prohibition in Islamic law. The Syrian government believed it had no option but to destroy the remains, and do so as quickly as possible, so it obtained a scholarly opinion allowing cremation under dire circumstances. The cremations began five days after the chaos had started. To mitigate opposition and criticism, the president ordered the ashes buried in a specially designated area consecrated as a Muslim graveyard.

As the panic began, the Syrian government had declared martial law and had prohibited everyone from leaving the country. Borders were sealed, and authorities gruffly questioned and monitored anyone roaming Damascus's streets. After the evacuation of the epicenter, the government caved to international pressure, grudgingly allowing foreigners to depart once people no longer exhibited any symptoms. The president also lifted martial law; the stunned and subdued population didn't need restraint, and military restrictions wouldn't help locate the perpetrator. Everyone knew the culprit's identity, but no one could find him, and no one could explain how he had executed the unbelievable attack. Government officials, scientists, and doctors around the world talked in disbelief about the insidious nature of the attack. No detonators, no debris, just death. It invaded, killing more than three hundred thousand people in one immense wave, and abruptly vanished, leaving a shocked and mortified population as the only proof it had ever struck.

Brannan remained in his one-room apartment watching worldwide news on his antiquated TV set by a rigged rooftop satellite dish. The dingy walls smothered him. When he opened the window seeking fresh air and sunlight, the stench of rot and death assaulted him, and he slammed it shut. Returning to the television, he found a station reporting in America, and turned up the volume when a reporter interviewed a man on a Dallas street.

"So what do you think about the attack in Damascus?" the reporter asked.

The man shrugged. "Well, obviously we need to find this American Terrorist. We can't have someone like this killing people.

I guess. But, I have to admit, he sure cured a lot of the rage I felt."

"What do you mean by that?"

"Well, I mean, that I would be beside myself with anger, and my gut would wrench for those people, if we hadn't been the victims of such horrendous attacks ourselves. But they have their terrorists, and now we have ours. You know, it seems like ours trumps theirs and that's the way it is."

"Thank you," the reporter said. "And, Bob, there are those outraged by this in our country, but I also have found a lot of people just like this man who see justice and retribution here. Back to you."

Brannan was also monitoring the international response. Condemnations were common, though the major thought he detected some indifference. He didn't know whether it was fear, or if the images of Damascus simply didn't evoke the visceral reaction of a typical terrorist scene with its fire and rubble. Carnage littering the streets didn't splatter televisions screens worldwide. Stacks of bagged bodies in an eerily serene but physically intact city perhaps dulled the replies. Maybe utter shock consumed the senses: impossible to think that so many people could die without a single building destroyed.

Six days after the crisis began, Brannan made final preparations for his departure. He hauled any identifying trash and documents to the trash can, pulled out a lighter, and burned them, carefully collecting the ashes in a plastic bag. After dressing in local attire, he slipped out the apartment having already paid, looking haggard and afraid. No one would wonder why he hadn't taken ill, since encoded waves didn't reach his neighborhood, and few if any people in the immediate area had died. The streets weren't as empty as they had been recently, and no one took notice when he stepped into his car.

As he drove along the winding highway toward the border of Jordan, Brannan rolled down his window, and every so often he would pinch some ash from the plastic bag and let the wind brush it from his fingertips. Predictably, as he approached the checkpoint about nine miles southeast of Dar'a, the traffic started to thicken; he wasn't the only person wishing to leave the country, and both Syrian and Jordanian governments had reinforced the checkpoint between the two countries, increasing the delay.

When the traffic came to a lull, Brannan casually took off his jacket. After a few moments, he replaced it with a coat purchased in

Nice, France. His shoes and belt were next, and he stuffed the exchanged garments in a duffel bag and withdrew a contact case. The green-tinted lenses slipped easily into his eyes; a little gel to restyle the hair and a pair of sun-glass completed the transformation. Brannan inspected his revamped visage in the rear-view mirror. Satisfied he looked the tired and harried European, Brannan next assumed an anxious though compliant demeanor. A Frenchman rushing toward the border to leave the stench of Damascus wouldn't raise an eyebrow.

The security officer sullenly held out his hand for Brannan's French passport once the major finally reached the gate. He passed it through a handheld scanner; his eyes skimmed the document and then Brannan's face. He was already looking at the next car as he waved Brannan through the gate, his expression suggesting a desire to join him. The major didn't blame him.

Brannan drove toward Amman with the window down on the surprisingly warm December day. As the afternoon faded into dusk, bringing a chill to the air, Brannan still felt uncomfortably warm, so the highway breeze kept him company as he drove toward the Jordanian capital.

Brannan wiped his mouth, detecting a small amount of moisture on his upper lip, and told himself it was just moisture in the air and not an indicator of his next target and its danger. Amman was the launching point for the third leg of the American Terrorist's attack. The idea of traveling to Tehran after the Damascus attack had troubled Brannan from the inception of his plan, but the exit from Syria to Jordan, the first leg of the perilous mission, had unfolded without disruption. The Amman-to-Iraq segment didn't concern him much; the Iraq-to-Iran journey did, since it was laden with pitfalls. With elevated alert levels, he risked delay and perhaps even detection at every turn. Brannan shivered, suddenly cold, and rolled up the window; he then subtly pressed down on the accelerator as dusk gave way to a starry night.

Chapter Twenty-Six

Thursday, December 13

The sun shone brightly through the Oval Office windows despite the bitter cold outside. Mel did a quick calculation: this was the fourth emergency meeting she had attended since the Damascus attack, but her first with the president. She crossed her legs as she stared at the curved walls, feeling a little uncomfortable and out of place. She liked it better when she was alone with the president. The crowd of important people made her feel lonely. No one talked to her or even looked at her; they all seemed immersed in private conversations too important to include a Special Agent from the FBI, even though she led the investigation on the American Terrorist hunt.

Failure to find him hadn't yet resulted in any recriminations; in fact, it hadn't warranted a direct call from anyone at the director level. She was a lone agent given anything she requested, except priority or attention from people in expensive suits. They had compartmentalized her Spencer role, cordoned it off completely. On her own, she continued the investigation, with technical help and databases her only tools. The expensive suits had limited her access to investigative human capital; even her crew appeared busy when she asked for support on Spencer. She didn't mind since she spent most of her time on Ghazali's trail anyway. And when she waved a Universal Jihad task under her crew's noses, they suddenly became immediately available. No one, of course, acknowledged the game they played, and she applied the "perfunctory" label to her official title of Supervising Lead Investigator of the American Terrorist.

With her official subject responsible for the death of more than three hundred thousand people, she thought she would walk into the Oval Office to face a maelstrom of governmental officials calling for her head. But while she sat there, picking up snippets of conversations, Mel quickly grasped two sides waged war in the upper echelons of government officialdom, and at the moment those who wished to see the American Terrorist run rampant were prevailing. Mel sighed.

A grim-faced president walked through the door and frowned at the crowd waiting for him. Andy Mahony, carrying a sleek tablet, was his usual one step behind. Instead of sitting in the empty chair around which everyone had converged, Halladan stood behind it, leaning on its back while Mahony shuffled behind the desk and stood silently.

Surveying the faces around the room, Halladan nodded as if confirming those who should be present were. "Well, here's the deal," he said. "A request has been made by several Middle Eastern governments that we send our criminologists, investigators, scientists, and any other person who could conceivably possess any knowledge even remotely relevant to this…this whatever it is that the American Terrorist is using to kill all these people, and they want as many as they can get over there now."

Mel frowned, surprised by the subject matter of the meeting. Several in the group exchanged perplexed stares. Secretary of State Mason Townsend immediately grasped the implication. "So they want to use Americans as shields. They want us to send them right on over there as hostages, as if we're in the Middle Ages sending royal family members to enemy princes as a deposit for good behavior." He shook his head, disgusted.

Halladan nodded. "Would it work?" he asked. "Would the American Terrorist stop an attack if he knew Americans were in a target area?"

No one answered.

"What's your analysis, Agent Dellendale?" the president demanded.

Startled at the president's direct address, Mel blinked a few times, and then answered succinctly, "The American Terrorist obviously avoids where Americans reside in targeted cities. Not a single American has been identified in either Gaza or Damascus. He's smart, Mr. President. Killing an American would put him in an entirely different light here at home, and I don't think he wants to jeopardize that."

"Agreed," Hanson said before the president could respond. "But he has increased the extent of his killing by almost an order of magnitude, Agent Dellendale. If he does that again, we're looking at millions of people, and wherever that target may be, Americans can hardly escape."

Mel gestured ambivalently. "For his next attack, he'll target where there is less risk to Americans."

The president shifted from one leg to the other. "Any ideas on where his next target might be?"

With all eyes on her, she leaned forward, crossing her legs at the ankles and glanced at President Halladan, who met her look with an earnest expression. He knew she hadn't concentrated on Spencer, but that didn't mean she hadn't thought about him, and a brief, astute comment from the American Terrorist's lead FBI investigator would enhance the charade. Tilting her head slightly, she moved easily from succinct analysis to pensive opinion, "The fact that he didn't kill an American in Gaza is expected, but in Damascus, with more than three hundred thousand dead, not killing a single American is a little surprising, even though the infected area was concentrated in the large Muslim sector. Undoubtedly Spencer has built a device that somehow helps mitigate American exposure. Now, I heard someone suggest he might have developed a serum that targets only Semitic people. I don't believe it. If he had some sort of racial component in his weapon, he wouldn't care at all about the targeted area. You'd have Semitic people falling down dead all over the world by now, not to mention the improbability of developing any kind of pathogen that could do that.

"But Secretary Hanson is correct. He will try to escalate the number of deaths with every attack, so he must find a place where he can inflict a high number of casualties while avoiding American presence. Identify a locale where we have no diplomatic ties and few American commercial interests, and we arrive at his next probable target. Iran comes to mind first."

The president looked at Brent Chalmers, Director of National Intelligence. Chalmers nodded agreement. "CIA's assessment is Iran also. I had NSA model it, and from a numbers perspective, they think Tehran is next, though other Iranian cities have to be considered."

"Agent Dellendale," the president pressed on, "I read a report stating you have personally met this American Terrorist, and you obviously have gathered a considerable amount of information. Please give us your professional opinion. Would Spencer still attack Iran if we sent Americans there?"

Dellendale didn't answer immediately. She doubted Thom Spencer would attack under those conditions. Yet she wasn't sure, so she decided to provide the president what he wanted: justification to refuse the Middle Eastern governments' request. Maintaining her tone, she continued, "Mr. President, Spencer will avoid Americans if possible, but if they're sent deliberately instead of already being there, that does substantially change the dynamics. Under those circumstances, there's a high probability he would still attack. I'd say there's a very good chance you'd be sending those Americans to their deaths."

The opinion had approval; heads around the room bobbed up and down. Since her blessing apparently mattered, Mel decided to elaborate with a conjecture she did believe. "Mr. President, there's something else I should mention."

Halladan snapped his eyes back to her, and this time they flashed a rebuke. She had performed her duty quite well, the look said, why endanger it? But the gallery had shifted its attention back to her, expecting additional commentary. "Yes, Agent Dellendale?" the president said evenly.

She couldn't back down now. "I must point out that I qualified my previous answer. I said Spencer would try to avoid Americans on his *next* attack."

Though Halladan didn't want this colloquy, Dellendale had piqued his curiosity. "You're implying that it doesn't mean all future attacks. Just his next."

Mel nodded. "Has anyone analyzed his timing and the target order?"

"Well, I hope you have, Agent Dellendale. That's your job," Townsend remarked icily, echoing the president's perturbed expression.

Halladan shot daggers at the secretary of state who suddenly found something of keen interest on the floor. The president turned back to Mel. "And what's the point, Agent Dellendale?"

"Gaza didn't pose much of a risk to Americans, but he still waited more than ten days after the deadline to attack. Why the delay? Damascus, where there was a higher American risk—though manageable, he waited more than a month to hit. Why?" She paused a moment; the silence stretched out until she answered her own question. "Mr. President, I think he's sending us a message. He's telling us, he's telling Americans to get out, and that he'll give us the time to do it. Now, I'm not claiming it's the only reason, but I think it is an important one. With Tehran or where ever, he'll give us time to get our people out, the few that are there. After that, he's running out of places where there is a visible lack of Americans."

"And we're supposed to get that message, and realize that inevitably his safeguard can't protect Americans when he escalates again, so we had better get everyone out of the entire Middle East now?" Townsend asked. Despite an even voice, his eyes apologized.

She gazed charitably at him. "Yes, Mr. Secretary. He's obviously not going to announce where his next target is, so we have to assume anywhere and everywhere in the Middle East."

This opinion didn't meet with the same approval, as evidenced by a sudden murmur and agitation in the room. The secretary of state turned to President Halladan and observed, "It's a different matter, Mr. President, not to send Americans over there than it is to call everyone home. Not to mention the economic and diplomatic complications, but how would it look to the world if we announced that all Americans residing in the Middle East should come home immediately, and then an attack ensued?"

His astute analysis startled Mel.

Halladan shook his head. "It would look as if we are working in concert with the American Terrorist, Mason," he answered quietly.

Again the room fell silent for several moments. President Halladan straightened up and smacked his hands on the chair. "Agent Dellendale, you said the American Terrorist will avoid Americans if possible?"

Mel nodded.

"Then there are diplomatic sectors of cities where he wouldn't attack," the president surmised, "so we, as quietly as we can, communicate to those who must remain in vulnerable areas to stay in those sectors, and hope it provides sufficient protection."

Everyone could tell Halladan didn't like his own solution, but had made his decision. "People," he continued, "my most important job is to protect our citizens, and I have no intention of subjecting Americans to that sort of risk demanded by our Muslim friends in the Middle East. Apparently, however, not everyone has the same responsibilities as I have holding this office, which presumably allows them to make promises and ask for volunteers without taking into account the risk it might present." Halladan nodded to Mahony, who quickly flung his fingers around his tablet. In mere seconds, a screen dropped from the ceiling, the lights dimmed, and a news clip rolled.

The speaker of the house, Wilma Thurlington, approached a podium and started speaking. "Today, I have formed a group to begin the process of sending US experts to the Middle East for the specific purpose of aiding Middle Eastern governments in searching for the source of this diabolical toxin. It is time to help these people find some sort of protection against this American Terrorist. It is time for America to take responsibility for these actions and to assist those vulnerable to this maniac's attacks. The United States must commit its resources to finding the perpetrator, and I will implement a plan to end this malevolent reign of terror. So far, I am not convinced we have done everything we can to find this man and stop him. The Halladan administration has been lackadaisical, to say the least, in its efforts. I will send teams to various cities deemed high probability targets...."

The president stopped the clip. "That presser occurred less than twenty minutes ago. She is trying to usurp the office of the president, and in so doing is putting Americans in extreme danger. I can't allow it, even though I will take it on the proverbial chin. I anticipate a barrage of recriminations ranging from racist to evil. But from my perspective, if I don't prohibit Americans from traveling to these 'high probability targets,' I'm a despicable president. Keeping those already there is nearly unacceptable."

Melissa couldn't believe Thurlington's audacity. Playing hardball politics in such explosive times disgusted her. The speaker knew the president wouldn't allow her to proceed with her plan, and his stance would provide further reason to rail against him. Thurlington was seizing the opportunity to gain political ground. Political power mattered more to her than good policy.

The president continued. "My expectation is for you to perform your duties diligently. I will not send Americans into the Middle East, and that is our official policy. I will respond to the speaker's statements by the end of the day. You will enforce my policy and prevent any American from traveling to an area at risk, despite the expected political pressure. These are your orders."

Without another word, Halladan turned his back on the group, indicating that the meeting had concluded. As Mel shuffled toward the door, she caught Halladan's eyes. They lingered briefly, subtly requesting her to remain. She stood back, as if respectfully waiting for the senior members of the administration to jostle their way out. When the last one had left, Mel approached the president.

Halladan rubbed his chin. "Agent Dellendale, do you really think Spencer is sending us these implied messages, or were you just enhancing the case against sending Americans over there?"

"I think Spencer is intentionally giving us the time."

"How is the Ghazali file coming along?" he asked abruptly.

She understood the implied accusation. Halladan wondered why she had apparently concentrated on Spencer when he had asked her to pursue Universal Jihad. She replied delicately, "Sir, it was only an afterthought."

The president sighed and looked at her kindly. "It's too hard not to have those afterthoughts. It's what makes you so damn smart. Have to keep your head in at least two games, right?"

Mel shrugged, "Please know I know which one is the big game, Mr. President."

"I know you do, but your little afterthought presents problems." He paused. "Someone will put two and two together, and make the accusation that we are working in concert with Spencer, that the administration is wholeheartedly accepting the signals from Spencer, and thanking him with silence. And you can bet that someone will raise the same *time delay* as proof."

Mel understood the problem. "Mr. President, I didn't intend to provide fodder."

Halladan interrupted her. "You didn't, Melissa. But if that someone is someone like Speaker Thurlington, then those accusations will not be of the quiet, diplomatic kind. She'll publicly hurl them and demand answers."

The uncomfortable silence between the president and the special agent confirmed the accusation's legitimacy, at least partially. A computer beeped loudly. Mahony, loitering in the background, looked pointedly at Halladan, who politely excused himself and dismissed Mel.

Special Agent Dellendale returned to her office without any change in her implied directive even though the specter of the Spencer collusion stifled her departure. She shed her coat as she took her seat and started reading holographic messages floating above her desk.

"Agent Dellendale," an assistant called urgently on the intercom.

Before Mel could answer, the door swung open and a woman marched into her office, shutting the door on the startled assistant's face, and turned toward the special agent and unctuously said, "Hello, Agent Dellendale. I was wondering if I could have a moment of your time."

Mel leaned back in her chair and sighed as she pursed her lips, wishing she had gone home instead. "And how can I help you, Madame Speaker?"

Chapter Twenty-Seven

Thursday, December 13

The heavyset, forty-nine-year-old speaker of the house had short brown hair, pointed features, and a perpetual smirk hanging on her lips. She cocked her head as she stood in front of Special Agent Dellendale and replied, "Perhaps it's not as much about what you can do for me, but what I can do for you. I'm here to talk about your future and your job, Agent Dellendale."

Instinct suggested dismissing Thurlington immediately, yet Mel had to tread lightly out of respect for the congressional officeholder. She replied aloofly, "As I think you know, Madame Speaker, working for the FBI places me under the attorney general, and that is a cabinet position. I'm not certain my job and my future are appropriate topics to discuss with the speaker of the house."

Thurlington grinned. "And so you've already taken sides, Agent Dellendale?"

Perplexed, Dellendale responded carefully. "Madame Speaker, I'm on America's side. As I hope we all are."

Thurlington shed the pretense and glared at her. She withdrew a small device from her pocket and started waving it as she moved briskly around the office. "I assume you don't have any listening instruments, but better check first."

The device beeped, confirming the clean status of Mel's office. The speaker of the house pocketed her detector and swung to face

Mel again. "Let's not play coy with each other. Have you seen the news lately?"

"Are you referring to your press conference?"

"I am."

"Yes, I saw it. The president showed it at a briefing."

"Puts our president in a bind, now doesn't it, Agent Dellendale?" she asked smugly.

The speaker's direct approach disturbed Mel, but she replied blandly. "As well as those Americans whom you want to send to the Middle East, Madame Speaker."

"Special Agent Dellendale, we both know the president can't allow any Americans over there."

Mel frowned, "Then why put it out there, Madame Speaker?"

The speaker's smirk deepened. "You think it's just politics?"

"It's not, Madame Speaker?"

"Partly. Mostly it's also forcing the president's hand. Agent Dellendale, I think something very sinister is going on in the president's administration, and I'm going to build a case against him."

"And what case is that?" Mel asked.

"That case, Special Agent Dellendale, is that the US government is involved with this American Terrorist. In fact, I think it just might be sponsoring him. Actually, I think he's a US operative. Obviously, the president won't allow Americans to travel to Middle Eastern countries. American deaths would undermine his operation."

Agent Dellendale furrowed her brow. "Or, the president doesn't know whether Spencer will attack, and he simply won't take the chance."

"That's one way to put it. I like how I've framed it better. Agent Dellendale, let's be serious here for a moment. How much effort have you put into the search for this Spencer fellow?"

"Madame, we have exerted tremendous effort toward finding Thom Spencer. The man is no fool. He planned his operation well, but I know we will eventually find him. My concern is not the 'if' but when."

"And you have had all resources at your disposal? No questions asked, and you have information, manpower, analysis? All of it at any time?"

Mel silently thanked her for the all-encompassing question; it allowed her to respond without deceit. "Of course not, Madame Speaker. Unfortunately the Bureau has limited resources just like every other agency, but I have been given the priority I need to find Spencer. And I will find him. Again, it's not if, but when I do."

Thurlington looked sharply at Mel. "Fair enough, Special Agent Dellendale. If you have the priority you claim, and you still can't find this man, then this proves something else is going on," the Speaker continued to press.

"And what would that be, Madame Speaker?" Mel asked, equally persistent in her abstruseness.

"He obviously has US resources behind him," she repeated, exasperated.

Mel remained silent.

Thurlington pressed her lips together and shifted tactics, resuming her smarmy voice. "Agent Dellendale...Melissa, I'm not here to chastise you. I'm here to help you. You've been made, unfairly, a pawn in this game, and you know it. I've read the reports. I know you've been working hard on this case, and I know you've had some resources put at your disposal. I also know other resources have been off-limits, resources that could be very effective in finding Spencer. You must have suspected some sort of covert operation or cover up, Melissa. All the evidence is right there, and that sort of thing isn't good for the country. I don't care what the situation is."

Mel stared at the speaker, deciding how to respond. The woman undoubtedly had gleaned some accurate information on her investigative protocol, so Mel couldn't continue the priority charade. Perhaps she could appeal to Thurlington's judgment with a tidbit of truth. After softly stroking her cheek, Mel leaned forward and tapped her fingers on the desk's edge. "Speaker Thurlington, I want you to listen very carefully to what I'm going to say. Maybe this will help you." Mel cleared her throat and swallowed. "I have been very thorough in my investigation. There's no doubt some resources have been off-limits. That of course raises red flags; anyone would wonder if somehow we were involved. But I had a CIA counterpart suggest to me that the US was not behind the American Terrorist in any way, shape, or form. I believed him, but I did some checking myself. Now, let me make this clear, if there are agencies wishing to conceal an operation, those agencies can do it. No one will find any evidence, no trail, no proverbial smoking gun. But when you're investigating something, even when you can't prove anything, you get a whiff of that smoke, a feeling, a gut reaction, that something is going on. Speaker Thurlington, there's no whiff of smoke. In fact, my gut instinct is telling me quite the opposite. I don't think the government is in any way sponsoring Spencer, and everyone wants it that way. You see, Madame Speaker, what he's doing is very nasty, filthy work, and their hands are clean, and they want to keep it that way. So maybe, it's quietly suggested, that we don't find him right now, and allow him to do those things the US can't. Beyond an accusation of a little indifference, there's nothing there. Now, I'm the FBI agent assigned the task of finding Thom Spencer, and I'm going to do just that, but I'm not going to find him with any government connections, Madame Speaker."

Thurlington looked at Mel thoughtfully, tapping a pudgy finger against her lips, and Mel thought she had placated her. But then the smirk reappeared, and she chuckled as she shook her head. "You're not listening to me, Melissa. You very well may be right, but I don't care about that. As I said, the evidence is there. I don't care whether it's true or not. I'm sure I can conjure up some sort of plausible connection that reveals the administration's collusion with or outright authorization of this American Terrorist's scheme.

"That's not, however, the reason I'm here, Agent Dellendale. I told you I'm here to talk to you about your job and your future. I'm here to recruit you, and you have to decide. Are you a part of this illegal and hideous operation, or are you a brave FBI agent who uncovers the plot? I know you are partial to the administration, but I also know you have ambition and smarts, and I just want you to think about that future of yours. That's all."

Mel's shoulders sagged. Appealing to this woman's judgment had exploded in Mel's face. She shook her head and leaned back in her chair. "You know what's ironic here?"

Thurlington stood silent with that smirk hanging on her flabby face.

"If I found Spencer, you'd detest me, since you then wouldn't have any conspiracy to hurl at President Halladan. Politics isn't all of it, is it? It's power. He has some, so do you, but you want it all. Do you really despise him that much?"

The smirk remained. "Well, Melissa," the speaker said as she turned and waddled toward the door, "you can either choose to be complicit in the plot, or be the one who uncovers it. Conspirator or heroine, it's your choice. Your job and future are at stake."

Melissa reciprocated the chuckle. "Speaker Thurlington, you keep threatening me with my job and my future. I do this job because I'm good at it and I like it, but mostly because I'm dedicated to my country. The moment those in government lose their dedication to the country's principles is the moment I reject that future and quit this job."

"Understood, Melissa. I just hope you give it some thought before destroying your career. You know, we women have to work together in this man's world to succeed. Good night."

Melissa massaged her temples. She glanced at the closed door in disbelief as she replayed the colloquy in her head. Slowly rising from her chair, she strolled toward the window and stared out, looking at nothing in particular. Frowning, Mel wondered who the greater enemy was, Thurlington or Spencer. She immediately rejected Spencer and asked the same question of Thurlington and Ghazali. Strangely and angrily, she found herself earnestly debating the question.

She buzzed her assistant. "Yes, Agent Dellendale?"

"I need to speak with the president. Now."

Chapter Twenty-Eight

Friday, December 14

Thom Spencer stared at his reflection in the stainless-steel door, thinking the distorted image depicted the truth about himself. The smeared portrait mirrored a thinner face and cold eyes. The founder of Nanoexelogy had changed; the American Terrorist had not only blurred but eclipsed that other man. News from Damascus continued to flow in, and weeks increased to months to finish the victim removal and disposal. Success measured by the body bags and the cloud of smoke swollen with the stench of victims' ashes didn't shake him at first. But when the figure hit more than three hundred thousand, guilt crept in, and Spencer swallowed, trying to suppress the bile rising in his throat. He tried to hide his emotions, not wanting to expose his vulnerability to anyone. Closing his eyes, he called up the images of severed heads until the bile disappeared. Maybe he wouldn't vomit anymore, he thought to himself, but maybe he didn't want to lose entirely the guilt. It assured him that a vestige of the Nanoexelogy founder remained.

Tyler walked out of the laboratory where he had just finished installing the last of the equipment just as Timothy Preston returned from a nearby grocery store.

"Good," Tyler greeted Brannan's right-hand man. "I need you to get me just a few more items to process the final serum. I don't think they'll be a problem, since the quantities are small and they're not hazardous or illegal." Although confident Preston and his organization wouldn't discover his process from the requested materials, Tyler threw in a few unnecessary ingredients just in case.

Distracted, Preston said, "Just give me a list, and I'll get on it, but right now we need to discuss another problem."

Spencer detected agitation in Preston's voice. "What's the matter, Timothy?"

"Saw this blaring on a TV at the store." Preston, shaking his head, went to the computer and double clicked the TV tuner program. A cable news station carried a press conference, and Speaker of the House Wilma Thurlington was fielding questions.

"Madame Speaker, in light of the president's decision to prohibit Americans from traveling to any high-probability target, effectively refusing to help them prepare for a possible attack, what do you do now?"

"I begin asking questions," Thurlington replied sharply. "Obviously we have a president who will not help these poor people subjected to horrible future terrorist attacks. We unquestionably have capabilities that could help these countries against this maniac, but this president won't allow it. Why? Why hasn't the government used its vast resources to find Thom Spencer? Something is behind the administration's reluctance to find this man, and I'm going to delve into it until I have the answers I want."

Preston grimaced. "I've confirmed that she approached an FBI agent and asked her to investigate the connection between the United States and you, Thom."

"Well, I hope there's no connection. Who really knows, though," Spencer said dryly.

"There's isn't. But, Thom, we need to be a realistic here. It's our opinion the government hasn't thrown all its weight behind finding you. We've detected some real resistance inside the administration about apprehending the American Terrorist. Apparently, we're not the only ones who understand this, and this little fact alone is creating a disturbing theory of sponsorship. With this sort of pressure mounting, 'the administration's reluctance' could disappear quickly, and that could make our job much harder."

Thom cast a speculative, accusatory glance at Preston, and finally asked the question they had danced around since Brannan had revealed the existence of his organization. "But is she right, Tim? Is there a government conspiracy? What is this organization you work for, Tim?"

Preston stiffened and abruptly squared off at Spence. "As I said, she's not right. But let me make something clear to you, Thom," his voice soft but threatening, "you control this operation, but that control does not extend to my employer. I'm not going to tell you who or what it is except that it's not the US government. And, Thom, my employer is not accountable to you. Now, we can proceed or not, but I will not answer any further questions about that."

Spence studied Preston; the man wasn't bluffing, and Thom still needed his help. He shrugged. "This means we need to move again, right?"

The tension waned and Preston nodded. "Yes. Another move will make it harder for them to find us. We'll move to a place hostile to Americans: Caracas. US agencies aren't welcome there."

Tyler raised his hand and waved to catch their attention. "Uh, I'm here too, guys. We can't go just yet; not since we just set up shop here. I have no desire to start all over again down there. I say we finish up here first. We have nearly everything we need."

Spence nodded. "Yes, we finish this batch, Tyler. Then we move."

Tyler started back toward his lab with a thumbs-up, but turned on his heel. "Hey, what did that reporter ask? Something about Americans and high-probability targets?"

Preston nodded. "Yes, Thurlington wanted to send Americans to cities deemed high probability targets. Use them as shields, in effect."

Spence jerked his attention toward Preston. "Are you kidding? That's what started this?"

"She wants you to kill Americans so you lose sympathy with the public, and then the administration will have to come after you with full force," Timothy surmised.

Tyler clenched and unclenched his jaw, his blood pressure rising. "That lady is more concerned about Muslims, fundamentalist or not, than she is about Americans. You know, you look at her and those big dopey brown eyes and hear what she says; you have to believe she hates America. I really think down deep she agrees with Ghazali that America's evil, and we deserve everything we get from those bastards."

Repressing unbidden images of severed heads, Thom bit his upper lip. "If she sends Americans to any of our targets, we're not moving forward. We planned it so they would have time to evacuate. I won't kill Americans like that."

The comment caught Preston off-guard. He concealed his surprise and furtively glanced at Spencer, gauging his resolve for several moments. "Well, for right now, I'm going to get these items you need, Tyler. It shouldn't take too long. I also need to start making preparations for Caracas. I'll be back soon."

Preston casually walked from the warehouse. Once he was out of eyesight, he picked up his pace. Turning several corners in quick succession, he lost all but himself in a maze of streets and alleys. Coming upon a small city square, he found an empty bench outside a café where several people were talking over a late lunch. Preston sat, pulled out his phone, and pressed a button.

"Preston here," he said quietly when the phone answered. He waited a moment until another voice asked for his progress. "We're moving to Caracas, but we have a bigger problem."

"What?" the voice asked.

"Thurlington."

No response.

Preston pressed, "Spencer has threatened to terminate the operation if any Americans are put in jeopardy."

"He has that capability, doesn't he?" the voice asked.

"Yes," Preston snapped. "He controls the serum. We're not to confiscate it or any other technology."

"Yes, I know." The voice paused again. "And you are convinced he would abort the entire operation?"

"Sir, I have studied Spencer for some time now, and I think I have a good read on him on this one. He'd abort it."

Sighing, the voice drawled, "Sending Americans abroad as shields infuriated the president, and I doubt very seriously he would ever do it. But with this investigation our Speaker is promoting, I can't say for sure he wouldn't."

Preston warned him. "We can't risk it, sir. I must return and handle this immediately."

Another silence suggested uncertainty.

"Sir, I shouldn't delay," Preston urged. "I'm going to have to come back. We have to deal with this immediately."

A longer pause and the voice finally committed, reluctantly. "Agreed."

After a few more phone calls for supplies, Preston returned to the warehouse to find Tyler and Spence working in the lab. "Tyler, your materials should arrive in four days, five at most," Preston announced. "How long to process it after that?"

Tyler could do it in two, though he preferred not to rush it. "Probably three days, maybe four. That's it."

"Then we plan to relocate two weeks from today. Shouldn't expose us too much, and it gives us a cushion. I'm going to make those arrangements. I'll be gone, but I'll be back in time for the move. You two don't worry about the logistics; I'll take care of that end. Have everything finished by the time I get back."

"I think we'll be fine," Tyler said tentatively. Spencer also nodded.

Preston handed a media disk to Spencer. "These are absentee instructions. They are detailed, yet succinct. If you have any questions while I'm gone, open it up. I've also provided numbers to call, if necessary. Just stay out of sight as much as possible, but not suspiciously so." A media card had just replaced Preston, and without another word, Brannan's right-hand man hurried out the door, leaving Thom and Tyler staring at each other, startled by his sudden departure.

Chapter Twenty-Nine

The black sedan crept through the wealthy Georgetown neighborhood toward Thurlington's estate. The large Victorian home stood prominently on a sizeable corner lot, fenced, digitally monitored, and guarded. The speaker declined protection from the Secret Service; instead, she purportedly paid for it with endless funds drawn from trusts created by her billionaire oil-magnate father, although rumors suggested campaign coffers paid many of the bills. The four men drove by without stopping. After twisting through several smaller avenues, they turned onto a busier street and returned to their nearby apartment.

John Smith, in the seat behind Timothy Preston, finished a quick calculation on his tablet. "It's measured correctly, Trenton." The three men knew Preston as Trenton; Preston doubted John Smith, Bill Jones, and Bob Johnson were authentic identities either. They belonged to a different division within the organization, and aliases provided protection in the event any one of them was compromised.

"Good," Preston answered taciturnly.

The four men entered a one-room apartment, empty except for some battered furniture, several maps, and one red box. They marched in single file to the large table covered with two sets of drawings. The first set outlined the horizontal sewer lines of the nearby neighborhood, and the second showed the floor plan of

Thurlington's residence. Preston grabbed the second set and studied the floor elevation of the Speaker's master bathroom. "And you're certain she's alone in that room?" Preston directed his question toward John Smith.

"She and her husband are estranged. Never around each other, especially in DC. No rumors of visitors, and I didn't detect any activity that would indicate otherwise. She arrives home alone, and, except for security, no one else is there."

"How long has she been watched?" Preston asked.

"We've monitored Thurlington for some time," Smith answered vaguely.

"In preparation for this?" Preston pried.

Smith didn't reply, imparting a look suggesting he had his orders just as Preston did, and Preston shouldn't ask any more questions along those lines.

Preston understood. When he arrived stateside, the organizational liaison explained the plan and forewarned him of the team's secrecy. He had felt uncomfortable; the plan had seemed hastily prepared, and he wondered who had the final review, pondering if it had cleared all channels. Still, he decided to proceed given the threat the target posed to the American Terrorist operation. Besides, the impressive technology could cover the deficiencies. "And your device can climb the two stories vertically?" he asked Bob Johnson.

Johnson, the vehicle designer, nodded confidently. "I'm not worried about the device working. It's the measurements that are most troublesome. We have to get those exact. Once it's programmed, that's it. It'll move in the programmed direction: north, south, east, west, up, down, whatever. But it will precisely move the number of millimeters encoded."

John Smith scoffed. "The measurements are accurate, and I'll most definitely program it with the right number of millimeters. The pressure-trigger just better work. That's going to be the trick."

Bill Jones, the pressure-trigger designer, smirked at the remark.

Preston strolled to the counter where the red box sat. The other three men followed. Preston opened it and peered inside. Preston stared at a tiny robotic vehicle, measuring a cubic inch at most. "How many tests did you perform?" he asked.

"We've model tested it hundreds of time. No live test yet,"

Jones conceded.

Preston frowned. "No live test? So it has no confirmed kills?" He hadn't left Mexico City for an experiment.

Smith, noticing Preston's annoyance, said reassuringly, "Live test, no, Mr. Trenton. But we've tested it in the lab many times, and have modeled it with the target's exact parameters with perfect success. We have been working on this design for a long time. Just been waiting for the right opportunity, and this target presents a perfect scenario."

Timothy had no choice given his time constraint.

"It's mostly nanotechnology, Mr. Trenton."

"I know." He also knew the three men had borrowed some parts from Nanoexelogy, but none of the three had any idea he operated on behalf of the American Terrorist. He had his orders too, and the organization had to maintain those Chinese walls.

He sighed heavily and picked up the box. Turning it in his hand, he studied its contents for several moments. They had named their miniature unmanned ground vehicle a nanogrone, since it was weaponized similarly to drones. The tiny vehicle inside could transform into nearly any shape and was equipped with gears, wheels, and a miniature hydraulic system, allowing it to move up, down, left, right, and at angles. All it needed was a surface to adhere to. The contorting vehicle carried a nano battery for power and had a small compartment for an explosive payload designed again with nanotechnology. It could kill several people in a ten foot radius. All of it was controlled by an on-board chip set. Preston's liaison had implied the software for the chip had had a setback.

"Have you corrected the software problem?" he snapped.

The software designer Johnson scowled. "There's no problem with my software. We have had problems because of improper measurement techniques. My software will work perfectly if all my external information is correct."

Smith glared daggers at Johnson. "I'm going to tell you one more time, my measurements are absolutely accurate. The plan is good, and if it fails, you're to blame, and you two will have to answer to me."

Tension in the room was palpable. Preston studied the three of them, realizing he dealt with highly intelligent specialists who competed among themselves. He couldn't tell whether professional one-upmanship or dedication to assassinate Thurlington motivated them; then again, he didn't care. Preston had to complete this mission by whatever means required, but the very technology he had expected to overcome the plan's deficiencies began to falter.

"Gentlemen, there is no room for failure here. Will this device work?"

Smith, the apparent team leader of the three, gave Preston a confident nod. "Mr. Trenton, please don't confuse our…our discussions with ineptness. This is how we operate. The device will succeed."

"All right, Mr. Smith, I'll take your word for it. How about the material it can adhere to. Copper or PVC covered with sewage? Any problems there?" Preston asked.

"PVC, copper, concrete, aluminum. Dry, wet, even with crap on it—it doesn't matter. The adhering process bonds with the surface."

"All right," Preston nodded. "So we send this…nanogrone through the street and up through Thurlington's sewer pipes right up into her toilet. Can we identify and confirm our target?"

This time Bill Jones grinned proudly as he rocked on his toes and chuckled. "With Mr. Smith's video imaging, we determined how much Thurlington weighs. The chip set includes sensory detectors. A person sitting on a toilet puts stress on it. The chip measures that stress, and when it detects the stress equivalent to that caused by a person of Thurlington's weight…boom. I guess it's possible someone else weighing the same as her might use her john at 5:00 in the morning, but after watching her habits and patterns, we doubt it very seriously. A risk we take, though."

"Does this nanogrone make a return trip?" Preston asked, indifferent to the risk.

Smith shook his head. "Better to destroy the evidence than chance that is stops or gets stuck somewhere on its way back. We can retrieve it if that happens before detonation, but not after."

Preston agreed; he mused softly, "So she sits down in the morning to go to the bathroom…"

"And we blow the fat bitch up," Smith finished with a snarl, revealing at least some of his motivation.

Forty-five minutes later, the four men pulled up next to a sewer manhole, and Smith stepped from the car onto a dark and deserted street. They had chosen this manhole for its seclusion and the lack of any monitoring devices in the vicinity. After prying open the lid, Smith climbed down, disappearing for a few moments and reappearing with no visible exertion. He climbed back into the car and motioned for Jones to drive.

Once back in the apartment, they monitored the grone's progress on the tablet. After two hours, it transmitted the beep, indicating that it had terminated its journey inside the correct toilet, lodged deep enough inside the siphon to avoid visual detection. There it insidiously sat, silently and patiently waiting for its victim. Satisfied with their night's work, they settled where they could to get a little sleep.

Sirens awakened them a few hours later, and before long local news teams confirmed the death of Wilma Thurlington, Speaker of the US House of Representatives. Preston, switching his attention from the television to the three other men in the room, didn't detect glee, but sensed satisfaction, and he finally decided it wasn't the professionalism but the dedication that motivated them. With a curt nod, he rose and without a word walked out the apartment, confident the assassination of Speaker Thurlington protected the American Terrorist's agenda.

Chapter Thirty

Thursday, December 27

With an index finger draped over her lower and upper lips, Special Agent Dellendale stared intently at a Lab 104 holographic e-mail displaying the components of the intricate device that killed Speaker of the House Wilma Thurlington. Pursing her lips, she shook her head. Some of the key nanotechnology inside the tiny bomb had come from Thom Spencer's company Nanoexelogy. In fact, it could not have been built without its technology, a fact that strongly implicated the American Terrorist in the speaker's death. Dellendale didn't believe it, but without doubt a reporter or political operative without clearance would gain access to the information, eventually draw that same conclusion, and make it headline news. Mel skimmed the distribution list, noting the e-mail had gone to nearly everyone inside the president's administration with the slightest hint of authority, increasing the likelihood of a leak. She sighed. More trouble ahead.

Daman Pryce strolled into the office and raised his eyebrows seductively. "What has you so enamored? Should I be threatened?" he smiled.

She gazed into those brilliant blue eyes, trying to mask the quiver she felt. Remembering a Dallas man's interview just two weeks ago, whose rage had dissipated because of the American Terrorist, Mel finally had to concede she felt the same. She still believed the FBI must capture and prosecute Spencer, but the country seemed to have exhaled a huge sigh of relief since his exploits. Though people didn't admit it, the American Terrorist had given them a sense of security and confidence. Most everyone claimed they wanted him caught, and few if any openly approved of what he did, yet, quietly, many had a guilty though an unmistakable gut-feeling of gratitude. America took refuge in Spencer's deadly temerity, and, despite Thurlington's assassination, nightlife had returned with robust laughter and lighthearted chatter bubbling up in bars and restaurants. Americans walked holiday streets with less fear and more cheer than they had since Miami and before, and Mel had joined the spirited reprieve and slipped into a relationship with her CIA counterpart.

But at work, there was no play, and linking Thurlington's assassination to Spencer would jeopardize the fragile American psyche. Destroying the American Terrorist's secretly revered, avenging-vigilante reputation could plunge America back into its depressed stupor.

"Have you seen your e-mails lately?" she asked.

Shrugging nonchalantly, the CIA agent reached for his phone and vetted his e-mails, doing a double take at one of the messages. He shook his head. "That bomb couldn't have been built without Spencer's technology, Mel. This could really change things."

"You think?" she asked with emphasized sarcasm.

Pryce stared at her for a few awkward moments. "You don't think he had anything to do with it, do you?"

"I know he didn't, Daman. He's too busy killing Muslims right now. And I don't think he would use his own technology to incriminate himself."

"Unless he didn't care," observed Pryce.

"It wasn't Spencer," Mel declared flatly. "He knows it would undermine everything he's trying to do."

"Then maybe it was made to look as if he did it."

Mel sighed again. Typical spook speak, she thought. "I doubt it, Daman. A device like this is bound to use something Nanoexelogy at least designed or even developed. All I can tell you right now is that Thurlington's coterie will claim it as proof that the American Terrorist has now killed, purposely, an American, and the speaker of the house no less. I'm concerned about the country's reaction."

Daman understood their romance had sparked with the change in the nation's mood. He hadn't determined whether its future was dependent on it until perhaps now. Daman detected the return of the previous aloofness in her tone. Early romance paranoia, Daman thought to himself, yet the office had assumed a sterile feel.

The land line light flashed, and Mel glanced at the caller ID. Anticipating the call, she nodded and picked it up promptly. "Special Agent Dellendale," she answered the summons. She stood a few moments, listening intently. Without responding, she placed the phone back in its cradle and reached for her satchel. With eyebrows raised, she looked at Daman and said, "Well, the president is none too happy."

"Wants to see you?"

"Right now."

An hour later, Mel found herself again in the Oval Office spinning her ring. President Halladan hastily entered through a side door and sat behind his desk. "Well, as you know, Spencer is now connected to Thurlington's death," he said by way of greeting.

Mel's expression soured at the president's abrupt analysis and opened her mouth to offer a different perspective. Halladan held up his hand, gesturing for her to save her breath; she stopped short. "We both know, Melissa, that Spencer didn't have anything to do with it. It's not his game, but it's going to play right into the hands of Thurlington's camp anyway, and you know what that means."

Mel frowned. "No, Mr. President, I'm not exactly sure what that means."

Halladan shrugged. "You're the lead investigator on Spencer, and now you'll have to concentrate on finding him. Agent Dellendale, this now won't be an investigation in name only where we wink and nod and put forth the perception that progress is being made. We're allocating resources to Spencer, substantial resources."

"That's understandable Mr. President. But take me off the case then. I'm better used on the Ghazali file. It's a mistake for me to drop that. As you know, we've made considerable progress."

Halladan nodded. "I know." He paused, evaluating both the predicament and her. "Recall the conversation you told me about when Thurlington accused me of using you as a pawn? I never denied it. I deliberately placed you between her and me, to be a buffer and give me credibility. You have a spotless, apolitical record with top-secret clearance, though you are just low enough on the bureaucratic totem pole to maintain defensible objectivity, and I can't destroy that. For either of us. How do you think it would play out with Thurlington's gang if I pulled the lead investigator now?"

"As if you cared more about catching Ghazali than Spencer. That Ghazali was more important, which by the way, I think he is. Don't get me wrong, Mr. President, we need to find Spencer. We obviously can't have Americans killing hundreds of thousands of people, but I work for the Federal Bureau of Investigation, which must concentrate on defending against domestic threats. And from that standpoint, my responsibility is to pursue what the Bureau deems the most likely threat to American domestic security. Mr. President, that threat is Ghazali, not Spencer."

"And that's also what your director said, Agent Dellendale. But I can't ignore this American Terrorist anymore, and we now have to make a determined effort to find him," Halladan said firmly. "Is this understood, Special Agent Dellendale?"

"Yes, sir, it is. I don't like it, but I understand." The president looked at Mel steadily without replying. "Is there anything more, Mr. President?"

Halladan's gaze softened sympathetically. "Yes. As this is a top priority for us now, I'll want you to brief me personally and others on a regular basis." He reached for a button and pressed it. "Please let the others in, Margaret, would you?" After a moment, the door opened, and the directors of the CIA, FBI, National Intelligence, plus the national security adviser, Special Counsel Harry Stanton, and Andy Mahony entered the office, each in turn politely greeting Special Agent Dellendale.

Watching the procession, Mel spun her ring. They expected a dog-and-pony show, and she had to provide a presentation right then and there on the investigation of the American Terrorist. Before the Nanoexelogy connection leaked, the president wanted to show the opposition that the administration officials, right to the top, were personally involved with Spencer's lead FBI investigator, and not simply sending orders through agency staff. Otherwise Thurlington's gang would spin the administration as detached and indifferent. Politics continued its inglorious pace.

Mel rose from her seat, pulling her tablet from her satchel as Halladan stepped from behind his desk to join the others.

"Mr. President, if you don't mind, I need to give you an overlay of the investigation from my electronic file. We've compiled a lot of data, and I have several visuals I'd like for you to see. Could you connect me up, Mr. Mahony?"

Andy Mahony nodded. The president couldn't hide his smile; Special Agent Dellendale arrived prepared.

Chapter Thirty-One

Sunday, December 30

Major Brannan burst into the Mexican laboratory, startling Spence and Tyler. At first they didn't recognize him; he looked more like the Arab Ali, the first victim of the serum, than the major who orchestrated their field operations. Even after the vaguely familiar visage registered, the surprise didn't subside. Brannan should have been in the Middle East. They hadn't seen him since Trinidad, and they hadn't planned for him to return before the next attack. Alarmed, Spence and Tyler expected dire news.

"Why are you here, Major?" Spence asked guardedly. "I didn't call you."

"You know about Speaker Thurlington?"

"Of course," both replied in unison.

"Do you know rumors in Washington suggest you're connected or responsible?"

Spence shrugged, puzzled by the major's intense demeanor. "It's just speculation, Major. From what we can tell from the news, not many people believe we had anything to do with it. It hasn't hurt that near-vigilante celebrity status we seem to enjoy, and people are willing to give us the benefit of the doubt. I don't see it affecting our operation at all."

Tyler shrugged. "Didn't like the woman anyway. She made my blood pressure rise whenever I heard that shrill voice of hers.

Someone finally decided to do us all a favor."

"You still haven't answered my question, Major," Spence said.

Brannan stared at them hard, shifting between the two men, searching for any clue their faces might reveal. "But neither of you had anything to do with it, did you," he finally surmised.

"Do with what?" Tyler asked in an incredulous tone. "Thurlington's murder? You serious?"

"And where was Preston?" Brannan asked sharply.

Spencer narrowed his eyes slightly, uneasy with the major's question. "Preston abruptly left right after Thurlington's press conference. We decided it would be best if we moved again. We assumed he was going to Caracas...." The coincidence of Thurlington's assassination and Preston's absence acutely sharpened his suspicion. He clenched his jaw in instinctive denial. "He returned...we're a few days late, but I never...what's going on, Major?"

"He led the hit squad that killed Thurlington. He thought if she persisted in threatening the president with investigations, she would succeed in forcing Halladan to rescind his initial policy, and if Halladan did do that and sent Americans to the Middle East, you might pull the plug on the next attack."

Spence's eyes glossed over for a moment and his blood started pounding through his veins. "So he killed Thurlington?" he asked faintly, his lip quivering in anger.

Preston may have accomplished what he had intended to avoid, Brannan observed. Spencer's raging eyes carried the threat of instantly terminating the operation. Might as well divulge the worst, so Brannan forged ahead. "There's something that's not been disclosed to the public yet." Spencer and Tyler looked anxiously at the major. "The hit squad used a nano-device."

It took a moment for the implication to sink in. Then Washington rolled his eyes and mumbled, "Nanoexelogy's fingerprints are all over it, right?"

Brannan nodded. "The device definitely had Nanoexelogy parts in it."

"And that substantiates all those rumors," Spencer groaned.

Brannan pressed his lips together firmly. "When this gets out, and it's snaking its way throughout the Beltway as we speak—so it will get out—that vigilante celebrity status you enjoy will disappear and disappear quickly. The target on your back suddenly got much, much larger."

"And it should," Spence seethed while grinding his teeth as he massaged his temples. "We don't kill Americans. We just don't."

The door opened, and Preston bounded into the laboratory holding a bag of groceries. He looked at Brannan, recognizing him after a moment. "Major!" he exclaimed, "what are you doing here?"

Brannan glanced at Preston and waved him in. "Have you seen the news lately, Timothy?"

"What news?" Preston replied, closing the door and placing the groceries on a nearby counter.

"Rumors about Spencer's involvement in Thurlington's assassination."

Preston shrugged. "Whackos, Major. No credibility; not even with the press. No one is giving it the time of day."

"Investigators have found Nanoexelogy parts in the bomb," the major announced deadpan.

"That seems unlikely, Major. By definition, they're too small to be found. Especially after exploding them. They purposely blew it up for that reason."

Brannan grimaced. "I've reviewed the operation, Timothy, and they're right. There were Nanoexelogy parts in the device. The FBI has become very sophisticated these days."

In an instant, Timothy Preston understood. He sighed. "They're suddenly not whackos anymore, are they? And I was the only one who knew both sides of the operation. I got approval from those in charge who obviously didn't know anything about the device, and the hit squad certainly had no idea about my involvement with Spencer. I was really the only one who had any idea Spencer could have been connected in any way...I pushed to move forward so rapidly...I should've..." He paused, holding his breath with eyes closed. "It's...it's...it's just inexcusable." Preston opened his eyes and gave a curt nod.

In one smooth movement, Brannan deftly reached inside his light jacket, withdrew a handgun with an attached silencer, and squeezed the trigger once, pumping one .40 caliber hollow-point bullet into Preston's head. Blood and brains splattered the door and wall behind the man who had just sanctioned his own execution. Spence and Tyler gaped in shock, wondering if they were next.

"He had to go," Brannan said quietly as he pulled out his satellite phone. "I need to get a crew in here to clean up the mess and properly dispose of the body."

Tyler and Spencer both covered their eyes and without Brannan's suggestion withdrew to the back storeroom, still trying to grasp the sudden sequence of events. Spence stole a glance at Tyler, whose lips were pursed as he stared distantly into a corner.

They sat in the storeroom for nearly an hour without exchanging a single word before they heard the warehouse door open. Two hushed voices quickly gave way to muted washing, scrubbing, and mopping. Tyler looked nervously at Spence, speculating whether Brannan would crash through the door with the gun pointed at them, but Spence stared absently at his own drumming fingers, seemingly indifferent to what had just happened on the other side of the door.

Tyler suddenly leapt from his chair. "What was he thinking?" Tyler exclaimed, his voice choked with anger as he paced around the room.

Spence raised an eyebrow without missing a drumbeat. "Who? Preston or Brannan?"

Tyler scoffed. "Preston, of course. I'm glad Brannan did it, Spence. Saves me from the chore, except it's a pretty good bet Preston would've gotten the best of me. Brannan is right. He had to go. Even dead, Preston still could blow it for us, Spence. Using our nanotechnology? Are you kidding? How stupid is that?"

Spence shrugged. "And he knew it. Did you see him nod, Tyler? He knew what Brannan was going to do."

"Yeah, I saw that, too." Tyler muffled a scoff as his eyes glazed. He paused for nearly a minute in thought and shrugged, looking at Spencer. "As stupid as it was, Spence, there's still something inside of me glad he killed her. Maybe I should have some remorse, but I don't." He looked defiantly at Spencer. "It's just not there. We're all better off without her socialist peace politics. Maybe Preston shouldn't have risked it, but good riddance." Tyler sighed heavily as he vigorously rubbed his jaw.

Spencer grimaced. He sympathized with Tyler, perhaps even to the point of feeling exactly the same about Thurlington. Yet, he knew he was ultimately responsible for the speaker's death, though Preston had acted as the executioner. Was he ultimately responsible for Timothy's death, too, he wondered? Doubt, qualms, and misgivings whispered to him.

Still drumming his fingers, he closed his eyes and recalled the image of severed heads. At first the images appeared hazy, as if in a dream, but then they abruptly came into sharp focus, taking his breath away for a quick moment. His mind instantly cleared and his resolve intensified. *Not all Americans were equally American*, he told himself. Reactions of anger and guilt quickly disappeared; Spencer now worried about the consequences of Preston's rash deed.

He pressed his lips together and clenched his teeth. *Time to lie*, he admitted to himself. He had to conjure up a message that would convince federal investigators he was appalled by Thurlington's assassination and loathed her assassin. An FBI special agent popped into his head, and he reached for his wallet where he guarded her card. Without consulting Tyler, Spencer marched into the formerly bloody laboratory, indifferent to a cleaning crew's presence, and gestured impatiently at Brannan, immersed in a phone conversation.

The major sensed Spencer's mood, ended the call swiftly, and followed Spencer into the back room. Spence's words came hard and fast. "Major, we have to send a message to someone. We have to let her know that we had no part in Thurlington's death, and that we made the person who was responsible pay for his actions."

Brannan looked at Spencer skeptically. "How do we do that?"

"Take the body to DC and pin this card on his chest."

Brannan took the offered card. "Special Agent Melissa Dellendale, FBI." The major paused. "Where'd you get this?" he asked.

"She gave it to me after my family was murdered."

Brannan rubbed his jaw. "We then admit he was connected to us, Mr. Spencer."

"They think that already. We have to disabuse them of the notion that we were willing participants in Thurlington's assassination, or in any American's death for that matter."

Brannan's eyes glazed over as he contemplated the idea. "I like it better than what I had intended to do, Mr. Spencer. I didn't terminate Preston out of anger or punishment."

"Really?" Tyler chimed in, relieved Brannan entered without a gun in hand.

Brannan hesitated.

"Then why, Major?" Spencer pressed.

Brannan sighed. "Because he increases the chances you will be caught. If you get caught, Mr. Spencer, then Timothy could have been apprehended as well."

Spencer scowled. "And you couldn't risk that he might give you or your organization up."

"We cannot have the government knowing anything about us, Mr. Spencer."

"So, what if Tyler and I were caught now, Major?" Spencer quipped.

"What could you give them? Me? I'm not worried about that, Mr. Spencer."

"So they could break Timothy, but not you?"

"How long do you want to debate this, Mr. Spencer?"

Spencer frowned and shifted gears. "I don't. So, by—as you call it—terminating Preston, you protect your organization. So his body showing up in DC doesn't change that?"

Brannan shook his head. "No. He can't talk. It also gives the FBI an out. They can offer Preston up as the assassin. Perhaps he had some ties to you, but there's no proof that he acted on your behalf." Brannan looked appraisingly at Spence. *He's learning to play the game well*, he thought. "They may reject the overture. But it's worth a try, most definitely worth a try. We have to move quickly."

Spence nodded. "We received the supplies, and everything's nearly processed, so we can leave soon."

Brannan's surprised look reminded Spencer that the major had been out of the loop. He explained what they had planned in his absence. "We have to be prepared, Major, to expand our operations beyond the original targets. You may have a longer visit than first planned. Right or wrong, Thurlington is dead, and so are her gambits. No one will be sending Americans to the Middle East now, and we need to press that advantage."

Brannan raised his eyebrow at Spencer's cool calculation, and, reflecting, agreed.

Chapter Thirty-Two

Thursday, January 3

"Special Agent Dellendale, you have a call."

Mel frowned at her intercom, annoyed with the interruption. She immediately returned her attention to floating documents, squinting and hoping it would improve the results she had just received. No trace of Spencer in the latest guess at his location.

"Special Agent Dellendale?"

Mel sighed. "I'm busy, Lynn. Take a message."

"I would, ma'am, but he's pretty persistent. It's a Lieutenant Rossi from MPDC Homicide Section.

"Metro Homicide?" she whispered to herself. "All right, I'll take it."

Lynn patched the Lieutenant through and Mel picked up the landline, spelling her from holographic images. "Special Agent Dellendale."

"Lieutenant Rossi, MPDC Homicide Section. Found something interesting on a body."

"And what's that, Lieutenant?"

"Your telephone number."

The lieutenant had her attention. "My telephone number? On a body? What do you mean by that?"

"The body has your card pinned to its chest."

Mel frowned, genuinely puzzled by the lieutenant's information.

"Really? Where's the crime scene?" she asked, already rising from her chair and reaching for her coat.

Special Agent Dellendale screeched to a halt at a Beltway motel known only for its location off the highway. No one admitted staying there, yet everyone knew where it was. She jumped from the car, and as she slammed the door another government-issued vehicle roared to a stop behind her. She peered at the tinted glass, but couldn't identify the driver. The door opened and out popped Daman Pryce.

"New car?" she asked.

"Actually, yes," he flashed his trademark smile.

Mel gestured with her palms up while shrugging, "Okay, but why are you here?"

"Called your office, Mel. Heard you caught a call from MPDC," he answered.

"Fine. So why are you here?" she repeated.

"Came to find out why you're here," he retorted, the smile morphing into a smirk. Throwing him a dubious glance, Mel decided against a futile argument about jurisdiction.

They entered the room to find several police personnel investigating the scene. A tall man with a moustache, wearing an elegant suit, silk tie, and expensive shoes, exited the bathroom. Noticing two newcomers carrying the aura of the federal government, he walked toward them with hand extended.

"Agent Dellendale, I'm Dan Rossi."

"Pleased to meet you, Lieutenant." Rossi glanced at Pryce, who kept smiling but said nothing. Mel rolled her eyes. "And this is Daman Pryce and he's with…well, let's just say he's with me."

Rossi shrugged. "Well, I hope you don't mind body parts because that's what we've got here. Hacked up into several pieces. Real professional job though, and we don't see any evidence from the killer. Obviously transported. Can't tell from where, but we're just getting started. When we saw your card, though, we called immediately. Have to admit, we don't get this one. No doubt someone specifically wanted you to know this guy was dead. Putting him in a motel tub so housekeeping can find him? Not exactly trying to hide the dirty deed."

They stepped into the tiny bathroom. A photographer snapped a couple more shots and shuffled out of the way so Mel could view the tub. She couldn't detect any blood except inside the plastic bags that covered several body parts. The killer had reassembled the parts to resemble a normal body; she didn't recognize him. On the torso, Mel saw her card neatly pinned to his chest. She leaned over to inspect it closely. Breathing over her shoulder, Daman followed suit, and when Mel reared back, she nearly smacked his jaw.

"Have you identified the victim yet, Lieutenant?" she asked tersely.

"No. Already have analyzed fingerprints. Nothing. Most likely we have a John Doe, here."

She spun and quickly exited the bathroom and headed straight for the door. Daman pursued her, and when they reached the balcony, Mel motioned with her head toward the far end of the walkway. Rossi had followed Pryce, but when Mel deliberately turned her back on him, he shrugged and ambled back to the crime scene.

"What's up?" Pryce asked.

"That card in there has a mud stain on it."

"So?"

"I don't give my card out much. And that one is older. I ran out of those a while ago. Right around the time Spencer's family was murdered. I dropped my card in the mud and didn't have any more, so I had to give him that one."

"Who? Spencer?"

Mel nodded.

Daman rubbed his jaw, contemplating the implication. "What? Are you saying Spencer sent you this body?"

Mel nodded again.

"Why?"

Mel looked at Pryce pensively. "Not sure. I wonder if he killed this guy."

Out of the corner of her eye, she noticed Lieutenant Rossi poking his head out of the doorway. Mel ignored him, but the head reappeared again. "Did you find something more, Lieutenant?" she hollered at him.

The detective jumped out and marched toward them. "Yeah, as a matter of fact we did. Have no idea what it is, but found it in the victim's mouth. Thought I would show it to you. Maybe you can identify it."

Lieutenant Rossi showed them a drawing. Mel and Daman

immediately recognized it from the email they both had received describing the device that had killed Speaker Thurlington. Before Daman said a word, Mel interrupted. "Lieutenant, would you mind bagging that and letting me take it for analysis. I think I know what it is, but I need to run a few tests that I don't think your department can."

"What? You think you feds can do a better job than us?" Rossi asked, irked.

Mel rolled her eyes. "It's not that, Lieutenant..."

"Just kidding you, Agent Dellendale. There's no doubt your machines are better than ours. Just let me log it for chain of custody purposes, and I'll bring it right back."

"Thank you, Lieutenant."

After Rossi disappeared, Mel and Daman exhaled. "That guy in there is Thurlington's assassin." Mel declared.

Daman blinked several times. "You're jumping to conclusions there, Mel."

"Really?" she pursed her lips. "I know Spencer sent the body, so I have to assume he put that drawing of the device that killed Thurlington in there for a reason. Why?"

Daman rubbed his jaw, contemplating the mystery, and then agreed. "It's reasonable to assume he did it to identify the assassin. But how would he know we'd recognize the device?"

Mel flashed Daman a curious expression. "Well, presuming he's really not working for you guys, and you didn't tip him off, then he probably believes we have some inkling of his connection given the accusations in the press."

Not amused by Mel's snide remark, Daman frowned. "I told you, I could smell the deal if it were stinking up our halls in any way. There's simply nothing."

She studied her counterpart. "So tell me, you've read Spencer's file, right?"

Daman nodded.

"Do you really think he can carve up a body like that one in there?"

Daman raised his eyebrows. "No. Not like that. So someone *is* helping him. No doubt about it. It's just not us."

She stared hard at Daman. "Worthless information to me, Daman. If your halls had any odor, you'd say the same thing to me."

Daman shrugged nonchalantly and glanced over the rail, staring reflectively.

"What is it, Daman?" Mel demanded.

Daman sighed. "Let's assume you're right. That Spencer knew that the John Doe in there killed Thurlington, and he had the body delivered to you. But how did Spencer actually find out that this guy killed Thurlington?"

Mel shrugged this time. "I'm not sure."

Daman chuckled. "Well, presuming someone or something is aiding and abetting the American Terrorist, I bet that someone or something is pretty sophisticated; certainly nothing from the amateur hour. And let's be clear here. Anyone like our John Doe in there who can coordinate the assassination of the speaker of the house also has to be very sophisticated himself and would need plenty of support with vast resources."

Mel's eyes widened. "So you think he comes from whomever or whatever is providing Spencer his support? You think that guy in there was part of Spencer's team in some way?"

Daman nodded pensively.

"So, what happened? They order that guy to kill Thurlington, but when some in the media suggest the American Terrorist might be connected to the speaker's assassination, they sacrifice him by sending the body to us, hoping somehow to preempt the bad press?"

"Maybe. Or the guy goes rogue, kills Thurlington, Spencer finds out, goes ballistic and kills the guy."

Mel considered the possibilities. "From what I know about Spencer, your alternative is more likely, Daman."

"Either way, he's obviously trying to clear his name with you first. I just don't know if that will work."

Mel cocked her head. "I wouldn't be so sure about that."

Chapter Thirty-Three

Friday, January 4

Special Agent Dellendale again found herself alone in the Oval Office. She wondered vaguely how many private meetings the president actually attended; she had always envisioned presidential meetings as chock-full of cabinet secretaries, counselors, and agency directors. Yet many of her meetings were one-on-one affairs.

Halladan entered the office a little short of breath, and, meeting Mel's expectation, he arrived alone. After taking his seat behind the desk, he placed his hands on the sides of the chair and leaned back with a neutral expression. "So you left me a cryptic message about Spencer. He's sent you some something?"

Mel described what Daman and she had found in the motel, trying to avoid unnecessary gruesome details, and offered their analysis. "So, Mr. President, as we believed, Spencer didn't have Thurlington assassinated," she concluded.

Halladan leaned forward and folded his hands on the desktop. "No. He just probably killed the person who did. Have you confirmed this John Doe killed Thurlington?"

Mel shook her head. "As much as we ever will. We can't identify him through fingerprints, dental records, or DNA. But the device drawing is pretty convincing, Mr. President. We have confirmed Spencer's fingerprints on my card. That's the only physical evidence we have, and I doubt I get much more."

Halladan scratched his cheek. "I don't see how this really changes anything, Agent Dellendale. I still think we have to concentrate on finding him, don't you? Thurlington's camp will claim the mere connection proves Spencer is responsible, and even if that doesn't have any traction, they'll claim he killed a man who is innocent until proven guilty, which neatly dovetails into their contention that Spencer's an insane vigilante who must be apprehended. And, Melissa, as you are well aware, the press despises the American Terrorist, and when it learns of the nano connection, it will be unrelenting. I think the days of the American Terrorist enjoying any kind of hero status are finished. I anticipate even greater pressure to find Spencer."

It was Mel's turn to lean forward. "You might be right, Mr. President, but what if we got out in front of the story first and controlled the narrative? What if we do that rather than waiting for the inevitable leak and then defensively responding to media accusations?"

"We play a little offense," Halladan mused.

"And we disclose it all," she nodded. "We call a press conference, a real dog and pony show. Reveal the nano connection ourselves, and explain that we thought it indicated the American Terrorist had the speaker of the house assassinated. But then we discovered a body with direct evidence linking Spencer to this unidentified dead man. Tell them our theory that this unidentified man and the American Terrorist are connected, and we believe this man chose to assassinate the speaker, and when Spencer found out, he killed him. We now have designated the dead man as our prime suspect in Speaker Thurlington's assassination, and have issued a warrant for Thom Spencer for the murder of the unidentified man."

Halladan rested his chin on his interlaced fingers, wide-eyed and smiling. "The truth?" he exclaimed.

"Our theory of it at least, Mr. President. We don't know for certain, but it has more than the feeling of mere plausibility. I don't feel foolish making this case."

"It's risky, Special Agent Dellendale." He chuckled, though apprehensively, and rose from his chair. After pacing around the back of the desk, he smiled. "I like it. As you said, we control the narrative. And, the arrest warrant is clever, Melissa."

"Whom do you want at the presser, sir?"

"You, directors of the CIA and the FBI, and the director of National Intelligence. Have support staff if needed, but no politicians from either side. Brief them first, but then have it immediately after. Do it by tomorrow, Melissa. I'll inform all the directors."

"Very well, Mr. President."

As Mel rose from her chair, Halladan resettled into his. Before she reached the door, Halladan stopped her. He leaned back, tilting the wheels. "Agent Dellendale, something in your briefing concerns me." Mel turned on her heel and returned to the front of the president's desk. Halladan continued. "I think you implied that Spencer really isn't acting alone. That he has help. Not just random help here and there, but organized, structural assistance. Something or someone with extensive resources. Not just money."

Mel grimaced. "That was my assessment as well as Daman Pryce's."

The president squinted, his eyes shifting back and forth as he reflected. "That is an interesting confirmation coming from his spooky neck of the woods. And that brings me to my next question."

"What's that, Mr. President?"

"Of course there's speculation out there that Spencer might have had something to do with Thurlington's assassination, but most don't believe it, and probably wouldn't unless the nano connection was made public. We haven't disclosed that to anyone yet; we've been able to keep it under wraps."

Melissa agreed with a nod.

Halladan sighed. "But your theory is that Spencer wasn't involved at all with Thurlington's assassination, that he didn't know anything about it, but somehow he discovered what this assassin did, and then killed him?"

She nodded again.

"And then he had this really bright idea to send the body to you, right? Just because of wild speculation? Somehow he knew enough not just to send the body, but to the person in charge of his investigation. How did he figure all this out?"

"I'm not sure. What are getting at, Mr. President?"

"Somehow it appears that Spencer knew the administration—and you—had made the Nanoexelogy connection, Agent Dellendale. He learned his connection wasn't simply rumor and innuendo, so he had to mitigate the damage, and sent you the body."

Halladan's deduction caught her off guard; it neatly and logically explained the sequence of events. She looked at the president and frowned. Both understood the implication: that whoever assisted the American Terrorist had an informant deep inside the government, providing Spencer with inside intelligence. The observation confirmed her previous suspicions, and the leak on Mel's desk was turning into a flood. She glanced at the man across the desk and wondered if he knew who the informant was, whether he'd authorized the leak himself to Spencer. Then, without changing her expression, it occurred to her the president might suspect she was the source. Her head began throbbing. "Maybe, Mr. President, Spencer doesn't know anything about any of it. Maybe his helpful associates have done it all."

Halladan sighed. "And maybe we're wrong, and he planned all of this from the get-go, Agent Dellendale."

The president's suggestion made her dizzy. "You mean he orchestrated all this just so he could kill Thurlington, but then blame our dead body, hoping we take the bait and take him off the public hook?"

Halladan's calculating eyes indicated he appreciated such cunning strategy, if Spencer had indeed employed it. Her headache worsened. They were interrupted by a discreet knock, and the President's aide entered the office with his tablet. "Sorry to interrupt, sir, but you did ask me to let you know when we had to leave for the SecDef's meeting."

Halladan nodded toward Mahony and stood up abruptly. "We could go crazy speculating, Agent Dellendale. We proceed as discussed."

"Understood, Mr. President."

When Mel arrived back at her office, she had convinced herself Spencer hadn't plotted Thurlington's death, despite the conjectures the president and she had just entertained. Her psychological profile of Thom Spencer told her otherwise, and she trusted her profile. Yet the headache persisted. Nothing could eliminate the obvious fact that Spencer had known about the FBI and her making the Nanoexelogy connection to the Thurlington assassination, and a national security leak threatened to consume her attention.

Chapter Thirty-Four

Saturday, January 5

Spence again scanned the front room of their laboratory, searching for any evidence that a man had been shot to death there several days ago, but it looked as if they had just walked in for the first time. Not so clean to prompt someone to wonder, yet nothing to indicate anything unusual had occurred. Biting his upper lip, he leaned against a cabinet, drumming his fingers in cadence.

The drama of Preston's murder had subsided. He thought he had accepted Brannan's unilateral action when it happened, and the operation to send the assassin's body to DC occupied his time. Since then, suspicion and anger sneaked into his thoughts, and they grew. Raising images of severed head didn't refocus his attention on the broader objective; instead, angst continually gnawed at him.

He detested Thurlington, but her assassination jeopardized his plan, and it was impossible that Preston had acted alone. Brannan's organization must have been involved to some degree, and Spence had transferred some of his anger to it, and he had subtly accused it as much. Brannan always remained tight-lipped, feigning he either didn't hear or didn't understand the indirect accusation. Yet, there was still more to his anger, and finally Spencer hit on what ate at his insides: Brannan's decision to kill Preston without Spencer's permission or even discussion. It called into question who made the decision, the substantive decisions. He wondered what he could do.

This organization had immersed itself too deeply into the operation for Spencer to eliminate it or Brannan now. He needed to reassert some sense of control, but didn't know whether he could without ruining their future success.

Since Preston's death, he had Tyler check their safeguard, trying to find comfort with that remaining strand of control. Major Brannan, as if sensing he had usurped Spencer's authority, tiptoed around him, attentively working without contradicting Thom or Tyler.

Spence rubbed his head, knowing the major had made the necessary decision and took the action neither he nor Tyler could have. And, again Spence had relied on the organization to facilitate Preston's final journey, thickening bonds joining the organization and him. Success indeed depended on Brannan and his organization, and that fact disturbed Spence, but reality was sinking in, and he tried to accept the partnership not just with the major but also his organization.

"It's on, Thom," Tyler shouted from the adjoining room. Spencer made a beeline through the door, where Tyler and Brannan stared at a satellite-fed TV. He recognized the woman standing in front of a lectern displaying an FBI seal.

"Turn it up, please," he requested.

Tyler complied. Thom heard FBI Special Agent Melissa Dellendale announce a John Doe—no one could identify the body— as the assassin of Speaker of the House Wilma Thurlington. She provided further details about the John Doe and then brought up Thom Spencer. The FBI had concluded from the evidence that Thom Spencer and John Doe were associates; that the John Doe apparently had become a rogue and killed the speaker on his own initiative; and that Spencer had him killed. The Bureau had issued a warrant for Spencer in connection with the assassin's death.

"Perhaps this FBI agent has conveniently saved that vigilante celebrity status of yours," Brannan remarked as the press conference finished.

"At least saving it from utter destruction," offered Tyler.

Tyler changed the channel, and they watched a political round table talk show discuss the FBI's press conference. One commentator obviously didn't agree with the FBI's assessment. "Now I've heard everything!" he exclaimed. "If they don't think this

American Terrorist planned this from the beginning, they're lying."

"Now what do you mean by that, Mark?" the anchor pressed.

"Look, Spencer ends up getting everything he wants. He has this John Doe fella kill Thurlington. Next, he conveniently sacrifices the assassin to make it appear he won't tolerate anyone hurting any American. Make it look like he's really a good guy. Who, by the way, has killed, what, over three hundred fifty thousand people? This is unbelievable, that there's this asinine effort to protect this maniac. My friends, he's killed over three hundred fifty thousand people, and this country is walking around as if this man is some of sort hero."

Another pundit interrupted. "Not a hero, Mark. That's unfair. Americans don't think what he's doing is right. They understand his actions, but that doesn't mean they condone it."

"Three hundred fifty thousand people, Phil. What? Am I the only one who understands that that is more than the number killed at Hiroshima and Nagasaki? My friends, we can't have an American walking around and deciding to take international law into his own hands and kill three hundred fifty thousand people."

"Why not?" Phil challenged. "And we heard the number the first time, Mark."

"Well, Phil, it's now three hundred fifty thousand and *one*, if this John Doe was an American…or doesn't that count?"

Spence inhaled deeply and exhaled slowly. "Well, maybe only partially saved," he said as he headed toward the outer room. "By the way, Major, was Preston an American?"

Brannan solemnly nodded.

"Thought so," he said, and the door slammed behind him.

The next morning, Tyler and Spence left the laboratory room. "Finished packing the pathogen. Had to be more careful doing that than processing the serum itself," Tyler grumbled.

Brannan looked up impatiently. "Good. We've been here too long," he said as he glanced toward Spencer. "Will you be ready with your broadcast, Mr. Spencer?"

"Yes, Major. We'll have everything ready to go."

The major paused a moment, inhaling deeply. "Mr. Spencer, Mr. Washington, we're going to have to give it another shot."

Perplexed, Tyler asked "And what do you mean by that?"

"After we update all the logistics, I'm going to leave someone else behind to take care of things. Someone replacing Preston. We can't do it without that support. But I can assure you that nothing like what Preston did will happen again."

Spence stared hard at the man. Undoubtedly he was sincere, but the time for subtlety had passed. "Major," Spence began, "I don't know how extensive your organization is. I am certain it is much larger and more powerful than I originally understood. Don't think for a second I think Preston acted on his own. There's no doubt someone sanctioned him to kill Thurlington. Not you, but a person in your organization pulled that trigger.

"Major, I remember telling you that I controlled this operation, and I had a similar conversation with Preston as well. Since then, I've had a reality check. We could not have done what we've done without you. My guess is that our selection of you for this job was the most important decision we made. But the job isn't finished. Tyler and I can unquestionably shut down the operation, but I'm committed to going as far as I need to go. I'm going to hell already. What's the difference between three hundred fifty thousand degrees and two million or more? All I see in my mind are my family's severed heads and a chance to make those responsible do as I say, or pay the price I set.

"But it's different with Americans, Major. An American may have died in Gaza or Damascus. God, I hope not—and it doesn't look like it happened or we'd have heard about it—but it's possible, and I will have to live with that. But, Major, we can't do anything like killing Thurlington again. Not because I think Thurlington deserved better. I don't. But what about the next American? Will he be so deserving? I know not all Americans are equally American, but what about Timothy Preston? How much of an American was he? He was committed to us, and yet he had to go, but I didn't sign you up to kill Americans. Now, I'm not going to threaten you and tell you we're shutting this thing down and all that. I'm just going to ask you, Major, to give me your word that it won't happen again. I know it sounds strange coming from a man who is responsible for killing three hundred fifty thousand people and probably more. But American blood can't be spilled by us, not in that way. I need you to look me in the eye and promise me that it won't."

Brannan stared directly at Spence and, leaning forward, shifted his weight to his other foot. "Mr. Spencer. Thom. You didn't see my expression when I learned what Preston did. I'm not going to lie to you. You're right, he did obtain approval, but not from me.

"I presumed my organization had something to do with it, so when I heard the news in Tehran, I got out. I had to come back to confirm my suspicion, and when I confirmed it, I…well, I sat in a chair for I don't know for how long, just sat there in disbelief. What were they thinking? I asked myself over and over again. Ultimately, though, I know who influenced the decision. I suppose it's possible that the three of us might be diagnosed with anti-social personality disorder or some other syndrome, but at times Timothy clearly exhibited those tendencies. Something would strike him in a certain way, and he wouldn't let it go. Couldn't let it go. Most of the time, a straight shooter. Smiling and reliable, but when something triggered that look, you knew something was going to happen. And it was exactly that trait that made him so useful and such a good operative most of the time. If I had been here, I would've seen it, and we could've stopped it."

"You think?" Spence asked skeptically. "I don't know about that, Major. Do you know I threatened not to proceed if Thurlington got her way and sent Americans to any of our targets? Did you know that?"

Brannan nodded. "Yes, Mr. Spencer, I knew that."

"And you would've allowed me to shut down the operation just like that?"

"Mr. Spencer, Thurlington was a political animal, and I don't mean that in an Aristotelian sense. She played the game hard and well. Do you really think there aren't other ways to touch those kinds of people? Mr. Spencer, you don't have to kill a Thurlington to touch her. She didn't need to die. But, Timothy also knew that any idea of sending Americans to the Middle East would die with her, and he was right about that. She's the only one who really could pull that off; no other dove has that kind of influence. Preston believed he had to terminate with extreme prejudice that threat as efficiently and quickly as possible, so he presented that option, and it was approved. Just like that, but it didn't have to be."

Spence sighed. "So you can assure me, Major, we're not going have another episode like that?"

"Yes. Nothing like that will ever again be approved, Mr. Spencer. And I have a man who is very reliable, yet doesn't have that instinctive reflex to kill like Preston had. He'll do the job and do it well, just a bit more even-keel."

"Why not him in the first place?" Spence asked.

"Because even-keel means serious and not delightful, if you catch my drift. Timothy's personality could be soothing and reassuring. I thought you would need more of that considering what we're all doing here. I've seen it help in other operations he was involved in."

"We'll take the hard-ass now," Spence said, deadpan.

Brannan nodded. He reached for his phone and then hesitated. "Mr. Spencer, I know it's about the Americans dying, but I also am aware your…disapproval is deeper than that. I think you're trying to say more."

"What do you mean by that?"

"We're running a very dangerous conspiracy here. Do you know why conspiracies fail?"

Spencer shook his head, expressionless.

"They fail because someone loses focus, becomes offended, hurt, mad or whatever with a co-conspirator and then invariably complains to someone who shouldn't be hearing it, and that's it. I've watched it happen many times, Mr. Spencer. You don't seem the kind to take things personally. Do you?"

"Take things personally?" Spencer asked.

"Yes."

"Are you serious? Why do you think I'm here, Major Brannan? I took it very personally when they murdered my family."

Brannan chortled, chiding himself for what now appeared to be a foolish question. Anyone in a conspiracy is taking something personally, he admitted to himself. "Touché, Mr. Spencer. Can you keep that the focus?" Without another word, Brannan reached for his phone to make the arrangements.

Brannan had just assessed Spencer's brooding as petty and unimportant, and Thom digested the soft rebuke without offense.

Tyler sauntered to Spence's side. "Three hundred fifty thousand degrees or two million, eh? No difference? Do you really still think you're going to hell, Spence?"

"Yes, I do, Tyler. Don't you?"

"Hell no! Nothing's changed. I'm still a scientist. And I don't believe in hell, or heaven for that matter."

Spence stared at Tyler without blinking for a moment and shook his head. "I envy you, Tyler. I envy you."

Twenty-four hours later, Brannan's team had decommissioned the entire laboratory, except for a lone computer in a side room. Brannan and Tyler asked whether Spence would address the Thurlington murder, and though he had considered it, he rejected mentioning it. It would clutter what he intended to convey.

Sitting, Spence withdrew a piece of paper with Richard Prednow's talk show telephone number. He punched the numbers on the key pad, and fortunately a busy signal didn't greet him and instead a friendly woman's voice answered.

"Where's Bruce?" he asked quietly.

"He's on the air with Richard. Can I help you?" she replied politely.

"This is Thom Spencer calling in to speak to your listeners."

The line went silent for a moment. "Yeah, right," she retorted in an uncertain voice. "The American Terrorist calling now?"

"Put Bruce on; he'll know me. But, ma'am, you'd better do it quickly. My guess is that we're being recorded right now and there's a tracer. Now, I can delay it, but not forever, so hurry, will you please?"

Less than a half a minute had passed when Bruce answered. "This is Bruce Mills."

"Bruce, the question is this: are you dedicated to your government or your profession? If you try to stall and play paddy cake so that the feds can try to locate me, and don't put me on right now, then I'll find a different place to make my statement."

Spence heard the producer swallow. "What is it Bruce, government or profession?" Thom asked.

Bruce cleared his throat. "Actually, Mr. Spencer, I'm for my country. That's why we're putting you through immediately."

After a click, the deep, resonate voice of the talk show host said, "The American Terrorist, I presume."

"Mr. Prednow, I am going to make a few comments. I am disappointed in the Middle Eastern Muslim countries' response to my demands. If within fourteen days I do not see the dismantling of the terrorist networks I identified previously, and if the previously identified terrorists aren't delivered to the proper authorities, I will strike again. Please understand that I will escalate the next attack.

Fourteen days, and the attack proceeds no matter what actions are taken. The attack may take place in fifteen days, a hundred days, or ten years, but I promise it will happen. Please understand that if any actions are taken against the United States, consequences will result. Deadly consequences. I think I have demonstrated my abilities, and I will execute these plans. In order to avoid substantial death, the demands must be met by my deadline. I will not call your show again with any further warning. I will continue to attack until the demands are met." Spence terminated the call.

Prednow's show remained silent on the air for several seconds, and then the host spoke. "And it is my opinion that we have just heard from the real American Terrorist and that he means to carry out these attacks if his demands aren't met. My humanity prevents me from wishing him well; my Americanism prevents me from wishing him harm. Mr. Thom Spencer has put me in a moral quandary. He needs to be caught, he needs to be stopped, and he needs to face the death penalty, yet it's as if I'm watching that good old American gangster movie where I'm cheering on the bad guy, hoping he gets away. But this time, it's real, and real people are dying, and I don't want them to die, but I think they must in order for them to understand. I know others think and feel the same way, and maybe that makes me a bad person. Maybe it makes us all bad people, but we bad people don't want to worry about getting blown up when we go to the store. We don't want to worry about exploding rafters at football games, and we don't want to fret about airplanes used as weapons. If we have to, well then our fellow human beings over there in the Middle East have to fret about Thom Spencer."

Spencer shut down the computer, and Brannan nodded. "Miles Wilbur, the hard-ass, has taken care of everything. I'm heading out. You should be in Caracas by late evening. We're in another warehouse district, in a nondescript building. My guess, you're not going to have to move from that location until I return."

Spence sniffed before answering. "You know the numbers now, don't you, Major," he said calmly while staring into a corner as if preoccupied. "Fairly easy to calculate."

"I'm fully aware of the number of deaths involved in these next attacks, Mr. Spencer. And I also think we may have to use that serum you and Mr. Washington just finished processing. Are you really prepared for that?"

"Three hundred fifty thousand or two million or more, Major. We're going to finish this, and if we have to blaze a path through the entire Middle East and beyond, so be it. Either I get caught or I get Ghazali and all those other bastards. It now has become as simple as that."

Chapter Thirty-Five

Sunday, February 8

Brannan changed his method of travel to Iran. Instead of entering the country covertly as he had previously from Iraq, the major had his organization forge Iranian and Turkish passports and visas, traveling first as an ordinary Persian merchant and later as a Turkish businessman. Forging foreign documents was always risky, but he had confidence his organization would produce them flawlessly. The real danger was the enhanced photographic apparatus every border authority had established because of the American Terrorist. Brannan couldn't avoid his face becoming part of an improved and integrated worldwide facial recognition database. Again, however, his organization had a solution: a new technology, never before deployed, and Brannan was the test case. The bio-engineer designers cautioned him about the dangers. If it malfunctioned, it could lead to a painful death. The major accepted the warning with the same aplomb as all other risks he accepted. He couldn't remember when painful death wasn't a possible outcome.

He was tired from the indirect route to Casablanca, but he decided to go straight through to Dubai. At his organization's Moroccan bank, Brannan retrieved the forged documents, US dollars, and Iranian rials from a safe-deposit box, and asked a bank associate to arrange the earliest United Arab Emirates reservation in the name of Farvad Ghadir Arki.

Ten hours later, Brannan's taxi rolled up to an exquisite new hotel in opulent Dubai. The open veranda's marble driveway flowed into an airy and bright lobby. Guests enjoyed state-of-the-art climate control, sophisticated lighting, and many other audacious accommodations in every room. But Brannan spent his one-night layover doing nothing but sleeping, ignoring the easily available amenities Dubai offered.

The enhanced security measures delayed the line at the Dubai airport longer than Brannan had anticipated. He wearily approached the counter and handed the agent his passport. The man slid it under a scanner, paused several moments while looking at nothing, and indifferently handed the passport and visa back to Brannan. He wondered how many video cameras had captured his image as he waited at the counter.

After eight hundred miles and four hours, the major found himself in a dilapidated motel near the Tehran airport. He unpacked his overnight bag, but left his larger duffel bag untouched, since Tehran wasn't the final destination. Because all connecting flights were already booked, Brannan traveled the next day as the same Iranian merchant on a holy pilgrimage to the intended target.

The following morning the Iran Aseman flight ended with a loud thud and a squeal of tires on the tarmac. Brannan hadn't enjoyed the turbulent flight from Tehran and was anxious to disembark. Sighing, he glanced around the cabin. Mashhad was a holy city in Shia Islam, and he had overheard several passengers talking about the religious nature of their excursion. It surprised him so many people would plan a pilgrimage at this time of year, despite claiming the same reason himself.

Brannan reached over a petite young woman who smiled at him as he grabbed his bag and his tattered woolen sweater from the bin. He returned the smile as he helped her with her luggage, wondering if she lived in or was just visiting the city. The unlucky denizens would die while the visitors would only witness the horror.

After renting a car, the major drove into the city in light traffic. His only familiarity came from his previous visit when he had dispersed the toxin, which sparked some anxiety. He pulled into a motel advertising vacancy, commonplace during February. The clerk absently handed him a key, and Brannan climbed the stairs to his room. A cool draft whistled past the doors and windows, so Brannan didn't remove his wool sweater. Sitting on his bed, he turned on the satellite TV.

He stared blankly at the screen, mentally reviewing the route he had planned before the first trip. Mashhad's street grid made it fairly convenient for his task. That was important, since he had a much larger area to cover than previous targets, increasing the number of stops to reach the desired coverage. Getting caught in congestion or wrapped up in an accident could disrupt the timing, affecting a portion of the population before he made it safely out. He had backup directions, but his lack of experience in the city would hamper him if something arose. Still, he thought to himself, he should have time. He pulled the tape from his duffel bag and programmed the strips—a simple process, though more time consuming since he had many more stops.

Rising from the bed after completing the task, Brannan moved restlessly to the sink and turned on the water. Looking at his reflection, he marveled at how excellent foreign language skills, a pair of contacts, and darkened skin and hair granted him access to so many countries up to this point. People might take him for a Tehrani or perhaps an Iraqi; no one paid him any attention. He feared the days of those simple disguises had disappeared. He splashed his face, patted it dry with a worn towel, and dug into his duffel bag again.

His inexperience in the city frayed his nerves again. Rubbing his chin, Brannan withdrew the map and spread it out on the small table. He couldn't chance a dry run; he didn't want to arouse any suspicion by visiting a place twice in such a short period of time. His memory would refresh itself from his last trip as he drove, but a review of the map would help his navigation tomorrow while quelling some of the nerves tonight.

His eyes probed the map. Spencer and Washington had pinpointed the locations the tape would maximize the effect of the toxin, calculating he would need to stop thirty-one times and travel nearly fifty-eight miles from the first stop to the last. With travel and stop time, they projected a conservative estimate of nine stops per hour. With a little cushion, he should have enough time to complete the circuit and return the rental vehicle in four hours, and then the difficult part would begin.

Once he placed the last strip of tape, he had twenty-four hours to land in Istanbul, his safe harbor. To make the only flight that met the deadline, he had to catch a bus to Ashgabat, Turkmenistan. But bus rides in these parts of the world weren't simple. He had to allow for unscheduled stops, mechanical breakdowns, flat tires, and worse. If he hadn't arrived in and departed from Ashgabat well before the first victim fell to the floor bleeding, the borders would likely close and he would find himself stranded in a remote part of the world. Transportation would come to a screeching halt, suspicion would flare, and his disguises might not help him. Shrugging, Brannan had to dispel these misgivings before they consumed the night. He closed his eyes, invoking his superb mental discipline. After a few moments, his jitters vanished.

He smiled. Nerves and adrenaline hit him before missions. It would undoubtedly surprise members of his organization that he would even acknowledge the presence of such feelings, but he would never admit it. His cold, dispassionate demeanor commanded respect, and it allowed him to operate under flexible parameters without question. He owed it to his father, who could have given him anything in the world, but his greatest gift was the lesson of mental discipline. Inculcated at an early age, Brannan knew he took to it naturally, and his dad cultivated it brilliantly, gentle when necessary, tough when needed. It served him well in athletics, in school, in the military, and it was an intangible, invaluable asset of the organization.

No doubt he felt compassion, happiness, anger, and rage, but what made him feel alive was the ability to control that emotion and channel it into hard, disciplined, objective conduct. He performed superbly because he could dismiss the vagaries of emotion at a moment's notice. They hadn't vanished; they still wrestled around in his soul when he saw a potential casualty, possible collateral damage, or an adversary deserving of immediate termination, but he could channel them at will. He always thought it ironic that what made him feel so alive, powerful, and capable was the ability to reject feelings. It was a rare quality he could recognize in others. When he sat in that bar in New York, he immediately saw the potential in Thom Spencer. The American Terrorist would have to endure a learning curve, but he had predicted Spencer would eventually conquer the feelings and execute without emotion. His first impression had proven correct. The next day would be another confirmation of the dispassionate alliance.

Brannan awakened at dawn and by the time he finished with his shower, sunshine had squeezed past the shades. He packed his gear methodically, readying himself for the race. After he dropped off the key and paid his bill, Brannan stepped into his vehicle, clutched the steering wheel, and turned the key. He looked at his watch and set the timer.

"Mark," he said aloud and drove onto the road.

The traffic cooperated for the first fifteen stops, and he finished those jobs under the time allotted. As he drove down a small arterial road, the line of cars came to a complete standstill. Brannan quickly scanned for exits to either side. If the traffic jam took more than a few minutes to clear he would skip this stop, believing coverage from other locations would bleed into the area. He anxiously tapped his fingers on the steering wheel until the line moved again. As he drove by his last escape route, his stomach suddenly fluttered, but the car ahead kept plodding along. He finally passed a vehicle stalled on the side of the street, and he noticed a man trudging down a side alley with a gas container in hand.

Just past the stalled car was a large public notice board. Brannan pulled over and quickly jumped out to tape a flyer—stolen from an approved public forum—to it. As he trotted back to his car, he clenched his teeth, thinking how fortunate the traffic jam had cleared and how unfortunate those around him were. Shoving those thoughts aside, he glanced at his watch and grimaced at the lost time.

The next fourteen stops were slow, and he gritted his teeth and scowled at the delays. Finally he reached the last location. Spotting a cafe, Brannan parked in a small lot and hopped out of the car. He headed straight for the bathroom and placed his final leaflet—an approved political poster—on a poster board with a deadly piece of tape.

On his way out, the proprietor threw him a stern look. "So," he complained, "you come in here with your posters and leaflets and clutter up my cafe and use my toilet and don't even pay for a cup of tea. You should at least have the courtesy to talk with me."

Brannan didn't need to look at his watch; he didn't have time to waste. But the man just might march into the restroom and flush the poster and tape, and he couldn't risk ruining the saturation at this location. Smiling pleasantly, he replied in perfect Farsi, "You're right, my friend. Mind if I have a cup with you at the counter?"

The man returned the smile and opened his arms. "Wouldn't have it any other way, my friend. Please, come join me." He poured Brannan tea and prattled on in a one-sided conversation as Brannan masked his impatience. The minutes ticked by, and Brannan knew his escape route frittered away. Finally, he begged the man's forgiveness, saying he had to leave.

Smiling broadly, the proprietor responded, "I know. You must go, and no doubt you're in a hurry or you wouldn't have rushed in and tried to rush out in the first place. But we have to slow down, you know, and you did this for me. You're a decent man, my friend. Courteous and polite. I thank you for taking the time to speak with an old man."

Brannan smiled without guile. "You're not an old man. And now how much do I owe you?"

The man glanced at Brannan's garb. "My friend, I can afford to buy you the tea more than you can afford to pay for it. That's all. I just wanted to buy you a cup of tea."

Brannan patted the man's forearm and nodded. "Thank you."

The man smiled again, and Brannan left the cafe, pulling his old sweater tighter around him as a cool, sharp wind gave him a chill. He tried to regain his callous efficiency from before, but it eluded him. The parley yanked at that deeply buried conscience, and his heavy breath condensed in the cold air. Relieved he had made his last stop, the major questioned the wisdom of having a near-certain victim buy him a cup of tea. He started the engine and drove to the car rental lot without interruption.

At the nearby bus terminal, he squeezed onto a small, narrow bus destined for Ashgabat, Turkmenistan. It smelled foul, but he found a seat near the back next to a window, thankful just to be on it. When the engine barely sputtered to life, Brannan's confidence wavered; it sounded as if it might not finish the journey. But busing remained the best and most discreet method of transportation to Ashgabat, and he couldn't switch now, especially if the terrorist attack materialized prematurely and governmental scrutiny descended quickly.

An elderly woman struggled up the aisle and wedged herself next to him just before the bus lurched forward and merged into traffic. Brannan smiled at her; she didn't appear to notice and sat staring straight ahead. The major glanced at his watch. The delays had eroded his cushion, but he was still within the allotted time window. Traffic thickened; he hoped it wouldn't last long.

The bus stopped and started again, lurching and grinding through the crowded city streets. Outwardly Brannan appeared to be an ordinary traveler, calm and resigned, enduring a ride that should take only a few hours, yet fully aware it would take longer. They eventually reached the city's edge, and the time between stops began to increase. He soon saw fewer buildings and more countryside. Farmland then whizzed by at a quicker pace. His traveling companion sat nearly motionless, seemingly oblivious. She suddenly turned toward him and smiled kindly, eyes twinkling with enviable mirth, and started extolling her glorious pilgrimage to the holy city. As a visitor, this elderly woman would most likely be spared a terrible death; he returned the smile, trying to smother the conscience that churned in his stomach again. He glanced out the window and found no reason to terminate the feeling with cold discipline, so he allowed the moment to linger. The kind elderly woman chatted on about the cold weather while he listened absently.

The bus traveled steadily down the road now. Brannan looked at his watch again; he remained on schedule, though with little time to spare. The bus brakes abruptly squealed, and the vehicle stopped, throwing Brannan forward with a jolt. The major grimaced; his elderly companion, noticing his clenched jaw, soothed, "Won't be too long. Happens every once in a while."

Two men with badges marched onto the bus and started down the bus aisle. Immediately alarms went off in Brannan's head. Not enough time had elapsed for any of the toxin's symptoms to appear. These officials couldn't be searching for him, yet something might have gone awry. They passed his seat, staring at him for only a moment, and halted at the row behind him. The officials grabbed a man and roughly escorted him off the bus.

Inside a regime like Iran's, the bus passenger had no rights; he was at the mercy of those who carried the badge, those who had the power. Outside the bus, the interrogation began. Brannan tried to watch casually, but the longer the episode continued, the more he squirmed in his seat. When the two officials suddenly started manhandling their captive, Brannan began considering his options.

Missing the plane out of Ashgabat, a Turkish Air night flight, would mean that Brannan would have to conceal himself in the Turkmenistan capital. He couldn't remain long if he were to reach the next target on time, so he would have to attempt a covert departure. He had planned for this possibility, but it was risky. The outbreak in Mashhad would place the entire area on high alert, and the Turkmenistan government could easily implement martial law. In Turkmenistan, he would make contact with known associates, but resources would still be scarce. He considered several hypotheticals, and debated their pros and cons. If he played it safe and gave up the fourth target, he could survive in Ashgabat, but he immediately rejected that option.

Rubbing his jaw, the major watched the two officers and the passenger talk in less strident tones. Surprisingly, they shrugged and allowed the passenger to return to the bus. He walked down the aisle with an indifferent expression, and not one person asked him a single question or even gave him a suspicious glance. In this country, people expected and accepted these episodes of arbitrary abuse of power. Costs of living under brutal regimes, Brannan thought to himself as the outlook just improved for him to make his Turkish Air flight.

Countryside scenery quickly surrendered to mountainous terrain as the bus approached the border, and with it the next test. Nestled in the desolate mountains, facilities erected jointly by Iran and Turkmenistan regulated all traffic, people, and goods between the two countries. Without proper documentation nothing passed, but Brannan had confidence in his papers. When the bus stopped at the checkpoint, two border agents hopped aboard. A congenial Iranian walked the aisle checking passports and visas with a handheld contraption while his aloof Turkmen counterpart monitored from the front with his own device. When the Iranian came to Brannan, he nodded as he accepted the documents. After scanning them, he handed them back and moved on to the next row without comment.

Brannan grimaced as the agent requested the abused man's documents. His papers might not share the impeccable aura of authenticity that Brannan's exuded. The agent processed what the man handed him with no incident. Relieved, Brannan smiled to himself as the agents departed, and the bus rolled through the border station. After nearly twenty miles of winding highway, the terrain started to flatten and city buildings reappeared.

The bus navigated the mildly congested Ashgabat traffic efficiently to other side of the city where a bus terminal had recently been constructed near the airport. The bus finally exited the expressway, made a few turns, lumbered into the station, and shuddered to a stop. The major quickly found a connecting shuttle to the airport, yet he wasn't ready to relax.

Brannan strode through the terminal doors of Ashgabat's fairly modern airport and headed straight for a bathroom. After searching for monitoring devices and finding none, the major stepped inside a stall and withdrew his Turkish passport, a mirror, a small black pouch, and his Dopp kit. Now was the time for him to counter the upgraded worldwide security measures with his organization's newest technology. Studying the supplied facial diagram the bio-engineers had given him, he identified his targets and assembled a syringe from several components pulled from his Dopp kit and black pouch. He took out an eye-drop bottle filled with saline and dropped a freeze-dried compound into the solution. After loading the syringe, he swallowed hard and injected his face under his left eye. He waited for a few moments. A burning sensation shot out from where he had punctured the skin. A sharp spasm then quickly erupted and dissipated, taking his breath away. Lurching for the mirror, he inspected his face, wondering it if had become contorted beyond recognition. Instead, he saw an area subtly morphed in color and shape under his left eye. After several more injections, with the same burn-and-spasm routine for each, he had become the image in the passport photograph in a few short minutes. Though similar to Botox, this substance contained compounds considerably more complex, and it changed his face not to beautify it, but to alter its three-dimensional appearance, even pushing apart the eyes just enough to frustrate a computer calculation. Brannan ended the procedure by injecting his ears, knowing his self-administered plastic surgery would foil the best facial recognition software, even programs written by CIA specialists.

Once he finished, he again compared his face with the photograph. No one would question him, and this face wouldn't cross match with the facial features he had when he entered Iran. Next he trimmed his hair, exchanged a few clothing items, and dropped his Turkish passport in a handy pocket before flushing the evidence of his alteration. Finally Brannan stepped out of the stall and gave one last appraising glance in the mirror. Thoroughly impressed with the bio-engineers, he left the bathroom and made a beeline for the Turkish Airlines counter. In Turkish, he greeted the agent cheerfully. "Hello. Is the Istanbul flight on time?"

The woman nodded. "Yes, could I have your name and identification?" she asked pleasantly. Brannan handed her the passport and visa, and ninety minutes later, as the jet engines hummed, Brannan comfortably leaned back his seat, knowing he would neatly tuck himself away in a nondescript hotel in a city he had visited often, and calmly wait for the right time to set out for the fourth target: Cairo, population twenty million.

Chapter Thirty-Six

Thursday, February 12

Mansur Ghazali stared at the television set as he ate his meal without tasting it. The reporter, in translated Farsi, spewed drivel about Thom Spencer. The American Terrorist's fourteen-day ultimatum had come and gone without an attack, but the previous two attacks hadn't immediately followed the deadline, so people were still afraid that at any moment someone would suddenly keel over on a sidewalk and hideously corrode from the inside out. Rattled nerves dominated the milieu, and governments flailed about, searching for any rhetoric to calm their subjects. Some regimes had taken more precautions than others; most didn't believe such actions would prove effective.

Ghazali agreed with this assessment. The American Terrorist had discovered something Ghazali could only dream of possessing. Whatever this weapon was, it mesmerized him, although he scoffed at Spencer's efforts to produce terror. With such capabilities, an authentic terrorist would have already killed tens of millions of people. Ghazali fantasized about destroying New York, Los Angeles, and Chicago with a single sweep of his hand: nearly thirty million Americans dead in a day. That kind of act spawned terror; Spencer had proven himself too craven, too weak to assert the power Ghazali coveted.

But he didn't have the technology to kill at that magnitude, and he admitted to himself that his attacks on the United States hadn't succeeded in terrorizing Americans. They hadn't inflicted enough pain on the hated infidels; the blood hadn't poured through American avenues in the wide rivers he had envisioned, and now the newscaster spoke about Thom Spencer instead of Mansur Ghazali.

Ghazali gritted his teeth, pushed aside his plate, and rose from his chair. Stalking to the window, he stared out at the city. Spencer had seriously jeopardized Ghazali's dream of unifying Islam and creating a Muslim military founded on the goal of destroying the Great Satan and capturing the Western world. It was Islam's destiny to overcome the infidel, and America stood as the greatest barrier to this destiny. He had believed he could eventually banish rifts between Shia and Sunni sects and merge ethnic Arab, Persian, and Turkic identities. Islam, true Islam, gave him the power, and the Great Satan provided the unifying cause. Universal Jihad had sown the seeds, and in his network the dream had started to flourish. In a generation, perhaps two, Islam would be unified, and the world would bow to Muslim power. Muslim warriors would lead Dar el Salaam, the people of Islam, to conquer Dar el Harb, the infidels.

With Spencer chiseling severe cracks in that dream, Ghazali had to act before it shattered. So he switched his strategy, opting for a plan he had held in reserve for years and developed for just such a time as now.

He hadn't heard from Mohammad since their last meeting, when his so-called friend informed him of how craven Muslim leaders wanted to avoid direct confrontation with the American Terrorist and the Great Satan. Ghazali wouldn't avoid that battle, and tonight he would meet with those he believed would support him. Indeed, the plot was risky and bold. His closest deputies—those who implemented his orders without question, and those inside governments who supported his vision—would receive instructions and, with Allah's grace, embrace the plan with passion.

He turned from the window, walked to a large map spread out on the table, and reexamined it. Westerners were so foolish, he thought. Of course Iran had developed nuclear weapons. Though they were crude, and, contrary to what some thought, couldn't travel a great distance, they would go far enough. The fear many Westerners had of a rogue nation delivering a nuclear weapon into the hands of a terrorist organization overlooked the more likely threat. It was more efficient for the terrorist to seize a government's nuclear weapon site. And Ghazali didn't need all the weapons, just a few or even one. Those who thought loyal soldiers of Universal Jihad couldn't infiltrate the Iranian nuclear defense establishment misunderstood how deeply his influence had penetrated the culture of the Muslim world and how far, how wide, and how deep his transcendent movement had evolved. His soldiers were more loyal to him than to their own government, and he believed they would follow him down the deadly path he envisioned. For many years, he had cultivated those fertile minds as youngsters inside the hallowed halls of the madrasas. It didn't matter what school of thought the madrasa preached; Ghazali's message was universal, and they embraced it, all of them, because it sang the song they wanted to hear: the destruction of the West, the vanquishing of the infidel. He gripped the edge of the table in exultant confidence.

Maybe a few in governments outside of Universal Jihad suspected Ghazali had infiltrated the nuclear missile program, but they shrugged with indifference and believed the essential launching technology was secure and protected at a nuclear launch site. Ghazali presumably couldn't penetrate that inner circle, which had denied him what he wanted. Not that they didn't want what he demanded; they were simply afraid of the West's retaliation. Ghazali had tolerated the cowardice until now.

The entire Middle East now lived in fear of the American Terrorist's death grip. Ghazali would obliterate that fear. Blood suddenly rushed to his head, and he felt a little dizzy. Inhaling deeply, he shook off the feeling and grabbed his jacket. Tonight, they would decide the fate of the world.

Ghazali strode briskly to a warehouse near his apartment. Most of the soldiers present had arrived from across the Islamic Ummah. A few of his local crew remained at the doors, guarding against any possible intruder. Though it was a cold evening, he felt warm in the cavernous warehouse and, surprisingly, felt a few butterflies tumbling in his stomach. They would disappear once he gauged the mood of the crowd, he convinced himself.

Chairs formed a circle, and Ghazali naturally strolled into the center, illuminated by a lone light. He waited a few minutes as the last stragglers were guided to their seats. One hundred fifty men, blindfolded to keep each man's identity secret from the other, sat silently waiting. Years ago, when Ghazali started devising his grand scheme, he had personally selected these men, and now they held positions of power, and a few had indeed infiltrated the inner circle of their government. He remained supremely confident of their unswerving loyalty in the time of need.

Clearing his throat, he began. "We are faced by an evil from the West as grave as we've ever encountered. The American Terrorist has rained death upon us unlike any witnessed before, and we all realize the West, and especially the Americans, at best idly sit by and watch, hoping he strikes again. More likely their governments orchestrate this despicable mass murder. And our governments are seized in fear. Many of you have secretly supported the overthrow of these governments, but you have been restrained. We have manipulated them as a tool, but now the time has come to cast them aside and seize what we need to eliminate the infidel. With Allah's help, we will strike a death blow to America and the West. This death blow requires a two-prong attack. The first is necessary, violent and destructive; it is more a ploy, a decoy, for the ultimate assault, the second prong of our salvation. We have people in this room capable of achieving both attacks. One is as important as the other, but without the first, we will not succeed. My brothers, the first attack is a nuclear missile strike."

Ghazali allowed his words to resonate. He couldn't see their eyes, though he sensed surprise, and a quiet surge of exhilarated energy infused the warehouse.

Feeding on their excitement, he continued. "We have a limited range here, so we can't touch Europe or America. So we strike, but instead of those distant lands, we strike at another enemy that has immorally invaded our Holy Land, and wipe them off the face of the earth. We target the vile nation of Israel, and we can reach the Jews with missiles and the launch pad we control with brothers in this warehouse."

The energy in the room elevated to palpable excitement. He had chosen his men wisely; he sensed their need to lash out, the lust to end their powerless frustrations.

"The Jews will retaliate. We know they have nuclear weapons, and they most definitely will respond, and lives will be lost. But I have learned from the Jews. They are our enemy, but they are also smart. That Mossad...well, the Mossad has had many successes.

Many of you have not heard of Eli Cohen, the notorious Israeli spy who infiltrated Syrian defenses to a greater extent than any in Syria wish to ever admit. His journey started in Egypt and Argentina, and he found his way to Damascus.

"Years ago, when I learned that story while placing our secret cells around the world, I traveled to Russia and recruited several families. They emigrated from Russia with Jewish credentials and blood, and reared their children outwardly as Jews, yet secretly prayed to Mecca five times a day. These children grew up, and many now occupy important positions inside Israel, but one in particular is very special to me…to us.

"He holds a position deep inside Israel's nuclear strike force. We have communicated only three times in his entire career. Security measures are as strict as you can imagine. In the first communication several years ago, he told me that he had devised a plan where he could, in the event of a nuclear launch from Israel, divert the path of the warheads. His intention was, of course, to save lives; to direct the missiles harmlessly into the sea, saving hundreds of thousands, perhaps millions of Muslim lives. A noble and useful purpose, and we might have needed him to perform that duty. But I have suggested a different plan. In our second communication, I asked him if he could and would divert three warheads to different locations. The third communication with this heavenly soldier was a simple one-word reply: 'yes'."

Mansur wiped his head, feeling the heat from the light. He didn't feel well; dizziness supplanted butterflies, but he had everyone's rapt attention; he had woven the story to solidify his support. No fire and no brimstone needed; pure substance had enthralled them, so he blinked a few times and shrugged off his ailments. "My plan," he said in a softer voice, "includes all my brothers. Though you can't see one another, you must understand that the man next to you could be Sunni or Shia or maybe a Sufi; he could be Turkic, Persian, or Arab. Universal Jihad includes all my Muslim brethren, and each has an important, an all-important job to do."

Ghazali scanned the room, searching for dissent or discontent among the various sects and ethnicities. He detected none; instead, he felt a passionate solidarity among these men. He had succeeded in transcending the sectarian and ethnic barriers with these soldiers, and his chest swelled with pride. Universal Jihad was indeed the path to glory.

"My Shia brothers will first launch a missile from the Natanz missile site and strike metropolitan Tel Aviv. The Israelis haven't deployed any of America's latest ABM technology yet, and we have a cruise missile. A surprise attack will penetrate any defensive measures, killing a third or more of the population. More than one million Jews killed in an instant."

The room nearly erupted in jubilation as Ghazali rubbed his chest. Without any dissent, the excitement continued to rise, so he proceeded. "Of course, Israel will respond. We want them to! They will launch warheads against Iran, but during their launch, the input codes will be changed and three missiles redirected to different targets. Our operative, our brother, will launch Israeli nuclear weapons against Mecca, Medina, and Cairo. Cairo is first, with its nearly twenty million people, and then Medina and Mecca for the symbolism and effect."

Though no eyes stared at him, Ghazali felt his audience stiffen in shock, but no one jumped out of his chair and objected. He had baited them, and now they eagerly waited for his explanation. Ghazali shrugged back his shoulders in confidence. "And a most splendid aspect of this plan: our Muslim brother has forged ties with radical right-wing Jews. Just like Yigal Amir claimed he killed Rabin for Israel, our brother will claim he purposely redirected those missiles, not as a Muslim Universal Jihadist, but as a right-wing Jew striking at the heart of Islam. Those deaths will never be attributed to us, and the historic, dreadful blame will always be on a Jew, on Israel and the West, forever justifying any and all retribution." He could tell his one hundred fifty soldiers liked this clever aspect. "Now, I know many of our Muslim brethren will die, and the brunt is borne more by Sunnis, but, my brothers, please realize that theirs is a sacrifice for Islam. Allah will greet them gloriously in heaven." Ghazali paused, waiting for the Sunni response. None arose; his entire audience sat hypnotized, and his Sunni brethren had embraced this extraordinary sacrifice with its immense suffering.

"All Muslim nations will immediately declare war on Israel. Perhaps they would accept retaliation against Iran, but they will not abide the unprovoked attack against Egypt and Saudi Arabia. It will also blunt the Great Satan's response. Easy for America to target

Iran, but when Israel is perceived to have escalated the war aggressively against the entire Middle East, the Great Satan may pause before launching its missiles. But I doubt that matters. I doubt America will care. It will be far too fixated on how to react to our second prong.

"My brothers, the nuclear strike is a complicated plan we have been implementing for years. It takes all of you to do as you are told. It took time and effort to place all the right people in all the right places. Of the two prongs, it is much more complex. My brothers, the second prong is easy…but it is the death blow.

"Listen to me, my brothers," he preached, his voice echoing of bare walls. "I have told our leaders to cut off the oil and gas to America and the West. Maybe killing Americans in shopping malls doesn't faze them, but destroying the shopping center itself will. And we can do this by depriving them of oil. America and its culture critically depend on energy, cheap energy all around the world, to sustain its commercial identity. You see, America's weakness is its commerce. Historically, commerce hasn't produced cultural strength. That comes from dedication, loyalty, and service to your religion and your culture. We can survive without the oil and gas; America and the West can't. Destroy that, and you destroy them. You must believe me.

"The financial fallout from the first attack would be severe, but their markets would recover. We've seen it many times over. To end this war with the West for eternity, we must end all access to the oil, and annihilate those markets forever. How do we accomplish this, you ask?"

He wiped the sweat from his brow, glad his audience remained blindfolded to his unusual anxiety. He inhaled deeply, steadying himself, knowing his voice conveyed calm confidence, and exhaled inaudibly. "In the horror of the nuclear strike, we will have the opportunity to destroy those fields.

"We all know the Saudis built explosive grids that can destroy their own oil fields. So now have the Iranians, Kuwaitis, Iraqis, as well other oil-producing countries, including our Central Asian brother nations. These explosive grids are controlled by sophisticated computerized systems with redundant security. But these countries guard an important secret about these grids. You see, brothers, a nuclear attack could damage the computerized system. If those systems are damaged in any way, they have no way of detonating the explosives, and the oil fields could end up in the hands of the Great Satan and the infidels. To avoid this catastrophe, these governments devised a strategy where they each independently transfer control of their explosive grid to a manual system, completely severed from any computerized network. Upon a nuclear attack, the computerized systems go off-line between twenty-five and twenty-nine minutes depending upon the country, allowing each nation the time to ascertain the threat and decide whether to destroy its fields. During this off-line period, the explosive grids on all these oil and gas fields can be detonated manually by simple wireless commands, if the nation determines their fields are in danger of being confiscated by the infidels. My brothers, men sitting among you right now control those command codes."

Ghazali felt the pride in the room swell. Every soldier immediately understood the effort and resources Universal Jihad had expended to obtain those codes. "Although these codes are completely useless unless there is a nuclear attack on one of these countries, when the first Israeli missile launches, and the alerts are transmitted, Universal Jihad suddenly becomes more powerful than any person, group, religion, or nation on the face of the earth. We have the power, and with that power we destroy all the largest oil and gas fields in the world. All our chosen brothers have to do is execute these simple wireless command codes, then the explosives detonate, and the oil and gas fields disappear. Many have never imagined we would destroy our own oil, but when we do, we forever demolish the West and its capitalistic regime. History will blame the Jews and the West for forcing us to resort to such a drastic act, since they chose to retaliate so immorally with unrivaled violent attacks upon peaceful Muslim cities and sacred symbols."

Ghazali detected the first hints of resistance and shifted into artful persuasion. For a moment, he faltered, his own fatigue shocking himself. Still, his audience was blind to the weakness, and he called up the inner strength Allah had always granted him. "We should reject oil as a source of wealth; it has been the seeds of America's wealth and the seeds of our own corruption. We end the corruption, and we end America and the West. With the oil destroyed, the financial and banking markets world wide will collapse. I know China, India, and Russia think they have found a third way, but their commerce economies will also implode. Our oil and gas fuel the entire commercial world; without it, the world's landscape changes, and the ensuing vacuum, that horrific void will be filled with the word of the Prophet.

"The Koran, the Sharia, and the Hadith will then envelop the entire world with the hope it needs, and we will rise from the ashes and sweep down on it as the Patriarchal Caliphs swept down on the ancient Middle East, conquering and converting those to the one true religion of the world. The moment has come, and we now must seize it!"

Ghazali stopped and listened to the silence. He didn't rant. He retained their entranced attention by virtue of his message; they would follow him to heaven or hell. Universal Jihad roused them; it was their time to act. Those terrorist cells inside America now gave way to the fervent cells inside the Muslim governments themselves. Revolution, true revolution, had been sown many years before and was now at hand.

The American Terrorist had thought himself so smart and so powerful, but now he had given Ghazali and his soldiers the reason to cast off their diffidence and forge a true revolution and remake the world with Allah's words. The time was now. Ghazali knew it, and the Muslim brothers in that warehouse agreed. They didn't cheer or cry; they sat in convicted silence, their demeanor resolutely committed. He had captured their hearts and minds.

"As I look into your faces, though I can't see your eyes, my brothers, I sense your commitment. You are all comrades in arms. The plan will proceed. Before each of you departs, you will be given a set of instructions. Each of you was chosen for your training, and more importantly for your loyalty. We know you will perform the instructions perfectly. When you read them, you will be surprised by their simplicity. But all your actions together will create out of the embers the righteous world we envision."

He felt a trickle of perspiration drip down his back. He dismissed it, knowing he was near the end. Allah's will, he thought to himself. "As I said, this plan was devised many years ago, and over the years we have implemented it, not as an immediate priority, but as a safeguard. Until recently. With the advent of this American Terrorist and the subsequent cowardly inertia from our governments, we refined it, and you were selected to execute it, my brothers. You are all the chosen few, the elite, and your names will be known among the greatest of Muslim soldiers, the Founders of the Muslim World Revolution. You are privileged, as I am privileged to know you, and together we make our new world. Once you leave here tonight, the wheels will be in motion. My brothers, I fear I have or will become the target, not just of the West and the Great Satan, but of our supposed brethren Muslim governments themselves. So what I start tonight no longer depends on me. It is a self-executing plan, and each of you needs to do only as you are instructed."

Ghazali surveyed his army, satisfied he had truly picked the future historical martyrs of his religion. He still had to dispel any seeds of doubt that might arise. "Now, I know as you have time to contemplate this plan, disturbing thoughts will arise. 'What if one of my brothers doesn't do what he is supposed to do?' you ask. We'll know, and we'll respond to that disloyalty; have no fear. And each segment of the plan has at least two redundant instruction sets to ensure execution. We also know you brothers are religious and you love Allah, and guilt sometimes creeps into men's consciences. We understand. We have also included a few sets of useless and inert instructions. If your heart falters, perform your duty and believe that Allah has chosen for you these instructions, absolving you of the guilt. But perform your task to prove your loyalty to Him. You will be rewarded here on earth and in heaven. I know hundreds of thousands or more of fellow Muslims will die, though they won't die in vain. The time has come when this price must be paid."

Ghazali paused a moment for effect. "When I leave this room tonight, my role in this task is complete. You, my brothers, will carry out the most glorious of all acts to rush in the everlasting glorious age of Allah!"

Chapter Thirty-Seven

Thursday, February 12

Ghazali waited until his soldiers had cleared the small warehouse. The plot was in motion, and no one could derail it. Waving one of his deputies over, he suddenly burst into a fit of coughing. Abdul Al-Barr trotted over, and Ghazali asked, "Did you notice anyone or anything that might lead you to think any of these soldiers aren't committed to the plan?"

The Arabic man shook his head. "We watched them closely when we directed them out and didn't notice any suspicious behavior. Mansur, they're dedicated and willing to perform what is necessary."

"I agree. I don't have a lot of energy tonight, but it seems I didn't need it. I thought they responded well. Very well. I just wanted to make sure I read them correctly." He swept more sweat from his brow.

"You did," Abdul Al-Barr confirmed.

"And since your arrival, you and the others understand what is needed?"

"Yes, Mansur. We have everything in place, but, as you have said, it is really self-executing."

"True, but trouble may arise, and after what Mohammad said in our last conversation, I may have worn out my welcome. Abdul, I've decided it's you. As you know, I'm leaving for a very remote location in Pakistan. No one may be able to contact me for some time. If questions arise, Abdul, you will make the decision. I have complete faith in you. You know me as well as if not better than anyone. You are my true brother, and you will make the same decision I would. I trust you, Brother. I have told those who need to know."

Abdul Al-Barr swallowed several time, trying to stop tears from welling up. The choice was among three of Mansur's inner circle captains, and Abdul couldn't help but feel pride. He cleared his throat. "It's an honor, Mansur. You can rely on me, but I just don't foresee any problems. We have an excellent plan that has been meticulously cultivated for years. And now is the best time to execute it. It is our time."

Mansur smiled. "You're sure no one is questioning your presence here?"

Abdul shook his head. "Not at all."

"Any problems with the Iranians?"

"My Persian brothers have been nothing but hospitable to your humble Arab."

Ghazali smiled. "Good. My Pakistani escort won't arrive until the morning after next, but it's better we don't have much contact. As usual, you will see the signal in my window when I leave. Nothing more."

Abdul nodded. "Good night, Mansur."

"Good night, Abdul."

Ghazali pulled his top coat tightly around him, hoping the cold drizzle wouldn't seep through. After returning to his apartment, he kept shivering after he peeled off the damp coat and sweater. Before settling on the couch to attempt another effort at his cold meal, Ghazali turned up the thermostat, hoping it would warm the room. He watched the news without listening, mentally reviewing the magnificent plan, believing they had considered all angles and that it would proceed smoothly. Massaging his temples, he tossed aside the unwanted food and decided to retire to the bedroom, hoping tomorrow he would feel more like his usual robust self. Spasmodically coughing as he slumped into bed, Ghazali fell instantly aslccp.

In the early morning, Ghazali bolted upright from a fitful sleep and violently vomited through netted fingers. He struggled to the

toilet, and, plopping down on the floor, heaved up bile. He leaned
back, trying to catch his breath; beads of sweat formed on his brow.
Grabbing a washcloth, he swabbed his forehead and wiped his face
with cold water, hoping it would cool his throbbing temperature.
Eerie sirens in the background serenaded his misery. His breath
came only in painful gasps, and his head pounded. He groped his
way toward the outer room as the sirens screamed louder, and
through a haze he saw the TV, still on from the night before,
brandishing the American Terrorist's name. Suddenly, pain seared
down his spine, and he crumpled onto the couch in agony. His breath
seized up in a throttled windpipe; the convulsion didn't subside, and
his lungs screamed for oxygen that wasn't there. Sweat poured all
over his body now, soaking his couch.

The pain leveled off after a few moments, and he reached for the
telephone. Blood started dripping from his nose; he touched his lips
and inspected trembling fingers. Blood there as well. Pain abruptly
shot though him again, racing down his back and into his kidneys. A
fresh wave of nausea washed over him, and bile and blood exploded
out his mouth. He finally grasped the phone with both hands, and
mustering all remaining strength, Ghazali dialed. It rang and rang
and rang and rang. The next time the pain lashed out, his arms
reflexively snapped back; the phone crashed to the floor while the
unanswered ring echoed in his ears.

It finally struck him. He had enough awareness to understand
what fatally confronted him. Though blurred eyes, Ghazali saw the
American Terrorist's face flash across the television screen. Thom
Spencer had attacked Mashhad, and Ghazali was one of his victims.
He convulsed again, more blood gushed out of his mouth, and his
chest heaved heavily.

Sirens blared outside his window, but they weren't rushing to
help Mansur Ghazali. 'How?' echoed in his mind. Surely Spencer
didn't know he hid in Mashhad. Luck, pure luck, Ghazali thought,
and his face twisted in a grotesque grin at the irony. A moment of
rest, and his only comfort was the knowledge he had already
executed his unstoppable plan; that this American Terrorist attack,
assaulting one of most holy cities in Iran, would only increase his
soldiers' zeal. He bared his red-stained teeth in a grimace and tried
to laugh, but all that came out was more blood.

His body contorted in agonizing pain, burning up through

stiffened legs and drilling through the groin into the stomach, and finally assailing his chest. His heart pounded erratically, and Ghazali's bloodshot eyes widened at the intense hammering. He prayed for Allah to call him to heaven and grant him entrance into a garden of rippling streams of water. He grasped blindly for his sacred Qur'an, but lurched off the couch to writhe on the floor without finding it. The final convulsion forced blood from his mouth and nose one last time, spewing out the last ounce of Mansur Ghazali's life.

Chapter Thirty-Eight

Thursday, February 12

He heard a man approach and felt his arm grasped firmly, but not roughly. The unknown escort guided him to a door into what sounded like an alley from sounds echoing off buildings and then to a busy street. There the escort took off the blindfold and asked him as a brother in a gentle whisper to keep his head turned the other direction. Tishtar Tahman Zandi nodded and waited a few moments. Realizing he was alone, he looked around and walked up the street, searching for a taxi. After a few minutes, he saw one and hailed it, climbed in gratefully, wiping the sleet off his hair and face.

The cab driver had pumped up the heat. He leaned forward and gave the driver the name of his hotel. The perspiring man stared at him with red-rimmed sunken eyes, and Zandi flinched back, fearing the cabby had caught a cold or the flu. Fortunately he wouldn't endure a long ride, since he had chosen a hotel near the warehouse.

Tishtar entered the stark, empty lobby and quickly walked through the silent hallways to his room. Once inside, he sat on the bed and unfolded his instruction sheet: just a few lines of text ordering him to set a specific duty rotation for the Natanz Missile Launch site, and five names appeared with dates. He didn't know whether all five men were Universal Jihad soldiers, or just two, or none. Other men could easily schedule these men at these times, but he did such rotations routinely. By virtue of his scheduling authority, the right person or people would occupy the seats to oversee the actual launch.

The next set of lines listing four dates—the first less than two weeks away—required his presence at the missile site. The instructions included no other commands.

Ghazali had said he would receive a simple set of orders, and so they were. Zandi understood exactly what Universal Jihad asked of him. A man with his rank, a full colonel in the Missile Forces of the Air Force of the Army of the Guardians of the Islamic Revolution, could offer valuable assistance on the day the command was given to launch on Israel. Undoubtedly a successful launch would require a complicit few above his rank, but his presence could avoid a command bottleneck and aid in the operation's efficiency. Zandi frowned, however; he immediately recognized he was an important cog, but not a necessary one. They could launch without him.

As Tishtar scanned the small sheet of paper, he nodded in appreciation of its elegance. Ghazali had probably scheduled a test on the first date, but perhaps not. And maybe others had different dates. As he reflected on possible scenarios launching a nuclear missile, he identified several men who could perform his role in the plot. Zandi calculated twelve stages, from the initial launch command to the missile launch itself, where Universal Jihad needed an executed order for success. He pinpointed particular men in each link of the command chain down to the soldier who would enter the code and turn the fateful key. Pondering these men, he nodded again, confident each one would perform the task without question. In fact, he suspected the commands would evoke delight. Each named soldier exuded the aura of a Universal Jihadist; all of them would face any consequence and embrace death to accomplish the mission and thus gloriously receive Allah's adulation. He envisioned a million Jews suffering by their hands.

Zandi then tested the redundancy of the plot. At each stage, he named to himself at least one other person who could perform the task, and each one again fit the profile of a Universal Jihad operative. Of course, he didn't definitely know whether any of them were members, just as no one definitively knew he was. Universal Jihad's brilliant structure purposely concealed these horizontal operatives.

Blindfolded, he couldn't determine the number of members

present at the warehouse meeting. However, based on the heat and breathing patterns he had detected, he had no doubt Ghazali had enough soldiers to insure the success of the operation, redundancy included.

Zandi stood, stretched, and sighed heavily. He stared at himself in the mirror, thinking first about the tactical logistics of the nuclear missile launch and then pondering the entire grandiose scheme. Mansur Ghazali just might achieve all he proclaimed he would.

Zandi filled a glass with water and drank deeply. The depth of Ghazali's network impressed him. The master terrorist had entangled America, several governments, including Iran's and Israel's, and an extensive number of nongovernmental organizations into his web of intrigue. Universal Jihad's penetration went further than he had originally thought.

But did Ghazali really believe he alone had the foresight to place agents inside the ranks of the enemy? Zandi smirked at the man's arrogance. Did he really believe the Central Intelligence Agency sat idly by without also implementing programs and operations to penetrate Iranian military forces or Universal Jihad?

Tishtar Tahman Zandi's parents had lived in Iran as CIA operatives for decades. His training began as a toddler, and when praying five times daily, he always silently finished each prayer with a glorious tribute to Abraham's God, Yhwh. He started a family himself and climbed the ranks of the military establishment, reaching colonel at a young age all the while secretly applying formidable game theory skills on the Persians. His star shone brightly, and he planned to ascend to even higher ranks; his idol, Eli Cohen, had nothing on him.

But Ghazali's revelation tonight changed everything.

Zandi brushed his teeth, still contemplating. He knew immediate communication with his handler could jeopardize his position. Too risky someone monitored him, and without the right equipment and safeguards, Ghazali's extensive organization might detect his communication. Besides, he mused, Universal Jihad might have enacted tonight's drama as a ploy to detect informants. Once home, he would devise a plan where he could safely contact and inform the CIA of Ghazali's deadly intentions.

As he tossed and turned in bed, Zandi wondered what the CIA would do to prevent the plot. He was not an inner-circle member of

UJ and had neither met nor seen Ghazali. Even tonight, he still hadn't seen him, but at least he could give the Agency Ghazali's location, though the terrorist surely had fled the city.

Ghazali's presence in Iran surprised Zandi; he thought he had enough clout to know whether Ghazali lived in the country. But it wouldn't shock the Agency. Despite Zandi's suggestion otherwise, his handler had implied the CIA believed Ghazali skulked somewhere inside Persian borders. Tonight's appearance confirmed the Agency's suspicion. It wouldn't matter. What he was about to divulge would shuffle the CIA's priorities; preventing a nuclear nightmare would replace the terrorist's capture at the top of the list. His eyelids started to droop and he finally slept, confident he could provide the Agency enough time to foil Ghazali's grand scheme.

Chapter Thirty-Nine

Friday, February 13

The loud knock on the hotel door startled Zandi awake. Screeching sirens nearly drowned out the next rap. He rubbed his eyes and shook his head, immediately devising an escape route. Someone, he thought, had discovered his true identity, and now he would have to face an unpleasant interrogation. Zandi cracked the shutter just slightly to peer out just as an emergency vehicle whizzed past. Maybe they weren't after him, so he rejected the suicide option. Another loud knock and Zandi decided to risk opening the door.

The moment after he tugged at the handle, a large, thick-chested man burst in, knocking Zandi against the wall. Zandi, surprised by the sudden action, instinctively lashed out, landing a blow to the invader's cheek.

Instead of retaliating, the huge man held up his huge hands, capitulating. "Stop! I'm here to help you! Don't you know? The American Terrorist has attacked Mashhad!"

Zandi hesitated, stunned by the news. The invader peered at him closely. "You don't look sick."

"I...I don't feel sick," he mumbled.

"No fever, no chills, no nausea?" the man gruffly inquired.

Zandi shook his head.

"You haven't contracted the infection then. Good. Get dressed. You're coming with me."

Zandi's internal alarms sounded, stiffening at the man's tone.

"Do you want to risk getting it? I can take you to a secure location," his enormous intruder offered.

Zandi frowned. "Why go with you? Who are you?"

"That's not important. But you're coming with me. Now, you got one good poke at my face, do you think you get another?" His unwavering stare and folded arms left no room for argument. Zandi felt trapped, but the wailing sirens reinforced the man's reason, and another capitulation in a second struggle didn't appear likely, so Zandi reluctantly complied.

His new escort guided him out of the hotel and into a parked vehicle with no further explanation. From the back seat, Zandi observed eerily echoing streets occupied only by first responders. No riots, no protests, no clamor of people demanding action, and it dawned on him. Most were dead or dying, and the few survivors didn't dare move, deathly fearful of contagion. Spencer had wiped out the entire city.

They drove in silence for nearly an hour to a hospital outside Mashhad. On arrival, his escort quickly ushered him though the emergency doors and to the elevators. On the fourth floor, a nurse shuffled him into a room and ordered him to disrobe. His clothes were gathered, and a doctor came in and performed a thorough examination with very few words exchanged. After the physical, the doctor departed without providing any further information. Several long hours passed. Nothing indicated his cover had been blown; Zandi waited patiently, knowing his best move was to cooperate. Finally his beefy escort barged through the door absent a knock and bluntly ordered him to await instructions, and that the staff would provide anything he needed. Just as he was leaving, the large man turned his head and grumbled, "Be prepared to stay here for a few days or more."

Zandi waited eight days. With no access to any media, he still knew nothing but the bare facts: the American Terrorist's death toll exceeded two million, and no one had died outside Mashhad. During those eight days, he displayed no emotion, mindlessly complying with minimal requests. The night before he had arrived at the hospital, he had fallen asleep confident he could advise the CIA of Ghazali's plan. He had always assumed he could safely navigate his family and himself out of Iran. His family knew nothing about his covert CIA identity, but he had conditioned his wife and son someday to expect a sudden departure, blaming unpredictable and dangerous policies as the reason. They accepted his warning, and never spoke of it with anyone. The American Terrorist's attack ruined his initial escape plan, and his mind constantly drifted toward his wife and son.

He loved them, but they were leverage he used to increase his worth. He had to risk a family; it created the necessary thickened societal bonds to engender trust over the years. A man without a family was smoke in the wind; his family had undeniably helped him attain his rank and position. But all leverage is a form of debt, and all debts had to be paid. So now he had to employ his considerable game-theory skills and remove the leverage to save their lives. Over and over again, he silently played out all the scenarios he could.

Despite no direct confirmation, it became clear Universal Jihad had rescued him from the hotel. The military had no idea he was in Mashhad, and no one but his UJ contact knew where he stayed. The hospital had no military presence, and he sensed the other patients had attended the meeting at the warehouse. None appeared sick, and they all exchanged the same discreet, conspiratorial looks. Of course, no one communicated, abiding by Universal Jihad's rule. And no one communicated with him about Ghazali's plan, but nothing indicated Universal Jihad had aborted its nuclear attack, and Zandi assumed the timetable would be kept.

As the days passed, he noticed his floor quietly emptied, and he harbored suspicions about where his fellow patients had gone. His sequestration precluded him from contacting his handler, and the clock ticked while he still fretted away in the hospital.

One night as the nurse entered his room with a tray of food, an unrecognized man—slim in build with a moustache and dressed in a knee-length dark leather jacket—slipped in behind her. With a pointed glance from him, the nurse scurried from the room. Zandi sprinkled some seasoning on his food, and, without looking up, declared, "I need to leave. Quickly. I've been away too long."

The man nodded. "Soon, but we have to talk first."

Zandi sighed. "After more than a week? I don't know anything. No TV's, no radios, no communication. Doubt I'm in prison, but it seems like it." he accused.

"No, you are not in prison. We just had to regroup. Colonel

Zandi, Mansur Ghazali is dead."

A knife clanged on the floor, dropped by a genuinely stunned Zandi. He didn't doubt his visitor's revelation, and he had to collect himself and respond appropriately, as if grief stricken. Putting his hand to his mouth, he slowly rose and staggered toward the window. The man allowed him a few moments of silence. Tapping the ledge, Zandi asked in an even voice, "The American Terrorist?"

Zandi saw the man's nod in the window's reflection, and nearly laughed at the irony, but forced it into a sob.

The reflection pressed its lips tightly together and shook its head. "We don't think Spencer had any idea Mansur was in Mashhad. It was just an awful fluke. Mansur was in and out of the city so often…Allah must have willed it and called him home."

Zandi wiped his eyes. "Of course we don't have time to mourn him properly, but tell me, was he at least appropriately washed, wrapped in cloth, and buried for his journey?"

"We don't think so. Not out of disrespect, but for health purposes. We're not certain how they disposed of the bodies, but we do know most didn't receive the proper rituals. It's horrible out there, and it couldn't be avoided."

Zandi feigned distress at the response. After pausing a few moments, he asked, "And so why are you here?"

"Because of Mansur Ghazali's self-executing plan."

Contorting his face in anger, Zandi wheeled and shouted, "So why am I still here? We're losing valuable time. We must act and respond to this filthy American Terrorist!"

The man lowered his head in respect. "After hearing of Mansur Ghazali's death, which we learned early the morning after the meeting, we had to determine who was dead and who survived. The plan was in motion, but if not enough men remained, it couldn't proceed. We retrieved you and others to make that determination. It took longer than expected. After several days, we realized only a few from the meeting didn't survive. Most of you had traveled to Mashhad, and that appears to be the difference between living and dying. If you were a Mashhad resident, you died. If not, you lived."

Zandi maintained his furious glare. "And the only thing I've heard is that two million people died. All in Mashhad. Is this true?"

"Yes."

"Then the plan has to proceed. Now more than ever," Zandi

exclaimed.

"Yes."

"And who's overseeing this?"

"It really hasn't been about overseeing anything, Colonel. As Mansur told us, it is really a self-executing plan. A few of us have helped those needed at distant places get there. We've been transporting men these last couple of days."

Zandi had his suspicions confirmed, and it didn't surprise him.

His slim visitor tightened the belt around his leather jacket and stuck his hands in the pockets. "I come now to ask if you remember your instructions. Do you know where you are supposed to be and what to do?"

"Of course."

"Very good."

"And so what now?"

"I take you there."

"And that's it. You don't know anything else?"

The man shrugged. "I only know that of the four dates given, only the first matters. I don't know your instructions. If you tell me where you need to be, I will take you there. It will happen."

Zandi read the man's expression. He lied. He knew exactly where Zandi had to go, and more than that. Demanding passage anywhere except the location in his instructions would have sentenced Zandi to death. But his captor did reveal one thing: only the first date mattered, which per the issued instructions meant Zandi must assume a three-day countdown to the launch. Many of the possible games that he had played out in his head imploded, and finding time to contact the CIA suddenly became even more difficult.

"Do you know where I work?"

"No," his captor lied.

"I work at an air force base. I need to contact it so they know I survived."

"We have contacted all necessary state agencies and notified them that you and others have survived. We were ordered to hold you in quarantine for obvious purposes. The quarantine period has ended, and you can return to work. We will accompany you there on the appointed day. We trust you are scheduled to work."

He nodded. "I should be there by nine in the morning on that day."

"Very well, Colonel."

"And my family. Has anyone had the decency to contact them?"

"Yes. They know you're safe."

Zandi slyly scrutinized the man's expression. He told the truth. "And I presume I cannot see them?"

"Not until after."

Zandi grimaced. "That means I might never see them."

His captor remained expressionless.

At Zandi's dismissive nod, the man rose and turned to depart. Zandi stopped him short. "Aren't you interested in which one?"

"Which one what?"

"Which air force base, of course," Zandi smirked.

Catching the man in the lie didn't change his expression; he simply stood there indifferently, his hand still on the doorknob. Zandi returned to his meal without saying another word, and his captor walked out the door.

Chapter Forty

Monday, February 16

The newly reconstructed war room beneath the White House vaunted an orchestra of ultra-high-tech equipment. Each wall was an immense super full high-definition screen, which could display a single interface or several at a time. Below the screens, three-dimensional holographic and virtual platforms delivered detailed graphic information, providing the analysts, technicians, and agents with powerful data. These experts sat at rows of modular desks, each with additional super full high-definition and virtual computing stations accessing the displayed information and all relevant databases. When the president wanted information, they quickly and efficiently retrieved it; when the president demanded analysis, they quickly and efficiently provided it; when he executed a command, they quickly and efficiently implemented it.

Behind these stations, on a large, raised dais, a huge table lorded over the war room. When the president entered, the flip of a switch transformed it into a secure logistical headquarters for all presidential operations. The table's granite veneer masked a translucent super full high-def touchscreen computerized interface, which could instantly offer individualized holographic keyboards, complete with tactile texture, where information was transferred from one station to another with simple conductor-like finger swipes—all accomplished in sound-proofed seclusion.

President Halladan sat at one end of the enormous interface with every other chair occupied and still more people standing behind them. A super full high-def ovoid monitor—called the Egg—where everyone on in the room had a perfectly angled view, held everyone's attention.

The numbers from Mashhad continued to grow. The most recent estimate of nearly two million deaths indicated the attack hadn't spared any sector, and journalists who risked traveling to the infected city displayed shocking photographs. Everyone watched aghast as bodies piled up. Mel somberly stood near the monitor, watching nearly in a daze. Her failure to capture Spencer had caused this catastrophe. She couldn't help but blame herself for these deaths, and she wondered how many around the dais stole an accusatory glance in her direction. She didn't notice any, but she probably had missed a few.

When the latest report finished, the president gestured for Andy Mahony to shut off the Egg. It silently retreated into the ceiling. With hands folded, Halladan spoke somberly. "The attack is unprecedented. Up until now, we have had good excuses. Frankly, when Ghazali retaliated with several terrorist attacks against our country after Gaza, the world expected us to prioritize Ghazali, despite believing Spencer would respond. We were justified in expending our resources to stop future terrorist attacks on our soil, and we succeeded. And when Spencer did infect Damascus, the weapon's efficiency really was the only surprise, not the attack itself. Now, after Mashhad, we don't have any more excuses. The magnitude and numbers can't be ignored. Strategic competitors, allies, trading partners, friends and foes alike will look to the United States and me to do something to find Spencer or counter his weapon, since we are the only nation that has the resources and capabilities to do so. I know many leaders, both foreign and domestic, blame me for Mashhad. But I reject that blame, and dismiss any guilt associated with it, and so must you. We didn't launch the attack, we didn't support it, we didn't know about it, and we couldn't have prevented it. Right now, we cannot sit around and wallow in our self-pity, our doubts, and start casting blame among ourselves. It's unproductive. It sounds callous, I know, but we must concentrate on what's ahead of us, and anyone can do the math. The American Terrorist will strike again, and if the next attack increases at the same rate, we're looking at ten million deaths, probably more. Somehow, Thom Spencer has developed an agent to inflict this magnitude of death. At this time, Dr. Meredith O'Brien will brief you on her findings and offer some direction."

The president nodded at a striking forty-five-year-old woman, dressed in a black skirt and silk blouse. She returned the nod and said, "Thank you, Mr. President." She stepped from the ring surrounding the table and walked to the president's left. "For those of you who don't know me, I am with Office of Science and Technology, and I work with the Centers for Disease Control and Prevention and the Department of Defense. My job has focused on nanotechnology and its applications in the biomedical field and biological warfare. When the American Terrorist first attacked Gaza, and we learned of Spencer's identity, the president brought me into the loop immediately. I was charged with finding the biological agent that could produce this kind of result.

"First, we needed to investigate the actual substance, or at least something it had infected. An American wishing to examine a victim of the American Terrorist presented a problem, but our Israeli friends helped, and we obtained a body. I flew to Tel Aviv and did an autopsy and in-depth analysis, and, candidly, what we found wasn't surprising."

She paused and swallowed before continuing. "Everyone in this room has top-secret clearance, and you need it for what I am about to tell you. It shouldn't come as a shock, and it wouldn't to the public, but we still must not publicly acknowledge or divulge any of this information. The United States hasn't been sitting on its haunches as everyone else develops bio-defense serums. There is little doubt we dominate the world in the technology. Our only surprise was that a private American citizen had developed it as well. But given the flow of technology and information in this day and age, it didn't test the limits of credibility. Spencer's serum and its effects are quite similar to those developed by us."

"And what were those effects, Doctor? Exactly how are these people dying?" an admiral sitting at the table blurted.

"Until now, only a few people besides the president know what we know. The victims die from a virus-like substance that generates Ebola-like and ALS-like symptoms. By that I mean that we see evidence of nerve and organ damage, accelerated so quickly that the body essentially begins decomposing while the subject is still alive. When the decay hits a critical level, the subject begins to experience pain, as we saw on the American Terrorist's video, but then dies relatively quickly."

"And what causes this decomposition?" another voice at the table asked.

She pursed her lips. "In general, here's what we think. It's similar to a retrovirus, but at the nano level. An agent is triggered in the body, and this agent is identified by the immune system as virus-like, and is attacked. The agent, this virus-like compound, recombines with phagocyte and lymphocyte cells in the immune system, and resequences them to attack the host instead of attacking foreign agents, as they are supposed to do. They apparently target the proteins in the major organs and the spinal cord. These toxic resequenced phagocytes and lymphocytes replicate at an extraordinary rate, and the result is death."

All the people around the table shifted uncomfortably and grimaced; she continued unemotionally. "Now, people, we have developed agents that cause similar resequencing, but that doesn't mean we can definitively identify what Spencer's serum is. Unfortunately, his agent, once it contacts the immune system, is then encoded by a sequence or a restriction enzyme of sorts, and dissolves into its bases, which can't be distinguished from human bases. It's tricky, but that appears to be exactly what Spencer and Tyler Washington have done, and as a result we can't backward engineer it to quantify the chemical composition."

Harry Stanton, special counsel to the president, abruptly leaned forward. "Dr. O'Brien, you said it has similar effects to the pathogens you have produced, correct?"

Dr. O'Brien, very worried about the next question, shrugged noncommittally, her face carefully neutral.

"How similar? Enough for someone to claim that it really is one of ours?" Stanton asked, alarmed.

So there it was. The question she had wanted to avoid, but couldn't. If the American Terrorist had coincidentally formulated the same or similar toxin her laboratories had produced, and if someone discovered this fluke, many around the world would immediately assert collusion between the United States and the American Terrorist in a state of accusatory hysteria. Despite evidence to the contrary, the international community would always inextricably link the appalling attacks with her government, creating endless diplomatic woe.

"Perhaps, Mr. Stanton," she answered with a grimace. "It's unlikely they're exactly the same, because we've traced back all of our chemicals to produce our toxin, and we can't detect any purchasing patterns that match ours. But, Spencer and our labs both could have independently developed similar formulas, and the technology will probably be very comparable."

Eyes bulged as everyone suddenly grasped the implication. Stanton scowled. "If this was ever leaked, do you realize the accusation we would have to refute? No one would ever believe that there was any independence of any sort. It doesn't matter if it's the same, similar or whatever, they would claim Spencer was working directly for us!"

"Yes, I know," she answered in a troubled tone, "but, Mr. Stanton, this isn't the primary concern we have now."

"What? Are you kidding?" Secretary of State Townsend asked incredulously, envisioning himself trying to explain the coincidence to heads of states, the UN, and the world in general. The vision quickly imploded into a nightmare. "And what could be worse than this?" Halladan waved off his secretary of state's question, and Townsend pressed his lips together firmly as he clasped his hands on the table in frustration.

Dr. O'Brien sighed. "Our present concern is how it's triggered; not with what, but how Spencer directly attacks the victims. Since we have a fairly good idea how the toxin works, we've done some extensive modeling. Spencer has shown he can surgically infect populations, wiping out targeted areas entirely." She motioned for Mahony to drop the oval screen again from the ceiling as she stepped forward and started the maestro finger manipulations on the translucent tabletop, which immediately appeared on the Egg. "This is the area affected, which as you can see is the entire city." Continuing the orchestration, she explained, "And this shows the progression of the infection from the information we obtained. Now, as you can see, it doesn't start in the north and move south or in the west and move east. Instead, it's uniform throughout the defined territory. And the other quirky nature of this attack: no one to date outside the defined territory has been affected. And that characteristic persists in all the attacks. Now, some outliers might pop up later, but basically you can draw a perimeter on the affected area, and no one dies outside that line."

The ability to control contagion with such precision incited even greater anxiety in the room. "When we model this," she said exhaling as she surveyed drawn faces, "we come up with a possible scenario that might accomplish it." Everyone hunched or leaned forward ever so slightly. "We think he emits an airborne pathogen, that it is spread from person to person over a period of time. Because of the way it interacts with the immune system, this agent probably lies dormant or inert in fatty cells. But then how does he trigger it? Time release? But metabolism rates differ, and we would notice significant staggering in the appearance of symptoms. After working through several possibilities, we finally discovered a plausible method."

"When you say trigger it," another table-sitter asked, "do you mean he personally delivers it or is it triggered by some sort of suicide bio-bomber?"

"Good question. We don't know. If there is an inoculation, then he might be able to do it himself. But we think he triggers it by a coordinated encoded emission of waves along the electromagnetic spectrum. We don't know how or what component he uses to emit the waves, just that it could very well work."

"You mean," Stanton said to clarify, "kind of like a garage-door opener, and the contaminated area is controlled by its range?"

She nodded. "More complex, but essentially yes. And now I'm going to turn the meeting over to Dr. Tray Dupree from NASA to explain this further."

A man wearing tailored clothes, a graying goatee, and nostalgic bifocal glasses rose from his seat as he tossed aside some papers. In a deep, rich voice he said, "I wish I could meet all of you in better circumstances. I am Tray Dupree from NASA. Many of you are probably wondering why someone from National Aeronautics Space Administration is here today. We helped launch the latest weather and advanced GPS satellite system. And since as my colleague has mentioned, everyone here has security clearance for this topic of discussion, I don't mind telling you that our weather satellite system can do a few more things than what is generally advertised, and that it assists other special agencies despite past directives to the contrary.

"Now, Dr. O'Brien approached me with a problem and wondered if I could help. She asked if I could formulate a method of detecting a complex wave signal like the one she proposed the American Terrorist is using. Of course, we don't know what his code is, but I don't think we need it. As Dr. O' Brien said, there aren't any cases outside a defined area, and we know all cases arise relatively at the same time, so it must be triggered by a code complex enough that it wouldn't be accidentally triggered by something such as the earlier-suggested garage-door opener. I wrote a program for our satellites that I think will detect such a complex signal. I can't state for a fact that it will work, but I've been working on it nearly day and night since Dr. O'Brien came to us, and we've just started running the initial program while we work out the bugs."

"So, once the agent has been triggered, you think you can detect it?" a table-sitter asked.

"Not the agent, but the trigger itself," he clarified.

"And how does that help?" Townsend asked politely.

"Well, in theory, the satellite will detect the emission. Agent Dellendale from the FBI has formed rapid deployment forces to be stationed around the globe. Upon detection, the nearest team will be mobilized with localized mobile electromagnetic traces to pinpoint precisely the location and destroy the trigger source. We hope to find Thom Spencer at that source."

Townsend grunted. "But it's an electromagnetic wave, Doctor. Once it emits, the cat is out of the proverbial bag, and that's it. It's triggering the toxin at literally the speed of light. You can't destroy it fast enough."

Dr. Dupree shrugged. "Not necessarily. If Spencer tests his trigger in a controlled environment, we have chance of capturing him before the next attack."

Townsend looked skeptically at Dupree. "Have you detected any possible emissions?"

Dupree nodded. "Actually, yes, Secretary Townsend. We detected two emissions almost immediately. However, before we deploy teams, we trace the code to see if we can find the source and confirm its origins. If we can't, then we deploy the team. In both instances, we confirmed the source in less than a minute. They were ours."

Townsend's expression soured. "What do you mean *ours*?"

Dupree shrugged. "US government signals. Actually DoD or NSA to be more precise. We have a large database with many codes already accounted for, but some of those are off-limits to most because of their top-secret nature. We figured we might run into a few of those issues, so we established communication lines with all agencies. We also have identified certain areas, inside Russia and China for instance, as undeployable. We doubt those codes would be Thom Spencer."

Townsend sighed. "Yeah, yeah, yeah, and what is the likelihood that Thom Spencer will really transmit one of these controlled test signals?"

Dupree shrugged once more. "That isn't my area of expertise. I'm just asked to detect them. I think I can."

Townsend shifted his inquisition to Dr. O'Brien. "So, Doctor, what do you think?"

She deferred as well. "That also isn't my area of expertise. Agent Dellendale, do you care to comment?"

All eyes on the dais shifted to Mel. Townsend's piercing set darted there first, but they softened with the secretary instantly remembering his previous sardonic exchange with the agent. Mel didn't hesitate. "It's a secondary tactic, Mr. Secretary. We don't think it is likely Spencer will transmit independent of an attack."

Townsend appreciated Mel's direct assessment. "So, that leaves our primary tactic at the point of Spencer's next attack. Not a controlled environment of any sort, but when he's actually killing people, correct?"

Townsend looked back at Dr. O'Brien, who rubbed her forehead and temple with her index finger and thumb. She exhaled heavily. "We think there's a chance that it requires significant exposure to the waves before triggered. If so, Mr. Secretary, then we can save many lives."

Townsend immediately recognized the doctor's skepticism about her latest assertion. "But that's not the only reason, is it, Doctor?"

"No, it isn't, Secretary Townsend."

"So does the subject have to be alive or dead?" he asked bluntly.

Eyes scattered and jiggled throughout the room. Everyone had followed the colloquy up to that point, but Townsend's strange question interrupted the logical flow.

O'Brien tried to remove the confusion. "If we can capture a subject before the toxin decomposes in the body, before it breaks down into those bases I earlier described, then we can trace its constituent parts. From that, we try tracing the origins of those chemicals. If it is anything like our serums, some of the chemicals might be rare enough that we can trace them to the manufacturer. There have to be physical deliveries, and maybe we can pick up a trail."

"You didn't answer my question, Doctor. Alive or dead?" Townsend repeated.

"Alive," she answered.

"And then dead to perform your procedure?" Townsend pressed.

"Yes, but the subject would've died no matter what from the pathogen."

"So it's really not murder if the subject is for certain dying at a later date. Boy, that's something any criminal defense attorney would love, since that sort of defense could logically apply to all murders, right? If you're only hurrying them along into the grave, it doesn't count anymore."

Secretary Townsend's self-righteous moral indignation snapped O'Brien's patience. "Apparently, Secretary Townsend, you're accusing me of murder."

Townsend nodded, inviting the possibility. "Dr. O'Brien, you're beating around the bush here. You have Dr. Dupree's array detect an attack so that you can rush to that location and kill a potential victim before the American Terrorist's pathogen does in order to harvest the chemicals before they decay."

Dr. O'Brien's shoulders slumped. "Yes, Mr. Secretary. And save that person from feeling the pain I witnessed on that video. I guarantee you that there will be no suffering."

"*You*, Dr. O'Brien, are still killing him."

Dr. O'Brien set her jaw. "I know. Risks and extreme actions are needed to find this Thom Spencer before he decides his next perimeter is the entire nation of Pakistan or worse."

"Just a single *him*?" Townsend persisted. "I doubt one will do. You will need at least two, a man and a woman, and probably more than one of each, right? If my science methodology is correct, you can't leave the operation to the chance of a single subject, can you?

How many, Dr. O'Brien?"

Dr. O'Brien swallowed under the prosecution. "That hasn't been determined yet," she mumbled.

Halladan intervened. "Mason, I don't like it either, but I don't think we can avoid some of these options. There's no sense in persecuting Dr. O'Brien under these circumstances."

Mason Townsend nodded his agreement. "I know, Mr. President. And I know, Doctor, you don't offer this plan lightly and without significant reservations. I just think it's important for everyone in this room to grasp the actions we might have to take and why. We need transparency. And I'm not just referring to the moral implications here. Obviously these subjects that Dr. O'Brien terminates in this operation are going to be Muslim people, and if it is revealed that we took these actions, there will be repercussions, despite all of the justifications we assert. Many will use it to further impugn us, even though we do it for their benefit, and it doesn't matter that the subject would have died irrespective. They will use it as political capital no matter the hypocrisy."

Some people appeared thoughtful, some skeptical, and some frustrated while all of them had concern, but no one voiced an opinion or question, so everyone's attention reflexively returned to the president. Halladan surveyed the congregation around the table. "I want to make it clear. We must find this trigger and this toxic agent. The magnitude of the latest attack presents huge risks for everyone. We simply cannot have anyone else possessing this technology. We cannot afford having Spencer captured and then turning over the information. We can't risk him turning on our allies, or worse yet, on us. It is imperative we locate Thom Spencer. Although different agencies and bureaus have taken various steps toward finding him, we will now adopt one coordinated effort to locate, contain, and capture him, and more importantly the toxin and trigger he has created. Each of you in this room will be responsible for a specific task. In some cases, it won't be much different from what you've been doing; in others, it will be entirely new. But, people, the stakes have been raised immensely, and, as you can imagine, all the world's eyes are on us. Fairly or unfairly, we must find this man, and quickly."

The president leaned back in his chair, and Chief of Staff Mac Stenberg started barking orders. After another hour of briefings, Mel finally could escape the war room. As she walked toward the door, someone touched her arm. She turned, finding Daman Pryce staring at her.

"I didn't see you in there, Daman."

"Didn't want to be seen," he replied.

"Oh. Playing the spook."

"That's my job."

"Yes, it is. And mine is finding Spencer. For real this time, I think."

Pryce pressed his lips together and cocked his head. "That directive seems to be on a sliding scale."

Mel dropped her eyelids slowly and sighed. Her resigned expression suggested the vacillating protocol had fatiguing effects.

Daman's blue eyes softened sympathetically. "Before you go and find him, how about we find a nice quiet spot and take a break from all this?"

She stopped just short of the door. Her crystal blue eyes twinkled. "Actually, I was requested to give a few people my detailed briefings. I finished those late last night, and until they respond, I have some free time, and I do need a break, Daman."

"And would those briefings have anything to do with finding a contaminated subject so that we can trace our terrorist's serum? Did you have something to do with that idea as well?"

Mel's shoulders slumped as she nodded. "It seems like Dr. O'Brien took all the blame. It was nice of her not to throw me under the bus."

Daman chuckled, recalling how quickly O'Brien claimed the primary tactic as hers, but deferred to Mel on the unlikely 'secondary tactic.' "Maybe, or she really thinks it will work, and she wants the credit."

Mel frowned. "Oh well. Good for her. I really don't care. It's simply the most promising lead I have, and if we don't pursue it, how many more Mashhads will we endure?"

"How promising is it, Mel?"

Mel pursed her lips. "It will be the beginning of Spencer's end, Daman. If I didn't think it would eventually lead to his capture, I wouldn't recommend such a...such a...." She couldn't finish her sentence.

"I know, Mel," he replied soothingly. "I understand."

She dropped her guard. "I know you do, Daman." That's another reason why she had attached herself to him, she thought to herself. "Do you have someplace close by? We can't be too far away."

The brilliant blue eyes danced and his smile indicated he was prepared. "I have just the place in mind."

Chapter Forty-One

Tuesday, February 17

As she lay there staring at Daman dozing, Mel tried to push the guilt away. Several months ago she couldn't take time for a rendezvous in a DC hotel when Ghazali had victimized Americans, yet when an American launched attacks, Daman and she suddenly had time to spark the latent flame kindling between them. And after two million died, they didn't extinguish it but further fanned it. The difference: America was on offense with the American Terrorist.

As shameful as it made her feel, she couldn't help reflect on the emotion that permeated the country. Americans, shocked by the Mashhad deaths, could and did sympathize. But below the surface, quiet determination quickly followed the perfunctory demands that America must apprehend Thom Spencer, satisfying the politically correct code of conduct. Pangs of guilt disappeared in images of a devastated Miami, exploding weddings, and decapitated children.

Americans fully expected retaliation from Ghazali and Universal Jihad, but they believed they still had the upper hand, and the American Terrorist would forcefully respond. An odd, quiet confidence had returned and swelled in her country. 'If it's going to happen, let's get it on,' was the mood, and she oddly expressed it herself, trysting at expensive hotels with Daman.

She had made the time to love Daman Pryce, dismissing her equivocations. And she did love him; he knew it, but she didn't know whether he loved her. He knew that fact as well. Behind the spooky persona was a passionate man she found mysteriously thrilling.

She stopped staring at his handsome profile and rolled over. As soon as she moved, Daman opened his eyes and immediately ran his finger gently down her spine. Her body tingled, aroused again by his silent offer. Smiling, she languidly leaned back, her thick blond hair grown longer flowing across their pillows. She caressed his face, staring into brilliant violet eyes, wondering how his eyes changed their color so subtly, yet so dramatically.

Her neo-pager buzzed; she sighed as coveted free hours fizzled to just a few minutes more. Sitting up, she waited, and as she had guessed the president's number flashed. Daman peered over her shoulder to see, and Mel slowly stroked Daman's nose with a slender, well-manicured finger. He gently kissed the tip and rolled over to reach for his clothes.

She answered the phone. "Agent Dellendale." The president requested her presence at the Oval Office immediately.

Again, sitting in the Oval Office, alone and a little tired, Mel's eyes wandered around the room, and the history embodied in those walls again dawned on her. Before the thought had time to penetrate, the door opened, and President Halladan entered, with Chief of Staff Mac Stenberg, Harry Stanton, National Security Adviser Dave Walters, and Andy Mahony all trailing behind him with somber expressions.

Standing, Mel smiled faintly at the president, who motioned for them all to take seats around the table near the center of the room. After sitting there for a moment, staring distantly, deep in thought, Halladan finally rubbed his eyes and focused on her.

"Agent Dellendale," he began, "we've just had some interesting diplomatic conversations with several nations. China and Russia were the two big boys, but several of our allies also chimed in. And basically, they're all sitting this ordeal out. They've expressed their deep concern that weapons possessed by Thom Spencer exist and all that, but they're working on them just as we are, and we all know it. I think they're very afraid that we have developed our bioweapons further than their intelligence sources have suggested, and they don't think the American Terrorist has done all his work by himself. Apparently, though, they've run their scenarios out and deem it possible, so no one is leveling any sort of accusations at us on that front. As a result, and contrary to what I said yesterday, much of the international pressure is off, and given our nation's attitude about Spencer, I'm indifferent to my domestic critics, and that presents options. To be blunt, one of these options is ugly, but it could be very effective."

From the insider glances the men visibly exchanged, Mel predicted more vacillation on that Thom Spencer sliding scale. She shifted her gaze among them impassively. "I'm assuming my American Terrorist protocol is about to change. I'm not to pursue him with as much vigor as requested yesterday?"

The president shrugged. "Perhaps, perhaps not. Given where we are with Russia, China, and others, there isn't much stopping us from simply allowing Thom Spencer to continue with his personal crusade. But we need to understand a few things first, which brings us to our current question for you, Agent Dellendale." He paused. "Is there a chance Spencer is…well…this is strange to say, but that he's actually sane, and that he does have only one goal, and that goal is retribution? Now obviously the man has problems, and what he's doing is atrocious, but I have to tell you, I've had those enraged feelings myself. Acting on them…well, he did it, and I didn't. I don't know, if I had the means, and if I weren't the president of the United States, I still probably wouldn't do it, but then again, I might if my family was murdered like his.

"But is he after something more than what he says? The power Spencer wields is enormous, and that power, once obtained, is intoxicating and rarely relinquished. And with terrorists, Islamic or American, the power and the thrill can transcend the ideology. I need to know if Thom Spencer is such a terrorist. You see, if he's not, then our risk decreases and for reasons that will be explained shortly, it might be in our best interest to place, shall we say, a different priority on Thom Spencer."

Mel blinked her eyes several times. President Halladan wasn't indecisive; the moving target on Thom Spencer just meant all the game pieces were changing rapidly. A new strategy had just emerged where international interference appeared very unlikely, except the president couldn't allow Spencer to transform into a megalomaniac, and suddenly become a danger to those nations who had just withdrawn, or to United States for that matter. That required assuming a mass murderer such as Thom Spencer was mentally stable and wouldn't deviate from his stated objectives.

Although she wasn't a Ph.D. in psychology or a psychiatrist, she had read several reports such specialists submitted. From those reports, and with what she had discovered about him, his background, how he functioned, and especially since she had met him personally, Mel knew Thom Spencer, even better than those specialists. Yet, in the back of her mind, a whisper asked, *But what if you're wrong, Agent Dellendale? How many people are at risk if you are wrong?* Mel considered the whisper and rejected it, staking her decision on one important piece of evidence. "Mr. President, gentlemen, Thom Spencer lost his family to a terrorist. He believed his government couldn't respond, so he did. He's not in this for power or glory; he's in it for revenge, and to eliminate Islamic terrorists from the world. If this is achieved, we would never hear from him again. Of course, we would continue searching for him, but we would be following a cold and stale trail. Now, we have all the reports and analysis to back this up not just from me, but other experts. In addition to all this, there is something he did that just tells me he's not that maniacal terrorist you fear." She paused a moment, staring into expectant faces. "It was the Thurlington assassination. By sending the assassin's body to me, he was sending the message that I—that we—could trust him; that he wouldn't do what you're suggesting. And I don't think it was a ruse or a clever maneuver; I think it was genuine."

They absorbed her analysis with calm expressions; they liked her assessment.

"And you're certain about this?" Harry Stanton asked.

Mel pursed her lips. "As certain as one can be about those sorts of questions, Mr. Stanton."

The president gave a curt nod. "Good. That is the exact case I want you to make for a few of our friends from the Middle East."

The president gestured at Dave Weathers; he took the cue. "Agent Dellendale, we've heard through several sources that many Middle Eastern regimes are destabilizing, and Spencer's attacks are the root of the problem. Tomorrow we want to fuel the fire. In order to survive, we think these governments' best strategy is to uproot and destroy the terrorist organizations and their internal influences. We have a chance to purge many of these governments and, therefore, countries of several layers of terrorists. And let me suggest, if we don't seize this chance, we will rue the day. Cleansing those governments of that influence will put these networks back decades, and they might never recover."

"So," Mel interrupted, "you agree with Spencer. You also think that Middle Eastern governments can purge their nations of these terrorist organizations."

"We do," Weathers answered. "They've always had that ability and still do. Maybe it'll be different in five or ten years, but, currently, terrorists have yet to co-opt these governments. They undoubtedly have their inside supporters, but fear can destroy that support, and we think fear is spreading in those regimes like a virus right now. Their leaders could quietly and efficiently obliterate these networks."

Mel understood their approach and instinctively believed they should exploit the opportunity, especially with China and Russia opting out. "So gentlemen, I am to report that the American Terrorist is solely focused on revenge, and that we don't think he poses any sort of danger to Americans or other friendly nationalities, that we have no certainty of capturing him before the next attack, that our incentives to pursue him aren't as great as they once were, and that maybe our friends from the Middle East should consider complying with his demands. We're just supplying them with a little motivation to act decisively."

"In a nutshell, yes, Agent Dellendale. They might assume we're in collusion with Spencer, but at this point, that might be worth the risk if we rid those countries of the terrorist threats," the president confirmed. "Are you able to do this?"

She chuckled. "Quite easily, gentlemen, since it's the truth." Before she rose to leave, Mel looked curiously at the president. "So, Mr. President, are you really considering changing my protocol again or am I just doing this for the benefit of our Middle Eastern friends tomorrow? Remember the secondary tactic from yesterday? What if Dupree could actually get a lead on Spencer performing some sort of test?"

Halladan rubbed his jaw. "Yes, I remember. We certainly would lose our leverage over those governments if we apprehended Spencer before the next attack, wouldn't we?"

Mel remained silent, refusing to venture into those murky

waters.

"You told us that it was unlikely that he would perform the test, right?" he asked in a pondering voice.

Mel nodded.

"Why?"

"Why would he, Mr. President? Everything seems to working pretty well so far. I don't think he has any reason for any controlled testing."

Halladan pondered a few moments, staring distantly. "Very well, maintain your current protocol, Agent Dellendale."

Chapter Forty-Two

Wednesday, February 18

The next morning, Mel arrived at the White House at the appointed hour, and the president introduced her to ambassadors from Egypt, Pakistan, and Saudi Arabia. The others from last night's meeting were present again, along with Secretary of State Mason Townsend. After the usual diplomatic remarks, the president asked Agent Dellendale to give the ambassadors a briefing on the American Terrorist investigation. Mel succinctly presented the case the president had requested.

At the conclusion of her presentation, Prince Nazir, Ambassador of Saudi Arabia and the apparent spokesman for the trio, looked Mel up and down coldly. "We are to believe that the United States has no affiliation, control, or knowledge of this Thom Spencer, and we are to believe it because you have a woman from the FBI tell us this?" he asked incredulously.

Waves of tension reverberated off the walls. Mel smiled inwardly. She now understood why the president had invited her to this meeting. He was informing the ambassadors that he wasn't contrite and wasn't going to play nice. Halladan had the upper hand, and they would have to accept the presence and the word of a woman FBI agent, not a man.

Secretary Townsend threw Mel a wink only she could see, confirming her thoughts. He then openly laughed, and all three ambassadors swiveled their heads toward him.

His voice low and menacing, Prince Nazir asked, "And what do you find so humorous, Secretary Townsend?"

Townsend rejected the true reason and shifted to another irony. "We all know why you're here. You're here demanding that we hand over Thom Spencer when we've been demanding the same from you with Ghazali. Everyone here in the room knows who more likely can do what. How ironic this situation is, isn't it?"

Halladan smiled. Townsend's blunt nature had a downside, but Halladan liked him and his straight forward assertions. Townsend had served the previous president as ambassador to Saudi Arabia. Halladan remembered how Townsend had answered a particular question during a meeting: 'What country is your primary responsibility?' Expecting the ambassador to blurt 'Saudi Arabia,' Townsend instead answered without hesitation, 'the United States.' He knew the deal.

Prince Nazir displayed pure hostility toward the secretary of state. Nazir, seething, said, "You don't have over two million Muslims dead, Mr. Secretary."

Townsend started to retort; Halladan waved him off. "No, but we have countless terrorist attacks. Regardless, Ambassadors, you've heard our current assessment of Thom Spencer. We can't find him. We are allocating resources to discover his location and stop any additional attacks; we simply cannot guarantee success."

Nazir glowered as he shifted uneasily in his chair. "Mr. President, I want you to know that our countries…and others, those countries that support the entire world oil and gas market, are wondering very much how we continue our production. If I may, I want to make it clear: world markets would be irreparably harmed if we withdrew our oil and gas. If we face these sorts of attacks, our only defense is to use our resources, Mr. President. We also think if we withdraw oil and gas from the markets, many other non-oil-producing countries would begin to side with our position."

There it was. The inner circle Middle Eastern 'oil and gas card' rumor and discussion had now become an official threat. The president, expecting it, answered deadpan. "What position is that, Mr. Ambassador? That they side with you demanding that we find Spencer? Great. Then I will tell those nations exactly what I'm telling you. Publicly. Publicly, so everyone, and I mean everyone, in the world will know exactly which nations made the original demand, and identify, publicly, these other nations willing to defend you in a global resource showdown."

Nazir understood the implication; everyone included the American Terrorist. If the American Terrorist turned his vigilantism toward nations supporting Nazir's position, that support would evaporate quickly. Nazir didn't appreciate how the president played the unfolding chess match. He stared hard at Halladan. "Mr. President, our people can surely withstand such a crisis much better than yours. What is the saying? 'The taller they are, the harder they fall.'"

Halladan leaned forward, nearly smiling. "We realize that, Mr. Ambassador. We know we have purchased your oil and gas to enrich our citizens' lives, while you've used it to suppress your subjects as you subsidize your own lavish lifestyle. But we are under no illusion that you spend your oil money on luxury only. This oil and gas of yours also finances the subversion and your desired destruction of the West. And we know it's a race, Mr. Ambassador. We use your oil to grow our economies right now, but do you know how much coal, oil, and gas our country really possesses? It takes time and money to develop, adapt, and convert it all, but we'll do it, and we'll use those fuels and our technology to create even cheaper and more efficient sources. In fact, that's your greatest fear. Because then you and your nations suddenly become quite impotent, and your subversion of the West a complete and utter failure."

Halladan leaned back and mused aloud, "Let me paint you a picture of the future political landscape you envision. Before we reach the point of self-sufficiency, you will hold us hostage with your oil resources. The West will be literally up in arms, but when it faces this war in thirty, maybe forty years, we'll find our cities populated by substantial Muslim minorities. And maybe some terrorist cell members have surfaced as political leaders, politicizing their seditious efforts just as Hezbollah and Hamas did in Lebanon and Israel, making it difficult or impossible to engage in this war of resources. Suddenly the balance of power shifts from the West to the Middle East. No longer is New York or London the financial capital of the world, but Dubai is. Financing for all fuels except yours dries up, leaving us even more reliant on the ever-decreasing oil and gas reserves that escalate daily in price. And over time, this political and economic landscape starts looking more and more like the current Middle Eastern landscape, except instead of just Middle Eastern people slavishly supporting your lavish princely lifestyle, you have the entire Western world doing so. A Muslim despotic monarchy at the center of the world. History repeating itself with the establishment of a new caliphate, and slowly but surely the conversions begin. Jews exterminated at first, and then Christian populations forced or bribed, like the Bogomiles, to convert. After this conquest, you turn then toward the East, but that might prove more difficult because unlike the West, the seeds of its destruction aren't woven into its political identity. Like you, it rejects republican principles and individual rights, those very principles you bastardized to help the West destroy itself. But that's all right, because by that time, you'll have the resources to confront China. It will be a war of despotic powers, and you believe you will have the advantage in that confrontation, because there will be more Muslims than Chinese. The inevitable war between Sunnis and Shias might interfere, but you'll delay that internal battle until your thousand-year march to world domination is complete. Does that sound about right?" He paused for effect. "Don't think we don't know Ghazali and you share many of the same goals, Mr. Ambassador. You just have different ways of getting there."

Prince Nazir sat in his chair piercing the president with an intense glare, conveying clearly the unbridgeable chasm between them. The president shrugged. "It doesn't really matter what you think, Mr. Ambassador. Because that is what I believe you desperately want. So what you have to understand, Mr. Ambassador, is that I'm willing, right here and right now, to have that resource war. Why would I risk the future I just painted? I won't. So, just give me a reason. And you may attempt to blow up your oil and gas fields. We think we can prevent that, and even if it happens, we have the technology to extract the oil regardless. The markets will fall, and times will be difficult, but only for a short while. So, when you start threatening us, you had better understand where I'm coming from, Mr. Ambassador."

Halladan had just dumped the chess board on the floor; Nazir and the other ambassadors didn't view the president's response as a gaming tactic. War would follow if oil and gas became a weapon, and with the American Terrorist galloping around the Middle East laying waste to wide swaths of population, the political landscape darkened severely for the three ambassadors, and they knew it.

In an attempt to salvage the meeting, the Egyptian ambassador cunningly changed his expression and demurely asked, "But what do you propose that we do, Mr. President? Sitting and waiting for your American Terrorist to strike isn't really an option, is it?"

"Maybe, Mr. Ambassador, you simply should comply with *my* American Terrorist's request. You can start with turning over Mansur Ghazali," Halladan replied firmly.

Secretary of State Townsend hid a smile. Whether the president truly believed the picture he had painted, the 'oil and gas card' threat had failed miserably. Townsend casually leaned back in his chair and studied the ambassadors. Frustration with the president's audacity had clearly surfaced, but something else was there too, hindering a coherent response. Although none of the three ambassadors looked at one another, Townsend sensed a common thread of uneasiness, even apprehension persisting among them. He searched their faces, and under his scrutiny, Prince Nazir slumped back in his chair, his shoulders sagging in defeat.

His eyes on the carpet, Nazir mumbled, "Mr. President, that is one demand no one can possibly meet."

The president leaned forward and studied the ambassador's transformed demeanor. "And why is that, Mr. Ambassador?"

"Mansur Ghazali is dead."

The president tried to look unimpressed, but his eyes widened slightly. "And I am supposed to believe this because…?" he asked skeptically.

Nazir hesitated for just a moment. "We can prove it, and we know you can confirm his identity through DNA analysis."

Townsend suddenly connected the dots. "Oh, I bet you can, Mr. Ambassador. He was killed in Spencer's last attack, wasn't he? You can produce his body, and we're going to see he most definitely met his demise at the hands of the American Terrorist. This puts the Iranian government in a very uncomfortable position, since it proves Ghazali has been living right inside one of its largest cities. Probably had a nice little apartment that even several Saudis like yourself knew about. What was his address, Ambassador Nazir? This just proves that Thom Spencer was right all along, doesn't it? You're *all* complicit."

Immediately Nazir stiffened in his seat, regaining his composure. "I'm offended by the questions, sir," Nazir icily responded.

"Are you kidding?" Townsend howled. "Why?"

The president leaned back in his chair, startled by the revelation. He looked at the three ambassadors and shook his head, nearly mesmerized by the irony. He finally asked, "So what in the world do you want us to do?"

Nazir gave the president a puzzled and then sardonic glance. "Mr. President, you now can call off your dog. Ghazali is dead. No one else needs to die."

The president laughed aloud, hearty and genuine. "One terrorist doesn't make a network, Ambassador Nazir. But," he said, still chuckling, "you haven't been listening to me. He's not our dog, and we can't call him off."

"Mr. President," Nazir glared at Halladan, "we can do the math. This maniac's next attack could reach ten million Muslims or more."

"And maybe some Jews, Christians, and Buddhists, but who cares about those people, not to mention the Muslims themselves? You don't really think we believe you care about them, do you? But ten million or more of them dead would put a serious dent in your ability to maintain credible power, wouldn't it?" Townsend interjected, his voice contemptuous.

Nazir didn't take the bait and pleaded calmly, "If he's not told that Ghazali is dead by someone he trusts, we know he has no qualms killing more innocent people. I implore you to find him, Mr. President. Tell him."

Halladan leaned forward with a resigned expression, "Mr. Ambassador, we will if we can. We have been, and we will continue to try. But let me tell you something. Maybe you personally didn't know Ghazali was walking the streets of Mashhad, but someone in your government did. In fact, I'd wager several people did. And those same people know where other terrorists are hiding, and they know how to dismantle those networks. And those people could do severe damage to those networks in a matter of days. You want to save those ten million Muslims, Mr. Ambassador? Clean your house, and clean it well. *That* will save those potential victims."

The meeting concluded in a cold cloud of silence as an aide escorted the three Muslim ambassadors from the office. As soon as the door closed behind them, Townsend exploded. "They've been lying all along. Just like Ghazali, they know exactly where all these terrorists are, Mr. President. Let them clean their houses, as you said. I suggest we simply sit on our hands until then. Don't pursue Spencer, and let their cleaning ladies get the job done. There's turmoil right now in every single one of those governments. We had better take advantage of our situation here. We owe them nothing, Mr. President."

"You've changed your tune a little since Monday, Mason. What about risking the world accusing us of aiding Spencer?"

Secretary Townsend scoffed. "Mr. President, I personally spoke with many of my counterparts from those other countries we were concerned about. They're not just looking the other way; they green-lit these regimes and their terrorists, and Spencer is their convenient executioner. Simply put, they've calculated that an efficient demise of those networks entangled with all of these Middle Eastern governments benefit them in the long run, especially with Spencer doing the dirty work. They're just as complicit as we are, and if we have to prove that, we can."

Halladan surveyed the room looking for objections; instead, he found quiet resolve. After rubbing his cheek for several moments, he exhaled and turned toward Mel. "In regard to your secondary tactic, Agent Dellendale, I am to assume that if we have an unidentified trace of a complex electromagnetic code that you send a rapid deployment team to that location, correct?"

"Yes, sir," Mel confirmed.

"Cancel that protocol, Agent Dellendale. Before any team is dispatched, you must obtain approval from me personally. Do you understand, Agent Dellendale?"

Mel nodded. "Yes, sir." The order met with silent approval from his advisors.

"Thank you," The president said, dismissing them.

Mel left the meeting, pondering how she would articulate the new protocol. After what had been revealed by the ambassadors, she knew Halladan had unleashed Spencer. They were to apprehend the American Terrorist's trigger, his pathogen, or Thom Spencer himself only after he had infected his next target, which conceivably jeopardized ten million or more people. And then another whisper in the back of her mind began speculating even about that permission if

Halladan's Middle Eastern adversaries didn't meet his demands. Mel dismissed the whisper with a frown, hoping she would never have to confront its implications.

Chapter Forty-Three

Tuesday, February 24

Zandi's eyes popped open, unsure of what awakened him. He looked at the clock: it read three-thirty a.m. Perhaps it was just the anticipation of returning to the Natanz missile base. A knock pounded on his door. He had expected the jarring interruption, so it didn't alarm him as did the last early-morning knock. Yet his stomach grumbled in a jumble of nerves and anxiety with the day of reckoning dawning in a few hours. He tried to quell the uneasiness.

Zandi had formulated a risky plan to contact the CIA during the night, rejected it, refined it, rejected it, and then finally adopted a finer variation. Sleep came in fits filled with strange dreams, and the knock actually came as a relief despite the queasiness.

His same mustached captor appeared when he opened the door, and Zandi asked him inside, but the man declined, handing Zandi a military uniform. It didn't belong to him, since he hadn't brought one with him to Mashhad. It appeared to fit, and Zandi presumed obtaining a uniform from a UJ agent inside the government wasn't difficult. His captor remained in the doorway while Zandi showered and dressed. After being escorted to an ordinary brown sedan, Zandi sat silently in the back seat without exchanging a single word on the chauffeured drive to the airport. When they landed at a Natanz airstrip and stepped out of the plane, the sun shone brightly, and the day had dawned beautifully. But Zandi's stomach still churned with nerves, and he feigned a cough to conceal a worried gulp. With a quick sniff and a brooding expression, he suppressed the anxiety.

The first hour at the missile base consisted primarily of somber greetings; most of the staff remained in a state of grief and shock over Mashhad. Stifled anger also infused the atmosphere, yet Zandi didn't notice any difference in the day-to-day operations. He casually assessed the crew staffing missile control; each would undoubtedly turn the key and launch on any command. But no stolen glances, nervous gestures, or awkward greetings signaled this day as one of destructive destiny. Perhaps the past few days had been a test, and today, except for the grief, would proceed normally.

Zandi continued to perform his duties for more than two hours without incident, and then he saw it. That one twitch from a communication officer sitting at a computer screen. He shifted in his chair, looked at the clock, and then at Zandi; he quickly averted his gaze. Slowly the officer's finger crept toward a button. He glanced around furtively before pressing it, and his body heaved heavily, releasing tension with the successful completion of his assignment. It had started.

Zandi rubbed his jaw momentarily, waiting for the inevitable alarm. It sounded, and the commanding general marched up behind him, evaluating the situation with intense eyes. "Colonel Zandi!" the commanding general barked, "we have authenticated launch orders and codes. Coordinates shall be forwarded immediately. You shall proceed with Missile Launch Lockdown One. This is not a drill."

"Yes, sir!" he responded automatically. No one could penetrate the command room and reverse the order once the lockdown occurred. One other command officer possessed lockdown authority if he failed to execute the order, so Zandi planned to comply. Ironically, the lockdown provided him the chance to contact his CIA handler.

The launch alarm had startled the men in the command room. Not because they weren't prepared for it, but the timing sent a shock wave through the somber atmosphere affected by Mashhad. Then it struck them; the mullahs had ordered retaliation for the American Terrorist's attack. They suddenly snapped to attention and executed their protocols with vigor and efficiency. Large screens flickered, and maps and logistics opened on the monitors. Men's fingers pounded the keyboards with purpose, and communication consoles hummed.

Three junior officers and three enlisted soldiers abruptly leaped in front of Zandi. He nodded curtly, "Captains, we have an authentic launch confirmed, and we at once move to Missile Launch Lockdown One. To your stations and execute the orders!"

The soldiers darted off in several directions. The general had rushed to his station where he and another ranking officer began the code confirmation and missile launch. The men who actually turned the key and pushed the button would confirm the order, and in just a few short minutes the warhead would launch. Zandi watched momentarily in eerie surreal suspension as soldiers bustled at their tasks with absolutely no ambivalence about launching a weapon of mass destruction.

He shook his head slightly, but strode toward a console with purpose, mimicking the observed determination, and started executing the lockdown protocol. Grimacing, he pounded the bulky machine on its side, nearly toppling it from the computer counter. Glaring, he leapt toward the stairs, glancing at the general who shot him a concerned look.

Zandi gritted his teeth in frustration. "Not accepting the code. I can override it from the upstairs office."

The general calmly nodded, but Zandi didn't wait for permission as he dashed up the steps. Once in the office, he quickly entered the lockdown code and started the confirmation process; he then reached for the secure phone line and dialed.

An operator answered. "Two four two, please give ID code."

"Two four two, WMT aka 233DMB AOP," Zandi said in perfect English.

"Password confirmed. Line is not recognized."

"Iran is the prefix. Natanz. I repeat, Alpha Omega Psi."

"Emergency code accepted, line conditionally held open, transfer in process."

"Pryce," the voice on the other end of the call answered promptly.

"WMT aka 0233DMB."

"Voice confirmed, Mr. Pryce," the operator interjected.

"What's going on, Tishtar. You've given us an AOP," Daman Pryce said calmly.

"Iranian nuclear launch underway on Tel Aviv. Ghazali's plot.

There is a UJ agent inside Israeli nuclear arsenal who will launch on Cairo, Medina, and Mecca upon Israel's retaliation. UJ agents then detonate all oil field grids. Confirmed by Ghazali. Ghazali is dead."

Silence answered Zandi. Perspiration formed on the undercover operative's brow. As he waited, he heard footsteps, and one of his captains appeared in the doorway. The man's face registered concern. "Colonel, we are in Missile Launch Lockdown One. No communications are permitted."

"Has the code been confirmed?" Zandi shouted. "The computer crashed downstairs."

"Yes, by you. We are in the confirmed lockdown. Put the phone down!" the soldier demanded as he approached, his hand hovering over his sidearm.

Zandi nodded and set the handset on the desk instead of its cradle. The captain, disconcerted, reached for the instrument to terminate the line, but Zandi grabbed his arm and twisted it behind him. Caught by surprise, he struggled, but Zandi yelled, "What is the meaning of this, Captain? Why are you using a phone?" Zandi shifted the captain's weight, finding the needed leverage, and gave a forceful jerk, snapping the neck instantly. The captain collapsed lifelessly to the floor.

He grabbed the phone and spoke rapidly. "Is this confirmed, Daman? You don't have much time."

"Confirmed, Tishtar."

Zandi terminated the call and placed the handset in the captain's hand, rubbing the mouthpiece across the dead man's mouth. DNA from the captain's saliva would support the illusion that he had last spoken on the phone. It might give him time, it might not, Zandi thought. As he stood, two enlisted soldiers entered the office.

Zandi pulled the handset from the dead captain's hand and threw it violently at his head. "Fool was trying to use the phone in lockdown!" he seethed, shaking his head. "Leave him. We'll dispose of that garbage later!" he shouted at the enlisted soldiers.

Zandi returned to the commanding general's side with beads of sweat rolling down his cheek. The general looked at him perplexed. "What happened?" he asked.

His voice shaking with rage, Zandi fumed, "Found Captain Azad on the phone after I confirmed the lockdown order."

"He went up after you," the general countered with raised

eyebrows.

"I passed him on my way back downstairs, and he said he was under orders from you to retrieve something from the office. I never trusted him, General, so I turned and followed him. Just a gut feeling. Sure enough, I walked in and he was on the phone. Pursuant to lockdown command authority, I eliminated him immediately."

Zandi's blunt explanation disturbed the general, but he recovered quickly. "Who was he calling?" he asked angrily.

Wiping the sweat from his brow, Zandi shrugged. "He didn't have the chance to dial. I just killed him, General. I didn't ask questions." Zandi shook his head, feigning incredulity. "What in the world was he thinking?"

Satisfied with Zandi's account and his preemptive initiative, the general returned his attention to the launch sequence and speculated indifferently, "What I know of the captain, probably warning family, Colonel. He was weak that way, but it makes little difference. Obviously it hasn't interfered with the launch."

The stark truth sent a shiver down Zandi's back. He asked solemnly, "Is the missile airborne yet?"

"Countdown is in progress."

Zandi searched the large wall monitors for coordinate confirmation; he found the numbers and nodded. "Tel Aviv."

"Yes," the general answered, his smirk indicating that he too was present at the Mashhad meeting.

Zandi nodded, and the general continued, "We're going to kill many Jews today. Not enough, but it feels good, doesn't it?"

Until now the adrenaline had masked the nausea. At the general's sneering words, Zandi rocked back on his heels, which the general interpreted as complete agreement. Zandi only did it to stop himself from vomiting violently.

Chapter Forty-Four

Tuesday, February 24

Daman abruptly threw off the covers and sat up; Melissa rolled over, startled by the jolt, eyeing Daman's intense expression. Pryce quickly dialed. "This is Daman Pryce, CIA. Please inform the president that I have received a confirmed AOP call."

As the operator contacted Halladan, Daman turned toward Mel and said, "Mel, can you go to the other room? You don't have clearance for this call."

"These days? You gotta be kidding, Daman. What's going on?" she demanded.

Daman didn't have time to argue, and he didn't respond. Anyway, who cared if she knew? He rose from the bed and started dressing, the phone wedged between his shoulder and ear.

The president finally answered the call. "Agent Pryce, you received an AOP call?"

"Yes, Mr. President. Our informant in the Iranian missile force has given me confirmation of an imminent launch on Tel Aviv."

"Understood. You need to get here as soon as possible."

"We're less than ten minutes away, Mr. President."

"We?"

"Special Agent Dellendale is present. Should she come?"

"Yes. Call your director with the details."

The line terminated and Daman, following protocol, dialed

another number. A CIA communication officer answered and immediately transferred him to the director who, already notified of the AOP code, awaited Daman's report with other officials conferencing into the call.

When they arrived at the White House, a Marine guard immediately escorted Daman and Mel to the War Room. It bustled with activity, and Daman and Mel stood near the large conference table as they watched officers and analysts scurry from station to station.

The president, disheveled from the early-morning AOP call, leaped up the stairs, strode to the computerized table, and pressed a communication button. "General Billington, do you have confirmation yet?" he asked, communicating with the general on the conference audio system.

General Billington, Commander of North American Air Defense, answered. "No, Mr. President. All Czech Republic Radar bases are up and operational. No detection."

"How about the unmanned aerial vehicles?" the president asked.

"Five launched, sir," Billington replied.

"And you have confirmed the Polish ABM interceptor bases are on launch alert?" the president asked.

"Yes, sir," Billington crisply responded.

A new interface appeared in the center screen. "Mr. President, please turn your attention to interface three. We have patched you into Czech Station Four's central electronic graphic map in real time. Sorry for the delay," a communications officer reported from the dais. The map focused on the stretch of land between Natanz and metropolitan Tel Aviv.

"Sir, the UAV signal will be the smaller display in the upper left," the officer advised.

Halladan nodded. Others crept onto the dais, silently waiting and watching.

Billington interrupted with a subdued announcement. "Mr. President, we have a confirmed launch."

"Secretary General, please authorize the transfer of authority to NORAD Command for the interception of the Iranian missile," Halladan requested.

Since the bases intercepting the missile resided inside NATO, the secretary general had to transfer formally logistical control. "Mr.

President, the transfer is complete," a man with a British accent acknowledged.

"General Billington, shoot down that bird!" President Halladan ordered.

Chills prickled Mel's neck. On the tactical screen she saw the location of the missile launch from Natanz.

An interface in the upper-left quadrant of the super full high-def screen suddenly flickered to life. An unmanned aerial vehicle had visual of the Iranian missile. To the right, a live satellite image appeared.

"CENTCOM, we have confirmation," Billington barked.

"CENTCOM confirmation," a man in Qatar responded.

"Czech Command Authority, we have confirmation," Billington snapped again.

"CCA confirmation," a woman in the Czech Republic replied.

"Interceptor bases Alpha, Beta, Omega, you have launch authority." The speaker magnified the sound of keys being punched. "Intercept that bird!" Billington commanded.

"Mr. President," the communication's officer interrupted, "the Prime Minister of Israel."

Halladan nodded, and the officer connected her to the dais's internal audio system. "Madame Prime Minister, President Halladan."

A voice with a heavy accent said calmly, "Mr. President, we have detected the launch." For a woman who was in the crosshairs of a nuclear warhead capable of destroying her administrative capital, she sounded surprisingly cool.

"We've detected it, Madame Prime Minister, and have issued the intercept command."

Suddenly the map lit up inside Poland, and in real time a super full high-definition computer-generated image of the interceptor travelled across the screen. Two additional lights burst on the screen, representing redundant launches if the first missile missed.

"Mr. President, several incoming calls from heads of state," his communication's officer reported.

"Understood, Major. Reissue the alert of our launch to destroy an Iranian missile attack on Tel Aviv and advise all nations to stand down their forces. Refer all other calls to the vice president. General Billington, DEFCON 3."

Mel understood the exchange. Other nations had detected the launch of the Iranian missile and the NATO interceptor response, and their protocols demanded they execute defensive measures. The president dutifully responded by raising the national defense readiness position to three from the peacetime DEFCON 5.

Silence abruptly descended on the room, and Mel shifted her gaze from the president to the huge screen, alternating between it and the UAV feed. The chills now cascaded down her spine as the blip representing the interceptor accelerated toward the Iranian missile. She didn't blink; the two dots merged and disappeared. She waited, unsure of what she had just seen. She looked at the upper left. The UAV feed showed a brilliant flash and the falling, inert missile; satellite imagery indicated success.

The CCA voice crisply announced, "Confirmed hit with interceptor one. I repeat, confirmed hit with interceptor one. Confirmation with UAV signal as well. Missile recovery ordered."

No one cheered, but a strange aura imbued the room. American technology had just saved hundreds of thousands of innocent people, and elation for those lives saved radiated from the sergeants to the president, along with pride in America. Mel felt it, and she couldn't help think about those who had scoffed at anti-ballistic missile theory and those who advocated for it. With this single show of force, and the saving of Tel Aviv, the program had instantly paid for itself and more.

The room's quiet ebullience quickly faded and tension returned. Mel glanced at Daman, who also noticed the vacillating extremes and shrugged in response. "Mr. President," the heavily accented voice of the Israeli Prime Minister cackled across the speaker. "We have confirmed target coordinates of that ballistic missile. Iran has launched on us. We must respond."

"Mr. President," Billington voiced on the conference audio system, "CENTCOM has submarines in place and ready to launch the SLBM's. Targets of Natanz and all other missile facilities are locked. We are ready for launch."

"General Billington, hold," he ordered.

"Yes, sir," Billington replied without hesitation, and Halladan asked the communication's officer to silence the NORAD line.

Halladan gestured toward Mahony, who with a push of a button soundproofed the dais. The president pulled out a chair and dropped into it, nodding to Daman, Mel, and the others to sit with him. Chairperson of the Joint Chiefs of Staff Admiral Lear, Secretary of State Townsend, Secretary of Defense Travis Mitchell, Harry Stanton, Chief of Staff Mac Stenberg, DNI Brent Chalmers, and National Security Adviser Dave Walters emerged from the shadows and joined them at the table.

"Visual, please," the president commanded. The Egg dropped from the ceiling, and several displays simultaneously appeared in the table interface. An elegant woman of sixty, with black hair graying at the side, and keen brown eyes nodded her greeting.

"Madame Prime Minister, I think you recognize everyone at the table," Halladan said.

Prime Minister Maayan Kahane tilted her head, considering and said, "Yes, except those two at the end."

Halladan nodded. "Special Agent Melissa Dellendale, Federal Bureau of Investigation, is the lead agent for the Ghazali and Spencer investigations. Daman Pryce is from CIA, Madame Prime Minister, concentrating on Middle Eastern affairs. Our man, we'll call him Wilson, contacted him with the information on the launch. Without that warning, Madame Prime Minister, we would have missed the interception. The operation was successful, because the interceptors and radar stations were alerted and prepared."

Prime Minister Kahane smiled gracefully. "We must give thanks to this operative, Mr. Pryce. Do you know where he is?"

"He's in Iran, Madame Prime Minister."

"Is he in danger?"

"I don't know," Daman answered honestly.

"But he said Ghazali orchestrated this launch?"

Since the president hadn't asked him to deflect the questioning, Daman answered the prime minister's question clearly and honestly. "Yes, Madame Prime Minister. The message was short but concise: Ghazali plotted this attack." Daman flicked his eyes to the president, who gestured for him to complete the report. "He also reported Ghazali is dead," Daman announced.

The president had ordered Ghazali's death kept secret. Reactions from around the table not privy to the information ranged from disbelief to relief to grim satisfaction. Mel watched the prime minister, who took the news deadpan.

"And so are we to believe that the Iranian government, or the mullahs, didn't authorize or have any part in this launch?" she asked pointedly.

Before Pryce could reply, the president spoke up. "Madame Prime Minister, we don't think they did officially. Of course, those governments are infested with terrorist informants and operatives, but we believe the attack was not officially sanctioned. Some simple facts confirm this."

"Could you explain, Mr. President?" the prime minister asked.

"Mr. Chalmers," the president, swinging his attention to his director of national intelligence, "what further reports do you have?"

Brent Chalmers redirected the question toward Daman, who had the latest intelligence. Pryce didn't hesitate. "CIA and NSA have been monitoring communications inside Iran. No other nuclear sites were placed in lockdown. Once Natanz went into lockdown, their communications board lit up, trying to contact that missile base without any success. Those attempts climbed the ladder very quickly, again without success. Iran next mobilized military units, which are headed to Natanz as we speak, which was confirmed by satellite."

Prime Minister Kahane exhaled. "Yes, yes, yes, we too intercepted the same intelligence. It all could be for show."

Pryce shrugged. "Additional chatter supports that mullahs and the government were taken completely by surprise. Our assessment right now is that the response is genuine and that the government did not officially sponsor this attack."

Kahane stared hard at Daman. She finally relented and shifted the interrogation. "I presume Natanz was chosen because it had the latest and most sophisticated technology."

"Yes," the admiral interjected. "But, as Mr. Pryce indicated, the early warning eliminated that advantage. With these distances seconds count, and without it, our anti-ballistic missile probably wouldn't catch up to their Natanz warhead in time."

"And did Ghazali know all this?" Kahane asked.

Attention returned to Daman. He folded his hands together. "Ghazali of course knew about the ABM system, and he knew Natanz was the best bet to succeed, and likely would but for advance warning. He undoubtedly had planned this operation for many years, Madame Prime Minister. It must have taken years to place the assets. But he kept it well hidden. It is fair to assume only his inner circle had any idea of its existence. But he quite clearly didn't know we had assets inside UJ that could give us warning."

Prime Minister Kahane sighed. "Assets. I was briefed by our liaison officer that Ghazali also placed someone in our missile corps? Is this true?"

"Wilson informed me that a man has penetrated your missile launch guard, Madame Prime Minister. Once you initiated launch protocol, this man would have programmed three missiles to target Cairo, Mecca, and Medina."

The prime minister quickly calculated the number of casualties and the symbolic damage of destroying those cities. "And of course we don't know who it is, but we can presume it is someone on duty today. I will have all of them removed and replaced immediately and proceed with a counterstrike on Iran."

The president nodded carefully. "It's certainly within your right. We have SLBM's ready for launch as well. However, Madame Prime Minister, I must advise you that we don't think Israel is under any current threat. We terminated the bird, and that one had the best chance of success. We think we can shield Israel from any further attack since we're operational."

Prime Minister Kahane placed her hands on the desk and pushed her chair slightly away from the camera. "And that means if we retaliate, it's really not in self-defense, is it?"

Everyone felt the discomfort of the dilemma. The prime minister of Israel stared intently into the camera. Despite the fact that many sitting around the table understood Israel's viewpoint, some did not, and she had a duty to explain fully her position and her country's worldview, since the ages would judge the moment. "You Americans are our friends, and we have a special relationship, but you don't live as close to this…this persistent threat. Now, I'm not minimizing what you have endured as a country, but we just had a terrorist launch a nuclear weapon at us. Without your help, and without this intelligence report, hundreds of thousands would be dead. My history tells me I must retaliate. We must take every opportunity to harm the enemy, not only to weaken them, but to communicate our resolve and our strength, even if the government didn't authorize it.

"You see, we view this differently than most Americans do. Ever since the Arab shed the yoke of the Turks, they've been striving to obtain Middle Eastern dominance. From the outset, amongst the Arabs, they have battled one another. On one side, you have those adopting a nationalist approach, using Islam as a buttressing rather than a primary force. These regimes promoted a socialist or Stalinist mentality, or in the least, a monarchy of some sort.

"On the other side, you have those groups advocating Arab identity through Islam, and Islam alone. These fundamentalists didn't initially dominate, but as the nationalist regimes devolved into despotic cults of personality and thoroughly corrupt parties, the hungry, disenchanted, and forgotten Arabs sought refuge with those offering help and an identity. This became the foundation of the Arab fundamentalist power.

"Meanwhile, in Iran, they played their monarchical nationalist politics while the fundamentalists gained power, and in 1979, as you know, the fundamentalists, the Islamic Revolution, successfully overthrew the Pahlavi dynasty. I don't think the West realized the subtle significance. Arab regimes had to respond to Shia fundamentalism. If they didn't succor fundamentalists, their regimes stood on a precarious precipice, and so these regimes started funding fundamentalist outlets. An odd competition persisted between the Arab Sunnis and the Persian Shiites with Arab Shias caught in the middle, all vying to prove their superior fundamentalism.

"Meanwhile, despite what some perceive, you still have Turkic people never straying too far from their Seljuk and Ottoman heritage, with millions of voices behind them, advocating for an active role in Muslim leadership worldwide, and again fracturing Dar el Salaam.

"Universal Jihad dramatically changed the relationships. It preaches that fundamentalism, Shia and Sunni, Arab, Turkic, and Persian, has much more to gain by cooperating against Jews and the Great Satan, and this unifying creed found cooperative zealots not only in the poor streets or angry madrasas, but right inside already susceptible governments, whether in Iran, Turkic nations, or in Arabia.

"From this perspective, we have thought it not only prudent, but necessary, to exploit every opportunity when one is presented. We incrementally eliminate, one by one, any threat. It is a war of attrition, and we persistently demonstrate to the enemy that we will perpetually retaliate, that our existence isn't negotiable, and that we will survive.

"So you see, our reality deteriorates yearly; we must defend, strike, and eliminate threats daily, and this is our existence, and we embrace it as our identity. Now, my friends, I am speaking for myself, and this is how I see it, but Israelis elected me because of this perspective, and I cannot deviate from it. When I have an opportunity to strike a severe blow at our avowed enemy, I have a duty I must satisfy."

Admiral Lear leaned forward. "So you now must strike back? With a nuclear response?"

Prime Minister Kahane held her hands open and shrugged. Clearly she didn't think other options offered a strong enough message.

Halladan understood her position. He shifted in his seat. "Prime Minister, I ask you to allow some time to pass. We think there might be some developments that could dramatically alter the Middle Eastern situation."

"The longer I wait, Mr. President," Prime Minister Kahane pressed, "the less justification I have. Besides, would it really alter Israel's situation? Would it provide any more security for us?"

The president nodded. "Yes, Madame Prime Minister. In the short term, yes. Then we just work on the longer-term solution, but maybe we do it under a less dangerous umbrella."

Kahane gravely regarded President Halladan, grimacing in response.

Chapter Forty-Five

Tuesday, February 24

Zandi stared at the wall monitors with the general next to him. He could smell the man's musky sweat; excitement exuded from every pore in his body.

The blurry electronic screen showed the Iranian missile start its trajectory; it quickly gained speed and zipped toward the dot labeled Tel Aviv. Suddenly, from the northwest, another blip invaded the screen, and tension instantly increased in the room. This unexpected signal had even greater velocity and flew directly toward their Iranian bird. Men scrambled franticly for information on the hostile signal, but everyone knew its origins. Just outside the brink of the Tel Aviv dot, the invading signal collided with and consumed the Iranian blip, and the screen went blank.

After a minute, a communications officer rose from his desk and crept up to the general wearing a stunned and frightened expression. "We think the missile was disarmed without exploding the nuclear warhead," he said quietly.

The general dismissed him with a curt, disgusted nod and turned toward Zandi with a bewildered expression. "Those damned Americans! They weren't supposed to be able to do that. Not without warning." The general looked at Zandi, alarmed. "You don't think Captain Azad contacted them, do you?"

Zandi feigned an incredulous look, meeting the general's eyes without flinching. "No, sir. You suggested family. Confirmation from Iranian authorities was my guess, but Americans? I don't think so. I didn't like him, but not because I feared that sort of betrayal. Anyway, as I said, he didn't get the call out."

Both men returned their gaze to the wall monitor. No doubt Israel had detected the launch, but each man had different expectations. Zandi was confident Israel had removed Ghazali's mole and had even odds between a strike on Iran and no nuclear strike at all. He hoped for the latter. The general, still believing Ghazali's plan could succeed, anticipated an Israeli launch where three diverted nuclear warheads would kill innocent victims in nations other than Iran and plunge the Middle East and the rest of the world into war.

The general waited impatiently, staring intently at the large monitors, praying for that missile launch from Israel. After ten minutes, he glanced worriedly at Zandi who shrugged in doubt. Another ten minutes, and the screen still remained empty. "The longer it is, the less likely they will strike, Colonel," the general said dejectedly.

Zandi nodded confirmation. "They suffered no casualties."

The general gritted his teeth. "But they always retaliate. That's what they do!" he exclaimed. "What are we going to do?"

The Middle East hadn't disintegrated in conflict. Regional war would have provided cover for the officers at the Natanz missile base. Once Israel had destroyed Cairo, Medina, or Mecca—or all three—the focus would have switched from the initial launch into a unified Muslim retaliation against Israel.

The general massaged his temples. "Government officials are on their way, Zandi. They must be. And we have no means out of here because of the lockdown."

Zandi found it ironic the general spoke of escape. "Yes, sir, and I am very disappointed the plan has apparently failed," he said deadpan.

The general turned and glared at Zandi. "Yes. Yes, and there's that, too."

Zandi remained expressionless. "If Israel doesn't launch, we have to hope someone inside the government will protect us. Maybe someone at the meeting the other night."

The general grimaced. "Maybe," he muttered doubtfully.

They kept their eyes on the wall monitor, but as time slipped by, confidence in an Israeli attack diminished. Another screen diverted their attention, this one from security cameras monitoring the four entrances to the missile base. A line of vehicles was streaming toward the main gate, trailed by several heavily armed helicopters. Since the mandatory lockdown period had expired, Zandi could open the base.

Zandi risked a sidelong glance at his superior. The general didn't notice, licking perspiration from his upper lip and anxiously wringing his hands. Having survived the day thus far, Zandi now required isolation from all the others, and the general's fear played into his hands perfectly. "I think," Zandi offered quietly, "that only one person here really needs to take responsibility, General."

The general rapidly shifted his eyes, incensed by the suggestion. "Why? I'm more important than you are, Colonel," he seethed.

"Of course you are, General. That's why I am the one. I take all the responsibility. I can easily convince the government that I deceived you. There's no need for both of us to take the fall."

The general swallowed, unsure of the idea, glancing skittishly at the colonel with a mix of fear and hope.

Zandi smiled faintly. "We all received orders that night in the warehouse, General. These are mine. A backup plan was carefully crafted, and I was trusted to be sacrificed. What an honor, General! But we have men of conviction here, and when the government troops commandeer the base, our UJ soldiers may resort to violence. We can't let that happen. You and they must all survive to continue the jihad another day. To stop this, you must declare right now that I have admitted to you that I, and I alone, have betrayed the government, and that I will be taken into custody for treason. I will announce that is my duty to take responsibility for the entire plot. Our Jihad brethren will understand, and I will quietly submit to the arriving officials without any commotion. Do you understand, General?"

The general had regained his composure and looked at Zandi squarely in the eye. "You can count on me, Colonel, and you, my brother, honor our cause."

"Thank you, General," Zandi humbly mumbled. Without delay, the general executed the plan. Zandi surveyed the room. He found surprise, solemn understanding, even admiration, and no defiance.

So far, his strategy was succeeding.

Scores of soldiers unloaded from the stream of vehicles and the airborne escort. When the gates opened, they swarmed in and took immediate control. Within a few minutes, Zandi was shoved into a small room with a defunct computer and a desk, and a guard locked the door behind. As he waited, Zandi prepared for the interrogator by playing out several scenarios in his mind, gaming every probable sequence he could imagine. Shrugging and then stretching his neck and arms, he grew impatient, wishing to begin the process.

The door finally opened, and he recognized the man: Mohammad Talebi, a well-connected government official who sympathized with Ghazali, but avoided open affiliation. Zandi leaned back in the chair, confident Talebi's rank and stature augured direct negotiations with the highest of authorities.

"Colonel Zandi," Talebi greeted him as he took a seat across from Zandi. "So you are the mastermind behind this entire fiasco? You're not working for anyone? You did this all by yourself?"

Zandi remained silent.

Talebi scoffed. "Because this aggressive attack—its complexity, how it was planned and implemented—smacks of Mansur Ghazali, we have concluded he had one last attack inside him before he died. Are we going to deny it? How are we going to play this game today?"

Zandi launched this game scenario with a grin. "Deny it? Absolutely not. Of course it was Ghazali's plan. But the nuclear strike was just the first part."

"What's the other?" Talebi asked patiently.

"If the Israelis counterstrike, which it doesn't appear they're going to do yet, Ghazali has an agent deep inside Israeli missile forces who will divert warheads to Cairo, Mecca, and Medina. If that happens, it will of course look like Israel has disproportionately retaliated, and the Muslim world will unite. Perhaps far-fetched, perhaps not. But that's not going to happen, even if the Israelis decide to launch. You know why?"

Talebi looked at the colonel with near indifference and shrugged. "Why?"

Zandi nearly laughed aloud. "Haven't you wondered why our nuclear missile was intercepted?"

"The question crossed our minds, but on the way here we were informed that a call was detected on a secure line to the United States, and then we found Captain Azad—I think that's his name—sprawled on the floor of the office where that call took place. What happened? Did Azad betray you?"

"No, Captain Azad didn't betray anyone," Zandi replied, "but here's your dilemma. I can tell you who did place that call, and warned the Americans about the launch and the rogue agent inside the Israeli nuclear missile force, but you're going to have to let the man go. What do you think of that?"

Mohammad Talebi stared at Zandi for several seconds; he had found not a Universal Jihadist as he expected, but something far worse: a traitor to Islam, a conspirator for the Great Satan. He braced himself internally, suppressing any sign of emotion. "And why would I have to release him?" he asked evenly.

The time for coyness had passed. Zandi leaned forward just slightly and said in a quiet but urgent voice, "Mohammad, you have only one option here. You must convince Washington, DC that Universal Jihad launched this missile, and not Iran. I can help. I know that Ghazali planned and orchestrated this entire episode, and DC will believe me. Iran is going to have to dismantle not only Universal Jihad, but all other terrorist networks. I know this will be a condition imposed to avoid retaliation. I don't want to debate whether you can do this; we both know you can. But, Mohammad, I must place a call to DC right now. If I don't, you can expect warheads exploding in Iran very shortly."

Talebi glanced at his watch with a perplexed look. "As you just said, it doesn't appear the Jews are going to retaliate. They would've done so already."

The odds Israel—or for that matter the US—would launch any attack had dropped to nearly zero from the earlier fifty-fifty in the last hour, but Zandi had to press his advantage with a bluff. "Mohammad," he said slowly and clearly, "I said 'yet.' They're waiting for my call. If they don't hear from me, I can guarantee if Israel doesn't launch, the US will. Do you really think a man like Halladan won't take this opportunity to demolish Iran? Don't be so naïve."

Talebi studied Zandi skeptically. "So let me get this straight. You will convince the Americans that we're going to…to eliminate terrorist networks entirely, and in exchange, they won't launch on us?"

"Talebi, you and I both know that you can demonstrate your commitment. The current prime minister must go, and now. Once replaced with someone DC likes, and once those responsible for this attempted strike are eliminated, and you start removing the networks, the US will have its answer, and quickly. But first, I must make the call and let them know the intentions before it's too late and they launch."

Talebi didn't like that he had lost his edge; he also recognized the number of lives at stake. His eyes shifted, searching for a loophole. Zandi anticipated the thought. "Don't stall, Mohammad. I know what you're thinking. If a day or two passes, Israel can't launch, but don't concern yourself with Israel. Let me assure you, Mohammad, the US will. If Israel hesitates, the US won't."

"And, as I said earlier, you must provide me safe passage. I'm your proof that Ghazali authored this attack, not Iran. By the time you finish your arrests and executions, no one will be around to confirm what occurred, except me, and this will be important for Iran."

"I must save a traitor like you?" Mohammad seethed. "You have to...."

Zandi interrupted the expected diatribe. "We're well beyond vapid recriminations, Mohammad," he declared.

"You could lie," Talebi observed, glaring at Zandi.

"On the phone? Shoot me if I do," Zandi retorted, chuckling.

"No. Not now, but after your release. You could lie about it, recant your entire story and claim our government was behind all of it," Mohammad persisted.

Zandi shook his head, "Look, Mohammad, if I make the call and then you remove your prime minister and start dismantling networks, it's not going to matter whether I lie. Your actions will count far more than any fabrications I could conjure up. If, however, I tell the truth, your credibility is enhanced even more. You win either way, but your inaction here and now will produce a swift and brutal retaliation."

Mohammad didn't respond immediately, pondering the predicament. The gleam in his eye flared as he suddenly thought of an advantage, but he quickly dismissed it, realizing Zandi would have a ready answer. He felt angry and uncomfortable inside the smothering box the traitor had placed him. Settling for hatred, Mohammad stared at Zandi without blinking.

Zandi shrugged, deciding this game sequence had run its course. He curtly summarized, "Mohammad, either you want to survive and save countless lives, in which case I survive, or you don't, and I die, but so do you along with those countless others. There's only one real alternative right now. Get me a phone."

The man swallowed hard and practically whispered, "I'll be back momentarily."

Momentarily became minutes and stretched into an hour. Zandi fidgeted, wondering if he had miscalculated. The Iranian government could attempt to prove its innocence without ever referring to him. Talebi might even offer Zandi's summary execution as proof of the government's purge of those responsible for the nuclear launch. Zandi was a full colonel, seemingly intimately involved with UJ and the launch. Suddenly images of his family popped into his mind. That leverage hadn't yet played a significant role. Enough time had elapsed for the Iranian secret police to snatch them up, and his calm demeanor became increasingly difficult to maintain. When Talebi finally returned, Zandi sensed triumph in his interrogator.

"We took your advice, but apparently we don't need your confirmation, so we don't need you," he smirked, reaching inside his jacket.

Zandi knew the risks and had prepared himself. He smiled wryly, "I may die, but at least I know I helped destroy you pathetic excuses for human beings. You and your government won't survive for long now."

"Maybe, but first I have the extreme pleasure of executing you personally without any trial or delay. You just die," Talebi sneered as he pulled out his gun.

Zandi jumped from the chair, ready to charge his executioner. "You're a worthless piece of…"

The door opened and an anxious soldier entered. Talebi, furious with the disruption, shouted, "I told you to remain outside!"

The soldier snapped to attention. "Sorry, sir. I was ordered to interrupt you. You have a call you must take immediately."

Mohammad dropped the gun to his side, frustrated but resigned. He looked at Zandi with contempt, but turned on his heel and stalked out. When he returned, the gun had vanished along with the triumph.

"You're wanted, Zandi. Someone believes you're the only one who can confirm it was Ghazali and not the government."

Zandi breathed a faint sigh of relief, but shot an arrogant grin at Mohammad. Somehow Daman Pryce must have made his release a condition in the negotiation. "And now you must understand, Mohammad, that my release includes my family as well."

Mohammad recoiled, as if Zandi had gut-punched him, and his eyes ever so slightly welled with tears of anger.

Zandi chuckled. "Ahh, you missed that piece of leverage during our little negotiation, didn't you? Too late now, but DC knows about them, and I assure you the deal includes them. Check it out. And I hold you personally responsible for their safe delivery to me."

Mohammad Talebi's world had changed drastically in the last several hours. Defeat mixed with humiliation sagged on his face as he walked out the room, knowing he would comply with the demand. Zandi, alone again, was confident he and his family would survive this ordeal. After disclosing his true identity to his wife and son, Zandi wondered if they would survive as a family. He shrugged to himself, content they at least would be alive and safe to give it a try.

Chapter Forty-Six

Tuesday, February 24

A gray haze hovered in the afternoon sky as Brannan strolled into the street, searching for news after failing to repair his satellite feed. People's expressions were intense and worried, and the atmosphere was more subdued, surprising him, since in the last few days the spirits of the people of Cairo had improved. When he first arrived a week ago from Turkey, it had been more like it was now: quiet and fear stricken.

Brannan had an uneventful stay in Istanbul in light of what just happened in Mashhad. When he deplaned at Ataturk airport, no urgent news had come from Iran. During the taxi ride, the radio station didn't interrupt the music with any breaking news. He found a hotel in the city's Muslim sector where he didn't expect any problem once the news from Iran spread.

When the reports from Mashhad finally flooded the airwaves, the death toll shocked the populace. Holed up in his small hotel room, Brannan watched all the news stations he could. Nerves started fraying in every major Middle Eastern city, and palpable fear suffocated the streets. Governments immediately grounded planes, halted trains, and closed borders. Angry mobs started congregating near official buildings in Ankara, Cairo, Tehran, Riyadh, and Islamabad. When the army or police arrived and demanded dispersal with guns drawn and several shots fired, frightened people cringed and returned home, shuttering businesses and emptying the streets. A few courageous souls ventured out, but their muted greetings communicated trepidation, and they held conversations in whispers. As the Mashhad death toll climbed, silence wrapped in fear smothered the Middle East. Government officials huddled in their capitals, wishing answers would materialize before the fear plunged their nations into the abyss.

The first twenty-four hours extended into another twenty-four-hour period of sullen silence. Finally, reports from Mashhad concluded the attack was contained within the city limits and no further. A perimeter drawing outlined the spread of the contagion; no one outside the identified area had reported any symptoms. To allay fear, the governments pumped the information as quickly as possible through all media outlets. Seventy-two hours after the attack, governments started reporting they would soften travel restrictions and allow specified international trade to resume.

The American Terrorist's name and face blanketed the Turkish and international news cycles. The numbers had escalated the anguish of terrorism to an unforeseen level. Many people wondered whether Ghazali and his ilk had ignited something they could not answer and had condemned the entire Middle East to a death sentence.

Brannan continued to monitor the reactions from the solitude of his room. As expected, Istanbul prohibited all travel in and out of the city. The military and police had significantly increased their presence, with armed guards patrolling the shipyards and docks, airport terminals, and train stations. After three days, Turkey, along with the other nations, started easing travel restrictions, and police and military presence began to recede.

Turkish merchants also warily opened their cafes and stands, and Brannan, shaking out the hotel jitters, took to the early-morning Istanbul streets. A somber milieu pervaded the city, but the major detected a desire to get back to work and forget—however briefly—the horror in Iran.

Fear that the Mashhad toxin would spread to other cities had dissipated, and a few Middle Eastern governments brazenly promised an antidote for their subjects before the next attack. Veiled threats against the West and especially the United States rolled off the lips of Middle Eastern ministers and ambassadors. They demanded the immediate capture and extradition of the American Terrorist. Open accusations that the US sponsored Thom Spencer became popular rhetoric.

Protests outside Western and particularly American embassies and consuls spread rapidly, but the United States and other governments had taken steps to protect their people abroad. Brannan had not yet heard of a report where a Westerner had been the victim of a retaliation killing, but he predicted in time that would change.

On the fourth day after Mashhad, Brannan discovered the bustle of commerce had started to compensate for the city-wide mourning. Morning streets echoed with normalized noises of traffic, horns, whistles, shouts, and greetings, although he noticed conversations still focused on Mashhad. Media outlets reported the Turkish and Egyptian governments had lifted the ban between Istanbul and Cairo effective the next day. Certain nationalities might be delayed, but Brannan felt confident he could book a flight to Cairo with his Turkish passport.

Still, the Egyptians warned the terminals, ports, and stations would post extra security, and visitors could expect careful document scrutiny.

The next day dawned bright and sunny, and the streets exuded even more confidence than the day before, despite the mounting death toll from Mashhad. The fear had evolved into anger, and Brannan expected worse in Cairo. Tempers flared and patience wore thin at the airport. The travel moratorium had stranded people for several days, and toughened security clogged the process even more. When he approached the counter, the airline agent asked for his ticket. Brannan shrugged and told him he didn't have one and subtly laid a stack of cash on the counter. The man raised his eyebrows and gave him a curious stare. He then efficiently typed on his keyboard and asked for an exorbitant sum. Brannan promptly handed him the money, and the ticket agent promptly produced a boarding pass, handing it to him with a wink and a smile. Brannan returned the smile, aware his cash had trumped passenger demands that the airline honor prior tickets.

The seven hundred seventy-five-mile flight ended with a bumpy landing at Cairo International Airport. Brannan took his time walking through the terminal but still found himself standing in a long customs line. Because he carried a Turkish instead of an

Egyptian passport, his wait was much longer, and as he approached the agent, the major sensed an impending ordeal.

The customs agent gestured for his passport and scanned it through a computer. After studying it for nearly a minute, he glanced up at Brannan and brusquely demanded the reason for visiting Egypt. Brannan immediately responded with a business explanation, since a vacation after the Mashhad catastrophe might raise a red flag. The seemingly unconvinced officer ordered him to stand where he was, as if Brannan had a choice, and called for a supervisor to inspect the passport. The major wondered if the Botox-like substance had failed him, though he hadn't noticed any change. The supervisor went through the same machinations, asking the same questions, but finally shrugged and nodded his approval. The man mimicked his supervisor with a nod of his own, and Brannan stepped through the security exit and walked to the bathroom. The mirror confirmed the ordinary visage staring back at him. Brannan suspected foreigners were delayed so the agents could take clear photographs. That possibility didn't bother him in the least; the face staring back at him from the mirror wouldn't match any in the relevant databases.

As expected, anger permeated the streets of Cairo. But so did anxiety. Citizens of Cairo feared the American Terrorist might target their city because of its size. Some dismissed the notion, since Cairo's diverse population would force Spencer to kill Westerners, even Americans. Others pointed out how the American Terrorist could draw neat lines around his intended victims. Quiet conversations suggested forcibly moving some available Americans inside those lines and announcing to the world that US citizens sat on those doorsteps.

Brannan monitored the city's attitude for several days. As the protests and rallies intensified outside the US and other Western embassies, he hoped the president had ordered the staff removed, but knew the ambassador would remain. But city activity slowly returned to a normal, busy pace, still with much animosity hurled at the American Terrorist in daily conversations.

Today everything had changed. Under the permeating pall, Brannan headed toward a nearby cafe and noticed a group huddled around a TV set sitting on an outside bar. Everyone looked agitated.

Brannan approached and tapped a man on the shoulder. "What's all the commotion?"

The man turned toward him, his expression lined with concern and fear, but different from that spawned by the American Terrorist. He answered in a trembling voice, "Iran just launched a nuclear missile at Israel."

Brannan gasped sharply with unfeigned surprise. The fear engendered by the American Terrorist abruptly dissolved and was replaced by an entirely new terror. The Cairenes now faced nuclear war in the Middle East. Everyone understood Israel could—and likely would—retaliate with utter devastation. Egypt nervously held its collective breath, and Brannan wondered if the Middle East would survive.

Chapter Forty-Seven

Wednesday, February 25

Brannan noticed changes evolving in the populace. Once people discovered Ghazali had orchestrated the launch, subjecting the Middle East to an all-out war, a new attitude arose. Anger against Ghazali ebbed into the street, and when the street learned he had died in the American Terrorist's attack on Mashhad, some cheered, though in a hushed tone. All Brannan could do was watch, listen, and wait.

The major continued with the plan. Spencer had scheduled the Cairo attack to follow soon after Mashhad with no warning. The clock was running, and eventually the US would find him. If the Middle East didn't meet his demands, he would continue attacking until he was captured. The next day was the last in Spencer's pre-established window of opportunity to launch in Cairo.

The American Terrorist still spooked the Arab street, yet Brannan acknowledged the emergence of a strange hope. The insane launch by Ghazali and his subsequent death had generated a noticeable rift between the street and the radicals. The major sensed a real disenchantment, which was confirmed by Arabic news reports around the Middle East. Still the window kept closing with no word from Caracas.

The window finally shut. Brannan intended to unleash the toxin on Cairo; then he awakened the next morning to additional news reports of mounting pressure on Arabic and Turkic governments to eliminate terrorist networks, violently if necessary. A stunning announcement from Tehran generated a tangible rather than just a strange sense of hope. The mullahs had replaced the militant prime minister with a moderate who proclaimed his government would take a different approach with the West, and especially the United States; his speech significantly didn't include any invective against Israel. Brannan pried the window open just a crack for a few more hours, wondering if he would hear from Caracas, but still the phone didn't ring.

Chapter Forty-Eight

Saturday, February 28

The president walked through the door of the Oval Office and glanced at Mahony, who nodded a greeting but didn't look up from his tablet. Harry Stanton, Brent Chalmers, Mac Stenberg, Admiral Lear, Mellissa Dellendale, and Daman Pryce followed him in single file. After a few minutes, a Marine announced the arrival of Prince Nazir, the Saudi Arabian ambassador, and the president dispatched two other Marines to escort him into the evening meeting.

Information obtained from Pryce through Zandi had confirmed Iran's housecleaning. The ruling mullahs had sacked the current prime minister and replaced him with a member of parliament, who conveniently found the resources to root out several terrorists and their networks. Iranian Universal Jihad was eliminated and its international presence decimated, since many of Ghazali's inner circle had loitered inside Iran during the Israeli launch. Those not immediately captured were hunted down.

Other collaborators inside the Iranian government abruptly changed their attitude and divulged all the information they could, while uncooperative terrorist associates suffered swift extermination. Iran, in the span of ninety-six hours, had undergone a transformation vastly different from the 1979 Iranian Revolution. Although the new prime minister considered himself a reformist fundamentalist, and the mullahs still retained the ultimate authority, the housecleaning message clearly signaled a new day had dawned.

"Any quick analysis before Nazir arrives?" the president asked.

"Just confirmed much of what was previously reported, Mr. President," Daman Pryce answered. "By our estimation, what the Iranians have done in the past few days counteracts decades' worth of allocated resources to terrorist networks. I don't think we could have accomplished it in years, if ever. Ironically, one might argue that Iran is now the most terrorist-free nation in the Middle East. We also are hearing of ramifications with Hezbollah and Hamas. Funding has been redirected."

"What do you mean by that?" the president asked.

"Money for the political arms remain, but not for the terrorists," Pryce replied.

"Anything else?"

Pryce massaged his chin as he glanced at Mel. Biting his lower lip, he returned his attention toward the president.

"Out with it, Mr. Pryce," the president demanded.

Clearing his throat, Pryce said, "There's another facet to the Iranians' actions these past several days. It's not only our nuclear subs in the Persian Gulf or a potential Israeli retaliation that's motivated them."

The president gestured for the CIA agent to continue.

"Well, sir, it's the American Terrorist. The death toll in Mashhad is approaching two and a half million people. Understandably they fear him as much as, if not more than, our retaliation. For purging all the terrorist networks, they now demand that Iran be removed from Spencer's target list. They made the demand to Zandi, but officially presented it to the Saudis, and I'll wager it's Nazir's priority today."

"So, they're still under the impression we can control Spencer?" he asked, grimacing.

Pryce nodded. "Zandi said they are claiming that their actions are louder than our words. If they can clean house, so can we."

"Well, haven't they thought that if the American Terrorist is so much more resourceful in inflicting harm than their own terrorist, he just might be that more resourceful in eluding us?"

"They don't see it that way. They think he must have had government sponsorship to do what he has. You see, from their perspective, unaffiliated individuals simply couldn't do what

Spencer has done."

"Well, that puts us in predicament, now doesn't it? And you think Nazir will broach this today?"

Pryce nodded again. "I think it's the primary reason he's here."

"Not that supposedly all-important comprehensive Middle East peace package?" the president asked wryly.

Pryce shook his head, lips tightly pressed.

"Well, I really wasn't expecting to talk peace with him," Halladan replied. "We might as well see him now."

Nazir stepped through the door with an entourage behind him. Halladan offered him the couch to his right with only two seats, and Nazir understood the invitation was for two only. He turned and dismissed several of those accompanying him, while one middle-aged man with sharp, penetrating eyes remained. They took their appointed seats.

"I think you know everyone here, Ambassador," Halladan declared instead of asking. Nazir nodded and began to introduce his associate, but the president proceeded without giving him chance. "As I am certain your intelligence agencies have confirmed, Iran has gone through, well let's say an extraordinary change in the past several days. From what I understand, you played an important role, especially communicating the need to protect our asset inside Iran. It was a fine piece of backdoor diplomacy, given the difficult relationship Saudi Arabia has with Iran, and we thank you for that."

Nazir bowed his head.

"And now you have requested to see me," Halladan said blandly.

"Yes, Mr. President. Informally."

"Didn't seem too informal with all those assistants following you," Halladan observed.

Nazir scanned the room and nearly objected considering the number of people Halladan included in his retinue, but fought back the retort. "Mr. President, as you know, we are here primarily about a comprehensive Middle Eastern peace package, but first we would like to discuss this Iranian transition. We are pleased by it; it does raise a few issues, however."

Halladan folded his hands in his lap. "All right, let's start with Iran's transition."

"Yes. Since you haven't any official channels with Iran, I was asked to bring a message to you. Iran wishes for you to remove it from the American Terrorist's target list."

Halladan shrugged with a fatigued expression. "Ambassador Nazir, we don't control the American Terrorist. Unlike our Persian friends, we aren't hiding terrorists, and we don't have anyone in the government who can miraculously reveal his location…or his plans. I'm afraid we're all still vulnerable to his attacks."

"Mr. President," Nazir responded, "as I'm certain you've been told, many inside Iran have already, well, how do you say, been neutralized. However, outside Iran, there are groups that can still inflict significant damage."

Halladan nodded. "We heard Iran was cutting funds to the terrorist branches of Hamas and Hezbollah."

"But that could change, sir," Nazir added without changing his expression.

Halladan glanced at Pryce, whose slight nod confirmed the ambassador's veiled threat.

Before Halladan could respond, the ambassador continued. "We also have other news that may not have been reported to you." Nazir glanced at his associate, who reached for his briefcase and withdrew several sheets of paper. He handed them to Halladan with a small flourish. "What you have in your hands, sir, is a list of individuals, that have been shall I say permanently detained or removed. They are from several Middle Eastern, Central Asian, and African countries. It isn't exhaustive, but it is extensive."

Halladan handed the list to Pryce. The CIA operative perused it for several moments, and whistled under his breath. "What do you think, Mr. Pryce?" Halladan asked.

"Mr. President, if this list can be confirmed, every major network has been either completely dismantled or seriously damaged. This actually is more thorough than what Iran did, sir."

Halladan glowered. "How is it, Ambassador Nazir, that all these governments suddenly discover and eliminate these terrorists and their networks? It's so obvious you could have done this many years ago."

Nazir's associate cleared his throat, and responded in a thick accent. "That's not necessarily true."

Everyone stared at him. "My name is Hadi Al-Jamil. I work as a liaison for many religious organizations inside and outside our country. Much of the information we needed to locate and apprehend those on that list came from several religious institutions that wished to eliminate terrorist threats, all of them. Rooting them out became a favored course of action only after Ghazali's near apocalypse. You must, however, understand that this American Terrorist cannot be allowed to make any further attacks, and he must be brought to justice."

The president leaned forward. "You're not listening, Mr. Al-Jamil. I guess no one is. We don't control the American Terrorist."

Al-Jamil shrugged haughtily, and replied stonily, "It doesn't matter what you say. His demands have been met, and all nations referenced on that list should be removed from his."

The truth blind-sided Halladan. He looked at Daman Pryce and Mel Dellendale for confirmation and they nodded in unison. Mel added, "That was Spencer's demand: eliminate the terrorists and their networks."

"But there's no way he would really know this, right?" Halladan muttered. "He has no idea his demands have been met."

A pall descended over the US contingent; the two Muslim men looked expectantly at Halladan. After a moment of contemplation, Halladan's impassive visage returned. "Mr. Nazir, Mr. Al-Jamil, at this time I don't think any of your governments can afford to announce that you have complied with Spencer's demands. Despite the necessity, too many of your unstable regimes would not survive that display of weakness. Besides, such announcements might not be perceived as credible. I have no solution for you. As I have said, we don't have any connection, any association, any communication, or any influence with Thom Spencer. As insensitive as this is to say, I can't help but think you gentlemen have made those beds, and now you must sleep in them. We will be in touch if we receive any information that could help you. Thank you."

Nazir trembled at his sudden dismissal. "And that is all you have to offer?" Nazir seethed.

Halladan met the ambassador's indignant question with smoldering eyes. "Mr. Ambassador, did you really expect me to wave a magic wand and conjure up Thom Spencer for you upon demand? Are you that naïve? I will not *ask* you to leave again."

Nazir stuttered in a fit of rage. "This…this…this…is…" Al-Jamil tugged at his companion's sleeve, shaking his head and whispering in Arabic to him. They rose and stalked out the room.

Halladan leaned forward. "Mr. Pryce, can you confirm those names and networks?"

Daman nodded. "I'll have it within in an hour, sir."

"Make it sooner," Halladan ordered and then exhaled. "Those Muslim governments can't make any announcement, but the fact these networks have been destroyed will eventually be revealed and confirmed. If we leak the information, that process can be hastened. Even with the leak, I still think we have a forty-eight to seventy-two hour window before everyone realizes that these terrorists have been destroyed. Anyone disagree?"

Everyone appeared to confirm the president's assessment.

The president abruptly directed his attention toward Mel. "Agent Dellendale, your analysis about Spencer hasn't changed, has it? You still think he'll stand down if he is convinced that these terrorists and networks have been eliminated?"

Mel nodded. "I do, sir."

"Then we have two to three days during which Spencer might attack again."

"We might be too late, sir," Daman observed. "He might have already infected his next target."

Halladan's brooding expression indicated he understood. "Agent Dellendale, your protocol is changing again. Did you dismantle the Dupree operation?"

Mel shook her head. "No. I was just to notify you before any deployment."

"Good," Halladan replied. "Sometimes presidential orders get confused and people take it upon themselves to overdo it. Glad you didn't, but I am now rescinding that requirement to notify me. Launch teams upon any indication of that trigger and then notify me. Andy, please help her implement that protocol now."

Andy Mahony was wildly tapping on his tablet and didn't immediately acknowledge the president. "Mr. Mahony, you need to assist Agent Dellendale. Right now!"

Mahony looked up, his face a mix of intensity and frustration. "Sir, sorry, sir, what can I do?" The president repeated the order. "No problem, sir. Agent Dellendale, please use my interface. I'll establish the connection." He tapped the tablet a few times and handed it to her. Mel began her orchestrations on the surface to implement the new orders.

"You still think it's unlikely Spencer will test his trigger?" Halladan asked.

Mel tapped, typed, and talked. "Yes, sir, it's unlikely. It's worth monitoring, but I don't think we can rely on it."

Halladan sighed. "So, we're too late if I receive any notification from you, right, Mel?"

Mel frowned. "I'm afraid so."

"Then we have a long couple of days to wait, don't we?" the president surmised.

Chapter Forty-Nine

Saturday, February 28

Eight hours later, Mel stepped out of the shower and jumped into her workout outfit. She glanced at herself in the mirror and shook her head, realizing for the first time her running suit was made with technology developed by Thom Spencer's Nanoexelogy. Too exhausted to worry about any irony, she eyed the couch, wanting to take a quick nap. Before she could even think about taking a break, she had to review several e-mails. The documents sprang into mid-air, and then they suddenly vanished as a Dupree alert flashed. It was surreal; she didn't think it would happen, but there it was. Dupree had detected a trigger. Fatigue disappeared as she pressed a button and Tray Dupree appeared. "Dr. Dupree?"

"Agent Dellendale," he immediately responded, "we've detected a possible trigger and can't confirm the source. Per your latest orders, we sent in the nearest team."

"Location, Doctor?"

"Cairo."

Mel shook her head. "Unlikely a test."

Dupree agreed with a nod. "And given the location, likely to be Spencer."

"Please hold."

On her holographic screen, she pressed another button. The president appeared.

"I assume we have detected a trigger, Agent Dellendale," he said evenly.

"Yes, sir. Cairo."

"Twenty million at risk," he declared. "Please come to the White House immediately, Agent Dellendale. I will have Nazir informed of the situation."

"Yes, sir. I'll call you in the car." She terminated both video calls and ran out her office door.

Chapter Fifty

Saturday, February 28

For nearly four days, media reports had leaked from Iran about the mullahs replacing the prime minister. Other sources claimed many Middle Eastern, Central Asian, and African governments had started purging terrorist networks at an unprecedented scale. Finally Iran confirmed it had a new prime minister and a different foreign policy. Yet no government had confirmed Ghazali's or any other terrorist's capture or elimination; only rumors circulated. Spence stared at the phone in his hand as he listened to the satellite TV. Should he attack Cairo with ten million lives or more at stake, or should he pick up the phone and call off the massive assault? The terrorist networks still presumably operated, so Cairo had to be sacrificed to further emphasize his point. No surrender.

Tyler entered the small TV room. "Strange, but I'm gettin' kinda used to these places." he offered as a distraction from the phone.

Spence nodded. "A warehouse is a warehouse wherever you are," he answered absently, knowing both of them avoided discussing the dilemma created by the news of the day.

Tyler glanced at the phone in Thom's hand. "Maybe the major decided against the attack, Spence."

"He may have delayed it, but he'll proceed unless he hears from me," Spence answered.

Tyler exhaled. "We may still have time to call him. Maybe you make the call, Spence. Let's see how all these news reports play out."

Spence took his eyes off the phone and stared at nothing as he reconsidered Cairo's sacrifice. As always, the vision of severed heads and his family's blood invaded the contemplation, and steel nerves swiftly returned. Without confirmation of the listed terrorist networks' destruction, he had to proceed not just with Cairo, but the other targets as well. With determination, he rose from the couch, leaving the phone behind. "No, Tyler, we don't rely on the rumor mill, and one prime minister isn't definitive. Maybe something has changed, but I can't be sure. We've come this far, and I'm not letting up. Even if we have to kill a hundred million or more," he whispered.

Tyler pressed his lips together. "I'm with you, Spence, but what if we're right on the verge? What if this ruins the chance? What if this galvanizes them?"

"Galvanizes them to do what?" Spencer asked without emotion.

Washington's shoulders slumped. "How many children have we killed so far, Spence?"

"How many of those children have learned to hate us, Tyler?"

Before Tyler could respond, Miles Wilbur entered the room, his face flushed and his eyes blinking urgently. "I've received a call, Mr. Spencer. We must call the major back, sir."

"What do you mean?" Spence asked in rapid cadence, shocked by the insistent request.

"Your demands have been met. I have confirmation from a reliable source." Wilbur further explained how all the terrorist networks—and more—identified by the media had been decimated.

Spence stared at Wilbur. Now something had definitively changed. He knew Miles would not utter such a statement without complete confidence in it, but it triggered a question. "Reliable source?" Spence asked slowly.

"We have a Washington contact, sir."

Tyler glanced at the taciturn man skeptically. "Now, that seems a little odd, don't you think, Miles?"

Miles's eyes returned to their usual stoic gloss. "Mr. Washington, a trusted person inside the administration made a call. We can recall Major Brannan. That is all I was told. Now, I wouldn't have been contacted if the information weren't reliable. Of course, the decision is yours, but it clearly is in our best interest to recall the major. Please believe, Mr. Spencer, Mr. Washington, that my contacts have the same interests you do. You must understand this by now."

Spence felt the organization's puppet strings pulling on his wrist, and he clenched his fists, trying to break the imagined constriction. He stared intently at Wilbur, trying to detect a scheme, an ulterior motive, something to belie his words, but he knew the man spoke the truth. Everything had changed in less than a minute. All the rumors floating around the news cycle had been instantly verified. Now was his chance to stop the killing, an opportunity to end his maniacal rampage, and a weird desolation descended on him.

Wilbur sighed, realizing he had nothing more to offer, and left Tyler and Spencer in a quandary. They looked at each other, and Washington, nodding toward the phone, silently urged Spence to make the call.

Spence hesitated, and he hated himself for it. The world could change, and Thom Spencer could change as well. He knew he could make the call, ending the gore and appalling death. But a strange resistance surged inside him, holding him back, gnawing at him from the inside. It wanted him to exact more than just revenge. It coursed through his body, all the way to his fingertips. He closed his eyes as he clenched his fists, feeling a transcendent rage bubbling up. A demon inside him taunted him to reject every reason why he had set out to destroy terrorism; the demon inside him wanted to dash over, pick up the phone, and throw it as hard as he could against the wall and let them all die in agony. He boiled with that rage, and in his mind's eye, Spence saw his face morph into Ghazali's. He had become what he wanted to destroy; the hate had consumed him, and that hate was all he could find in his soul, and killing the only relief for it.

But hate was a choice. Spence opened his eyes and looked at Tyler; he then walked to the phone and dialed. When the line was answered, he said clearly, "Major Brannan, please return."

Chapter Fifty-One

Saturday, February 28

Brannan stood in a Cairo city square under a clear moonlit sky momentarily stunned by the telephone call he had just received from Thom Spencer. The call itself didn't surprise him, but he looked at the tape in his hand, and more than half of it was gone. He had already placed many of the strips around the city.

As in the previous attacks, he had staggered all the strips to emit the signal at the same time to eliminate any detectable pattern. He glanced at his watch. The timing gave him only three hours to retrace his steps and destroy every strip. Seemingly the point of no return had passed; and he didn't have time to get them all.

Despite evening time, the streets of Cairo remained crowded. Brannan abruptly turned on his heel, and without bringing attention to himself headed to the last location he had visited.

After destroying six strips, the major knew he would have to take a few chances. When an opportunity arose, he ran. Taxis were plentiful, and Brannan hired them wherever available, ordering them to wait if needed. At a few stops, he "borrowed" unlocked bicycles. On the nineteenth posting, he rode right into an armed soldier with beads of sweat bubbling on his forehead.

"What's the hurry?" the soldier demanded.

Brannan bowed his head and profusely apologized, breathing heavily. "I am sorry, so very sorry. My wife and child have called me home. I only hurry for them."

The soldier stared hard at the Arab-looking middle aged man and shrugged. "It is getting late. Just please watch where you're going so you don't hurt yourself or someone else, sir," he politely requested.

Again Brannan apologized, surprised at the soldier's demeanor, and jumped back on the bike and quickly rode away.

He looked at his watch again; he had made excellent time, and it appeared he could reach every location, despite his initial calculation. At the final location, he exhaled in relief and peeked at his watch yet again. Just enough time. As he turned the corner into a square, a muezzin called everyone to an evening prayer at a local mosque. The throng of people blocked him from where the tape was sticking on a fence near the side of the holy sanctuary, innocently conspicuous. He could even see it through bobbing heads. He looked at his watch again, and the seconds ticked away. Frustrated, he jostled a man shuffling toward the mosque. Others beside the elderly Muslim glared at Brannan, wondering what provoked his rudeness. Brannan didn't meet the angry stares, but slid by them as gently as possible, mumbling apologies. Just as he burst through the crowd, the watch beeped. Brannan ignored the infuriating sound and lunged toward the tape, crumpling it in his hand as soon as he ripped it from the wall. Dismissing the curious looks, he quickly jogged past, furtively burning the tape as he wondered how many Cairenes had just died.

Chapter Fifty-Two

Saturday, February 28

The car bolted into the street before Mel had a chance to settle into the backseat, lights flashing and siren shrieking. Just before she pressed the button to call the president on her phone, another priority call from Dupree flashed across the screen. Before the ringtone sounded, she answered. "Dupree?"

"Agent Dellendale, it's disappeared!"

"What? What's disappeared?"

"Our red dot that represents the emission. It was there. As I said before, we couldn't confirm the source, which means it's likely Spencer, and then suddenly it disappeared."

Mel scowled at Dupree. "So there was not an electromagnetic emission in Cairo?"

Dupree frowned. "No. I think there was, but then it was abruptly destroyed."

She now understood Dupree's confounded expression. "Did you check for any malfunction?"

He nodded. "We cross-checked all systems. All running at a hundred percent. We have to assume, Agent Dellendale, this was a genuine trigger by the American Terrorist that was terminated for whatever reason."

"Can you estimate the radius and the possible number of people infected?"

"I have sent the data to Dr. O'Brien. She is better equipped to calculate that."

Mel nodded. "Have her forward it immediately to me. Even preliminary numbers."

Dupree again nodded. "I sent the rapid deployment force immediately. Do you want me to recall the team?"

"No. I will obtain clarification from the president, but we had strict orders to launch the team upon an American Terrorist attack. We can always recall them. I will be in touch."

She terminated the call and pressed the presidential button on her phone, but she couldn't get through. "What is more important than this?" she muttered to herself. Her phone rang again. Thinking it was President Halladan, she answered reflexively, "Mr. President?"

"No, Meredith O'Brien. I made those calculations. There may be some damage, but I think it will be minimal. Perhaps fewer than a hundred, maybe even fewer than fifty. Once we confirm more detailed assumptions, I'll let you know."

"Thank you, Doctor." Mel sighed heavily. She felt relieved when O'Brien mentioned one hundred deaths and elated at fifty, and then sullen and sad at one.

Upon her arrival at the White House, a Marine immediately escorted her to the Oval Office. When she entered, she understood why the president hadn't responded. Nazir and his companion had beaten her to the White House.

Nazir lurched forward, eyes glaring at Halladan. "You're able to detect the toxin?" he fumed, outraged.

"The trigger, not the substance, Nazir. And quit the indignation. You've put yourself in this position, and I don't want hear your inane recriminations."

Nazir had to suffer the insult; he found the nerve and asked, "Where?"

Halladan looked at him with compassion. "Cairo."

Nazir's shoulders slumped. "But that's twenty million people," he whispered. "What do we do?"

Halladan surveyed the room, looking to no one in particular for an answer. Mel quickly scanned the room. Everyone at the last meeting was present and bearing dire expressions. They hadn't been notified of Dupree's latest update. Before the tension exploded, she interrupted. "Maybe not twenty million people, Mr. President. The trigger seems to have disappeared. We still believe there was an emission, but it was very limited in duration, and the early estimate is perhaps fewer than one hundred deaths, maybe even fewer than fifty."

Halladan took Mel's information in stride. "You confirmed there was not a malfunction?" Mel nodded. "And you and Dupree think it was Spencer?" Mel nodded again. "But you cannot determine the reason why it was terminated." Another nod by Mel. "Could this have been one of those controlled tests?"

Mel shrugged. "I don't know, Mr. President.

Halladan exhaled and closed his eyes, leaning his head on his fingertips. "We have to assume Spencer is in Cairo and is attacking that city. I know this will cause utter chaos and widespread panic, but Ambassador Nazir, you must tell the Egyptian government…what are you doing, Andy?" Mahony had shoved his tablet under the president's nose and urged him to read it. Halladan squinted at the screen and did a double take; then he leveled his eyes at his information advisor, bewildered. "Ambassador…Ambassador Nazir, hold off on that, and please give me moment with my staff."

Addled by the president's abrupt change in demeanor, Nazir declined an objection, and nodded toward Al-Jamil and left with only a slight bow.

Once the two men had departed, Halladan, mouth slightly agape, turned the tablet screen toward Mel. "I've found our damned leak!" In large letters, the screen read: *I HAD THOM SPENCER NOTIFIED THAT HIS DEMANDS WERE MET.*

Halladan's suspicions were finally confirmed. But he had never suspected Andy Mahony, yet it made perfect sense. His information technologist had access to every meeting and nearly every piece of information coming into and going out of the Oval Office.

From all the stunned expressions, no one else had suspected Mahony either, and then the president noticed the subtle nods when they connected their own dots. The quiet, demur Andy Mahony transformed in front of their eyes. His posture assumed a more confident pose, and his eyes deadened like a soldier's in the heat of battle. He folded his arms, and said evenly, "I'm just a contact, nothing more."

"A contact for whom?" the president demanded.

"I'm just a contact placed here for this… and other purposes. Senseless killing had to be avoided."

Pryce rose from his chair. "The American Terrorist infiltrated the Oval Office!" he exclaimed incredulously.

"No, sir, the American Terrorist did not," Mahony countered firmly.

"Then who?" the president asked in a low voice.

"Mr. President, I simply answer to an unknown person who represents an organization that operates to protect the interests of the United States when those interests are threatened. This is all I can and will say. Let me be clear, I did not hurt, harm, or endanger you or any in your administration at any time, but I also want you to understand my loyalties are with those I notified. You perhaps can successfully interrogate me, but I promise you that you will only obtain the information I give to you now. People in my position simply are not entrusted with anything more in order to protect against this very situation."

Halladan recognized the demeanor of a professional military man. Somehow their vetting had missed something in this man's background, or those for whom he worked were just that good. And, of course, the American Terrorist hadn't operated by himself. He had help. Maybe not from the beginning, but at some point he had enlisted the services of something larger with the ability to implement, on a grand scale, a scheme of the magnitude they had witnessed over the past several months. And that organization had the power and capability to plant someone deep inside the administration.

Halladan sighed as he massaged his cheeks. "Why did we detect an emission, Andy?"

Andy Mahony shook his head. "I don't know. I have no personal knowledge of Spencer or his operation. I just know that the emission's disappearance confirms he was notified that his demands were met and that he terminated his mission. If that weren't the case, we wouldn't be having this conversation."

"Why are you telling us this now?" Mac Stenberg asked, still dumbfounded.

Mahony's expression softened slightly. "So you can inform Ambassador Nazir. There is no reason to create panic in Cairo. The city and the country wouldn't survive it. That wouldn't be good for us or anyone."

Halladan agreed. "Get Nazir back in here."

The ambassador stood again at the president's desk. "Ambassador Nazir, we've just had direct confirmation of Agent Dellendale's report. The loss if any will be very limited; perhaps fewer than fifty people. You need to contact the Egyptian government with me so we can explain the situation. Anyone who was exposed will show symptoms, but the Egyptians should have time to quarantine the small infected area. If they can keep any victims from the general population, they can probably avoid widespread panic. We'll provide them and you any assistance you need. We can have a team…" Halladan discreetly glanced at Mel for confirmation. She nodded. "A special kind of team at the toxin epicenter in minutes, if requested."

Nazir, relieved, exhaled. "All right. It'll be better if I have a preliminary conversation first. Can you provide me a direct line?"

"Of course. We will provide you an unsecured line immediately." Halladan recalled a Marine to escort the ambassador and his assistant to a nearby room.

After they had departed, Halladan looked at Andy Mahony, who nodded his approval. Halladan scoffed. "Yeah, glad you approve, Andy, and I have one of those Marines for you too, but you're not going to the same room as the ambassador did. Got a different place for you. Not nearly as comfortable."

"Understood, Mr. President," Mahony replied deadpan.

Despite facing a severe leak in his administration, and an organization hidden deep inside his own country with breathtaking resources, Halladan allowed himself a faint smile, quietly thanking God Cairo wouldn't endure a disaster of an epic proportion. And by the expressions staring back at him, he wasn't alone in his ineffable relief.

Chapter Fifty-Three

Monday, March 2

In the TV room, Tyler and Spence paced back and forth as the news anchor continued reporting on the Cairo attack. The American Terrorist had struck again, but the number of casualties had remained at less than thirty, and no one had reported symptoms for many hours. Information about the attack had leaked despite the quarantine of the infected area, and fear spread quickly through the streets of Cairo. Government and military officials assured the people that the situation was under control and theirs was not another Mashhad. Still, frightened people started to quarrel and riot; crowds gathered around hospitals and government buildings; angry mobs targeted the US embassy with rocks and Molotov cocktails. As the hours passed and no one else showed any symptoms, tension began to wane. Violence subsided with anxiety its substitute.

The media tried squeezing another sensationalized story out of the attack. Many accused it of wanting another several million dead so it could have a never-ending headline. Finally, even the most aggressive reporters recognized the death toll would not exceed the reported number, and the question swiftly switched to why Cairo was spared. Most concluded the American Terrorist had pulled the plug on his killing operation because of the reports from Tehran and rumors of decimated terrorist networks across the entire Middle East, Africa, and Central Asia.

Tyler finally dropped down on the couch. "Well, I think we called off the major in time. Looks like there is minimal damage. I think it's over, Thom."

The words echoed off walls, emphasizing the emptiness and desolation Spence felt as he listlessly nodded. "Yes, but now what do we do? You know they're coming for us."

Tyler shrugged. "Hey, our job is finished. We don't need to do anything more. We just fade away. Maybe they find us, maybe they don't."

"Us?" Spence asked. "You know, I don't think I've ever even heard your name mentioned, Tyler."

"Really? And do you really believe they think you concocted all of this own your own, pathogen and all? You're good, Thom, but I'm not sure they'll believe you're that good. I go where you go."

"I'm not sure that's wise. Anyway, the first thing to decide is what we do with the serum. We have some left. More importantly, what do we do with the formula? Do we keep it? Destroy it?"

Before Tyler offered an answer, the door burst open and Major Brannan entered. Again, they barely recognized him. The reunion didn't generate any feelings of joy or accomplishment, only a sense of finality. They exchanged nods, and Spence mumbled, "Well, Major Brannan, you've had an interesting trip."

The major nodded. "I nearly didn't get out of Cairo. Had to backtrack for several hours to retrieve all the tape. Obviously I didn't get one piece, or at least all of it. After that, with bags packed and ready to go, I went directly to the airport. I had enough time to perform a few facial alterations right before my flight. Before the havoc even started, I had already landed, switched flights, and taken off from Barcelona."

Spence chuckled. "I didn't mean just that leg, Major Brannan."

Brannan nodded, his face stoic.

"You were able to get all but one piece of our tape," Tyler observed curiously. Again Brannan nodded. Washington raised his eyebrows, thinking how serendipity had spared so many lives.

Spence eyed the major a little suspiciously. "And why are you here, Major? Are you here to tie up two loose ends?"

The major pressed his lips together. "Yes, actually I am, Mr. Spencer. And as you correctly suspect, you and Mr. Washington are those loose ends."

Tyler started up from his seat, fear and anger contorting his face. The major held up his hand, palms outward. "Nothing sinister, Mr. Washington, but we have to figure what to do with the two of you."

"We were just talking about that," Spence replied coolly, uncertain whether he believed the major's assurance, vividly recalling Timothy Preston's bloody demise. "In fact, Major, we were just discussing what to do with the serum. Maybe we destroy what is left as well as the formula."

Major Brannan, shrugging casually, strolled to their small refrigerator and took out a cola. He offered both Spence and Tyler one; Spencer refused, Tyler accepted. Brannan lowered himself into a chair, opened the can, and took a long drink before answering. "Mr. Spencer, Mr. Washington, I will help you do what you need to do. The operation is complete, and we need to close it down. If you want to destroy the serum and the formula, just tell me what's required. I'll still need to know where you want to go. But once we've moved you to your chosen destination, you'll never see me again. Unfortunately we can't help you after that. You'll be pursued forever. You could be caught in one month, one year, ten years, or never, but you'll always be on the run in some way or another."

Spence nodded. "I understand. Any advice, Major Brannan, how we might avoid that kind of life, at least to a certain extent?"

Major Brannan subtly sighed. "Yes, Mr. Spencer, I have some. It might be unacceptable to you. If so, fine. Again, I will do whatever you want."

Spencer gestured for Brannan to continue.

"Destroy the existing serum and send the US government the formula with a 'so sorry, but you didn't do your job, so I did,' explanation. Then move just once from here, each to different locations. Create an alternate identity; don't move around. Establish yourself under that identity with documents, stories, and awareness of local events and relations that predate your actual arrival so everyone assumes you have lived there much longer than you actually have, and just live. If they come, so be it, they come, but don't keep running."

"And you can help us with that identity?" Washington asked.

"Yes. Of course."

Spencer leaned against the far wall, his arms folded, with a smirk spreading across his face. Brannan, noticing the quirky expression, asked, "And why are you smiling, Mr. Spencer?"

Spence blinked several times before answering. "Well, I don't know whether I believe you, Major Brannan. It seems incredible."

"What does?" the major asked.

"You mean to tell me that if Tyler and I took you up on this offer, and right now destroyed the serum and delivered all our work to the US government, not only would you refrain from stopping us, but you would help us? Come on, Major Brannan, that's unbelievable."

"And why's that?"

"You don't want it, Major? You mean to tell me that you haven't been helping us ultimately to get the serum and the formula for your organization?"

"Mr. Spencer, if you gave us both the serum and the formula, it would end up with the US government anyway."

Washington let out his breath in a gasp. "Oh…my…God. Oh my God! I can't believe it, Spence. We should've known from the beginning. Our major is the US government! What agency, what black ops outfit are you working for?"

Brannan calmly shook his head. "Mr. Washington, if you're caught, the first question the government will ask is, 'Who helped you?' We're not the government. And it very well may be that the government at this moment has just become aware of our existence, and I can guarantee you that a massive search for us will begin. One as large, if not larger, than the one coming for you. We don't want the serum. That would be just another reason for them to pursue us. Anyway, it's just as safe, maybe safer, with them."

Spencer accepted Brannan's answer. He had never really believed the major or his organization was affiliated with the government since the day he had confronted Timothy Preston with the same accusation. "So what agency would we give it to, Major?" Spence asked.

"Your choice."

"The FBI?" Spence offered.

"Why not?" Brannan answered.

Spence pursed his lips. "All right, I have another question. What if one of us surrenders? What do you think happens to other?"

Brannan didn't hesitate. "If it's you, Mr. Spencer, who surrenders, I think Mr. Washington goes free. If they have you, it's over in their minds. They'll spend some insignificant resources searching for Mr. Washington, but if they don't find him in the first couple of years, they'll drop it. With the identity we establish for him, he'll be safe."

"Whoa, Thom. That's not going to happen. We're in it together. If you go in, I go too." Tyler said firmly.

"I don't think so, Tyler. This was my fight first. You joined me, because they brutally murdered my family. I now have to answer for what I've done. But I do so with you as my insurance policy."

Both Brannan and Tyler stared curiously at Spence. He returned the looks with a glare. "I nearly smashed the phone instead of calling you, Major, when Miles came in and told us that we could salvage Cairo. I wanted to kill them anyway. My soul hardens by the moment, callous and cold. My body temperature drops daily, and once you hate like I have hated, it blisters your insides beyond repair. Reclaiming any other emotion becomes impossible. I'm nearly dead as it is, so my sacrifice isn't much of a sacrifice at all.

"Major Brannan, I don't think Muslims will ever enter the modern world. Once Tyler and I are captured and served up, their little terrorist organizations will start up again, and then in another decade or two, maybe three, we're back to square one. But if I surrender alone, and let them know that one of us is still out there, the one with the real brains, the one who can actually make the virus and kill them all…well, that just might keep them honest. I'm dead, but they live in fear of you, Tyler. Whether or not you would ever do it again, the threat remains."

Brannan cleared his throat. "You put him in greater jeopardy, Mr. Spencer, if you make that threat."

"Then it's in your organization's best interest to make sure nothing happens to Mr. Washington, isn't it?"

Brannan thought about that for a moment, and then nodded his agreement with tightly pressed lips. "Yes, you're right."

Spence offered a small, tight smile. "It just keeps everyone a little honest if they think a man capable of killing all of them remains at large."

"Whether or not I turn myself in with you, Spence, the man really capable of killing them all will remain at large regardless, won't he, Major Brannan?" Tyler asked pensively.

Brannan folded his hands and rested them in his lap. "Yes, Mr.

Washington, I will remain at large."

Spencer sighed. "I need to surrender on my terms, Major. Can you help me get back into the country?"

"Of course, Mr. Spencer," Brannan answered succinctly. "That won't be a problem. What's your plan?"

Spencer shook his head, declining any further explanation. "No plan, just get me back in."

Chapter Fifty-Four

Wednesday, March 18

Mel, absorbed by several holographic charts, still couldn't locate the American Terrorist. Although fatalities in Cairo had remained low, the Middle Eastern governments maintained pressure on the US to capture Thom Spencer. The destruction of the terrorist networks had given them the moral grounds to make demands. Publicly the president rebuffed much of their sanctimonious rhetoric; privately he insisted that every relevant agency make serious and concerted efforts to find the American Terrorist.

The president walked a fine line. In his press conference after the nuclear tension had subsided, Halladan emphasized how the Muslim governments had helped themselves by removing destructive and dangerous elements from their respective societies. But he couldn't deny the importance of apprehending the American Terrorist. A nation founded on and bound by the rule of law, and constantly espousing the value of this all-important principle, couldn't ignore its responsibility to bring the American Terrorist to justice.

Resources had been spread thin since the revelation of an inside job in the White House. Of course this item wasn't for public consumption, but the administration allocated significant time and energy trying to discover the extent of the penetration. The president had implied discreetly that he wanted Mel to include it in her

Spencer investigation. In the past few days, she had found herself more engrossed in ferreting out the secret organization than Spencer's location, believing this link would ultimately lead to the thread exposing both. Frustratingly, the mysterious organization had covered itself as well as if not better than the American Terrorist.

She took a sip of coffee and leaned back in her chair, massaging the muscles in her neck and shoulders. When she leaned forward, an e-mail alert flashed on the screen. It landed in her personal FBI quarantined inbox with an attachment. She didn't recognize the sender's address, but the subject line caught her attention with the name Thom Spencer and a date. She considered deleting it, but the date tugged at her. She opened her calendar. It was the day she had met Thom Spencer, the day his family had been murdered. The email and the attachment tested clean, and she opened it. After deciphering some of its contents, she read the e-mail again and shook her head in disbelief, her heart pounding. Pressing a holographic button with a trembling finger, Mel asked her assistant to connect her with the president immediately.

An hour later, a Marine escorted her into the Oval Office. The president, Chief of Staff Mac Stenberg, and Special Counsel Harry Stanton sat around the coffee table, seemingly awaiting her arrival. "All right, Agent Dellendale, what's so urgent?" the president asked, forgoing any greeting.

"Mr. President, I think I have received an e-mail from Thom Spencer. He has asked for me to meet him at the US District Court, North Texas District in Dallas, where he said he will surrender himself."

Stunned silence and wide eyes answered the special agent. She looked at Halladan, prompting him for some sort of response.

But Harry Stanton spoke first. "How do you know it actually is Spencer, Agent Dellendale?" he asked with lawyer-like skepticism.

"I don't know for sure, yet, Mr. Stanton, but he also sent an attachment that I think will confirm it's he."

"What's the attachment?" the president asked.

"He's sent me all the data on his serum, sir. Now, I'm not a scientist, but I've been around long enough to know real scientific expressions from drivel, and this looks authentic. I haven't shown it to anyone yet, but we can confirm it. However, we should think carefully about what agency actually tests it."

Shocked silence continued for a few more moments before Stenberg suggested, "Maybe the FBI lab isn't the right place, Mr. President."

Halladan shook his head. "Agreed. I think O'Brien and our friends in NSA should have the first look. The FBI has different legal responsibilities." Mel understood. Bio-nano-weapons still were banned. Under a national defense rubric with the NSA, disclosure decreased and latitude increased for the handling of the American Terrorist's pathogen.

Stanton grimaced. "This could complicate many things, Mr. President, if it is ever leaked that we have this serum. We're going to be in some serious trouble. No doubt Middle Eastern governments would view it as evidence we sponsored this maniac's terrorism."

"Not much different than the quandary Dr. O'Brien revealed to us already, is it?" Halladan asked rhetorically.

Dellendale jumped in almost before the president finished speaking. "Spencer recognizes this risk, sir, and he has solution that just might solve both problems. He is willing to surrender even if we fabricate a story that we finally hunted him down and confiscated all his data. He thinks that if other governments know we now have this weapon, it might give us an advantage. Just his opinion though. In the end, he doesn't care if you disclose we have the serum or not. It's ours no matter what…but he does place two conditions on his surrender."

The president raised his eyebrows, pursed his lips, and leaned back in his chair, wary of any demands. Finally, he gestured for her to proceed.

"First, we must accept that he is solely responsible, and that he won't surrender anyone else."

"Unacceptable," Stanton instantly responded. "He didn't act alone, and now we know we have some sort of cabal organization lurking around the White House halls, and this…this terrorist has information we need. And what about the other fella who worked with him? What's his name?"

"Washington. Tyler Washington," Mel answered, her voice indifferent.

"We need him," Stanton said sternly, glaring at her and then looking askance at the president's silence.

In an even-keeled voice, Mel replied. "Spencer claims it's in his best interest and maybe the nation's best interest that one of them remains at large. It keeps our friends in the Middle East in check."

Halladan chuckled. "It sure does. If the number-two man remains in hiding and inactive, but still out there somewhere, he just might come out of the woodwork if they get a little too comfortable and those networks start popping up again. An insurance policy of sorts."

Mac Stenberg shook his head. "We simply can't let that other man go, Mr. President."

"I don't think that's what Spencer is saying," the president answered thoughtfully. "Spencer knows he can't stop us from searching for him. He's just telling us he's not going to help. He's the big fish, and once he's hooked, most of the pressure is off, and maybe it's in our best interest to leave the other one out there." Halladan had found another fine line to walk.

"But he has to give up this…this…group or whatever it was that helped him," Stanton pressed.

Time again for Dellendale to intercede, and she shook her head ever so slightly. The president took the bait and invited her input. "What do you think, Agent Dellendale?"

"Mr. President, since our last meeting, I've been investigating both this organization and, obviously, Spencer. I've created a rough narrative of what I think has gone on between the two. Of course, I can't be certain, but I don't think they're all that connected."

"How can you say that, Agent Dellendale?" Stanton admonished. "Of course they're connected. They've been working together."

Mel pressed her lips firmly together. "Currently, yes, Mr. Stanton," she replied. "But I think this organization has been around much longer than the American Terrorist. Spencer's family was killed. That's what started it for him. And there simply has not been enough time since their murders to penetrate, as you've described, these White House halls. No, the organization surely predates Spencer."

Stenberg squinted, puzzled by Mel's analysis. "So who do you think actually developed the serum? Do you think it was the organization or Spencer?"

"I think Spencer and Washington developed it on their own. The organization then contacted them, or maybe they contacted the organization, perhaps even accidentally. But they both began independent of each other."

Halladan leaned forward. "You know, that makes sense. You have these two guys who concoct this serum, have this plan, but to implement it, someone else comes in and runs the show. Or at least helps run the show."

"From what I can gather, Mr. President," Mel answered, "that is the most likely scenario."

Stanton clenched his folded hands. "Well if that's the case, then he probably couldn't help us even if he wanted. They would have insulated themselves from him as much as possible, wouldn't they?"

"Yes, Mr. Stanton, they would," Mel replied. "Spencer and Washington were their tools."

Halladan smiled. "And vice versa as well."

Mel, eyelids closing slowly, nodded in agreement.

"Okay," Halladan said, "we probably can't get any information from him on our penetrated White House halls and he tells us nothing about Washington. You said he had two demands, Agent Dellendale."

"The second is more difficult, in my opinion. He's asking that the US doesn't surrender jurisdiction, and that we don't extradite him to any Muslim country."

"That's not surprising," Stenberg remarked.

"I don't think it's out of fear, Mr. Stenberg," Mel said. "He says he's not afraid of what they would do to him, but he cannot endure the thought of them gloating over him and his demise. He doesn't respect them enough to allow this to happen, and he also thinks it would injure the US in the future."

Again resistance came from Harry Stanton. "Jurisdiction clearly lies with Iran or Syria. Palestine is a little different, but it's a tough argument to deny the other two."

"What about Thurlington's assassin, the one he pinned your card on, Agent Dellendale?" Stenberg offered. "That gives us jurisdiction."

"I don't know if we could get the death penalty on that one," Stanton opined.

Mac Stenberg frowned. "You know, I think in one of the reports I saw a naturalized Iranian-American citizen on one of the Mashhad victim lists."

Stanton looked at the chief of staff, considering. "Well, that might give us jurisdiction over that death. It's still a tough case, Mac."

Halladan shook his head. "No, it's not. We have crimes against terrorism in this country, domestic or foreign. I'm not standing for reelection, and I don't have any plans to visit any of those other countries. I have no intention of surrendering that man to any other nation. Before he goes anywhere, he's tried, convicted, and sentenced here. We carry out that sentence…and there is only one sentence, and that is death."

Dellendale nodded. "Yes, Mr. President, he concedes that the death penalty would apply. In fact, he made it clear that he deserved and would only accept execution."

The president, sitting quietly, searched the others' eyes. The denouement had come so suddenly everyone felt strange and anxious. They exchanged tentative looks, but no one had anything else to add, so the president shrugged. "Accept the conditions and meet him in Texas, Agent Dellendale."

Chapter Fifty-Five

Monday, March 23

Agent Dellendale sat alone on the outside steps of the courthouse, twisting her ring again. She immediately recognized the man walking slowly toward her, though the public wouldn't. He seemed to have aged beyond his years: thinner, and with longer hair, and lines had appeared. As he stood in front of her, not saying a word, she looked up into deadened eyes. The intense cold seared in her memory had vanished; all life seemed to have evaporated from them.

She stood. "Mr. Spencer."

"Agent Dellendale."

She had prepared a speech, preaching to him the brutality of his acts, the hatred of his deeds, the evil of his ways. No need, she knew. He already knew it all, and her wasted words offended the moment.

He sighed. "Hard to be around the likes of a Hitler or a Stalin or a Pol Pot, isn't it?" he asked without emotion.

She nodded slowly. "Yes, Mr. Spencer, it is in many ways."

"I know. It's been hard to be around myself. I wonder if any of them felt the way I did when looking in the mirror." His eyes flickered for a moment as the image of severed heads suddenly reappeared, and just as quickly went dead again.

"Probably not," she answered.

He shrugged. "It wears on you insidiously."

"What's that, Mr. Spencer?"

"Hatred. Hatred does this to you. It makes you feed yourself on itself, perpetuating yourself all the way to a figurative and perhaps even a literal hell. You know in the end, all the people in Cairo?"

"All the people in Cairo?"

"I almost killed them. Even though I didn't have to, I almost did it. Out of pure hatred. Out of spite. Out of evil. I nearly did it to them because they did this to me."

Mel cocked her head, curious. "Did what?"

"Made me this way. Destroyed who I was and made me hate. I didn't have these emotions before, Agent Dellendale. I wasn't like this."

"I know you weren't, Mr. Spencer, but you made the choice."

"Yes, I did. And I chose to act on that hatred. And what if I hadn't acted, Agent Dellendale? If I hadn't made the choice to become a Hitler, a Ghazali, would your job be harder or easier now?"

She had rehearsed her response to this very question. She looked sternly at him and opened her mouth, but the words didn't come.

He offered a small, sad smile. "See, a part of even you, deep down inside, is glad that I did what I did. And my guess is that many Americans share the same feelings. If the world wants to play with the big boys, then let it know when a real big boy gets into the game, he doesn't play for fun, but plays to win, and to finish it and kill them all if he must. And I hate that I had to play the game, but even now, beyond the hate, beyond the drained emotions, there still lies a soul—damaged undoubtedly, but still holding a conscience whispering that I would do it again."

With an impromptu, honest response, Mel said, "Mr. Spencer, I do think in the wake of all the attacks here, everywhere after Miami and the other cities, Americans were searching for an answer, and you provided many of them with that answer. And yes, there is a sense of satisfaction, but I don't think very many of those people would condone what you've done. I think that if any one of them had the chance to serve you up, they would. I don't think you're a hero."

"Of course I'm no hero. I don't even condone what I've done, and that is why the people of this country must convict me and put me to death. But I wonder."

"Wonder what?"

"What would happen in a trial if I pled self-defense," he said with another flicker in his eyes. "National self-defense. I did it partly to defend my own country," he said with a trace of defiance in his voice.

A breeze swept a few strands of blond hair in front of Mel's eyes. She brushed them aside without any expression while Spencer scrutinized her. She pressed her lips firmly together. "They're still collecting bodies in Mashhad, Mr. Spencer, and they have several more weeks, maybe months, ahead of them."

Spencer scoffed. "And I wonder how many years it will really take to clean up Miami. How many people will walk into a doctor's office in five years with cancer?" Mel had asked herself that question when surveying the rubble. "I bet there was more blood and gore at my home than a thousand in Mashhad. I wonder how long it will take them clean that blood, or the blood staining that church in Houston or that post office in San Diego. But that doesn't matter, does it?"

Mel frowned. "So you're somehow justified, morally superior, because your kind of death left a city quarantined not because of flowing blood or destroyed buildings, but because it must be cleared of two million decomposing bodies? Seriously?"

"Yes."

Mel, not sure how to respond, eyed Spencer skeptically and exhaled.

Then the defiance and the flicker faded, and he said dispassionately, "No matter. The world must know we don't condone my actions at all. I am a moral outrage of immense proportions. And you're right, Agent Dellendale, I can't shirk my responsibility; I won't deny it was my hand that killed all those people. I did, and I embrace what I did. I authenticate my authorship, so I must also embrace the consequence."

Mel nodded. "And that is what will happen, Mr. Spencer."

TURN THE PAGE TO ENJOY
THREE PREVIEW CHAPTERS
of
THE AMERICAN TERRORIST
BOOK TWO: FREEDOM'S TWILIGHT

Chapter 1

The day was warm for November, the sun bright in the early afternoon, with a few wispy clouds floating in an azure sky. Alone, President Mark Dominick Halladan stared at a super high-definition television in the Oval Office and glanced out the window, shaking his head. Storm clouds were forming, and he could see them obscuring the light, turning day into night. And winter was coming, cold, sterile, and brutal, and with it freedom's demise. The voters had just decided against his vice president, Dillon Wright, and had elected Franklin D. Whitten to succeed him as president of the United States. Halladan had just apologized to his vice president.

They should've won. After the American Terrorist had decimated terrorism, Halladan seized the opportunity, implementing polices significantly reducing regulation, taxes, and trade barriers, and the economy exploded. Everyone was getting rich, everyone was doing better, and America was exceptional again. Yet, out of the prosperity a specter rose. A flamboyant attorney, Franklin D. Whitten, discovered an exploitable wound in American politics.

Thom Spencer, the American Terrorist, elicited ambivalence from Americans, and Whitten knew exactly what emotion he could ride to power: guilt. Despite the fact terrorists attacked with blood pouring in stadiums and churches, despite the fact the entire world

1

benefited from the destruction of the terrorist networks, Americans could still be convinced of their guilt, and of their undeserved prosperity.

Whitten began his campaign by attacking Halladan, claiming the president violated law by not extraditing Thom Spencer to the Middle East. Halladan ignored him, so the attorney hustled to The Hague and filed a case in the International Court of Justice against the United States and Mark Dominic Halladan for harboring the international terrorist Thom Spencer. The ICJ, accommodating the unusual claim, granted jurisdiction and allowed the case to proceed. The United States and Halladan would not consent, and Whitten returned to the United States with all the fuel he needed to inflame the country over Halladan's refusal to submit to a lawful tribunal.

Charges of abuse of power and corruption soon followed, and the crusade eventually ignited emotions at college campuses across the country. The crusade spread to state capitals and morphed into a full-blown historical movement, collapsing a mainstream political party along with several activist organizations under its skyrocketing banner. The appointed leader, Whitten, fueled the fire by promoting new policies anointing international law as the supreme law of the land. Next came the resurrection of climate politics and a call for an electronic currency, free health care, equal income, and a host of other programs ultimately capped with a symbolic, militant demand for Thom Spencer's extradition. Whitten had the gift and the charisma, giving currency to a message demonizing the principles that afforded the prosperity allowing for so many to protest rather than to subsist, and the movement advanced its platform with an alluring name, the New Agenda.

When the next presidential campaign started, Whitten announced his candidacy to an adoring mainstream media under the New Agenda banner. Regardless of a media coronation, the New Agenda candidate had an uphill battle; the economy, worldwide and domestically, had continued to thrive under Halladan policies. Although Franklin Whitten had the million dollar smile, and he attracted huge crowds, the country was too comfortable and too prosperous to embrace change. So the polls showed the New Agenda candidate trailing in the race, and Whitten needed money to change the tide. Instead of trolling domestic coffers, he brazenly solicited international sources for donations to political action committees, dismissing murky legal waters by claiming American politics should be globalized. Middle Eastern nations were his first target. To capture their support, he promised his administration would raise oil prices, share US technology, and provide access to weapons, professing that the agreements were simply a way of distributing wealth and knowledge.

The mainstream media loved it, and it pushed what it defined as the most brilliant and far-sighted policy ever to come from a candidate. Whitten's plan helped solve alleged climate problems by giving the oil regimes money to reduce oil production while spreading wealth and knowledge to those entitled to it. The Middle East held out for more plunder, and more it received. Whitten asked the Syrian regime to invite him to Damascus where he could re-launch the issue that had originally brought him fame. He would apologize for America and its refusal to surrender Thom Spencer to Middle Eastern governments, where he deserved to be judged. During the speech, he announced he would extradite Spencer immediately upon his election to the presidency. The Middle Eastern nations bit, and the money flowed.

The New Agenda's opposition, appalled at the audacity of the extradition announcement, thought Whitten had made a fatal error. The media disagreed, promoting Whitten's campaign gambit to a near frenzy. Spencer still resonated ambivalently in America: an avenging hero, but a vigilante who must face the ultimate consequence. The media seized on the ambivalence, hyping those consequences, and the extradition declaration found support. Polls slowly shifted in Whitten's favor.

If the Opposition—the tag the media attached to the New Agenda's opponents—had acquiesced to the extradition, they might have smothered the surge and regained the lead. But President Halladan, in a fateful press conference, trapped the Opposition in its own conscience. He declared the extradition a capitulation of American sovereignty, the right to judge its own citizens for crimes they commit, and just as he would not submit to the ICJ, he would not recognize New Agenda campaign demands either. The decision this time came during the scrutiny of the presidential race, and the media's howl reverberated even more than when he rebuked The Hague. Of course America should capitulate to international demands and norms, the media roared.

The Opposition bristled, claiming America would surrender its sovereignty over their dead bodies; Thom Spencer would stay put and die on American soil if its candidate prevailed. With the influx of Middle Eastern cash, the New Agenda held the lead for four weeks, and it looked as if they would win. Countering Whitten's surge, Vice President Dillon Wright had a flash of genius. An onslaught of radio, television, the internet, print, and other media ads listed all the names of people killed by terrorists on American soil. Nothing else, just names. The elites guffawed at the notion, but the ads quickly reminded Americans what Thom Spencer had stopped. Despite the subsequent mainstream media outrage, the New Agenda lead withered, and rapidly.

Then came another news conference. A reporter hurled a question at President Halladan about a presidential pardon for Thom Spencer. When Halladan impertinently ignored it, the mainstream media went berserk, accusing Halladan of entertaining thoughts of actually releasing the American Terrorist. The mere mention of pardoning the mass murderer generated unease in the American psyche, and the world press unmercifully blasted the president, Dillon Wright, and America. The issue, exploding globally, created the momentum the New Agenda needed to climb back into the lead. Whitten, in a contrived sullen speech, declared he would search for the American Terrorist if pardoned, without the intention of lethally injecting him on American soil, but to deliver him to the Organization of Islamic Cooperation Council of Foreign Ministers, and allow it to determine Spencer's fate. The pardon would be nominally respected, and justice would be served. Without time for Dillon Wright to react, the election occurred, and he lost to the New Agenda candidate with a million dollar smile, Franklin D. Whitten.

President Halladan had wondered if his vice president would accuse him of sabotaging his opportunity; instead, the man graciously thanked Halladan for the opportunity to serve.

Turning away from the sun drenched window, Halladan picked up the phone to answer the reporter's question precipitating his vice president's loss. "Agent Dellendale, could you please meet me at my office?"

Chapter 2

Special Agent Melissa Dellendale, nearly a household name, famous for apprehending the American Terrorist, Thom Spencer, on the steps of the U.S. District Court in Dallas, walked into the Oval Office. President Halladan sat on a couch and offered Mel a seat opposite of him. Accustomed to Oval Office visits, Mel calmly settled across from the president. He sighed heavily, and from behind the couch, revealed the drink he held in his outstretched hand. "Would you like a drink, Mel?"

Mel shook her head. "No thanks, Mr. President. On duty, you know."

Halladan chuckled. "So am I. Always am."

Mel smiled. "Well, I'll still pass, sir."

Halladan nodded and took a sip. Leaning forward, he set his drink on the table and turned over a single sheet of paper with an official heading and a presidential seal. Mel glanced at it, but not invited to read it, she left it untouched.

A strange doubt, even fear, clouded Halladan's face. He rose from the couch, slowly, the years in the Oval Office having taken a toll. "Mel, what do you make of the New Agenda?"

Mel inhaled deeply at the loaded question. Letting out the air furtively, she bit her lip. Unable to conceal her true feelings from

5

the man whom she had grown to trust, she gritted her teeth. "Not much, sir. I am going to be working for an administration I don't know I can believe in or trust. Yet, I don't think I should resign."

"You can't, Mel. Without the likes of you, we don't have a chance." Halladan sighed and glanced ponderingly at Mel. "This New Agenda is something that has been in the works for years. Actually decades, many decades. It's influenced by powers greater than Franklin Whitten, and they see an incredible opportunity to change our country drastically."

"They, sir? Who are they?" she asked curiously.

Halladan shook his head. "I can't directly identify them, Mel. They lurk in the shadows. Funny thing: when Spencer defeated the terrorists, everyone believed the threat from the Middle East would disappear. I knew better. The deeper threat comes from the Islamists, those who strive to implement a Caliphate in stages, thinking and planning in years and decades and even more, if necessary, using the Ghazalis and terrorists like him when convenient. These Islamists are working through evolution rather than revolution, and they work in the shadows, everywhere insinuating themselves into the fabric of society, into the fabric of reality. The power behind the New Agenda is like that, Mel. What you need to understand about these people is that they don't care about the law or rights or morality. None of that matters to them. They care about their agenda, and changing words and meanings and ideas in order for them to get what they want, well...that's what they'll do. Property will become what they define it as—maybe the shirt on your back, maybe not. Our private homes are transformed into public places where everyone has a new right to shelter. Rights are manipulated and defined any way they want. And expressing contrary political views will be hate speech prosecuted to the full extent of their power. With them, liberty and the fate of America are up for grabs."

Mel furrowed her brow, frustrated. She looked directly into the president's eyes. "Sadly, sir, I can't disagree."

Halladan nodded. "So, we have to be willing to fight in the shadows as well; we have to be willing to employ weapons we wouldn't usually consider justified. We have to be willing to use people and organizations that operate more in the dark."

At the mention of 'organizations,' Mel perked up. "I assume

you're talking about that secret organization we think is connected to Thom Spencer."

Halladan grimaced. "Yes. But I believe that organization is different than the New Agenda; in fact, I think it is its nemesis. It better be, because if I'm wrong, we're in a lot of trouble."

Given Halladan's demeanor, Mel glanced at the official document with the presidential seal, sensing the conversation revolved around it.

Halladan slid it toward her slowly, and she gingerly lifted it. Her eyes bulged at its contents: she held in her hands Thom Spencer's presidential pardon. She then lifted her head to meet the president's stare.

Before she asked any questions, Halladan interjected, "You may wonder if that document matters, given what Whitten and the New Agenda have promised to do if I issued his pardoned. They will surrender him to a Muslim authority of some sort while pretending to respect the pardon. That can't happen. That's why, Mel, you need to get Spencer out of that federal prison and conceal him, and do it now."

She blinked several times. The silence between them thickened with tension, which she snapped by clearing her throat. "Sir, are you kidding?" she asked, confused. She scolded herself immediately for the idiotic question. "Of course you're not kidding, Mr. President," she stammered. "I'm sorry. Only...I'm not sure that it's...feasible."

"It is. I have arranged it," he answered sharply. "No one will connect the two of us. I've made sure of that. I can protect you, but I can't know what happens to him after you get him out."

Then she understood. "So when you say for me to conceal him, you actually mean the organization, don't you?"

He nodded.

Questions crowded her mind, confusing her usual clarity. Repressing the swirling thoughts, she asked calmly, "Mr. President, I agree sending Spencer to Damascus or Tehran isn't right. I just don't really see how saving him helps us. Is he worth it?"

Halladan laughed mirthlessly. "Right now the face of our most immediate enemy is Whitten and his New Agenda, and we need a weapon to stop them. Mel, I'm not saving Spencer from the Muslims; I'm saving America from the New Agenda, and Thom Spencer is my weapon."

Swirling thoughts stopped; confusion vanished; and Mel's clarity materialized: the American Terrorist, the man who had devastated international terrorism would stop the New Agenda. Thom Spencer was Mark Halladan's last line of defense. The gloomy gravity of Halladan's expression imprinted itself on her mind. Mel faced a critical decision. Did she believe the man who had so often demonstrated keen insight, or did she ignore his dire predictions this one time? Intuition, supported by reason, won out. She trusted President Mark Halladan, and bizarrely she trusted his weapon.

Chapter 3

Her flat-soled shoes scuffed the white tiles of the dull hallway. An indifferent guard escorted a plain-looking Mel, dressed in a forgettable outfit, through the federal prison outside Florence, Colorado. Without showing any identification, she had been granted access to Thom Spencer by orders from DC. The guard showed her into a small interrogation room cased in white-painted cinder blocks.

When Thom Spencer arrived, Mel probed the steel-blue eyes to see if they still had a deadened look, but she found nothing: no spark of life, but no veil of death either. His look was disinterested, nothing more. After taking his seat, he leaned on the table. "Agent Dellendale, you look different." Mel didn't respond; he remained impassive. He asked without guile, "How can I help you?"

Her emotions fluctuated. Something in the honesty of the mass murderer confirmed Halladan's trust, yet she couldn't help but feel guilty conspiring with him.

She offered Spencer a copy of the presidential pardon.

He read it, laid it on the table, and slid it back to her with a shrug. "Don't need that, Agent Dellendale," he said vacantly. "I've accepted my fate, and that's that. I know you understand. I can see your...your ambivalence toward me. There is some...affinity, I suppose, maybe understanding, but mostly hate. I deserve my fate."

9

She dismissed the analysis. "What about the threat that Whitten will hand you over to the Muslims?"

He scoffed. "So?"

"I remember you telling me how you wouldn't tolerate Muslims judging you. Not because you were afraid of them, but because you said it wasn't good for the nation. Something like that, right?"

He shrugged again, steel-blue eyes still impassive. "They allow me to watch the news these days, Agent Dellendale. I'm not sure the nation survives with this Whitten nightmare. It makes me wonder if my efforts were in vain, a worthless, futile attempt to save our country."

So he knew about the New Agenda. Dellendale furrowed her brow and launched into a recitation of her conversation with Halladan. As she talked, an ambivalent look dawned on Spencer's face, which slowly turned into an angry glare. Concluding, she stared straight into an intense stare. "President Halladan believes you are his and America's last line of defense—a weapon—against what he sees as an assault against our country with this New Agenda. I get the sense he truly believes you are the only one who can stop them."

Then she saw it. A flare in the eye sparked, removing any remaining cobwebs of indifference, as if awakening a dangerous giant, and he muttered, "Not all Americans are equally American."

"What?" she asked.

He smirked. "Never mind. I understand who these people are, Agent Dellendale. They're worse than the terrorists. Terrorists don't lie when they destroy you. These people do. They're more dangerous, more insidious." Out of the depths of prison, another fire blazed in the American Terrorist's eyes.

"All right," Mel said, "but I need your help, Mr. Spencer. I can't do this through the government. We have to get you out of sight, off the grid, without help from the FBI or anyone in the administration. I told you President Halladan has real concerns about that."

Spencer's eyes narrowed, and he chuckled, "The organization?"

Mel stared at him deadpan.

"Is this some sort of elaborate scheme for me to reveal my connection to the organization so you can root it out?"

"No."

Spencer sighed, contemplating the agent sitting across from him.

"I need help here, Mr. Spencer. I can't do this without it. Hiding you will be an extraordinary feat."

He rubbed his check vigorously. "I need a secure line. Can you get me one?"

She nodded.

"Agent Dellendale, if it isn't secure, the other side of that conversation will know, and I guess I'm on way back to my cell, and eventually Syria or Iran."

"I know."

Mel quickly arranged a secure line for Spencer. After placing the call, he returned to the interrogation room and handed her a piece of paper with a name: Major Jacob Brannan.

Mel returned to Washington, DC, under the ruse she had left her off-the-record interview empty handed. The visitor's list was scrubbed of any visits to Thom Spencer, and no one admitted they remembered any.

On a night with a moon barely peeking out behind hazy clouds, Thom Spencer walked alone through the exit gate of the super max prison and stepped into a dark SUV. When President Halladan announced the pardon, his disappearance blazed through the media. A manhunt was called, yet for what reason? The man had a presidential pardon, and no law enforcement agency had any cause to apprehend him. By the time Franklin D. Whitten entered the Oval Office, Thom Spencer had become a ghost, vanishing into the night without a trace, and the world resumed its business, yet wondering if it would ever feel the presence of the man who had devastatingly terrorized terror.

JOIN US ONLINE!

TheAmericanTerrorist.com
Follow Thom Spencer on Twitter:**@HiTechTerrorist**
The American Renaissance Publishing Company: **TARPC.com**

Copyright © 2014 R. Carl Irwin
All rights reserved.

THE
AMERICAN RENAISSANCE
Publishing Company

Denver • Colorado • USA